William Havard

King Charles I

A Historical Tragedy

William Havard

King Charles I
A Historical Tragedy

ISBN/EAN: 9783743392557

Manufactured in Europe, USA, Canada, Australia, Japa

Cover: Foto ©Andreas Hilbeck / pixelio.de

Manufactured and distributed by brebook publishing software (www.brebook.com)

William Havard

King Charles I

B E L L's

BRITISH THEATRE,

Confifting of the moft efteemed

ENGLISH PLAYS.

VOLUME THE TWELFTH.

Being the Sixth VOLUME of TRAGEDIES.

CONTAINING

King Charles I. by Mr. Havard.
The Gamester, by Mr. Moore.
Don Sebastian, by Dryden.
Œdipus, by Dryden and Lee.
The Revenge, by Dr. Young.

LONDON:

Printed for John Bell, at the British Library, Strand.

M DCC LXXX.

BELL'S EDITION.

KING CHARLES I.

AN HISTORICAL TRAGEDY.

As

VARIA   THE   TRE,

Thea

Regulate   Prom

By PERMISSION of the MANAGERS.

———————— *Quis talia fando*
Temperet à lachrymis?————————   VIRG.

LONDON:

Printed for JOHN BELL, near Exeter-Exchange, in the Strand.

MDCCLXXVII.

To Her Grace the

DUCHESS

OF

MARLBOROUGH.

Madam,

ADDRESSES, unauthorifed by merit, are too frequent, and (what fhould be more furprifing) often fuccefsful.

I would willingly approach in what I think the beft fhape, and choofe rather to appear dreffed in the opinion of the town, than my own.

I have been favoured with the general approbation, yet am ftill confcious of weaknefs, and know not where to fue more properly for protection, than to your Grace: believe this, Madam, when I affure you, that I will always facrifice my intereft—to my fincerity.

I am an enemy to flattery; and, therefore, to be fure to be thoroughly difengaged from it, apply to a perfon who wants it not.

The greatnefs of mind I have conftantly confidered beyond that of the perfon; and when I fay that you are a good woman, I think I fay more than I fhould by ftiling you a great duchefs. By confirming yourfelf the firft, you have eminently proved yourfelf the latter. In this laft opinion I apply myfelf to the world—not to your Grace, confcious that you are the only perfon that will not join in it.

I have little title to addrefs your Grace, more than in the affurance that the fmalleft merit does not go unre-

A 2

garded

garded by you. I confefs myfelf obfcure; but fhall not think fo, if your Grace looks upon me with the eye of favour: for, believe me, I have more ambition to merit your Grace's efteem, than any other confideration that may be fuggefted; and fhall ever think myfelf honoured in fubfcribing myfelf,

Your Grace's moft devoted,

Moft obedient,

And moft humble fervant.

THE

[5]

THE

PREFACE.

TO obviate any criticism that may justly fall upon
the inaccuracy of this play, I judged it necessary
to publish a few lines as an apology for the liberties I have
taken with the history, and the faults that may appear to
the judicious reader. And though the uncommon and
general applause it has met with in the representation
may seem to make it unnecessary, yet, without it, I could
not acquit myself to my own judgment.

And first, as to the liberties I have taken with history,
I hope I may be forgiven my introducing the queen, who
was in France at the time I have laid the action of the
play; but it being a story barren of female characters, I
was induced to make her appear; and because I thought
there would very naturally arise a pleasing distress at their
parting, which I have introduced at the beginning of the
fourth act.

Again, to heighten the distress in the last act, and to
bring on one supposed to receive and convey the advice
better, that the king sends by him to his eldest son,
Charles, James appears, who, at that juncture, was in
Holland. I have made an excuse for Cromwell's coming
to the king, because I thought an interview between them
was necessary, and would add to the spirit of the whole.

I am not conscious of any other liberties I have taken,
except heightening the characters of Fairfax and his lady;
which has added a warmth to the piece, and in some mea-
sure supplied the want of real matter to constitute five
acts. The other persons in the drama are as strongly
characterised, and as impartially, as I had ability, and
the shortness of the time would permit.

A 3

There

There were some speeches omitted in the representation, which I have restored in print; and the reader may particularize them, if he thinks it worth while, by remarking a comma prefixed to each line.

I must now do myself the pleasure to addrefs those gentlemen of known judgment and great candour, whose corrections (though in so short a time for making them) have done me honour, and given reputation to the piece. Some I have not an opportunity of thanking personally; and therefore do it thus publicly, and declare, that nothing could equal the justness of their remarks, but their sincerity and humanity in delivering them.

I now throw the piece before the reader; and hope it will prove as agreeable an entertainment in the closet, as it seemed to be upon the stage.

PROLOGUE.

Written by a FRIEND.

IN former times, when wit was no offence,
And men submitted to be pleas'd with sense——
Then was the stage fair virtue's fav'rite school,
Scourge of the knave, and mirror of the fool.
Here oft the villain's conscious blush would rise,
And fools become, by viewing folly, wise.
Our bard, as then, despises song and dance,
The notes of Italy, and jigs of France :
With home distress he nobly hopes to move,
And fire each bosom with its country's love——
So much a Briton——that he scorns to roam
To foreign climes, to fetch his hero home——
Conscious, that in these scenes is clearly shown
Britain can boast true heroes of her own.
Murder avow'd by law he boldly paints,
Heroes and patriots, hypocrites and saints ;
Rebellion fighting for the public good,
And Treason smiling in a monarch's blood.
Party, be dumb——in each pathetic scene,
Our muse, to-night, asserts an honest mean ;
Shews you a prince triumphant o'er his fate,
Glorious in death, as in misfortunes great ;
By nature virtuous, tho misled by slaves,
By tools of power, by sycophants and knaves.
When Charles submits to faction's deadly blow,
What loyal heart but shares the monarch's woe ?
Nor less Maria's grief, ye gentle fair,
Claims the sad tribute of a tender tear.
From British scenes to-night we hope applause,
And Britons sure will aid a British cause.

DRA-

DRAMATIS PERSONÆ.

MEN.

	Drury-Lane.
King *Charles*.	Mr. Giffard.
Duke of *York*,	Mafter Giffard.
Duke of *Glouceſter*,	Mafter W. Hamilton.
Biſhop *Juxon*,	Mr. Havard.
Duke of *Richmond*,	Mr. Bardin.
Marquis of *Lindſey*,	Mr. Richardſon.
Oliver Cromwell,	Mr. Wright.
Fairfax,	Mr. Johnſon.
Bradſhaw,	Mr. Roſco.
Ireton,	Mr. W. Giffard.
Colonel *Tomlinſon*,	Mr. Hamilton.

WOMEN.

Queen,	Mrs. Giffard.
Princeſs *Elizabeth*,	Miſs Norris.
Lady *Fairfax*,	Mrs. Roberts.

SCENE, partly at *St. James's*, and partly at *Whitehall*.

KING CHARLES I.

⁎ *The lines marked with inverted commas, 'thus,' are omitted in the representation.*

ACT I.

Enter Bishop Juxon *and Duke of* Richmond.

JUXON.

GOOD day, my Lord, if, in a time like this,
 Aught that is fortunate or good can happen;
When Desolation, wedded to Despair,
Strides o'er the land, and marks her way with ruin:
Plenty is fled with Justice; Rage and Rapine
Have robb'd the widow'd matron, England, quite,
And left her now no dowry—but her tears.

Rich. Is it then certain that the lawless Commons
Have form'd a court of justice (so they call it)
To bring the King to trial?

Jux. 'Tis most true;
And tho' the Lords refus'd to join the bill,
Yet they proceed without them. Lawless man!
Whither, at last, will thy impieties,
Thy daring insolence extend, when kings
Feel from a subject-hand the scourge of pow'r?
Where may an injur'd monarch hope for safety,
If he not find it in his people's hearts?

Rich. Oh, Naseby, Naseby, what a deadly stroke
Was thy ill-fated field to royalty!
On thy success depended monarchy;
The fate of rebels, and the fate of kings
Hung on thy battle; but thou, faithless too,
Conspir'd with faction to o'erthrow us all,
And bring to sight these more than bloody times.

Jux.

Jux. To-morrow does the black tribunal fit;
When majefty is cited to appear
Before his tyrant fubjects.   Oh, prepofterous!
Is't not as bad as if thefe rebel hands
Should from their feats tear forth their ruling eyes,
Whofe watch directs the body's ufe and fafety?
   Rich. It cannot be! 'Tis not in cruelty
To think of fpilling royal blood.   Mercy, fure,
And the pretended juftice of their caufe,
Will fave them from the weight of fo much guilt.
   Jux. What added guilt can that black bofom feel,
That has fhook off allegiance to its king?
Whole feas of common and of noble blood
Will not fuffice; the banquet muft be crown'd,
And the brain heated with the blood of kings.
But fee where Cromwell comes! Upon his brow
Diffimulation ftamp'd.   If I can judge
By lineament and feature, that man's heart
Can both contrive and execute the worft
And the moft daring actions yet conceiv'd.
Ambitious, bloody, refolute and wife,
He ne'er betrays his meaning till he acts,
And ne'er looks out but with the eye of purpofe.
His head fo cool, that it appears the top
Of Alpine hill, clad with flow-wafting fnow;
His execution rapid as the force
Of falling waters thund'ring down its bafe.
Let us avoid him; for my confcious foul
Fears him in wonder, and in praife condemns him.
                                   [*Exeunt.*

Enter Cromwell.
   Crom. Now thro' the maze of gloomy policy
Has fire-ey'd Faction work'd her way to light,
And deck'd ambition in the robe of power.
Our fears in Charles's fafety are remov'd,
And but one blow remains to fix our ftate ——
The lopping off his head.   No more the royal tree
Shall, from legitimacy's root, prefume
To fprout forth tyrant branches.   Commonwealths
Own no hereditary right, unlefs our worth
Shine equal to our birth.   Wherefore, at once,
Down with nobility—the Commons rule!
                                   Avaunt

Avaunt prerogative and lineal title,
And be the right fuperior merit.
Enter Fairfax.
Fair. I was to feek you, Sir; fome lab'ring doubts,
Which, in th' uncertainty of thefe ftrange times,
Call for the ray of clearnefs, make me prefs
(Perhaps unfeafonably) to your ear.
You will forgive th' impatience of a man,
Who labours to be right—by your example.
Crom. Good Fairfax, fpare me; I am ill at words,
And utter badly where I mean refpect:
Uncouth my anfwers are to truth and plainnefs;
But to a compliment I 'ne'er could fpeak:
Yet could you look into my fecret mind,
There my foul fpeaks to Fairfax as to one
Book'd in the faireft page of my efteem,
And written on my heart——But to your doubts.
Fair. You may remember, Sir, when firft my fword,
My fortune, life, and ftill, yet more—my honour,
Were all engag'd to fight the caufe of juftice;
You thought, with me, the wrongs to be redrefs'd,
Were the attempts upon the fubjects' right,
The unregarded laws, and bold defign
To ftretch prerogative to boundlefs rule.
Defign full fair and noble! and th' event
Has crown'd our utmoft wifhes.   England owns
No arbitrary fway; the King's adherents
Are all difpers'd, or the remains fo few,
They are not worth a fear; the King himfelf
In clofe confinement. Now, let reafon judge,
And blend difcretion with fuccefs.
Let us be juft—but let us ftop at juftice,
Nor by too hafty zeal o'erfhoot the mark.
The Roman fpirits, favage as they were,
When they determin'd to abolifh kings,
Shed not the blood of Tarquin, but expell'd him;
And fhall we, owners of the Chriftian law,
Where mercy fhines the foremoft attribute,
Be harder to appeafe? If not more mild,
Let us not be more cruel than barbarians.
Charles grafp'd, we own, at arbitrary fway,
And would have been a tyrant—for which crime,

The

The kingdoms he was born to we have feiz'd.
But let us not defpoil him of his life.
Crowns, as the gift of men, men may refume;
But life, the gift of Heaven, let Heaven difpofe of.

Crom. Well have you weigh'd each growing circum-
And held difcretion in the niceft fcale.   [ftance,
Our fears remov'd, the fubject right reftor'd,
What have we more to do, than to fit down,
And each enjoy the vineyard of his toil?
'Tis true—but yet fome clamours are abroad;
Petitions daily crowd the parliament,
That loudly call for juftice on the King,
Imputing to his charge the guilt of murders,
The defolation that has bared the land,
And fwept the crops of plenty from our fields.

Fair. What, fhall the rabble judge; thofe fervile curs,
Who, as they eat in plenty, fnarl fedition?
Are thefe to be regarded?

Crom. You miftake me.
'Tis not their outcries only; but, indeed,
Thofe who fee farther, and with better judgment,
Fear, while he lives, his friends will never die;
But, by fome foreign force or home defign,
May fometime fhake the fafety of the ftate.
Befides, they fpeak of an approv'd good maxim,
Remove the caufe, and the effect will ceafe.
Oh, worthy Fairfax, thou art wife and valiant!
I have feen thee watch occafion, till advantage
Came fmiling to thy arms, and crown'd thy patience:
And then, in fight, I have beheld thy fword
Out-fly the pace of peftilential air,
And kill in multitudes.

Fair. Good Sir, forbear.

Crom. Blufh not to hear a truth, when Cromwell fpeaks
My uncouth manner, ill at varnifhing,   [it:
Beggars my will, and dreffes praife uncomely.
Methinks I fee thee in the rage of battle,
When Nafeby's field confefs'd thy victor arm,
And thy decifion was the fate of kings.
Methinks I view thee in the buftling ranks,
Where danger was the neareft—(for you brought it)
Unhelm'd, encounter armies, and defpife
The fafety that the meaneft foldier wore;

                      And

And when a private man, with bold affertion,
Challeng'd a conquest which your arm had gain'd,
And was reprov'd; methinks, I hear you fay,
I have enough of glory, let him own it.
   Fair. Whither does all this tend? I pray forbear—
I never fought in hopes to have it told:
'The man whofe actions fpeak, expects no anfwer.
   Crom. I do but barely tell thee what thou art,
And what the world may yet expect of Fairfax.
'The diamond, Merit, in the quarry hid,
Being-unknown, unfeen, attracts no eyes,
But digg'd up by the lab'rer's curiofity,
And polifh'd by the hand of gratitude,
It fhines the ornament of human life.——
Think therefore what you are, and what this juncture:
The faireft lock of fortune is difplay'd,
And fhould be feiz'd on by the bold and worthy.
   Fair. You talk in clouds above my purpofe quite;
Which was but to enforce the caufe of mercy,
And fhew how much is gain'd by ftopping he e;
To tell you what my confcience makes opinion,
And ftrengthen that opinion by your voice.
   Crom. 'Tis true indeed—I had forgot myfelf;
But whither was I hurried in my zeal?
E'en I can defcant on a pleafing theme:
Can you forgive me? though 'tis hard indeed;
Exalted virtue can with eafe forgive
A calumny, but not a praife.——No more,
Heav'n can witnefs for me, with what true accord
My thoughts meet yours! How willing I would ftop
The arm of violence, and make the law,
Stern as fhe is, affume a face of fmiles.
The death of Charles is far from my defign—
And yet the general outcry is for juftice:
He has been much to blame, you know he has;
And (but I foften thofe unruly thoughts)
Were I to fpeak the dictates of my heart,
I could not find a punifhment too great
To fall upon the man, who fhould, like Charles,
Forget all right, and wafte with lavifh hand
The rich revenue of his people's love.

B

Fair.

Fair. Dearly he fuffers for mifguided fteps,
And knows that mifery he meant to give ;
He feels the bondage he defign'd for us,
And by the want of freedom counts its value.

Crom. I pity him ; and would the commons think with
He were as fafe as Cromwell ; and, brave Fairfax, [me,
We will endeavour it ; and may that power,
Whofe arm has fought the battle of our caufe,
Incline 'em all to think like you,—or me ;   [*Afide.*
I will about it.   Yet remember, Fairfax,
The pofture of thefe times : confider too,
How great your expectations ought to be :
Would Fairfax liften to the voice of Cromwell,
He fhould have nearer hopes than Charles's life :
Somewhat as great as your defert fhould crown you,
And make you partner of the higheft honours.   [*Exit.*

Fair. The higheft honours ! what can Cromwell mean ?
Acquit me, Heav'n ! I fought not but for juftice,
Rage fir'd me not, nor did ambition blind ;
No party led me, and no intereft bound :
My tie was confcience, and my caufe was freedom.
When Fairfax liftens to another call,
May his next ftroke in battle be his laft.

Enter Ireton.

Ire. Fairfax, I come, commiffion'd by the army,
To know your pleafure, if you think it meet
That they fhould march and quarter nearer London :
The public fafety makes it requifite :
But they attend your orders ere they move.

Fair. The public fafety ! Say what new alarm,
What danger fo awakes fecurity,
That in her fright, fhe thus lays hold of caution ?

Ire. The fafety of the commons, of yourfelf,
Of the high court of juftice ; who to-morrow
Againft a tyrant proves the people's pow'r,
And brings offending majefty to juftice :
This may excite his yet remaining friends,
Arm'd with defpair, to fome attempt of danger.
Who can be too fecure ? The man whofe pillow
Prevention guards, may fleep in eafe and fafety.

Fair. To bring offending majefty to juftice ?
Ire. To the fcaffold.

Fair.

Fair. Ha!

Ire. Why do you ftart?

Fair. Your zeal too much tranfports you.
Ireton, farewel,—and let me gain belief,
When I affirm this moral to thy ear:
Confcience than empire more content can bring,
And to be juft, is to be more than king.   [*Exit.*

Enter Cromwell.

Crom. It is enough, good kinfman, let him go——
And yet I could well wifh that he was ours—
But 'tis no matter—You began to warm,
And the good caufe fat burning on thy cheek;
Thou haft a well-turn'd tongue: but lift thee, Ireton,
Hear my defign (for ftill my heart is thine)
The commons moft are ours: the weeder's care
Has, from the garden of our enterprize,
Thrown out the rubbifh that difgrac'd the foil:
And now our growth looks timely. This you faw,
When by my means a hundred doubted members
Were by the army feiz'd upon their entrance,
And fince expell'd the houfe. Independency
Roots itfelf faft; while prefbytery force
Withers unfeen. Would Fairfax had been ours!

Ire. I cannot fee that his adherence to us
Could profper much our caufe, or his defection
Make us decline one moment from our purpofe.

Crom. You miftake, Ireton, Fairfax ftands the firft
In intereft with the very men I hate:
Therefore his joint endeavour would be found
The eafieft means to bring my point to bear;
Befides, he ftands the faireft in the love
Of our whole party. Were we link'd together,
The army too were ours; and their keen fwords
Are powerful arguments. We fhall thrive however—
I have it—He fhall hence, and on an expedition
Not the moft juft; I know his fqueamifh honour,
If it furmife an action the leaft tainted,
Will throw up this employment: then 'tis mine:
And while I have Dame Fortune, fhe fhall pleafe me.

Ire. But the main turn of all your enterprize
Hangs on to-morrow, on the death of Charles:

                            'Tis

'Tis from his scaffold only you must mount
To what your wishes aim at.
   Crom. Fear not that.
I have to do with men, upon whose tempers
I know to work—Those who love piety,
I with the vehemence of prayer encounter,
And through the spirit practise on their passions.
Those who are crafty, I subdue with fraud,
And wile them to my purpose. To the bloody
I promise slaughters, deaths and executions:
Gold gains the covetous; and praise the proud.
There is another sort—but they are easy;
Your honest men, who never wear distrust;
For honesty's the jaundice of the mind,
That makes us think our neighbours like ourselves:
Let us together. Ireton, here it lies;
When fools believe, wise men are sure to rise. *[Exeunt.*

END of the FIRST ACT.

A C T. II.

Enter Fairfax.

OH, glory! how deceitful is thy view!
   Such are thy charms, that o'er th' uncertain way
Of vice or faction, thou, to hide the danger,
Dost to the outward eye shew fair appearance:
Which when the follower steps on, down he sinks,
And then too late looks backward to the path
Of long neglected virtue.

Enter Lady Fairfax.

  Lady Fair. My dearest Fairfax, call not this intrusion;
Long has obedience combated with love,
Ere I would press upon your privacy:
If love has conquer'd, love may be forgiven.
The faults of tenderness (if faults they are)
E'en in offending wear the seal of pardon.
Why are you thus alone; and why thus chang'd?
  Fair. My gentle lady, thoughts of deep concern,
That to the last recesses of my soul

Travel

Travel, with pain and penitence their guides,
At length have found the company they like;
Bufy Reflection, moping Melancholy,
And Silence the fure guard that keeps the door.

Lady Fair. I cannot blame your griefs; but come to
Indeed the caufe is juft: but good my Lord,   [fhare 'em,
Let not defpair take hold of that brave heart,
And boaft a conqueft which your foes ne'er could.
If (as I long have thought) the King be wrong'd,
Seek to redrefs, and not lament his fortunes.
I am a woman, not defign'd for war,
Yet could this hand (weak as you think its grafp)
Nerv'd by my heart's companion, refolution,
Difplay the royal banner in the field,
And fhame the ftrength of manhood in this caufe.
Forgive this warmth: I ne'er till now, my Lord,
Gave you unafk'd my thoughts, but I perceive
Your heart is wounded, and I came to heal it:
To offer you the balm of wholefome counfel,
And temper my perfuafion with my love.

Fair. Thou haft been more than I could hope in woman:
Thy beauty, thy leaft excellence.   Thou appear'ft
Like a fair tree, the glory of the plain,
The root thy honour, and the trunk thy friendfhip,
(That ftands the rudeft blaft of cold adverfity)
From whence branch out a thoufand different boughs;
Candour, humility, and angel truth,
And every leaf a virtue.   True, my love,
While I conceiv'd our liberties in danger,
I fought in their defence; but cannot bear
This bold defign upon the life of Charles.
We took up arms to keep the law entire,
Not to defend its open violation.

Lady Fair. I know thy honeft heart, it hates a wrong;
'Twas principle, not party, urg'd thee on
To fight their caufe: but Cromwell's fpecious wiles
Pervert the juftice of thy fair defigns,
And make thy virtue pander to his will.

Fair. Cromwell has art—but ftill I think him honeft:
Yet in our late difcourfe his fpeech, methought,
Appear'd disjointed; and he wav'd the theme
I fpoke about—The fafety of the King——

At parting too, his words betray'd a purpose
Beyond the limits of a commonwealth ;
And talk'd of highest honours—but I hope
That my suspicions wrong him.

    Lady Fair. No, my Lord ;
Rather increase 'em, keep 'em still alive
'To arm against his black designs : discretion,
At the surmise of danger, wakes incessant ;
Nor drops the eye-lid 'till she sleeps in safety.

Enter a Servant.

    Serv. The duke of Richmond and a reverend bishop
Desire to see you.

    Fair. Wait upon them hither ;
I guess at their desires, and wou'd to Heav'n
My pow'r could grant 'em what my wish confirms !

    Lady Fair. And wherefore not, my Lord ? The army
        yours,
Who can dispute your will ? Command them hither.
And be their threats the safety of the King.   [ness.

    Fair. Betray my trust ! Thou canst not mean such base-
Should I (which much I doubt, for Cromwell's faction
Equals my pow'r, and more, among the soldiers)
Make 'em revolt, what would my conscience say ?
'Twould be a mountain crime, a molehill good.
The whiteness of my fair design to Charles,
Spread o'er the visage of the means that gave it ;
Like thinnest lawn upon an Æthiop face,
Would cover, not conceal the blackness. No, my love,
Virtue and baseness never meet together.

Enter Bishop Juxon *and Duke of* Richmond.

    Juxon. A mournful errand, good my Lord of Fairfax,
Makes us thus rude. My gentle Lady, stay ;——
Your voice will help the music of our plaint,
And swell the notes to moving melody:
Ill-fated Charles, deserted as he is,
Lives in your fair report (or fame has err'd)
Join in our concert, as you are next his heart,
You know to touch the string that sounds to pity.

    Fair. My Lords, I guess your purpose, and assure you
If my persuasion or my wish avail,
Charles feels no stroke, 'till nature gives the blow.
Long may the fruit of health adorn the tree,
And ripen with his years in warmer times !

4

Rich.

Rich. 'Tis truly fpoke, my Lord, and worthy Fairfax;
Whom I have ftill confider'd in this light;
As nobly juft, and but at worft mifled.
    Juxon. How would this man adorn the royal caufe.
Who makes rebellion wear the face of virtue!
                                    [*Afide to* Richmond.
How I am pleas'd to find you feel this woe,
And ftrive for its prevention—Let thefe fpeak——
                                            [*Weeps.*
Thefe eyes muft elfe have known the difmal office
To fee the widow's and the orphans' forrows:
Complaint had been my language, care my bed,
And contemplation my uneafy pillow.
Now by your hopes of mercy plead this caufe;
Know it a labour that will pay itfelf,
E'en in this world—and when you mount above,
You will behold it of fo vaft a value,
It will out-weigh th' offences of your life.
    Fair. Without this interceffion, good my Lord,
I had done all within my feeble pow'r;
Yet think what outcries din the parliament,
How many zealots call aloud for juftice!
Then think what you may hope, and what not fear.
    Lady Fair. No matter, Fairfax; 'tis a virtuous caufe,
And Heav'n will blefs the purpofe with fuccefs.
    Juxon. There mercy fpoke, and in her fofteft voice:
And Heaven, I doubt not, figns the prophecy.
                    Enter Cromwell.
    Crom. Indeed! Does Fairfax keep fuch company?
Shame on his pitying heart! His foul's unmann'd,
His refolution dwindled to a girl's:
Now, in the name of fight, is this the man
Whom armies fled from, and whom conqueft lov'd?
Behold him now crept to a private corner,
Counting out tears with priefts and women.   [*Afide.*
    Fair. See
Where Cromwell comes, I will once more affail him,
And be yourfelves the witnefs of his anfwer.
Good Cromwell, welcome! And let my petition,
Join'd with thefe lords, prevail upon your pity;
Let Charles have life: is that fo hard a boon?
In lieu of three fair kingdoms, give him life.
                                            Crom.

Crom. Why this address to me? Am I the parliament?
'Tis they who justly call him to account,
And form this high tribunal.
    Juxon. Justly, Cromwell!
    Crom. Ay, good bishop, justly!
I cry you mercy! By the good old cause!
It is but gratitude in you to plead:
Episcopacy was the rock he split on;
And he has ventur'd fairly for your lawn:
How learnedly did he uphold your cause,
When Henderson inveigh'd against your miters,
Did he not write full nobly? Say'st thou, bishop?
    Juxon. His conscience prompted him to what did;
His zeal for us can never be forgotten.
    Crom. His conscience! you say true—his conscience
He would have stretch'd to arbitrary sway,   [did it:
And swallow'd down our liberties and laws:
His conscience would have soon digested them.
    Fair. Let us not into insult turn our pow'r;
Good fortune is not wedded to our arms:
Conquest, like a young maiden with her lover,
If roughly treated, turns her smiles to frowns,
And hates where once she lov'd.
    Crom. I stand corrected.
To me then you apply in Charles's favour,
And wait my answer, which is briefly thus:
I am but one, and (as the weaker must)
Flow in the current of majority:
My single voice be it against, or for,
Avails him little: if the rest incline
To think of mercy and of Charles together,
'Tis fairly done, and e'en to Cromwell's wish:
This is the sum of all I can deliver——
Fairfax, I have matter for your private ear.
    Juxon. We humbly take our leaves.
    Fair. My lords, farewel!
                    [*Exeunt* Jux. Rich. *and* Lady Fairfax.
    Crom. How can you waste your time on trash like this?
Were Fairfax' honour to be doubted, this might make
The child suspicion grow to certainty;
But we are confident in you: your actions speak.
Yet, Fairfax, do not let thy noble eye

Catch

Catch the contagion of weak-judging pity,
And sympathize with beggars. To my purpose:
The council, at whose head your wisdom sits,
Weighing some depositions 'gainst the King,
Would have your judgment's sanction : they request
Your presence there ; I bear their will with pleasure.
    Fair. It is not needed, Sir.
As to the purpose of their meeting, say,
If they incline to mercy, let their charge
Be weaker than it is ; but if to rigour,
They have, I fear, too much of that already :
Let 'em (if friendly Fairfax may advise)
Judge with that candour, they expect of Heaven.
    Crom. You will not go then ?
    Fair. Say I cannot go.
My reason pleads against so bad a deed,
And inclination holds me ; nay, yet more,
A secret impulse strikes upon my soul,
Which, though I had the will, would yet detain me.
    Crom. Folly and superstition ! Drive 'em hence;
And in exchange, wear honours and renown :
Of this I've said—And, noble Fairfax, believe me,
That when the wind of promise and of hope
Stretches the canvas out of resolution,
The bark, Design, flies swift before the gale,
And quickly anchors in Good-fortune's bay ;
Then we unlade our freight of doubts and fears,
And barter 'em for happiness and glory.   [*Exit.*
    Fair. He who embarks himself in Cromwell's ship,
Out-sails fair truth and ev'ry honest purpose.
'Tis now too plain—How could I doubt so long ?
My honesty has made me Cromwell's tool :
His arts have turn'd my virtue to a sword,
And now 'tis bared against me.
But say, shall Fairfax, who in open field
An army could not conquer, fall a prey,
To the ambitious prospects of one man ?
No, Fairfax, rouse up thy resentment's force,
And rescue thy renown from infamy.   [*Exit.*

SCENE.

SCENE, *a Chamber.*

King Charles *difcovered reading.*
   King. What art thou, life, fo dearly lov'd by all ?—
What are thy charms, that thus the great defire thee,
And to retain thee part with pomp and titles ?
To buy thy prefence, the gold-watching mifer
Will pour his bags of mouldy treafure out,
And grow at once a prodigal.   The wretch
Clad with difeafe and poverty's thin coat,
Yet holds thee faft, though painful company.
Oh, life ! thou univerfal with, what art thou ?—
Thou'rt but a day—a few uneafy hours :
Thy morn is greeted by the flocks and herds,
And every bird that flatters with its note,
Salutes thy rifing fun ; thy noon approaching,
Then hafte the flies and every creeping infect
To bafk in thy meridian ; that declining
As quickly they depart, and leave thy evening
To mourn the abfent ray : night at hand,
Then croaks the raven confcience, time mifpent ;
The owl Defpair fcreams hideous, and the bat
Confufion flutters up and down—
Life's but a lenghthen'd day not worth the waking for.
            Enter Queen.
My deareft Queen !
I have been fumming up th' amount of life,
But found no value in it, 'till you came.
   Queen. Do not perplex yourfelf with thoughts like
Ill fortune at the worft, returns to better,   [thofe :
At leaft we think fo, as it grows familiar.
   King. No, I was only arming for the worft.
I have try'd the temper of my inmoft foul,
And find it ready now for all encounters :
Death cannot fhake it.
   Queen. Do not talk of death :
The apprehenfion fhakes my tender heart ;
Ages of love, I hope, are yet to come,
Ere that black hour arrives : fuch chilling thoughts
Difgrace the lodging of that noble breaft.
   King. What have I not to fear ? Thus clofe confin'd ;
To-morrow forc'd to trial.   Will thofe men,
                        Who

Who infolently drag me to the bar,
Stop in the middle of their purpofe ? No.
I muft prepare for all extremities :
And (be that Pow'r ador'd, that lends me comfort)
I feel I am—Oh, do not weep, my Queen ;
Rather rejoice with me, to find my thoughts
Outftretch the painful verge of human life,
And have no wifh on earth—but thee ! 'Tis there
Indeed I feel : peace and refignation
Had wander'd o'er the rooms of every thought,
To fhut misfortune out, but left this door
Unclos'd, through which Calamity
Has enter'd in thy fhape to feize my heart.

   Queen. Be more yourfelf, my Lord ; let majefty
Take root within thy heart, nor meanly bend
Before ill fortune's blaft.

   King. Oh, doubt me not !
'Tis only on the fide where you are plac'd,
That I can know a fear. For Charles's felf,
Let fierce encounter with the fword of danger
Bring him to bloodieft proof ; and if he fhrinks,
Defpife him. Here, I glory in my weaknefs.
He is no man whom tendernefs not melts,
And love fo foft as thine. Let us go in.
And if kind Heav'n defigns me longer ftay
On this frail earth, I fhall be only pleas'd,
Becaufe I have thy prefence here to crown me.
But if it deftines my immediate end ;
(Hard as it is, my Queen, to part with thee)
I fay, farewel, and to the blow refign,
That ftrikes me here—to make me more divine.

END of the SECOND ACT.

ACT

ACT III.

Enter Cromwell *and* Bradshaw.

CROMWELL.

IT shall be better, Bradshaw: do not think
Desert, though lowly plac'd, escapes our eye;
To me it is as precious in the valley,
As glittering on the mountain's top:——
I praise myself that I have found thee out:
'Tis not my favour, Bradshaw, but thy worth
Brings thee to light; thou dost not owe me aught.
Now, Bradshaw, art thou our high president.
Thou hast a heart well temper'd to the cause:
Thou look'st on monarchy in a true light:
And where the cause is just wilt shut out pity.
Pity!
The fool's forgiveness and the mother's tear:
The indiscretion of th' unpractis'd maid,
Who through that organ hears her lover's plaint,
And listens to her ruin.
   Brad. My good Sir,
Think not of Bradshaw thus.   My soul is firm;.
The melting eye and the relenting heart
Ne'er wrong'd my resolution.   As to kings,
To monarchy, and to superior state,
That I disclaim'd; 'till your exalted merit
Alter'd my purpose in my own despite,
And when I meant to level, rais'd you high.
   Crom. Spoke in a hearty zeal for our good cause.
That I have the same thoughts of thee, let this,
Thy present weighty office, speak, which should,
If Cromwell's nature bent to partiality,
Have fallen upon my kinsman, Ireton; one
Of good regard and hearty in the service:
But Cromwell's heart points only to desert,
The north of all his purpose.   Thou art ours;
And though thy modesty at first declin'd
To sit our head, and lead our counsels right,

Yet I determin'd not to lofe thy worth,
If importunity could win it.
  Brad. True, Sir ;
I own I thought myfelf unequal to it ;
Nor am I yet convinc'd : yet what I want in merit,
I will make out in rigour on the King.
In juftice to the people and to Heaven.
  Crom. Bradfhaw,
Thou art the very finew of our caufe ;
The fpirit of defign and warmth of zeal
Glow in thy purpofe. I adore that man,
Who, once refolv'd, outflies e'en expedition.
Thou art the glory of our brotherhood !
And fpare not to reproach, to taunt and blacken,
T' infult their party; nay, the King himfelf:
Mindful that all his dignity is loft,
And he, for monftrous crime, brought forth to juftice.
Seek an occafion too, to talk with Fairfax,
And urge to him the ftrong neceffity
Of the King's death—Perhaps he may prove angry—
But do not thou regard it. The time preffes ;
And thou haft liv'd too long to fquander that.
  Brad. Good Sir, farewel ! my love would offer more,
But my hafte wrongs it.   *[Exit.*
  Crom. Go too, Bradfhaw.
Such are the tools with which the wife muft work :
And yet he too is wife, and might cajole
A weaker than himfelf, and does.
He is my proper inftrument
To operate on thofe below my notice.
Thus by comparifon are all things known ;
And by fuch under-fteps as him, and lower,
Do the ambitious mount to fame and honour.
Befides, I choofe me thofe whom zeal inflames,
Who failing to convince you, will compel :
Such, prompted by enthufiafm's force,
And in predeftination's armour cas'd,
Will to the mouth of danger plant their breafts,
And out-fight frenzy and defpair. But lo !
Where Ireton comes !
C

Enter

Enter Ireton.

My trufty friend,
What look wears our defign ?
   Ire. Such as a bride,
The morning after blifs; fhe fmiles upon us,
And laughs at what fhe fear'd.   Petitions call
For juftice on the King—Our faction thrives ;
Murmur increafes to a public outcry.
All are 'gainft Charles, fave a few pitying hearts,
Who melt with Fairfax, and incline to mercy.
   Crom. 'Tis well.   Send poft unto the army, Ireton,
And let thofe fums of money I have order'd,
Be fecretly difpers'd among the foldiers ;
It will remind them of their promifes :
Gold is fpecific for the memory.
O gold ! wer't not for thee, what great defign,
What bold ambition, that outftretches juftice,
Could have fuccefs ? Thou buy'ft our very prayers :
Thou art the heart of oppofition,
And the tooth of faction.   Wer't not for thy aid,
Succefs would vary like the uncertain wind,
And honefty might profper ! Hie thee, Ireton ;
I muft to the King ; I have fome bills to offer him,
Which for the life of Charles, Charles would not fign ;
And his refufal turns to our advantage.
Thou fhalt know more hereafter—Now difpatch.
   Ire. Good Sir, I fly.   [*Exit.*
   Crom. Ha ! who have we yonder ?
O ! 'tis the wife of Fairfax : once as hearty,
As zealous for the caufe, as Cromwell's felf,
And wrought her lord to think fo.   Now, O woman,
Such is thy varying nature, that the waves
Are not more fluctuating than thy opinions,
Nor fooner are difplac'd.   To her is owing
The wayward pity of her vaffal lord.
Oh, 'tis certain danger to have fuch a woman,
Who, when man leaves himfelf to toy with her,
Knows how to win, and practife on his weaknefs.
But let me think—All women may be won.
The dame of Ephefus, the Anne of Richard,
Shew us a woman's grief and refolution.

                                         Why

Why may not she be wrought up to my purpose,
I can approach in what they like, in flattery ?
Enter Lady Fairfax.

Lady Fair. Stay, worthy Cromwell, and attend my
Hear me, and may thy answer be propitious,   [prayer,
As this kind hour that favours my address.
O may my falling tears that plead for mercy,
Drop on thy heart, and melt it to compliance,
Nor disregard the suit because a woman's.
Cromwell is noble ; and the noble soul
Grants the most free indulgence to the weak,
Because its generous nature pleads their cause.

Crom. Such is a woman's weakness, that she thinks
T' impose on us, by what allures herself :
But I must turn this project upon her,
And fairly put it to an equal proof,
Who best dissembles, Cromwell—or a woman.   [*Aside.*
Lady, I must esteem a compliment,
When from a tongue that seldoms errs that way.
From what I know, and what I oft have heard,
You can dress praise like truth : that praise I mean,
Which from our liking to the theme we speak of,
Swells to extravagance (tho' still our thoughts)
Such warmth is virtue's fault ; and such, I hope,
May be your kind excuse for praising me.

Lady Fair. Talk not of praise, good Sir, your merit
When from a woman's mouth.   [shames it,

Crom. Well turn'd again.   [*Aside.*
O lady, were I but to speak my thoughts
Of you, and your brave lord, you would conclude
'Twere praise indeed—for virtue looks within
For her faults only, not for her perfections.
Hear some of those : you once espous'd our cause,
E'en with persuasion's warmth ; and well you su'd.
We have not, sure, o'erlook'd desert so far
To merit opposition !
The state is busy—but the time will come
When her best office shall be pleasing you.

Lady Fair. You mock me, Sir ; I do not wish that
Vain as you think my sex. I came to say——   [time,

Crom. E'en to that purpose, to the life of Charles.
It cannot be, the people cry for justice :
C 2

Would

Would I could stop its course ! But, gentle lady,
Think it more wife to fly a falling pile,
Than strive to prop its ruin.   Charles must die.
    Lady Fair. O gracious Cromwell !——
    Crom. Nay, but hear me on.
Why will you thus employ your eloquence,
Which our whole council would with liking hear,
To help impossibilities ? Good lady,
Rather employ it (and you know the way)
To teach your lord to value rising fortune,
And make his fame——
    Lady Fair. As black as yours will be.
Shame on thy dark designs, and the whole cause,
If only such a deed can make it prosper.
Be the heart bloodless that conceives the act,
The tongue accurst that dares avow the purpose,
And the hand blasted that obeys the order !
May his life here be all the hell we think of,
Yet find a greater in the other world.   [*Exit.*
    Crom. How wayward and pervese a thing is woman !
How much unlike the softness we expect,
When rage and trifles vex 'em. In the heat
And the full vigour of their first enjoyment,
Distrust succeeds their love ; and he who pleases,
Is hunted by their jealousy to hate.——
Fairfax and Bradshaw earnest in dispute !
I will not interrupt them, but to Charles.   [*Exit.*
            Enter Fairfax *and* Bradshaw
    Brad. Why all this heat, my Lord ; because I said
That Charles deserves to die ? Why, I repeat it :
And would you master this unmanly rage,
I might to reason prove it, but not frenzy.
    Fair. Well, I am calm—Speak out your bloody pur-
What hell devises, and what Bradshaw thinks.   [pose,
    Brad. Cast your eye backward then, and let us view
E'en the beginning of this Charles's reign ;
In the first year a raging plague destroy'd us,
And was prophetic of our woes to come :
Did it not sweep whole multitudes away
Fast as the sword, which Charles has since unsheath'd ?
' Did he not follow still his father's steps,
' Retain his ministry, pursue his aims ?

                            ' Would

‘ Would he, tho’ pray’d and threaten’d by the parliament,
‘ Give up thofe men, whofe counfels had mifled him ?
‘ And is not that prince weak—to fay no more—
‘ Who from a general outcry guards the man,
‘ Whofe bold ambition ftrikes at liberty,
‘ At native freedom, and the fubjects right ?’
　　Fair. You but this moment blam’d my warmth,
And art thyfelf tranfported.
　　Brad. Grant I be:
’Tis in the caufe that liberty approves,
And every honeft Englifhman muft own it ;
But to proceed—Thofe men he ftill held faft,
Or parted with ’em, as the heart drops blood :
‘ Witnefs the earl of Strafford :’ tax’d the land
By grievous impofitions; levy’d war
Againft the commons, and the kingdom’s peace.
But I forget me that I fpeak to Fairfax,
Who has fo often fought againft his arms,
And taught fuccefs to know the caufe of right.
　　Fair. I fought for reparation of our wrongs——
But cannot think that it confifts in murder.
I would not have him die.
　　Brad. By the good caufe,
It does portend fome more than common change,
When generals plead for mercy ! Shame it hence,
And let your vifage wear the glow of rage;
Let Prynn’s undaunted foul inform thy breaft,
And drive weak pity thence.
　　Fair. I’ll hear no more :
Thy fervile tongue may fpare its hireling office,
It roots my purpofe firmer : In thy fpeech
I read defign, tho’ oratory’s flowers
Strive to conceal the rancour of the heart.
O Eloquence ! thou violated fair,
How art thou woo’d, and won to either bed
Of right or wrong ! O when Injuftice folds thee,
Doft thou not curfe thy charms for pleafing him,
And blufh at conqueft ? But the juncture calls,
Nor will I leave one moment unemploy’d,
’Till the King’s fafety be confirm’d.　　　　　[*Exit.*
　　Brad. ’Tis well.
I muft to other folk, here time is loft.

　　　　　　　　　　　　　This

'This man has ftep'd into the ftream of mifchief,
Juft like the boy, who tries the water's cold,
And fhrinking pulls his foot to land : men, like me,
Plunge boldly in, and weather to their point.   [Exit.

SCENE *changes to the* King's *apartment.*

Enter King *and Bifhop* Juxon.

Juxon. Why does your highnefs feem fo loft in thought?
Confider not fo deeply, good my Lord.

King. The purport of my dream this afternoon,
Has fet this vifage on.   I'll tell thee, Juxon——
Finding my fpirits faint, I laid me down,
And courted fleep to eafe me ; to my wifh
It quickly feiz'd my eye-lids, and methought
(So fancy painted) former times return'd,
Grandeur encircled me, and regal ftate ;
My people's love flew round about my throne,
On acclamation's wing ; 'twas glory all,
And fuch a reign as Charles has pray'd for. Homage,
The bond of friendfhip, and the oath of truft,
Were all before me : ftraight the pleafing fcene,
Quick as the fearful eye can wink, was chang'd ;
And in its room, a vaft and dreary plain,
Comfortlefs, wild, without inhabitant,
Stretch'd out a difmal length that tir'd the eye ;
I was about to go,——when kind Adverfity
Pull'd me behind, and as I turn'd around,
Shew'd me where Innocence ftood weeping by ;
He whifper'd in my ear, that fhe alone
Of all my boafting friends, had ftaid with me.
The thought ftruck deep, I wak'd, and good my Lord,
I found my weeping queen within my arms.

Enter Cromwell.

Crom. If I difturb you, Sir, I afk your pardon :
Neceffity will fometimes be importunate,
And out-go compliment.

King. Your bufinefs, Sir ?

Crom. Know then, whatever may be thought of Crom-
He pays this vifit to approve his love,   [well,
His fair defign and honefty of heart
To Charles—Solicitous to bring you good,
Behold two bills, in tenor much the fame

                                        With

With thofe before prefented ; I prefume,
The eye in danger more diftinctly fees,
Freed from fecurity's thick film : Thefe fign'd,
Rigour may break her fword, and concord join us.

   King. Can the low peafant mount his thoughts with
The fervile judge of all men by themfelves.   [kings ?
But know, miftaken man, the noble mind
Rifes above diftrefs ; and terms, perhaps,
Which in the day of power I might accept,
Muft be refus'd in this : but thefe can never.
There is no good that equals the exchange
Of peaceful thoughts and an untainted mind.

   Crom. Where were thofe thoughts in Charles's former
When to defpotic fway you ftretch'd your view,   [days,
And would have pull'd up laws ? When to that end
You fo carefs'd your fav'rite Buckingham,
The tool of your defigns. What were your thoughts
When from the fair impeachment of the public,
You fhelter'd up that monfter minifter,
And hid him in the bofom of your fondnefs ? [fpeak'ft ;

   Juxon. Infolent Cromwell ! Know to whom thou
Think what a diftance Heaven has fet between you ;
And be your words as humble as your ftate.

   Crom. Diftance ! good bifhop ! But I cry you mercy ?
' For thus the clergy will ftill argue on,
' Deny from pique, affert from prejudice ;
' Shew us the leffon, feldom the example,
' And preach up laws which they will ne'er obey :'
But thou art trafh below the note of Cromwell :
To thee I fpeak, protector of black Buckingham.
' What muft that monarch be, who lets one man
' Ingrofs the offices of place and pow'r,
' Who, with the purloin'd money of the ftate,
' Buys popularity, and whofe carelefs eye
' Sees our fair trade deftroy'd by corfair force,
' And pirate violence : who merchandifes trufts,
' And higheft pofts—and whofe unbounded pow'r
' Does on his worthlefs kindred lavifh titles ?'

   King. Were I the perfon that thy malice fpeaks,
I fhould deferve this treatment. Thy bafe charg
Strikes at my honefty as King and man,
And forces me to anfwer. Well I know,

That

That for my actions here, to Heav'n alone
I stand accountable ; yet stooping thus,
(Low as to thee) I thus avow my justice ;
Have I not still maintain'd the subjects rights,
Preserv'd religion pure ; nay, struggled for it,
E'en to this hour, the witness of thy insolence ?
What would your faction have ? If monarchy ;
Must I not govern by the acts of state ?
I am a monarch else without a council.
Would you reduce the state to anarchy ?
You are a council then without a pow'r.
   Crom. You feel our power (as slightly as you term it.)
   King. Such as a robber's, by surprise and force :
Where is your right from Heav'n ?
   Crom. Power !
The right of nature and the free-born man.
   King. Leave me.
   Crom. You speak as if you still were king.
   King. If not : what am I then ?
   Crom. Charles Stuart, nothing more.
   King. Well may the servile herd insult and threaten,
When they behold the lion in the toils.
   Crom. You may complain as much as suits your will,
You've still that comfort left—So fare you well. [*Exit.*
   Juxon. Thus is good Fortune treated by the base :
O did she know how much they shame her favours,
She would confer 'em only on the great !
Be chearful, Sir ; he is not worth a thought.
   King. O Juxon ! think what majesty must feel,
Who bears an insult from a subject tongue :
But let him hence—I am compos'd again,
And for the worst prepar'd.   All-gracious Heav'n !
You gave me power, and you may take it back ;
You gave me life, and may reclaim the gift ;
That as you please—But spare this luckless land,
And save it from misfortune's rugged hand !
My ev'ry wish is for its joys increase,
And my last pray'r shall be my people's peace. [*Exeunt.*

END of the THIRD ACT.

ACT

ACT IV.

Enter King Charles, *the* Queen *and Lady* Fairfax.

QUEEN.

IS it like love thus to perfuade me hence?
  Is it like love, alas! in me to go?
Can fhe be faithful to her lucklefs Lord,
Who will be abfent in affliction's hour?
Is it not then the lenient hand of love
Proves its beft office? Then the virtuous wife
Shines in the full meridian of her truth,
And claims her part of forrow: O, my Lord,
Have I been fo unthrifty of thy joy,
That you deny me to partake your woe?

King. No, my beft Queen——You wrong my heart's
'Tis not my wifh advifes—but my fear,   [defign.
My fears for thee, the tendereft part of Charles;
When thou art fafe beyond their barbarous pow'r,
I cannot feel misfortune.

Queen. But I fhall,
More than to fhare e'en death with thee :——
My forrows will be doubled if I go :——
The pangs of feparation muft be great,
And my conceit of what my Charles may feel
Exceed reality—O let me ftay——
I was prepar'd to fuffer all things with you,
But not the fhock of parting.

Lady Fair. Welcome tears!
Who that have virtue can behold this fcene,
And not be actors in it?

King Now 'tis paft.
I would have fooner fpoke, but pow'rful Nature
Firft claim'd my tears, ere fhe would lend me words:
It muft not be, my love; thy pray'r to ftay
(The growing proof of thy eternal love)
Argues againft thee to my tender heart,
And forces thee away: this worthy Lady
Has found the means, and made the generous offer,
Her care prepares your flight: the prefent hour

That

That forces me before their black tribunal,
Will hold all eyes regardless of your steps,
And make security thy guide :—farewel ;
'Till we shall meet again, thy dear idea
Shall in my waking fancy still revive,
And fill up every dream.
　Queen. My dearest Lord,
Can you so easily pronounce—farewel,
When that farewel may be perhaps—for ever ?
O can you leave me thus ?——
Methinks our parting should affect the world,
And nature sympathize with griefs like ours——
O let me stay, at least, till this black day
Be past, that I may know the worst.
To be in doubt is worse than to be certain ;
My apprehension will increase my woe,
And bring the blackest scenes of death before me.
　King. No more, my queen ! that were to risk thy safe-
And make me more unhappy in thy danger :　　[ty,
Farewel.
　Queen. O, yet a little longer !
Each moment now is worth an age before.
Thou never-resting time ! 'tis only now
I count thy value.　O, my dearest Lord !
Who could believe when first we met in love,
That we should know a parting worse than death ?
Do not go yet.
　King. Heav'n knows I would not go——
But dire necessity must be obey'd :
And see where he appears in his worst form.
Keep in thy tears, my love, lest he suspect——
And teach thy heart to say farewel at once.
　　　　　　Enter Colonel Tomlinson.
　Tom. My Lord, I have orders to attend your Majesty
To Westminster.
　King. A moment spent in private,
And I am ready.　　　　　　　　　*[Exit.* Tom.
Do not droop, my queen,
Exert the strongest vigour of thy soul,
Call up thy piety, thy aweful virtue,
Thy resolution, and thy sex's pride,
And take their friendly counsel ; they will soon

　　　　　　　　　　　　　　　　Deter-

Determine you to think of Charles, as one
Beyond the power of faction in this world,
And ready for another—Fare thee well ;
I have this compliment to pay thy worth,
That now I leave thee with more tender thoughts
Than first I met thy love—this tear—adieu !
Now, Sir, lead on.   [*To Col.* Toml. *entering.*
    Queen. O stay ; my dearest Lord !
                            [*Exeunt* King *and Col.* Toml.
Let me assure thee of my faith and love——
Witness thou aweful Ruler of the world,
How much I feel in parting—how my heart
Labours to break to prove its constancy ;
How my affection still has call'd thee dear ;
Never unkind, 'till in this parting moment.
What do I say ? Alas ! my Charles is gone——
Fancy presented him before my eyes,
And my tears wrong'd my fight—he's gone for ever.
    Lady Fair. Good Madam, think your safety calls upon
Your very forrows are not here fecure ;   [you ;
Tho' you neglect your own, yet think his eafe,
The eafe of Charles, depends upon your flight ;
I have provided every proper means,
They wait your will.——
    Queen. Kind Lady, I will go——
But Oh, be just to nature, and to pity,
And own 'tis hard—I thank your friendly tears,
They fpeak my meaning—but I weary you.——
The wretch who feels misfortunes will complain,
And I have won'drous reafon—O, my Charles !
Since I muft go, may every adverfe ftar
Dart on my wand'ring head, and leave thy fky
Deck'd with propitious planets only.—May thy life,
Clear as thy innocence, adorn the world,
And be the theme of wonder.—O my heart !   [*Exeunt.*
Enter Marquis of Lindfey, *meeting the Duke of* Richmond.
    Lind. Saw you the King pafs by ?
    Rich. I did, my Lord:
As to his coronation, not his trial :
Such was his look—fuch aweful majefty
Beam'd out on every fide, and ftruck the gazer.
No mark of forrow furrow'd up his face,

                                        Nor

Nor ſtopp'd his ſmiles to his ſaluting friends ;
Clear as his conſcience was his viſage ſeen,
The emblem of his heart.   As I approach'd,
Richmond, ſaid he, commend me to my friends ;
Say, tho' my pow'r is gone, my wiſhes reach 'em,
And ev'ry prayer that riſes, breathes their welfare.
'Tis not in faction to ſubdue the ſpirit,
Or break the noble mind : his ſpeaking eyes
Repeated his commands, and pierc'd my heart :
E'en the baſe rabble——licens'd to inſult,
Struck with the dignity of kingly awe,
Forgot their hire, and roſe from praiſe to wonder.

   Lind. Will you not follow, Sir ? 'twere worth remark,
How he deports himſelf.

   Rich. O fear not Charles :
Let him encounter with a hoſt of kings,
And he ſhall ſtand the ſhock without a terror :
Will he then ſhrink beneath a ſubject-brow,
Tho' wrinkled with rebellion ?—No, good Lindſey,
The lion cannot loſe his kingly nature,
The ſun its heat, nor Charles his noble firmneſs ;
Perhaps indeed, his generous heart may feel,
Not for himſelf, but for his tyrant judges ;
He may lament deprav'd humanity,
And bluſh to be miſtaken in his people.
See, what a mournful viſage Fairfax wears,
The ſun of pleaſantry eclips'd by thought :
Now judgment combats inadvertency,
And makes him curſe ſucceſs—but thus 'tis ever
When courage wildly ſtarts out by itſelf,
Nor aſks conſideration's friendly aid ;
Confuſion joins him ; then he wanders thro'
The thicket Doubt, the maze Perplexity,
And finds at laſt Repentance.

                   Enter Fairfax.

   Fair. Now the ſcene
Of bloodieſt purpoſe is on foot, and acting ;
Now Murder mounts the bench, array'd like Juſtice,
And points the ſword at Charles——ill-fated man !
Ha ! who are thoſe ? The friends of Cromwell's faction ?
No, they are with their huntſmen on the ſcent

Of

Of royal blood, uncoupled for deſtruction,——
If ſorrow blinds me not——the duke of Richmond.
  Rich. Good Sir, how fare you?
  Fair. Wond'rous ill, my Lord.
Could I but tell you what I feel,——yet live,
You would conclude me danger-proof——O, Sir!
Reflection ſhews me the vaſt tract I've paſt,
And ſtern Impoſſibility denies
One ſtep return—yet (be my witneſs Heav'n)
This dreadful day was never in my wiſh.
  Rich. We do not think it was. But, gentle Lord,
Think of ſome means to ward this fatal blow,
And ſave the King. Would you but go, my Lord,
Your ſtruggle might——
  Fair. Alas! what can I do?
Was ever army routed by one man?
I have an army there to combat with.
Should I go there in order for prevention,
Failing, my preſence would be made conſent,
And I ſtill more unhappy. O the change!
This is the curſe of independent pow'r,
For preſbytery never meant it. Yet, my Lords,
You ſhall not ſay, that Fairfax only talks;
He will approve his honeſty by deeds;
Somewhat he will attempt to ſave his honour,
And clear it to the view of future times.
  Rich. We do not doubt you will, nor yet your power.
My Lord, farewel.   [*Exeunt* Rich. *and* Lind.
  Fair. My pow'r!——ſay, what is pow'r?
The vain extent of title and of land;
The barbarous impulſe to the inſulting wretch,
To uſe his fellow-creature like a ſlave;
The woman's idol, and the man's misfortune,
As it too often robs him of humanity.
This is the worſt degree——behold the beſt,
And now 'tis lovely; the redreſs of wrongs,
Hunger's repaſt, and the large draught of thirſt,
The poor man's riches, and the rich man's wealth,
When thus apply'd—The means to ſtop the death,
The death of Charles——This is my wiſh for pow'r.
                     [*Exit.*

      D   SCENE.

SCENE *draws, and discovers the High-Court.*

King, Bradſhaw, Cromwell, Ireton, *&c.*
  King. Sir, were my perſon all the danger here,
I ſhould not think it worth the pain of ſpeech ;
Your charge 'gainſt me is of the ſmalleſt force,
But 'tis my people's liberties I prize,
At which, through me you ſtrike : impeachments run
In the King's name, and therefore cannot lie
Againſt the King himſelf ; what earthly pow'r
Can juſtly call me to account ?   By what law
Have you erected this pretended court ?——
The houſe of commons ? – Say, is that alone
A court of judicature ? Where are the lords
To lend their aid ? the King to ſit ſupreme,
And paſs the nation's laws ? Are theſe your means
To bring the King to meet his parliament ?
To force him hither like a criminal ?
I lately did require, and preſs'd it warmly,
Stoop'd almoſt to intreaty, to be heard
Before both houſes in the painted-chamber ;
I told you what I had to offer there
Concern'd the kingdom's ſafety more than mine :
I was refus'd—Is this your boaſted juſtice ?
Conſider of it yet—and hear your King ;
If you do not, remember where it lies,
The weight of this day's guilt ; if you refuſe,
Do as you pleaſe—I have no more to ſay.
  Brad. The court has ſomething then to ſay to you,
Which, though it may not pleaſe you, muſt be ſpoke :
You have been charg'd with tyranny and murder,
With levying arms againſt the commonwealth,
And joining in rebellion 'gainſt the people.
  King. Sir, give me leave to ſpeak, ere ſentence paſſes,
Againſt thoſe imputations—
  Brad. By your favour,
Your time is paſt, and ſentence now approaching.
  King. Am I not to be heard ?
  Brad. 'Tis now too late ;
You have diſown'd us for a court of juſtice ;
We have too long been trifled with already ;
And muſt proceed—Attend your ſentence, Sir :

The

The commons, in behalf of the whole people,
Have conftituted this high-court of juftice,
To try Charles Stuart, lately king of England.
He has thrice heard his charge, and thrice deny'd
The pow'r and jurifdiction of the court;
For which contempt, and proof of his high crimes,
It does pronounce him tyrant, traitor, murderer,
Adjudging him to death, by fevering
His head and body—This is the joint act,
The fentence, judgment, and the refolution
Of the whole court.

> [*The whole court rifes in token of their affent.*

King. Will you hear me, Sir?
Brad. Not after fentence.
King. No, Sir?
Brad. It is too late. Withdraw your prifoner.
King. ' May I not fpeak ?—I may, Sir, after fentence.
' Your favour, Sir, I may, Sir, after fentence.
' *Brad.* Adjourn the court.

> [*The King is brought forward; the Scene clofes.*

King. Deny'd to fpeak !—Why have I lived to this?
When I had power, the meaneft of my fubjects,
Not heard by me, would ftraight arraign my juftice,
And brand me with the hated name of tyrant.
Will future ages, looking back to this,
Credit the record? They will rather deem it
The black invective of a partial pen,
And curfe his memory that libell'd England.
Sir, I am ready to attend your will,
Do your worft office; if 'tis your commiffion,
Then lead me down this inftant to the block;
'Twill be a joyful hearing, for believe me
I would not live in longer fellowfhip
With men, whom my beft thoughts muft call ungrateful.

Tom. Sir, my commands are to attend you back;
I have no more in charge.

King. I follow you.

> [*As he goes out, Fairfax enters.*

Fair. Sir, let me trefpafs for a word or two,
Ere you remove your prifoner.   [*To* Tomlinfon.
Tom. I obey, Sir.
King. Your pleafure, Sir? If you come here t'infult,

                                        Spare

Spare not the taunt, nor the opprobrious fmile:
I have to-day already borne fo much,
That an addition will be fcarcely felt.
  Fair. Wrong me not fo; I bear a fairer purpofe:
My heart, detefting this accurfed day,
Comes to approve its honefty to Charles:
If I have often fought againft thy arms,
My confcience dictated, and not my hate;
Acquit me to thyfelf of this laft act,
And judge the former as you pleafe.
  King. Good Fairfax,
The prefent times are liable to error,
I am a fatal inftance; then forgive me.
I had forgot how lately I had caufe
To think you now no enemy to Charles;
But forrow forc'd down her lethargic draught,
Which had clos'd up the eye of memory.
  Fair. Ill-fated prince! how does thy firmnefs fhine,
And make affliction glorious: Oh, 'tis thus,
The truly great exert their refolution,
And make calamity a virtue: Cromwell now
Lofes the barb'rous joy of his defign,
To fee misfortune's arrow fail to pierce thee.
  King. Believe me, Fairfax, 'tis not innate firmnefs,
The dame morality, the Stoic patience,
That furnifh true ferenity of mind:
I had try'd all thefe helps, but prov'd 'em weak,
And found the beft philofophy in virtue.
Can the fond teacher's leffon, conn'd by rote,
Change the dark lodging of the murderer's breaft,
To the fun-lighted rooms of innocence? Oh, no!
As to the agents of my prefent fate,
I look upon them with the eye of thanks;
Who from this life of forrow wing my parting,
And fend me fooner to an happier throne.
  Fair. Such refignation wears the noble mind,
And triumphs over death: but, gentle Charles!
Think not of death fo foon, live long and happy
Fairfax will try his utmoft ftretch of power,
But you fhall live, though this black day has happen'd;
Perfuafion, pray'r, and force, fhall all be us'd,
To make my promife good.

King.

King. Good Fairfax, hear me;
Nor indiscreetly throw thyself away,
To save the man whose wishes are to die.
I had remov'd my thoughts from earth, and now
'Twill be such pain to call 'em back again——
Life is not worth the trouble: yet I thank thee.
   Fair. This was but half my purpose: hear me on—
If in the hurry of intemp'rate zeal,
I have outgone the justice of the cause,
And, erring in my judgment, fought in wrong,
Let this intreaty win thee to a pardon.
   King. If to have my forgiveness, makes thee clear,
Thou art as white as virtue.
   Fair. Glorious Charles !
But I will hasten to preserve his life,
And make my gratitude my thanks; farewel !
It is the common interest of mankind
To let him live, to shine out an example.
   King. Who dresses in good fortune's gorgeous ermine,
Looks not so comely to a virtuous eye,
As he who clothes him in repentant black.
I tire your patience. Come, Sir, lead the way ;
Lighter than fancy does my bosom feel,
My thoughts are mercy, and my quiet conscience
Tranquility's still calm ; no anxious fear
Beats in my pulse, or ruffles me with care:
If the bare hope of immortality
Knows peace like this, what must the full enjoyme
         be ?

E*ND* of the F*ourth* A*ct.*

ACT V.

Fairfax solus.

WHY did I conquer—to repent of conquest ?
   Who, though I fought for liberty alone,
Will yet acquit me of the guilt that follows ?
Will future ages, when they read my page,
(Though Charles himself absolves me of the deed)
Spare me the name of regicide ? Oh, no !
I shall be blacken'd with my party's crimes,

And damn'd with my full fhare, though innocent.
In vain then 'gainft oppreffion have I warr'd,
In vain for liberty uprear'd the fword ;
Pofterity's black curfe fhall brand my name,
And make me live in infamy for ever.
Now, valour, break thy fword, thy ftandard victory,
Furl up thy enfigns, bold hoftility,
And fink into inaction : fince, alas !
One tainted heart, or one ambitious brain
Can turn the current of the nobleft purpofe,
And fpoil the trophies of an age's war.
But fee where, to my wifh, ftern Cromwell comes ;
Now urge him ftrongly for the life of Charles,
And, if intreaty fails, avow thy purpofe.

Enter Cromwell.

Crom. Fairfax in thought ! My noble Lord, good day.

Fair. To make it good, let Cromwell grant my prayer,
So mercy and the fun fhall fhine together.

Crom. Still on this paltry fubject ! Fairfax, why,
Why will you wrong intreaty by this caufe ?
Fairfax is wife, and fhould not afk of Cromwell
To grant what juftice ftops ; yours are not years
When childhood prattles, or when dotage mopes :——
Pardon the expreffion.

Fair. I forgive you all,
All you can think, but rigour to the King.

Crom. Pr'ythee no more : this mercy that you pray for,
As ill becomes the tongue, as my feverity ;
Nay, worfe. Would you obftruct the law
In its due office ; nor permit the axe
To fall upon offenders, fuch as Charles ?
Would you fee tyranny again arife,
And fpread in its foundation ? Let us then
Seize on our general, Liberty, who ftill
Has in the front of battle fought our caufe,
And led us on to conqueft ; let us bind him
In the ftrong chains of rough prerogative,
And throw him helplefs at the feet of Charles :
He will abfolve us then, and praife our folly.

Fair. This is a fophiftry too weak for reafon :
You would excufe the guilt of Charles's death,
By fhewing me the oppofite extreme ;

But

But can you find no mean, no middle courfe,
Steering between the danger of the laft,
And horror of the firft? I know you can.
    Crom. It is not to be done: would Fairfax now,
When he has labour'd up the fteep afcent,
And wafted time and fpirits; would he now,
When but one ftep exalts him to the fummit,
Where to his eye the fair horizon ftretches,
And ev'ry profpect greatnefs can command;
Would he now ftop, let go his fearful hold,
And tumble from the height?
    Fair. I aim at none;
Damn'd be all greatnefs that depraves the heart,
Or calls one blufh from honefty—no more——
I fhall grow warm to be thus trifled with:
Think better, Cromwell—I have given my promife
That Charles fhall live.
    Crom. A promife may be broke;
Nay, ftart not at it—'Tis an hourly practice;
The trader breaks it—yet is counted honeft;
The courtier keeps it not—yet keeps his honour;
Hufband and wife in marriage promife much,
Yet follow fep'rate pleafures, and are—virtuous.
The churchmen promife too, but wifely, they
To a long payment ftretch the crafty bill,
And draw upon futurity: a promife!
'Tis the wife man's freedom, and the fool's reftraint;
‘ It is the fhip in which the knave embarks,
‘ Who rigs it with the tackle of his confcience,
‘ And fails with ev'ry wind: regard it not.'
    Fair. Can Cromwell think fo bafely as he fpeaks?
It is impoffible, he does but try
How well fair fpeech becomes a vicious caufe,
But, I hope, fcorns it in the richeft drefs.
Yet hear me on, it is our intereft fpeaks,
And bids us fpare his life; while that continues,
No other title can annoy our caufe,
And him we have fecure; but grant him dead,
Another claim ftarts up, another king,
Out of our reach—this bloody deed perhaps
May roufe the princes of the continent,
(Who think their perfons ftruck at in this blow)
To fhake the very fafety of our caufe.

Crom.

Crom. When you confult our int'reft, fpeak with free-
It is the turn and point of all defign.   [dom ;
But take this anfwer, Fairfax, in return ;
Britain, the queen of ifles, our fair poffeffion,
Secur'd by nature, laughs at foreign force ;
Her fhips her bulwark, and the fea her dike,
Sees plenty in her lap, and braves the world.
Be therefore fatisfy'd ; for Charles muft die.

Fair. Wilt thou be heard, tho' at thy utmoft need,
Who now art deaf to mercy and to pray'r ?
Oh, curs'd Ambition, thou devouring bird,
How doft thou from the field of honefty
Pick ev'ry grain of profit and delight,
And mock the reaper, Virtue ! Bloody man !
Know that I ftill have pow'r, have ftill the means
To make that certain which I ftoop to afk ;
And fix myfelf againft thy black defign,
And tell thee, dauntlefs, that he fhall not die.

Crom. Will Fairfax turn a rebel to the caufe,
And fhame his glories ?

Fair. I abjure the name ;
I know no rebel on the fide of virtue.
This I am fure of, he that acts unjuftly,
Is the worft rebel to himfelf ; and tho' now
Ambition's trumpet and the drum of pow'r
May drown the found, yet confcience will, one day,
Speak loudly to him, and repeat that name.

Crom. You talk as 'twere a murder, not a juftice.
Have we not brought him to an open trial ?
Does not the general cry pronounce his death ?
Come, Fairfax dares not.

Fair. By yon Heav'n, I will——
I know thee refolute ; but fo is Fairfax.
You fee my purpofe, and fhall find I dare.   [*Going.*

Crom. Fairfax, yet ftay. I would extend my pow'r
To its full ftretch, to fatisfy your wifh ;
Yet would not have you think that I fhould grant
That to your threats, which I deny'd your pray'r——
Judge not fo meanly of yourfelf and me.
Be calm, and hear me——What is human nature,
When the intemperate heat of paffion blinds
The eye of reafon, and commits her guidance

                                                    To

To headlong rashness? He directs her steps
Wide of success to error's pathless way,
And disappointments wild; yet such we are,
So frail our being, that our judgment reaches
Scarce farther than our sight——Let us retire,
And, in this great affair, intreat his aid,
Who only can direct to certainty.
There is I know not what, of good presage,
That dawns within, and lights to happy issue.

   Fair. If Heav'n and you consider it alike,
It must be happy.

   Crom. An hour or two of pray'r
Will pull down favour upon Charles and us.

   Fair. I am contented; but am still resolv'd
That Charles shall live—I shall expect your answer
With the impatience of desiring lovers,
Who swell a moment's absence to an age.   *[Exit.*

   Crom. This was a danger quite beyond my view,
Which only this expedient could prevent.
Fairfax is weak in judgment; but so brave,
That, set determination by his side,
And he ascends the mountain top of peril.
Now time is gain'd to ward against his pow'r,
Which must be quickly thought on—To my wish—

Enter Ireton.

   Ire. I but this instant met the general, Fairfax,
Who told me his intreaty had prevail'd
To save the life of Charles—'Tis more than wonder—

   Crom. Ireton, thy presence never was more timely.
I would disclose; but now each moment's loss,
Is more than the neglect of future years.
Hie thee in person to St James's, Ireton,
And warn the officer, whose charge leads forth
The King to execution, to be sudden:
Let him be more than punctual to the time;
If his respect to us forerun his warrant,
It shall win greatness for him; so inform him——
That done, repair o'th' instant to the army,
And see a chosen party march directly,
(Such as can well be trusted) post them, Ireton,
Around the scaffold——My best kinsman, fly.
[*Exit* Ireton.
Why

Why, now, I think I have fecur'd my point ;
I fet out in the current of the tide,
And not one wind that blows around the compafs,
But drives me to.fuccefs. Ambition, now,
Soars to its darling height, and, eagle-like,
Looks at the fun of pow'r, enjoys its blaze,
And grows familiar with the brightnefs ; now I fee.
Dominion nigh ;. Superiority
Beckons and points me to the chair of'ftate ;
There Grandeur robes me.   Now let Cromwell boaft
That he has reft the crown from Charles's brow,
To make it blaze more awful on his own.   [*Exit.*

SCENE, *the* King *difcovered on a couch.*

King. Kind Sleep, farewel !
Thou haft been loyal in the nightly care,
And always fmooth'd my pillow : at our parting,
As to a faithful friend, I fay, farewel,
And thank thee for thy fervice.   Here's another,
Enter Bifhop Juxon.
Whofe better care gives quiet to the mind ;
Who gives the rich opiate of content,
That makes us fleep in hope, and wake to mercy ;
Him too, the bankrupt Charles can only pay
As he has done the former ; no return,
But the poor gratitude of thanks, warm from the heart.
Say, my good Lord, have you fo foften'd rigour,
That I may fee my children ere I die ?

Jux. It is permitted, Sir ; they wait without ;
I would not let them enter, till I knew
You were prepar'd, and ready for the interview.
[*Exit* Juxon.

King. Good Juxon, lead them hither. Now the father,
Spite of my firmnefs, fteals into my eye,
And melts my manhood. Heart, thou haft no temper
Proof againft nature, fpeaking in a child !
Enter Bifhop Juxon, James, Glo'fter, *and* Elizabeth.
James. My royal father !
King. Good Juxon, make them rife ;
For if I look that way I fhall kneel too,
And join with them in tears. A chair, good Juxon.
[Juxon *brings a chair forward, and raifes the children.*
Come

Come hither, James; nay, do not weep, my boy;
Keep thy eyes bright to look on better times.
    James. I will command my nature if I can,
And stop these tears of sorrow; for, indeed,
They drown my sight; and I would view thee well,
Copy my royal father in his death,
And be the son of his heroic virtues.
    King. Thou art the child of duty; hear me, James,
And lay up this last lesson in thy heart:
When I am dead, look on thy brother Charles
Not as thy brother only, but thy king;
Pay him fraternal love, and subject duty;
Nor let ambition, or the thirst to reign,
Poison thy firm allegiance.   When thou seest him,
Bear him my blessing, and this last advice:
If Heav'n restores him to his lawful crown,
Let him wreak no revenge upon his foes,
But think it his best conquest to forgive;
With kindness let him treat Success, so shall she be
A constant guest; his promise, when once given,
Let no advantage break; nor any view
Make him give up his honesty to reach it:
Let him maintain his pow'r, but not increase it;
The string, prerogative, when strain'd too high,
Cracks like the tortur'd chord of harmony,
And spoils the concert between king and subject:
' Let him regard his people more than ministers,
' Whose interest or ambition may mislead him.'
These rules observ'd, may make him a good prince,
And happier than his father——Wilt thou, James,
Remember this?
    James. Oh, doubt not, royal Sir!
Can what my father says escape my memory;
And at a time when he shall speak no more?
    King. Come to my arms, my boy.
    James. Would I could weep the blood that warms my
For water wrongs my sorrow.   [heart;
    King. My dear Elizabeth,
Draw near, and take thy dying father's blessing.
Say to thy mother, (if thou e'er shalt see her)
That my thoughts never wander'd from her; that my
Holds her as dear, ev'n in this hour of death,   [heart

    I   As

As when my eyes firſt languiſh'd on her beauties;
Tell her, that Charles is only gone before
T' inherit an immortal crown, and ſhare it with her.
Farewel, Elizabeth ; and let thy love
And thy obedience wait thy brother Charles.

   Eliz. Alas, my father, I but now have found
A paſſage for my words, and yet you ſay,
Farewel, already ! .

   King. Come, my little Glo'ſter,
Come to my arms, and let me kiſs thy cheek.

   Glo'ſter. Alas, my Lord, tis cold and wet with tears !
I'll wipe it dry, and warm it with my hand,
That it may meet your kindneſs as it ought.

   King. Glo'ſter, when I am dead, your brother Charles
Is then your King and maſter—Love and obey him.
Theſe men who ſhall cut off thy father's head,
When I am dead, perhaps, may make thee King ;
But do not thou, I charge thee, on my bleſſing,
Accept the crown while thy two brothers live ;
Conſider, Glo'ſter, they were born before thee,
And have an elder title—Wilt thou, Glo'ſter ?

   Gloſter. A King ! No, they ſhall tear me firſt in pieces.

   King. Oh, Nature, Nature, do not ſtrike ſo deeply !
This ſcene is worſe than death——I am ready, Sir.
                        [Tomlinſon *at the door.*

  James. Oh, Sir !
  Eliz. My Lord !
  Glo'ſter. My father !
  King. Oh !
  Glo'ſter. I cannot part from you, my deareſt father.
Would not thoſe bloody men that cut your head off,
If I ſhould beg it, cut off mine ?

   King. Heart, thou art marble, not to break at this—
Yet I muſt go ; for dire neceſſity
Has ſtruggled long with my paternal fondneſs,
And has at length prevail'd. Farewel, at once.
                        [*Going, returns.*

I thought I had taken my laſt leave of them ;
But find that nature calls me back again,
And aſks another look, another parting kiſs.
Be virtuous, and be happy.   [*Embrace.*

   Glo'ſter. Oh, my poor father !——   [*They are led off.*
                                    King.

King. So, now 'tis over—Let thy friendly aid,
Good Juxon, bear me company to death—
Now, Sir, lead on ; ere long I hope to fee
A world more glorious ; where no difcord lives,
Nor error rifes, and no faction thrives :
There the unfetter'd mind perfection knows,
And looks with pity upon human woes.   [*Exeunt.*
   Enter Duke of Richmond, *and Marquis of* Lindfey.
   Rich. Oh, fatal day ! now horror is on foot
In her worft garb, and ftern calamity
Can do no more to England : Charles's fun
Sets in his blood, and blufhes for his people.
   Lind. What aweful majefty his vifage bears,
Nor deigns the tribute of one forrowing look,
To grace misfortune !
   Rich. Look where Fairfax comes ;
His motion wild, and his diftemper'd eye
Shoots fire around, and fpeaks fome ftrange emotion.
          Enter Fairfax.
   Fair. Curs'd be the villain's arts, and every wile
That wrought me to believe him : Oh, Credulity,
Thou haft as many ears as Fame has tongues,
Open to every found of truth and falfhood !
'Tis now too late, impoffible to fave him :
Fool that I was, I knew him for a villain,
Yet trufted to him, to the monfter Cromwell.
   Rich. Fairfax, the world acquits thee of the deed ;
Thy pow'r has labour'd ftrongly for his fafety :
Behold where Juxon, the good bifhop, comes,
Return'd from his laft fervice to his mafter.
   Fair. I will not ftay to hear the fad relation.
But think on my revenge on Cromwell ;
May the mercy which he deny'd to Charles's mortal part,
Ne'er light upon his foul, though at his laft intreaty.
          Enter Juxon.
   Rich. Charles is at peace.
   Juxon. He is, my gentle Lord ;
And may we all meet death with equal firmnefs !
Patience fate by him in an angel's garb,
And held out a full bowl of rich content,
Of which he largely quaff'd : then came Charity,
And in behalf of Charles, with hafty hand,

E.   Dealt

Dealt round forgiveneſs to the world: his pray'r
Was for his foes more earneſt than himſelf,
Becauſe their wants were greater.   Thus fell Charles——
A monument of ſhame to the preſent age,
A warning to the future.   His example
May prove this maxim's truth to all mankind;
The ſubject's reverence, and the prince's love,
Graſping and graſp'd, walk hand in hand together,
Strengthen'd by union: then the king's command
Is loſt in the obedience of the ſubject:
The king, unaſk'd, confirms the people's rights,
And by the willing gift prevents the claim.
Theſe are the virtues that endear a king,
Adorn a people, and true greatneſs bring.

                             [*Exeunt.*

END of the FIFTH ACT.

E P I L O G U E.

Written by a FRIEND.

AT length our bard has told his difmal ftory ;
   He thinks—without offence to *Whig* or *Tory*,
He writes not from a fpirit of contention ;
And only on third night expects—his penfion.
Ladies, when civil dudgeon firft grew high,
And the good folks fell out—they knew not why——
A ftubborn race, no doubt on't, were thofe *Round-heads*,
Rebels at once to female power, and crown'd-heads :
But now, blefs'd change ! our heroes give their votes
For government of kings, and petticoats.
Had we then liv'd—What crowds of volunteers !
Down with the *Rump*, and high for *Cavaliers* !
In thofe prim times, our grandmothers of yore,
Preferr'd a pray'r-book to a matadore :
At court, each turtle only lov'd her mate,
And no intrigues went on—but thofe of ftate.
What odious Salique law ('twas none of nature)
Excludes us women from the legiflature ?
Could we affemble once in convocation,
How purely would we fettle all the nation !
Lovers and op'ras fhould employ our cares,
Cards, mafquerades, and fuch-like ftate-affairs :
Debates, like a male-fenate, we could handle ;
And move, as well as they, to—fnuff a candle :
Our ay's and no's with one fhrill voice declare ;
And none be mutes, but all, all fpeakers there.
Now, on our ftage, while *Charles* once more is try'd,
He hopes none here can prove a regicide ;
A milder fentence to receive, his truft is,
Tremendous pit, in your high court of juftice.
If bravely you'd fupport the good old caufe,
Atone your fathers crimes by your applaufe ;
Lay not a harb'rous tax on your good-nature,
Nor raife in fpleen the funds of wit, by fatire.

I. Roberts del.   Pub.Night for Bells British Theatre May 22d 1777.

Mr. PALMER in the Character of STUKELY.
"But here, he comes!___I must dissemble!"

THE
GAMESTER.

A TRAGEDY.

As written by Mr. MOORE,

DISTINGUISHING ALSO THE

VARIATIONS OF THE THEATRE,

AS PERFORMED AT THE

Theatre-Royal in Drury-Lane.

Regulated from the Prompt-Book.

By PERMISSION of the MANAGERS.

By Mr. HOPKINS, Prompter.

LONDON:
Printed for JOHN BELL, near *Exeter-Exchange,* in the *Strand.*

MDCCLXXVII.

TO THE

RIGHT HONOURABLE

HENRY PELHAM.

SIR,

IT was a very fine piece of oratory of a young lawyer at the bar, who, as council againſt a highwayman, obſerved that the proſecutor had been robbed of a certain quantity of ore, which being purified by fire, cut into circular pieces, and impreſſed with the image of a king and the arms of a ſtate, brought with it the neceſſaries, the conveniences, and the luxuries of life. I'll be hanged, ſays an honeſt country gentleman who was ſtanding by, if this flouriſhing fool does not mean money. But if he had ſaid it in one word, would not all the reſt have been implied?

Juſt ſuch a cenſure as this ſhould I deſerve, if in an addreſs to Mr. Pelham, I endeavoured to enumerate the qualities he poſſeſſes. The characters of great men are generally connected with their names; and it is impoſſible for any one to read the name of Mr. Pelham, without connecting with it, in his own mind, the virtues of humanity.

It is therefore ſufficient that I deſire his acceptance of this play; that I acknowledge the obligations I owe him, and that I ſubſcribe myſelf

His moſt grateful,

And moſt obedient ſervant,

EDW. MOORE.

A 2

PRO-

PROLOGUE.

Written and spoken by Mr. GARRICK.

LIKE fam'd La Mancha's knight, who launce in hand
   Mounted his steed to free th' enchanted land,
Our Quixote bard sets out a monster taming,
Arm'd at all points, to fight that hydra—Gaming.
Aloft on Pegasus he waves his pen,
And hurls defiance at the caitiff's den :
The first on fancy'd giants spent his rage,
But this has more than windmills to engage.
He combats passion, rooted in the soul,
Whose powers at once delight ye and controul ;
Whose magic bondage each lost slave enjoys,
Nor wishes freedom, though the spell destroys.
To save our land from this magician's charms,
And rescue maids and matrons from his arms,
Our knight poetic comes—And, Oh, ye fair !
This black Enchanter's wicked arts beware !
His subtle poison dims the brightest eyes,
And at his touch, each grace and beauty dies.
Love, gentleness and joy to rage give way,
And the soft dove becomes a bird of prey.
May this our bold advent'rer break the spell,
And drive the dæmon to his native hell.
Ye slaves of passion, and ye dupes of chance,
Wake all your pow'rs from this destructive trance !
Shake off the shackles of this tyrant vice :
Hear other calls than those of cards and dice :
Be learn'd in nobler arts than arts of play,
And other debts than those of honour pay.
No longer live insensible to shame,
Lost to your country, families and fame.
Could our romantic muse this work achieve,
Would there one honest heart in Britain grieve ?
Th' attempt, though wild, would not in vain be made,
If ev'ry honest hand would lend its aid.

A 3

DRA.

DRAMATIS PERSONÆ.

MEN.

		Drury-Lane.
Beverley,	—— ——	Mr. Reddish.
Lewson,	—— ——	Mr. Brereton.
Stukely,	—— ——	Mr. Palmer.
Jarvis,	—— ——	Mr. Aickin.
Bates,	—— ——	Mr. Packer.
Dawson,	—— ——	Mr. Norris.
Waiter,	—— ——	Mr. Everard.

WOMEN.

Mrs. *Beverley,*	—— ——	Miss Younge.
Charlotte,	—— ——	Miss Hopkins.
Lucy,	—— ——	Miss Platt.

THE

THE GAMESTER.

*** *The lines diftinguifhed by inverted comas, ' thus,' are omitted in the reprefentation.*

ACT I.

Enter Mrs. Beverely *and* Charlotte.

MRS. BEVERLEY.

BE comforted, my dear; all may be well yet. And now, methinks, the lodging begins to look with another face. Oh, fifter! fifter! if thefe were all my hardfhips; if all I had to complain of were no more than quitting my houfe, fervants, equipage, and fhew, your pity would be weaknefs.

Char. Is poverty nothing, then?

Mrs. B. Nothing in the world, if it affected only me. While we had a fortune, I was the happieft of the rich: and now 'tis gone, give me but a bare fubfiftence and my hufband's fmiles, and I'll be the happieft of the poor. To me now thefe lodgings want nothing but their mafter. Why do you look at me?

Char. That I may hate my brother.

Mrs. B. Don't talk fo, Charlotte.

Char. Has he not undone you?——Oh, this pernicious vice of gaming! But methinks his ufual hours of four or five in the morning might have contented him; 'twas mifery enough to wake for him till then. Need he have ftaid out all night? I fhall learn to deteft him?

Mrs. B. Not for the firft fault. He never flept from me before.

Char. Slept from you! No, no, his nights have nothing to do with fleep. How has this one vice driven him from every virtue! Nay, from his affections, too! ——The time was, fifter——

Mrs.

Mrs. B. And is. I have no fear of his affections. Would I knew that he were safe!

Char. From ruin and his companions——But that's impoffible. His poor little boy, too? What muft become of him?

Mrs. B. Why want fhall teach him induftry. From his father's miftakes he fhall learn prudence, and from his mother's refignation, patience. Poverty has no fuch terrors in it as you imagine. There's no condition of life, ficknefs and pain excepted, where happinefs is excluded. The hufbandman, who rifes early to his labour, enjoys more welcome reft at night for't. His bread is fweeter to him; his home happier; his family dearer; his enjoyments furer. The fun that roufes him in the morning, fets in the evening to releafe him. All fituations have their comforts, if fweet contentment dwell in the heart. But my poor Beverley has none. The thought of having ruined thofe he loves, is mifery for ever to him. Would I could eafe his mind of that!

Char. If he alone were ruined, 'twere juft he fhould be punifhed. He is my brother, 'tis true; but when I think of what he has done; of the fortune you brought him; of his own large eftate too, fquandered away upon this vileft of paffions, and among the vileft of wretches! Oh, I have no patience! My own little fortune is untouched, he fays. Would I were fure on't.

Mrs. B. And fo you may—'twould be a fin to doubt it.

Char. I will be fure on't—'twas madnefs in me to give it to his management. But I'll demand it from him this morning. I have a melancholy occafion for't.

Mrs. B. What occafion?

Char. To fupport a fifter.

Mrs. B. No; I have no need on't. Take it, and reward a lover with it. The generous Lewfon deferves much more. Why won't you make him happy?

Char. Becaufe my fifter's miferable.

Mrs. B. You muft not think fo. I have my jewels left yet. I'll fell them to fupply our wants; and when all's gone, thefe hands fhall toil for our fupport. The poor fhould be induftrious——Why thofe tears, Charlotte?

Char. They flow in pity for you.

Mrs.

Mrs. B. All may be well yet. When he has nothing to lofe I fhall fetter him in thefe arms again ; and then what is it to be poor ?

Char. Cure him but of this deftructive paffion, and my uncle's death may retrieve all yet.

Mrs. B. Ay, Charlotte, could we cure him. But the difeafe of play admits no cure but poverty ; and the lofs of another fortune would but encreafe his fhame and his affliction. Will Mr. Lewfon call this morning ?

Char. He faid fo laft night. He gave me hints too, that he had fufpicions of our friend Stukely.

Mrs. B. Not of treachery to my hufband ? That he loves play, I know ; but furely he's honeft.

Char. He would fain be thought fo ; therefore I doubt him. Honefty needs no pains to fet itfelf off.

Enter Lucy.

Mrs. B. What now, Lucy ?

Lucy. Your old fteward, Madam. I had not the heart to deny him admittance, the good old man begged fo hard for't.   [*Exit* Lucy.

Enter Jarvis.

Mrs. B. Is this well, Jarvis ? I defired you to avoid me.

Jar. Did you, Madam ? I am an old man, and had forgot. Perhaps, too, you forbad my tears ; but I am old, Madam, and age will be forgetful.

Mrs. B. The faithful creature ! how he moves me.
[*To* Char.

Char. Not to have feen him had been cruelty.

Jar. I have forgot thefe apartments, too. I remember none fuch in my young mafter's houfe ; and yet I have lived in't thefe five and twenty years. His good father would not have difmiffed me.

Mrs. B. He had no reafon, Jarvis.

Jar. I was faithful to him while he lived, and when he died, he bequeathed me to his fon. I have been faithful to him, too.

Mrs. B. I know it, I know it, Jarvis.

Char. We both know it.

Jar. I am an old man, Madam, and have not a long time to live. I afked but to have died with him, and he difmiffed me.

Mrs.

Mrs. B. Pr'ythee no more of this! 'Twas his poverty that difmiffed you.

Jar. Is he indeed fo poor, then?—Oh! he was the joy of my old heart——But muft his creditors have all?—And have they fold his houfe too? His father built it when he was but a prating boy. The times that I have carried him in thefe arms! And, Jarvis, fays he, when a beggar has afked charity of me, why fhould people be poor? You fhan't be poor, Jarvis; if I was a king, nobody fhould be poor. Yet he is poor. And then he was fo brave!—Oh, he was a brave little boy! And yet fo merciful, he'd not have killed the gnat that ftung him.

Mrs. B. Speak to him, Charlotte; for I cannot.

' *Char.* When I have wiped my eyes.'

Jar. I have a little money, Madam; it might have been more, but I have loved the poor. All that I have is yours.

Mrs. B. No, Jarvis; we have enough yet. I thank you, though, and will deferve your goodnefs.

Jar. But fhall I fee my mafter? And will he let me attend him in his diftreffes? I'll be no expence to him; and 'twill kill me to be refufed. Where is he, Madam?

Mrs. B. Not at home, Jarvis. You fhall fee him another time.

Char. To-morrow, or the next day—Oh, Jarvis! what a change is here!

Jar. A change indeed, Madam! My old heart akes at it. And yet, methinks——But here's fomebody coming.

Enter Lucy *with* Stukely.

Lucy. Mr. Stukely, Madam.   [*Exit.*

Stu. Good morning to you, ladies. Mr. Jarvis, your fervant. Where's my friend, Madam? [*To Mrs.* Bev.

Mrs. B. I fhould have afked that queftion of you. Have you feen him to-day?

Stu. No, Madam.

Char. Nor laft night?

Stu. Laft night! Did he not come home then?

Mrs. B. No. Were you not together?

Stu. At the beginning of the evening; but not fince. Where can he have ftaid?

Char. You call yourfelf his friend, Sir; why do you encourage him in this madnefs of gaming?

Stu.

Stu. You have afked me that queftion before, Madam; and I told you my concern was that I could not fave him; Mr. Beverly is a man, Madam; and if the moft friendly entreaties have no effect upon him, I have no other means. My purfe has been his, even to the injury of my fortune. If that has been encouragement, I deferve cenfure; but I meant it to retrieve him.

Mrs. B. I don't doubt it, Sir; and I thank you——But where did you leave him laft night?

Stu. At Wilfon's, Madam, if I ought to tell; in company I did not like. Poffibly he may be there ftill. Mr. Jarvis knows the houfe, I believe.

Jar. Shall I go, Madam?

Mrs. B. No, he may take it ill.

Char. He may go as from himfelf.

Stu. And, if he pleafes, Madam, without naming me. I am faulty myfelf, and fhould conceal the errors of a friend. But I can refufe nothing here.

(Bowing to the Ladies.

Jar. I would fain fee him methinks.

Mrs B. Do fo, then; but take care how you upbraid him—I have never upbraided him.

Jar. Would I could bring him comfort! [*Exit* Jarvis.

Stu. Don't be too much alarmed, Madam. All men have their errors, and their times of feeing them. Perhaps my friend's time is not come yet. But he has an uncle; and old men don't live for ever. You fhould look forward, Madam; we are taught how to value a fecond fortune by the lofs of a firft. [*Knocking at the door.*

Mrs. B. Hark!—No—that knocking was too rude for Mr. Beverley. Pray heaven he be well!

Stu. Never doubt it, Madam. You fhall be well, too —Every thing fhall be well. [*Knocking again.*

Mrs. B. The knocking is a little loud, though—Who waits there? Will none of you anfwer?—None of you, did I fay?—Alas, what was I thinking of! I had forgot myfelf.

Char. I'll go, fifter—But don't be alarmed fo. [*Exit.*

Stu. What extraordinary accident have you to fear, Madam?

Mrs. Bev. I beg your pardon; but 'tis ever thus with me in Mr. Beverley's abfence. No one knocks at the door, but I fancy it is a meffenger of ill news.

Stu.

Stu. You are too fearful, Madam.; 'twas but one night of abfence; .and if ill thoughts intrude (as love is always doubtful) think of your worth and beauty, and drive them from your breaft.

Mrs. B. What thoughts? I have no thoughts that wrong my hufband.

Stu. Such thoughts indeed would wrong him. The world is full of flander; and every wretch that knows himfelf unjuft, charges his neighbour with like paffions; and by the general frailty hides his own—If you are wife, and would be happy, turn a deaf ear to fuch reports. 'Tis ruin to believe them.

Mrs. B. Ay, worfe than ruin. 'Twould be to fin againft conviction. Why was it mentioned?

Stu. To guard you againft rumour. The fport of half mankind is mifchief; and for a fingle error they make men devils. If their tales reach you, difbelieve them.

Mrs. B. What tales? By whom? Why told? I have heard nothing—or if I had, with all his errors, my Beverley's firm faith admits no doubt—It is my fafety, my feat of reft and joy, while the ftorm threatens round me. I'll not forfake it. [Stukely *fighs and looks down.*] Why turn you, Sir, away? and why that figh?

Stu. I was attentive, Madam; and fighs will come we know not why. Perhaps I have been too bufy—If it fhould feem fo, impute my zeal to friendfhip, that meant to guard you againft evil tongues. Your Beverley is wronged, flandered moft vilely—My life upon his truth.

Mrs. B. And mine too. Who is't that doubts it? But no matter——I am prepared, Sir——Yet why this caution?——You are my hufband's friend; I think you mine too; the common friend of both. [*Paufes.*] I had been unconcerned elfe.

Stu. For heaven's fake, Madam, be fo ftill! I meant to guard you againft fufpicion, not to alarm it..

Mrs. B. Nor have you, Sir. Who told you of fufpicion? I have a heart it cannot reach.

Stu. Then I am happy—I would fay more—but am prevented.

Enter Charlotte.

Mrs. B. Who was it, Charlotte?

Char. What a heart has that Jarvis!——A creditor,

fifter.

fifter. But the good old man has taken him away——
Don't diftrefs his wife; don't diftrefs his fifter, I could
hear him fay. 'Tis cruel to diftrefs the afflicted——And
when he faw me at the door, he begged pardon that his
friend had knocked fo loud.

Stu. I wifh I had known of this. Was it a large demand, Madam?

Char. I heard not that; but vifits, fuch as thefe, we
muft expect often—Why fo diftrefs'd, fifter? This is no
new affliction.

Mrs. B. No, Charlotte; but I am faint with watch-
ing—quite funk and fpiritlefs—Will you excufe me, Sir?
I'll to my chamber, and try to reft a little.

Stu. Good thoughts go with you, Madam.

[Exit Mrs. Bev.

My bait is taken, then, [*Afide.*]—Poor Mrs. Beverley!
How my heart grieves to fee her thus!

Char. Cure her, and be a friend, then.

Stu. How cure her, Madam?

Char. Reclaim my brother.

Stu. Ay, give him a new creation, or breathe another
foul into him. I'll think on't, Madam. Advice, I fee,
is thanklefs.

Char. Ufelefs I am fure it is, if thro' miftaken friendfhip, or other motives, you feed his paffion with your
purfe, and footh it by example. Phyficians, to cure fevers, keep from the patient's thirfty lip the cup that
would enflame him. You give it to his hands. [*A knocking.*] Hark, Sir!——Thefe are my brother's defperate
fymptoms——Another creditor.

Stu. One not fo eafily got rid of——What, Lewfon!

Enter Lewfon.

Lew. Madam, your fervant——Yours, Sir. I was
enquiring for you at your lodgings.

Stu. This morning! You had bufinefs, then?

Lew. You'll call it by another name, perhaps. Where's
Mr. Beverley, Madam?

Char. We have fent to enquire for him.

Lew. Is he abroad then? He did not ufe to go out fo
early.

Char. No, nor ftay out fo late.

B

Lew.

Lew. Is that the cafe? I am forry for it. But Mr.
Stukely, perhaps, may direct you to him.

Stu. I have already, Sir. But what was your bufinefs
with me?

Lew. To congratulate you upon your late fuccefles at
play. Poor Beverley!——But you are his friend; and
there's a comfort in having fuccefsful friends.

Stu. And what am I to underftand by this?

Lew. That Beverley's a poor man, with a rich friend;
that's all.

Stu. Your words would mean fomething, I fuppofe.
Another time, Sir, I fhall defire an explanation.

Lew. And why not now? I am no dealer in long fentences. A minute or two will do for me.

Stu. But not for me, Sir. I am flow of apprehenfion,
and muft have time and privacy. A lady's prefence en-
gages my attention. Another morning I may be found
at home.

Lew. Another morning, then, I'll wait upon you.

Stu. I fhall expect you, Sir. Madam, your fervant.

[Exit Stu.

Char. What mean you by this?

Lew. To hint to him that I know him.

Char. How know him? Mere doubt and fuppofition!

Lew. I fhall have proof foon.

Char. And what then? Would you rifk your life to be
his punifher?

Lew. My life, Madam! Don't be afraid. And yet I
am happy in your concern for me. But let it content
you, that I know this Stukely——'Twould be as eafy to
make him honeft as brave.

Char. And what do you intend to do?

Lew. Nothing, till I have proof. Yet my fufpicions
are well-grounded—But, methinks, Madam, I am acting
here without authority. Could I have leave to call Mr.
Beverley brother, his concerns would be my own. Why
will you make my fervices appear officious?

Char. You know my reafons, and fhould not prefs me.
But I am cold, you fay; and cold I will be, while a poor
fifter's deftitute——My heart bleeds for her; and till I
fee her forrows moderated, love has no joys for me.

Lew. Can I be lefs a friend by being a brother? I

would

would not fay an unkind thing—But the pillar of your houfe is fhaken; prop it with another, and it fhall ftand firm again.   You muft comply.

Char. And will, when I have peace within myfelf. But let us change this fubject—Your bufinefs here this morning is with my fifter.   Misfortunes prefs too hard upon her; yet, till to-day, fhe has borne them nobly.

Lew. Where is fhe?

Char. Gone to her chamber.   Her fpirits failed her.

Lew. I hear her coming. Let what has pafled with Stukely be a fecret—She has already too much to trouble her.

Enter Mrs. Beverley.

Mrs. B. Good morning, Sir; I heard your voice, and, as I thought, enquiring for me.   Where's Mr. Stukely, Charlotte?

Char. This moment gone——You have been in tears, fifter; but here's a friend fhall comfort you.

Lew. Or, if I add to your diftrefles, I'll beg your pardon, Madam.   The fale of your houfe and furniture was finifhed yefterday.

Mrs. B. I know it, Sir; I know too your generous reafon for putting me in mind of it.   But you have obliged me too much already.

Lew. There are trifles, Madam, which I know you have fet a value on; thofe I have purchafed, and will deliver.   I have a friend, too, that efteems you—He has bought largely, and will call nothing his, till he has feen you.   If a vifit to him would not be painful, he has begged it may be this morning.

Mrs. B. Not painful in the leaft.   My pain is from the kindnefs of my friends.   Why am I to be obliged beyond the power of return?

Lew. You fhall repay us at your own time.   I have a coach waiting at the door—Shall we have your company, Madam?   [*To* Char.

Char. No; my brother may return foon; I'll ftay and receive him.

Mrs. B. He may want a comforter, pérhaps.   But don't upbraid him, Charlotte.   We fhan't be abfent long. Come, Sir, fince I muft be fo obliged.

Lew. 'Tis I that am obliged.   An hour, or lefs, will

B 2

be

be sufficient for us.   We shall find you at home, Madam.
　　　　　　[*To* Char. *and exit with Mrs.* Bev.

Char. Certainly.   I have but little inclination to appear abroad.   Oh, this brother, this brother! to what
wretchedness has he reduced us !　　　　　　[*Exit.*

SCENE *changes to* Stukely's *Lodgings.*

Enter Stukely.

Stu. That Lewson suspects me 'tis too plain.   Yet why
should he suspect me ?——I appear the friend of Beverley
as much as he.   But I am rich, it seems ; and so I am,
thanks to another's folly, and my own wisdom.   To what
use is wisdom, but to take advantage of the weak ?   This
Beverley's my fool ; I cheat him, and he calls me friend.
But more business must be done yet——His wife's jewels
are unsold ; so is the reversion of his uncle's estate : I must
have these too.   And then there's a treasure above all——
I love his wife——Before she knew this Beverley I loved
her ; but, like a cringing fool, bowed at a distance, while
he stepp'd in and won her——Never, never will I forgive
him for it.   My pride, as well as love, is wounded by
this conquest.   I must have vengeance.   Those hints,
this morning, were well thrown in——Already they have
fastened on her.   If jealousy should weaken her affections,
want may corrupt her virtue ——My heart rejoices in the
hope——These jewels may do much——He shall demand them of her ; which, when mine, shall be converted
to special purposes——What now, Bates ?

Enter Bates.

Bates. Is it a wonder, then, to see me ? The forces
are all in readiness, and only wait for orders.   Where's
Beverley ?

Stu. At last night's rendezvous, waiting for me.   Is
Dawson with you ?

Bates. Dressed like a nobleman ; with money in his
pocket, and a set of dice that shall deceive the devil.

Stu. That fellow has a head to undo a nation ; but for
the rest, they are such low-mannered, ill-looking dogs, I
wonder Beverley has not suspected them.

Bates. No matter for manners and looks.   Do you supply them with money, and they are gentlemen by pro-
fession——The passion of gaming casts such a mist be-
　　　　　　　　　　　　　　　　fore

fore the eyes, that the nobleman shall be surrounded with sharpers, and imagine himself in the best company.

Stu. There's that Williams, too. It was he, I suppose, that called at Beverley's with the note this morning. What directions did you give him?

Bates. To knock loud, and be clamorous. Did not you see him?

Stu. No, the fool sneaked off with Jarvis. Had he appeared within doors, as directed, the note had been discharged. I waited there on purpose. I want the women to think well of me; for Lewson's grown suspicious; he told me so himself.

Bates. What answer did you make him?

Stu. A short one——That I would see him soon, for farther explanation.

Bates. We must take care of him. But what have we to do with Beverley? Dawson and the rest are wondering at you.

Stu. Why, let them wonder. I have designs above their narrow reach. They see me lend him money, and they stare at me. But they are fools. I want him to believe me beggared by him.

Bates. And what then?

Stu. Ay, there's the question; but no matter; at night you may know more. He waits for me at Wilson's. I told the women where to find him.

Bates. To what purpose?

Stu. To save suspicion. It looked friendly, and they thanked me. Old Jarvis was dispatched to him.

Bates. And may intreat him home——

Stu. No; he expects money from me; but I'll have none. His wife's jewels must go——Women are easy creatures, and refuse nothing where they love. Follow to Wilson's; but be sure he sees you not. You are a man of character, you know; of prudence and discretion. Wait for me in an outer room; I shall have business for you presently. Come, Sir;

Let drudging fools by honesty grow great?
The shorter road to riches is deceit.

[Exeunt.

END of the FIRST ACT.

B 3

ACT

ACT II.

SCENE, *a Gaming-houfe, with a Table, Box, Dice, &c.*

Beverley, *difcovered fitting.*

BEVERLEY.

WHY, what a world is this! The flave that digs for gold, receives his daily pittance, and fleeps contented; while thofe for whom he labours, convert their good to mifchief, making abundance the means of want. Oh, fhame, fhame! Had Fortune given me but a little, that little had been ftill my own. But plenty leads to wafte; and fhallow ftreams maintain their currents, while fwelling rivers beat down their banks, and leave their channels empty. What had I to do with play? I wanted nothing. My wifhes and my means were equal. The poor followed me with bleffings, love fcattered rofes on my pillow, and morning waked me to delight——Oh, bitter thought, that leads to what I was, by what I am! I would forget both——Who's there?

Enter a Waiter.

Wait. A gentleman, Sir, enquires for you.

Bev. He might have ufed lefs ceremony. Stukely, I fuppofe?

Wait. No, Sir, a ftranger.

Bev. Well, fhew him in.   [*Exit Waiter.*

A meffenger from Stukely then; from him that has undone me! yet all in friendfhip——And now he lends me his little, to bring back fortune to me.

Enter Jarvis.

Jarvis!—Why this intrufion?—Your abfence had been kinder.

Jar. I came in duty, Sir. If it be troublefome——

Bev. It is——I would be private——hid even from myfelf. Who fent you hither?

Jar. One that would perfuade you home again. My miftrefs is not well; her tears told me fo.

Bev. Go with thy duty there then——' But does fhe ' weep?, I am to blame to let her weep.' Pr'ythee, begone: I have no bufinefs for thee.

Jar. Yes, Sir; to lead you from this place. I am

your

your fervant ftill.   Your profperous fortune bleffed my old age.   If that has left you, I muft not leave you.

Bev. Not leave me ! Recall paft time, then ; or thro' this fea of ftorms and darknefs, fhew me a ftar to guide me——But what canft thou ?

Jar. The little that I can I will.   You have been generous to me —I would not offend you, Sir—but——

Bev. No.   Think'ft thou I'd ruin thee, too ? I have enough of fhame already—My wife, my wife ! Wouldft thou believe it, Jarvis ? I have not feen her all this long night——I who have loved her fo, that every hour of abfence feemed as a gap in life.   But other bonds have held me——Oh, I have played the boy ! dropping my counters in the ftream, and reaching to redeem them, loft myfelf.   ' Why wilt thou follow mifery ? Or if thou wilt, ' go to thy miftrefs : fhe has no guilt to fting her ; and ' therefore may be comforted.'

Jar. For pity's fake, Sir !——I have no heart to fee this change.

Bev. Nor I to bear it——How fpeaks the world of me, Jarvis ?

Jar. As of a good man dead.   Of one, who, walking in a dream, fell down a precipice.   The world is forry for you.

Bev. Ay, and pities me.   Says it not fo ? But I was born to infamy——I'll tell thee what it fays ; it calls me villain, a treacherous hufband, a cruel father, a falfe brother, one loft to nature and her charities ; or, to fay all in one fhort word, it calls me—gamefter.——Go to thy miftrefs ; I'll fee her prefently.

Jar. And why not now ? Rude people prefs upon her ; loud, bawling creditors ; wretches, who know no pity— I met one at the door ; he would have feen my miftrefs : I wanted means of prefent payment, fo promifed it tomorrow.   But others may be preffing, and fhe has grief enough already.   Your abfence hangs too heavy on her.

Bev. Tell her I'll come then.   I have a moment's bufinefs.   But what haft thou to do with my diftreffes ? Thy honefty has left thee poor ; and age wants comfort—— Keep what thou haft ' for cordials,' left between thee and the grave, mifery fteal in,   I have a friend fhall counfel me——This is that friend.

4   *Enter*

Enter Stukely.

Stu. How fares it, Beverley? Honeſt Mr. Jarvis, well met; I hoped to find you here. That viper Williams! Was it not he that troubled you this morning?

Jar. My miſtreſs heard him then?————I am ſorry that ſhe heard him.

Bev. And Jarvis promiſed payment.

Stu. That muſt not be. Tell him I'll ſatisfy him.

Jar. Will you, Sir? Heaven will reward you for't.

Bev. Generous Stukely! Friendſhip like yours, had it ability like will, would more than balance the wrongs of fortune.

Stu. You think too kindly of me————Make haſte to Williams; his clamours may be rude elſe.   [*To* Jar.

Jar. And my maſter will go home again————Alas! Sir, we know of hearts there breaking for his abſence.
                                        [*Exit.*

Bev. Would I were dead!

Stu. ' Or turn'd hermit, counting a ſtring of beads in ' a dark cave; or under a weeping willow, praying for ' mercy on the wicked.' Ha! ha! ha!—Pr'ythee be a man, and leave dying to diſeaſe and old age. Fortune may be ours again; at leaſt we'll try for't.

Bev. No; it has fool'd us on too far.

Stu. Ay, ruin'd us; and therefore we'll ſit down contented. Theſe are the deſpondings of men without money; but let the ſhining ore chink in the pocket, and folly turns to wiſdom. We are Fortune's children———— True, ſhe's a fickle mother; but ſhall we droop becauſe ſhe's peeviſh?————No; ſhe has ſmiles in ſtore. And theſe her frowns are meant to brighten 'em.

Bev. Is this a time for levity? But you are ſingle in the ruin, and therefore may talk lightly of it. With me 'tis complicated miſery.

Stu. You cenſure me unjuſtly————I but aſſumed theſe ſpirits to cheer my friend. Heaven knows he wants a comforter.

Bev. What new misfortune?

Stu. I would have brought you money; but lenders want ſecurities. What's to be done? All that was mine is yours already.

                                        Bev.

Bev. And there's the double weight that finks me. I have undone my friend, too; one, who to fave a drowning wretch, reached out his hand, and perifhed with him.

Stu. Have better thoughts.

Bev. Whence are they to proceed? I have nothing left.

Stu. [*Sighing.*] Then we're indeed undone. What nothing? No moveables, nor ufelefs trinkets? Bawbles locked up in cafkets to ftarve their owners? I have ventured deeply for you.

Bev. Therefore this heart-ake; for I am loft beyond all hope.

Stu. No; means may be found to fave us. Jarvis is rich. Who made him fo? This is no time for ceremony.

Bev. And is it for difhonefty? The good old man! Shall I rob him too? My friend would grieve for't. No; let the little that he has, buy food and cloathing for him.

Stu. Good morning then.   [*Going.*

Bev. So hafty! Why then, good morning.

Stu. And when we meet again, upbraid me. Say it was I that tempted you. Tell Lewfon fo; and tell him I have wrong'd you——He has fufpicions of me, and will thank you.

Bev. No; we have been companions in a rafh voyage, and the fame ftorm has wreck'd us both. Mine fhall be felf-upbraidings.

Stu. And will they feed us? You deal unkindly by me. I have fold and borrow'd for you, while land or credit lafted; and now, when fortune fhould be try'd, and my heart whifpers me fuccefs, I am deferted; turn'd loofe to beggary, while you have hoards.

Bev. What hoards? Name 'em, and take 'em.

Stu. Jewels.

Bev. And fhall this thriftlefs hand feize them too? My poor, poor wife! Muft fhe lofe all? I would not wound her fo.

Stu. Nor I, but from neceffity. One effort more, and Fortune may grow kind. I have unufual hopes.

Bev. Think of fome other means then.

Stu.

Stu. I have ; and you rejected 'em.

Bev. Pr'ythee let me be a man.

Stu. Ay, and your friend a poor one. But I have
done. And for these trinkets of a woman, why, let her
keep 'em to deck out pride with, and shew a laughing
world that she has finery to starve in.

Bev. No; she shall yield up all. My friend demands
it. But need we have talk'd lightly of her ? The jewels that she values are truth and innocence————'Those
will adorn her ever ; and for the rest, she wore 'em for
a husband's pride, and to his wants will give 'em. Alas !
you know her not. Where shall we meet ?

Stu. No matter. I have chang'd my mind. Leave
me to a prison ; 'tis the reward of friendship.

Bev. Perish mankind first——Leave you to a prison !
No; fallen as you see me, I'm not that wretch. Nor
would I change this heart, o'ercharged as 'tis with folly
and misfortune, for one most prudent and most happy,
if callous to a friend's distress.

Stu. You are too warm.

Ber. In such a cause, not to be warm is to be frozen.
Farewel. I'll meet you at your lodgings.

Stu. Reflect a little. The jewels may be lost. Better not hazard 'em—I was too pressing.

Bev. And I ungrateful. Reflection takes up time. I
have no leisure for't. Within an hour expect me.

[Exit.

Stu. The thoughtless, shallow prodigal ! We shall
have sport at night, then—But hold——The jewels are
not ours yet—They lady may refuse 'em—The husband
may relent, too—'Tis more than probable—I'll write a
note to Beverley, and the contents shall spur him to demand 'em——But am I grown this rogue thro' avarice ?
No ; I have warmer motives, love and revenge—Ruin
the husband and the wife's virtue may be bid for. ' 'Tis
' of uncertain value, and sinks or rises in the purchase,
' as want or wealth, or passion governs. The poor part
' cheaply with it ; rich dames, tho' pleased with selling,
' will have high prices for't. Your love-sick girls give
' it for oaths and lying. But tender wives, who boast
' of honour and affections, keep it against famine—Why,
' let famine come then ; I am in haste to purchase.'

Enter

Enter Bates.

Look to your men, Bates; there's money ftirring. We meet to-night upon this fpot. Haften, and tell 'em fo. Beverley calls upon me at my lodgings, and we return together. Haften, I fay, the rogues will fcatter elfe.

Bates. Not till their leader bids 'em.

Stu. Come on, then. Give 'em the word and follow me; I muft advife with you——This is a day of bufinefs. [*Exeunt.*

SCENE *changes to* Beverley's *Lodgings.*

Enter Beverley *and* Charlotte.

Char. Your looks are chang'd, too; there's wildnefs in 'em. My wretched fifter! How will it grieve her to fee you thus!

Bev. No, no——a little reft will eafe me. And for your Lewfon's kindnefs to her, it has my thanks; I have no more to give him.

Char. Yes; a fifter and her fortune. I trifle with him, and he complains—My looks, he fays, are cold upon him. He thinks too————

Bev. That I have loft your fortune——He dares not think fo.

Char. Nor does he—You are too quick at gueffing. He cares not if you had. That care is mine—I lent it you to hufband, and now I claim it.

Bev. You have fufpicions then.

Char. Cure 'em, and give it me.

Bev. To ftop a fifter's chiding?

Char. To vindicate her brother.

Bev. How if he needs no vindication?

Char. I would fain hope fo.

Bev. Ay, would and cannot. Leave it to time, then; 'twill fatisfy all doubts.

Char. Mine are already fatisfied.

Bev. 'Tis well. And when the fubject is renewed, fpeak to me like a fifter, and I will anfwer like a brother.

Char. To tell me I'm a beggar. Why, tell it now. I that can bear the ruin of thofe dearer to me, the ruin of a fifter and her infant, can bear that too.

Bev.

Bev. No more of this——you wring my heart.

Char. Would that the misery were all your own! But innocence muſt ſuffer——Unthinking rioter! whoſe home was heaven to him; an angel dwelt there, and a little cherub, that crowned his days with bleſſings.——How he has loſt this heaven to league with devils!

Bev. Forbear, I ſay; reproaches come too late; they ſearch, but cure not. And for the fortune you demand, we'll talk to-morrow on't; our tempers may be milder.

Char. Or, if 'tis gone, why farewel all. I claimed it for a ſiſter. ' She holds my heart in her's; and every ' pang ſhe feels tears it in pieces'——But I'll upbraid no more. What Heaven permits, perhaps, it may ordain; ' and ſorrow then is ſinful.' Yet that the huſband! father! brother! ſhould be its inſtruments of vengeance! ——'Tis grievous to know that.

Bev. If you're my ſiſter, ſpare the remembrance—— it wounds too deeply. To-morrow ſhall clear all; and when the worſt is known, it may be better than your fears. Comfort my wife; and for the pains of abſence, I'll make atonement. The world may yet go well with us.

Char. See where ſhe comes!——Look chearfully upon her——Affections ſuch as hers are prying, and lend thoſe eyes that read the ſoul.

Enter Mrs. Beverley and Lewſon.

Mrs. B. My life!

Bev. My love! how fares it? I have been a truant huſband.

Mrs. B. But we meet now, and that heals all—Doubts and alarms I have had; but in this dear embrace I bury and forget 'em. My friend here [*Pointing to* Lewſon] has been indeed a friend. Charlotte, 'tis you muſt thank him: your brother's thanks and mine are of too little value.

Bev. Yet what we have we'll pay. I thank you, Sir, and am obliged. I would ſay more, but that your goodneſs to the wife, upbraids the huſband's follies. Had I been wife, ſhe had not treſpaſſed on your bounty.

Lew. Nor has ſhe treſpaſſed. The little I have done, acceptance over-pays.

Char.

Char. So friendſhip thinks——

Mrs. B. And double obligations by ſtriving to conceal 'em——We'll talk another time on't.——You are too thoughtful, love.

Bev. No, I have reaſon for theſe thoughts.

Char. And hatred for the cauſe—Would you had that too!

Bev. I have——The cauſe was avarice.

Char. And who the tempter?

Bev. A ruined friend——ruined by too much kindneſs.

Lew. Ay, worſe than ruined; ſtabbed in his fame, mortally ſtabbed—riches can't cure him.

Bev. Or if they could, thoſe I have drained him of. Something of this he hinted in the morning—that Lewſon had ſuſpicions of him——Why theſe ſuſpicions?

[Angrily.

Lew. At ſchool we knew this Stukely. A cunning, plodding boy he was, ſordid and cruel, ſlow at his taſk, but quick at ſhifts and tricking. He ſchemed out miſchief, that others might be puniſhed; and would tell his tale with ſo much art, that for the laſh he merited, rewards and praiſe were given him. Shew me a boy with ſuch a mind, and time, that ripens manhood in him, ſhall ripen vice too—I'll prove him, and lay him open to you ——Till then be warned——I know him, and therefore ſhun him.

Bev. As I would thoſe that wrong him.——You are too buſy, Sir.

Mrs. B. No, not too buſy——Miſtaken, perhaps—— That had been milder.

Lew. No matter, Madam. I can bear this, and praiſe the heart that prompts it—Pity ſuch friendſhip ſhould be ſo placed!

Bev. Again, Sir! But I'll bear too—You wrong him, Lewſon, and will be ſorry for't.

Char. Ay, when 'tis proved he wrongs him. The world is full of hypocrites.

Bev. And Stukely one—ſo you would infer, I think. ——I'll hear no more of this——my heart akes for him ——I have undone him.

C

Lew.

Lew. The world fays otherwife.

Bev. The world is falfe then——I have bufinefs with you, love. [*To Mrs.* Bev.] We'll leave 'em to their ran-cour.   [*Going.*

Char. No ; we fhall find room within for't.——Come this way, Sir.   [*To* Lew.

Lew. Another time my friend will thank me; that time is haftening too.   [*Exeunt* Lew. *and* Char.

Bev. They hurt me beyond bearing————Is Stukely falfe ? Then honefty has left us! 'Twere finning againft Heaven to think fo.

Mrs. B. I never doubted him.

Bev. No ; you are charity. Meeknefs and ever-du-ring patience live in that heart, and love that knows no change.——Why did I ruin you ?

Mrs. B. You have not ruined me. I have no wants when you are prefent, nor wifhes in your abfence but to be bleft with your return. Be but refign'd to what has happened, and I am rich beyond the dreams of avarice.

Bev. My generous girl !—But memory will be bufy ; ftill crouding on my thoughts, to four the prefent by the paft. I have another pang too.

Mrs. B. Tell it, and let me cure it.

Bev. That friend————that generous friend, whofe fame they have traduced————I have undone him too: While he had means he lent me largely ; and now a pri-fon muft be his portion.

Mrs. B. No ; I hope otherwife.

Bev. To hope muft be to act. The charitable wifh feeds not the hungry——Something muft be done.

Mrs. B. What ?

Bev. In bitternefs of heart he told me, juft now he told me, I had undone him. Could I hear that, and think of happinefs ? No ; I have difclaimed it, while he is miferable.

Mrs. B. The world may mend with us, and then we may be grateful. There's comfort in that hope.

Bev. Ay ; 'tis the fick man's cordial, his promifed cure ; while in preparing it the patient dies.——What now ?

3

Enter

Enter Lucy.

Lucy. A letter, Sir.   [*Delivers it and Ex.*

Bev. The hand is Stukely's.

                    [*Opens it and reads it to himself.*

Mrs. B. And brings good news——at leaſt I'll hope ſo——What ſays he, love ?

Bev. Why this—too much for patience. Yet he directs me to conceal it from you.   [*Reads.*

" Let your haſte to ſee me be the only proof of your eſteem for me. I have determined, ſince we parted, to bid adieu to England; chuſing rather to forſake my country, than owe my freedom in it, to the means we talked of. Keep this a ſecret at home, and haſten to the ruined   . R. STUKELY."

Ruined by friendſhip!————I muſt relieve or follow him.

Mrs. B. Follow him, did you ſay ? Then I am loſt indeed !

Bev. O this infernal vice ! how has it ſunk me ! A vice, whoſe higheſt joy was poor to my domeſtic happineſs. Yet how have I purſued it ! turned all my comforts to bittereſt pangs, and all my ſmiles to tears. Damn'd, damn'd infatuation !

Mrs. B. Be cool, my life ! What are the means the letter talks of ? Have you——have I thoſe means ? Tell me, and eaſe me. I have no life while you are wretched.

Bev. No, no; it muſt not be. 'Tis I alone have ſinned; 'tis I alone muſt ſuffer. You ſhall reſerve thoſe means to keep my child and his wronged mother from want and wretchedneſs.

Mrs. B. What means ?

Bev. I came to rob you of 'em——but cannot—dare not——Thoſe jewels are your ſole ſupport——I ſhould be more than monſter to requeſt 'em.

Mrs. B. My jewels ? Trifles, not worth the ſpeaking of, if weighed againſt a huſband's peace ; but let 'em purchaſe that, and the world's wealth is of leſs value.

Bev. Amazing goodneſs ! How little do I ſeem before ſuch virtues !

C 2

Mrs. B.

Mrs. B. No more, my love. I kept 'em till occasion called to use 'em; now is the occasion, and I'll resign 'em chearfully.

Bev. Why we'll be rich in love then. ' But this ex-
' cess of kindness melts me. Yet for a friend one would
' do much—He has denied me nothing.'

Mrs. B. Come to my closet——But let him manage wisely. We have no more to give him.

Bev. Where learnt my love this excellence? ' 'Tis
' Heaven's own teaching: that Heaven, which to an an-
' gel's form has given a mind more lovely.' I am unworthy of you, but will deserve you better.

Henceforth my follies and neglects shall cease,
And all to come be penitence and peace;
Vice shall no more attract me with her charms,
Nor pleasure reach me, but in these dear arms.

[Exeunt.

END of the SECOND ACT.

A C T   III.

SCENE Stukely's *Lodgings.*

Enter Stukely *and* Bates.

STUKELY.

SO runs the world, Bates. Fools are the natural prey of knaves; Nature designed them so, when she made lambs for wolves. The laws that fear and policy have framed, Nature declaims: she knows but two, and those are force and cunning. The nobler law is force; but then there's danger in't; while cunning, like a skilful miner, works safely and unseen.

Bates. And therefore wisely. Force must have nerves and sinews; cunning wants neither. The dwarf that has it shall trip the giant's heels up.

Stu. And bind him to the ground. Why, we'll erect a shrine for Nature, and be her oracles. Conscience is weakness; fear made it, and fear maintains it. The dread of shame, inward reproaches, and fictitious burn-

ings

ings fwell out the phantom.   Nature knows none of this;
her laws are freedom.

Bates. Sound doctrine, and well delivered!

Stu. We are fincere, too, and practife what we teach.
Let the grave pedant fay as much.—But now to bufinefs
—The jewels are difpofed of : and Beverley again worth
money.   He waits to count his gold out, and then comes
hither.   If my defign fucceeds, this night we finifh with
him—Go to your lodgings, and be bufy—You underftand conveyances, and can make ruin fure.

Bates. Better ftop here.   The fale of this reverfion
may be talked of—There's danger in it.

Stu. No, 'tis the mark I aim at.   We'll thrive and
laugh.   You are the purchafer, and there's the payment.
[*Giving a pocket-book*] He thinks you rich; and fo you
fhall be.   Enquire for titles, and deal hardly; 'twill
look like honefty.

Bates. How if he fufpects us.

Stu. Leave it to me.   I ftudy hearts, and when to
work upon them. Go to your lodgings; and if we come,
be bufy over papers.   Talk of a thoughtlefs age, of gaming and extravagance; you have a face for't.

Bates. A feeling too that would avoid it.   We pufh too
far; but I have cautioned you.   If it ends ill, you'll
think of me—and fo adieu.   [*Exit.*

Stu. This fellow fins by halves; his fears are confcience to him.   I'll turn thefe fears to ufe.   Rogues that
dread fhame, will ftill be greater rogues to hide their
guilt——This fhall be thought of.   Lewfon grows troublefome——We muft get rid of him.——He knows too
much.   I have a tale for Beverley; part of it truth, too
—He fhall call Lewfon to account—If it fucceeds, 'tis
well; if not, we muft try other means—But here he
comes—I muft diffemble.

Enter Beverley.

Look to the door there! [*In a feeming fright.*]—My
friend!—I thought of other vifitors.

Bev. No; thefe fhall guard you from them—[*Offering
notes.*] Take them, and ufe them cautioufly—The world
deals hardly by us.

Stu. And fhall I leave you deftitute? No: your wants
are the greateft.   Another climate may treat me kinder:
The fhelter of to-night takes me from this.

C 3

Bev.

Bev. Let thefe be your fupport then—Yet is there need of parting? I may have means again; we'll fhare them, and live wifely.

Stu. No: I fhould tempt you on. Habit is nature in me: ruin can't cure it. Even now I would be gaming. Taught by experience as I am, and knowing this poor fum is all that's left us, I am for venturing ftill——And fay I am to blame—Yet will this little fupply our wants? No, we muft put it out to ufury. Whether 'tis madnefs in me, or fome reftlefs impulfe of good fortune, I yet am ignorant; but——

Bev. Take it, and fucceed then. I'll try no more.

Stu. 'Tis furely impulfe; it pleads fo ftrongly—But you are cold——We'll e'en part here then. And for this laft referve, keep it for better ufes; I'll have none on't. I thank you though, and will feek fortune fingly—One thing I had forgot——

Bev. What is it?

Stu. Perhaps, 'twere beft forgotten. But I am open in my nature, and zealous for the honour of my friend ——Lewfon fpeaks freely of you.

Bev. Of you I know he does.

Stu. I can forgive him for't; but, for my friend, I'm angry.

Bev. What fays he of me?

Stu. That Charlotte's fortune is embezzled—He talks on't loudly.

Bev. He fhall be filenced then—How heard you of it?

Stu. From many. He queftioned Bates about it. You muft account with him, he fays.

Bev. Or he with me——and foon, too.

Stu. Speak mildly to him. Cautions are beft.

Bev. I'll think on't—But whither go you?

Stu. From poverty and prifons——No matter whither. If fortune changes you may hear from me.

Bev. May thefe be profperous, then. [*Offering the notes, which he refufes.*] Nay, they are yours——I have fworn it, and will have nothing——Take them and ufe them.

Stu. Singly I will not. My cares are for my friend; for his loft fortune, and ruined family. All feparate interefts I difclaim. Together we have fallen; together

we

we muſt riſe. My heart, my honour, and affections, all will have it ſo.

Bev. I am weary of being fooled.

Stu. And ſo am I—Here let us part, then—Theſe bodings of good-fortune ſhall all be ſtifled; I'll call them folly, and forget them——This one embrace, and then farewel. [*Offering to embrace.*

Bev. No; ſtay a moment——How my poor heart's diſtracted! I have theſe bodings too; but whether caught from you, or prompted by my good or evil genius, I know not—The trial ſhall determine—And yet, my wife.

Stu. Ay, ay, ſhe'll chide.

Bev. No; my chidings are all here.

[*Pointing to his heart.*

Stu. I'll not perſuade you.

Bev. I am perſuaded; by reaſon too; the ſtrongeſt reaſon; Neceſſity. Oh, could I but regain the height I have fallen from, heaven ſhould forſake me in my lateſt hour, if I again mixed in theſe ſcenes, or ſacrificed the huſband's peace, his joy and beſt affections, to avarice and infamy.

Stu. I have reſolved like you; and ſince our motives are ſo honeſt, why ſhould we fear ſuccefs?

Bev. Come on, then—Where ſhall me meet?

Stu. At Wilſon's—Yet if it hurts you, leave me: I have miſled you often.

Bev. We have miſled each other—But come! Fortune is fickle, and may be tired with plaguing us——— There let us reſt our hopes.

Stu. Yet think a little——

Bev. I cannot——thinking but diſtracts me.

When deſperation leads, all thoughts are vain;
Reaſon would loſe what raſhnefs may obtain.

[*Exeunt.*

SCENE *changes to* Beverley's *Lodgings.*

Enter Mrs. Beverley *and* Charlotte.

Char. 'Twas all a ſcheme, a mean one; unworthy of my brother.

Mrs. B. No, I am ſure it was not—Stukely is honeſt too; I know he is—This madnefs has undone them both.

Char. My brother irrecoverably—You are too ſpirit-

leſs

lefs a wife—A mournful tale, mixed with a few kind words, will fteal away your foul. The world's too fubtle for fuch goodnefs. Had I been by, he fhould have afked your life fooner than thofe jewels.

Mrs. B. He fhould have had it, then. [*Warmly.*] I live but to oblige him. She who can love, and is beloved like me, will do as much. Men have done more for miftreffes, and women for a bafe deluder: and fhall a wife do lefs? Your chidings hurt me, Charlotte.

Char. And come too late; they might have faved you elfe. How could he ufe you fo?

Mrs. B. 'Twas friendfhip did it. His heart was breaking for a friend.

Char. The friend that has betrayed him.

Mrs. B. Pr'ythee don't think fo.

Char. To-morrow he accounts with me.

Mrs. B. And fairly——I will not doubt it.

Char. Unlefs a friend has wanted——I have no patience——Sifter! Sifter! we are bound to curfe this friend.

Mrs. B. My Beverley fpeaks nobly of him.

Char. And Lewfon truly—But I difpleafe you with this talk.——To-morrow will inftruct us.

Mrs. B. Stay till it comes then——I would not think fo hardly.

Char. Not I, but from conviction——Yet we have hope of better days. My uncle is infirm, and of an age that threatens hourly——Or if he lives, you never have offended him; and for diftreffes fo unmerited he will have pity.

Mrs. B. I know it, and am chearful. We have no more to lofe; and for what's gone, if it brings prudence home, the purchafe was well made.

Char. My Lewfon will be kind too. While he and I have life and means, you fhall divide with us——And fee, he's here!

Enter Lewfon.

We were juft fpeaking of you.

Lew. 'Tis beft to interrupt you then. Few characters will bear a fcrutiny; and where the bad out-weighs the good, he's fafeft that's leaft talked of. What fay you, Madam? [*To Charlotte.*

Char.

Char. That I hate fcandal, though a woman—there-fore talk feldom of you.

Mrs. Bev. Or, with more truth, that, though a wo-man, fhe loves to praife——Therefore talks always of you. I'll leave you to decide it.   [*Exit.*

Lew. How good and amiable! I came to talk in pri-vate with you ; of matters that concern you.

Char. What matters ?

Lew. Firft anfwer me fincerely to what I afk.

Char. I will——But you alarm me.

Lew. I am too grave, perhaps ; but be affured of this, I have no news that troubles me, and therefore fhould not you.

Char. I am eafy then—Propofe your queftion.

Lew. 'Tis now a tedious twelve-month, fince with an open and kind heart you faid you loved me.

Char. So tedious, did you fay ?

Lew. And when in confequence of fuch fweet words, I preffed for marriage, you gave a voluntary promife that you would live for me.

Char. You think me changed, then ?   [*Angrily.*

Lew. I did not fay fo. A thoufand times I have preffed for the performance of this promife : but private cares, a brother's and a fifter's ruin, were reafons for delaying it.

Char. I had no other reafons.—Where will this end ?

Lew. It fhall end prefently.

Char. Go on, Sir.

Lew. A promife, fuch as this, given freely, not ex-torted, the world thinks binding ; but I think other-wife.

Char. And would releafe me from it ?

Lew. You are too impatient, Madam.

Char. Cool, Sir—quite cool—Pray go on.

Lew. Time and a near acquaintance with my faults may have brought change—if it be fo ; or for a moment, if you have wifhed this promife were unmade, here I ac-quit you of it—This is my queftion then ; and with fuch plainnefs as I afk it, I fhall entreat an anfwer. Have you repented of this promife.

Char. Stay, Sir. The man that can fufpect me, fhall find me changed——Why am I doubted ?

Lew.

Lew. My doubts are of myself. I have my faults, and you have observation. If from my temper, my words or actions, you have conceived a thought against me, or even a wish for separation, all that has passed is nothing.

Char. You startle me—But tell me—I must be answered first. Is it from honour you speak this? Or do you wish me changed?

Lew. Heaven knows I do not. Life and my Charlotte are so connected, that to lose one, were loss of both. Yet for a promise, though given in love, and meant for binding; if time, or accident, or reason should change opinion—with me that promise has no force.

Char. Why, now I'll answer you. Your doubts are prophecies——I am really changed.

Lew. Indeed!

Char. I could torment you now, as you have me; but it is not in my nature—That I am chang'd, I own: for what at first was inclination, is now grown reason in me; and from that reason, had I the world; nay, were I poorer than the poorest, and you too wanting bread, with but a hovel to invite me to—I would be yours, and happy.

Lew. My kindest Charlotte! [*Taking her hand.*] Thanks are too poor for this——and words too weak! But if we love so, why should our union be delayed?

Char. For happier times. The present are too wretched.

Lew. I may have reasons that press it now.

Char. What reasons?

Lew. The strongest reasons; unanswerable ones.

Char. Be quick and name them.

Lew. No, Madam; I am bound in honour to make conditions first——I am bound by inclination too. This sweet profusion of kind words pains while it pleases. I dread the losing you.

Char. Astonishment! What mean you?

Lew. First promise, that to-morrow, or the next day, you will be mine for ever.

Char. I do——though misery should succeed.

Lew. Thus then I seize you! And with you every joy on this side heaven!

Char.

Char. And thus I feal my promife. [*Embracing him.*] Now, Sir, your fecret?

Lew. Your fortune's loft.

Char. My fortune loft!——I'll ftudy to be humble then. But was my promife claimed for this? How nobly generous! Where learned you this fad news?

Lew. From Bates, Stukely's prime agent. I have obliged him, and he's grateful—He told it me in friendfhip, to warn me from my Charlotte.

Char. 'Twas honeft in him, and I'll efteem him for't.

Lew. He knows much more than he has told.

Char. For me it is enough. And for your generous love, I thank you from my foul. If you'd oblige me more, give me a little time.

Lew. Why time? It robs us of our happinefs.

Char. I have a tafk to learn firft. The little pride this fortune gave me muft be fubdued. Once we were equal; and might have met obliging and obliged. But now 'tis otherwife; and for a life of obligations, I have not learned to bear it.

Lew. Mine is that life. You are too noble.

Char. Leave me to think on't.

Lew. To-morrow then you'll fix my happinefs?

Char. All that I can, I will.

Lew. It muft be fo; we live but for each other. Keep what you know a fecret; and when we meet to-morrow, more may be known.————Farewel.   [*Exit.*

Char. My poor, poor fifter! how would this wound her! But I'll conceal it, and fpeak comfort to her. [*Exit.*

SCENE *changes to a Room in the Gaming-Houfe.*

Enter Beverley *and* Stukely.

Bev. Whither would you lead me?   [*Angrily.*

Stu. Where we may vent our curfes.

Bev. Ay, on yourfelf, and thofe damned counfels that have deftroyed me. A thoufand fiends were in that bofom, and all let loofe to tempt me—I had refifted elfe.

Stu. Go on, Sir——I have deferved this from you.

Bev. And curfes everlafting——Time is too fcanty for them——

Stu. What have I done?

Bev.

Bev. What the arch-devil of old did——foothed with falfe hopes, for certain ru:n.

Stu. Myfelf unhurt; nay, pleafed at your deftruction —So your words mean. Why, tell it to the world. I am too poor to find a friend in't.

Bev. A friend! What's he? I had a friend.

Stu. And have one ftill.

Bev. Ay; I'll tell you of this friend. He found me happieft of the happy. Fortune and honour crowned me; and love and peace lived in my heart. One fpark of folly lurked there; that too he found; and by deceitful breath blew into flames that have confumed me. This friend were you to me.

Stu. A little more, perhaps—The friend who gave his all to fave you; and not fuccceding, chofe ruin with you. But no matter, I have undone you, and am a villain.

Bev. No; I think not—'The villains are within.

Stu. What villains?

Bev. Dawfon and the reft——We have been dupes to fharpers.

Stu. How know you this? I have had doubts as well as' you; yet ftill as fortune changed I blufhed·at my own thoughts——But you have proof, perhaps.

Bev. Ay, damned ones. Repeated loffes—Night after night, and no reverfe—Chance has no hand in this.

Stu. I think more charitably; yet I am peevifh in my nature, and apt to doubt—The world fpeaks fairly of this Dawfon, fo it does of the reft. We have watched them clofely too. But 'tis a right ufurped by lofers, to think the winners knaves—We'll have more manhood in us.

Bev. I know not what to think. This night has ftung me to the quick—Blafted my reputation too—I have bound my honour to thefe vipers; played meanly upon credit, 'till I tired them; and now they fhun me to rifle one another. What's to be done?

Stu. Nothing. My counfels have been fatal.

Bev. By heaven I'll not furvive this fhame—Traitor! 'tis you have brought it on me. [*Taking hold of him.*] Shew me the means to fave me, or I'll commit a murder here, and next upon myfelf.

Stu. Why do it then, and rid me of ingratitude.

Bev. Pr'ythee forgive this language—I fpeak I know

not

not what—Rage and defpair are in my heart, and hurry me to madnefs. My home is horror to me—I'll not return to it. Speak quickly; tell me, if in this wreck of fortune, one hope remains? Name it, and be my oracle.

Stu. To vent your curfes on—You have beftowed them liberally. Take your own counfel; and fhould a defperate hope prefent itfelf, 'twill fuit your defperate fortune. I'll not advife you.

Bev. What hope? By heaven I'll catch at it, however defperate. I am fo funk in mifery, it cannot lay me lower.

Stu. You have an uncle.

Bev. Ay, what of him?

Stu. Old men live long by temperance; while their heirs ftarve on expectation.

Bev. What mean you?

Stu. That the reverfion of his eftate is yours; and will bring money to pay debts with—Nay more, it may retrieve what's paft.

Bev. Or leave my child a beggar.

Stu. And what's his father? A difhonourable one; engaged for fums he cannot pay—That fhould be thought of.

Bev. It is my fhame——The poifon that enflames me. Where fhall we go? To whom? I am impatient 'till all's loft.

Stu. All may be yours again—Your man is Bates—He has large funds at his command, and will deal juftly by you.

Bev. I am refolved——Tell them within we'll meet them prefently; and with full purfes, too—Come, follow me.

Stu. No. I'll have no hand in this; nor do I counfel it—Ufe your difcretion, and act from that. You'll find me at my lodgings.

Bev. Succeed what will, this night I'll dare the worft. 'Tis lofs of fear, to be completely cure'd.

[*Exit* Beverley.

Stu. Why, lofe it then for ever—Fear is the mind's worft evil; and 'tis a friendly office to drive it from the bofom—Thus far has fortune crowned me— Yet Beverley is rich; rich in his wife's beft treafure, her honour and affections. I would supplant him there too. But 'tis the curse of thinking minds to raise up difficulties. Fools only conquer women. Fearless of dangers which they see not, they press on boldly, and by persisting, prosper. Yet may a tale of art do much——Charlotte is sometimes absent. The seeds of jealousy are sown already. If I mistake not, they have taken root too. Now is the time to ripen them, and reap the harvest. The softest of her sex, if wronged in love, or thinking that she's wronged, becomes a tygress in revenge——I'll instantly to Beverley's——No matter for the danger——When beauty leads us on, 'tis indiscretion to reflect, and cowardice to doubt.　　　　　　　　　　　　　　　　　　　[*Exit.*

SCENE *changes to* Beverley's *Lodgings.*

Enter Mrs. Beverley *and* Lucy.

Mrs. Bev. Did Charlotte tell you any thing?

Lucy. No, Madam.

Mrs. B. She look confused, methought; said she had business with her Lewson; which, when I pressed to know, tears only were her answer.

Lucy. She seemed in haste, too—Yet her return may bring you comfort.

Mrs. B. No, my kind girl; I was not born for't— But why do I distress thee? Thy sympathizing heart bleeds for the ills of others—What pity that thy mistress can't reward thee! But there's a Power above, that sees, and will remember all. [*Knocking.*] ' Pr'ythee sooth me ' with the song thou sungest last night. It suits this change ' of fortune; and there's a melancholy in't that pleases ' me.

' *Lucy.* I fear it hurts you, Madam. Your goodness, too, ' draws tears from me—But I'll dry them, and obey you.

' S O N G.

' When Damon languish'd at my feet,
　' And I believ'd him true,
　' The moments of delight how sweet!
　' But, ah! how swift they flew!
' The sunny hill, the flow'ry vale,
　' The garden and the grove,
' Have echo'd to his ardent tale,
　' And vows of endless love.

　　　　　　　　　　　　　　　　　　　　　' The

‘ The conqueſt gain'd, he left his prize,
  ‘ He left her to complain,
‘ To talk of joy with weeping eyes,
  ‘ And meaſure time by pain.
‘ But Heav'n will take the mourner's part,
  ‘ In pity to deſpair;
‘ And the laſt ſigh that rends the heart,
  ‘ Shall waft the ſpirit there.

‘ *Mrs. B.* I thank thee, Lucy; I thank Heaven, too,
‘ my griefs are none of theſe. Yet Stukely deals in
‘ hints; he talks of rumours; I'll urge him to ſpeak
‘ plainly.'——Hark! there's ſome one entering.

Lu. Perhaps 'tis my maſter, Madam.   [*Exit.*

Mrs. B. Let him be well, too, and I am ſatisfied.
[*Goes to the door and liſtens.*] No, 'tis another's voice;
his had been muſic to me. Who is it, Lucy?

     Re-enter Lucy *with* Stukely.

Lu. Mr. Stukely, Madam.   [*Exit.*

Stu. To meet you thus alone, Madam, was what I
wiſhed. Unſeaſonable viſits, when friendſhip warrants
them, need no excuſe—therefore I make none.

Mrs. B. What mean you, Sir? And where is your
friend?

Stu. Men may have ſecrets, Madam, which their beſt
friends are not admitted to. We parted in the morning,
not ſoon to meet again.

Mrs. B. You mean to leave us then; to leave your
country too. I am no ſtranger to your reaſons, and pity
your misfortunes.

Stu. Your pity has undone you. Could Beverley do
this? That letter was a falſe one; a mean contrivance to
rob you of your jewels—I wrote it not.

Mrs. B. Impoſſible! Whence came it then?

Stu. Wrong'd as I am, Madam, I muſt ſpeak plainly.

Mrs. B. Do ſo, and eaſe me. Your hints have troubled
me. Reports, you ſay, are ſtirring—Reports of whom?
You wiſhed me not to credit them. What, Sir, are theſe
reports?

Stu. I thought them ſlander, Madam; and cautioned
you in friendſhip, leſt from officious tongues the tale had
reached you with double aggravation.

Mrs. B. Proceed, Sir.

Stu. It is a debt due to my fame; due to an injured wife too——We are both injured.

Mrs. B. How injured? And who has injured us?

Stu. My friend, your hufband.

Mrs. B. You would refent for both then——But know, Sir, my injuries are my own, and do not need a champion.

Stu. Be not too hafty, Madam. I come not in refentment, but for acquittance. You thought me poor; and to the feign'd diftreffes of a friend gave up your jewels.

Mrs. B. I gave them to a hufband.

Stu. Who gave them to a——

Mrs. B. What, whom did he give them to?

Stu. A miftrefs.

Mrs. B. No, on my life, he did not.

Stu. Himfelf confeffed it, with curfes on her avarice.

Mrs. B. I'll not believe it——He has no miftrefs; or if he has, why is it told to me?

Stu. To guard you againft infults. He told me, that, to move you to compliance, he forged that letter, pretending I was ruin'd, ruin'd by him too. The fraud fucceeded; and what a trufting wife beftowed in pity, was lavifhed on a wanton.

Mrs. B. Then I am loft indeed! and my afflictions are too powerful for me. His follies I have borne without upbraiding, and faw the approach of poverty without a tear——My affections, my ftrong affections, fupported me through every trial.

Stu. Be patient, Madam.

Mrs. B. Patient! The barbarous, ungrateful man! And does he think that the tendernefs of my heart is his beft fecurity for wounding it? But he fhall find that injuries fuch as thefe, can arm my weaknefs for vengeance and redrefs.

Stu. Ha! then I may fucceed. [*Afide.*] Redrefs is in your power.

Mrs. B. What redrefs?

Stu. Forgive me, Madam, if, in my zeal to ferve you, I hazard your difpleafure. Think of your wretched ftate. Already want furrounds you—Is it in patience to bear that? To fee your helplefs little one robbed of his birthright? A fifter, too, with unavailing tears lamenting her

loft

loft fortune? No comfort left you, but ineffectual pity from the few, outweigh'd by infults from the many.

Mrs. B. Am I fo loft a creature?——Well, Sir, my redrefs?

Stu. To be refolv'd is to fecure it. The marriage vow, once violated, is, in the fight of Heaven, diffolved—Start not, but hear me. 'Tis now the fummer of your youth; time has not cropt the rofes from your cheek, tho' forrow long has wafhed them——Then ufe your beauty wifely, and, freed by injuries, fly from the cruelleft of men, for fhelter with the kindeft.

Mrs. B. And who is he?

Stu. A friend to the unfortunate; a bold one too, who, while the ftorm is burfting on your brow, and lightning flafhing from your eyes, dares tell you that he loves you.

Mrs. B. Would that thefe eyes had Heaven's own lightning, that, with a look, thus I might blaft thee! Am I then fallen fo low? Has poverty fo humbled me, that I fhould liften to a hellifh offer, and fell my foul for bread? Oh, villain, villain!——But now I know thee, and thank thee for the knowledge.

Stu. If you are wife, you fhall have caufe to thank me.

Mrs. B. An injured hufband, too, fhall thank thee.

Stu. Yet know, proud woman, I have a heart as ftubborn as your own; as haughty and imperious; and as it loves, fo can it hate.

Mrs. B. Mean, defpicable villain! I fcorn thee and thy threats. Was it for this that Beverley was falfe? that his too credulous wife fhould, in defpair and vengeance, give up her honour to a wretch? But he fhall know it, and vengeance fhall be his.

Stu. Why fend him for defiance then. Tell him I love his wife; but that a worthlefs hufband forbids our union. I'll make a widow of you, and court you honourably.

Mrs. B. Oh, coward, coward! thy foul will fhrink at him. Yet, in the thought of what may happen, I feel a woman's fears. Keep thy own fecret, and begone. Who's there?

Enter Lucy.

Your abfence, Sir, would pleafe me.

Stu. I'll not offend you, Madam.

[*Exit* Stukely *with* Lucy.

D 3

Mrs.

Mrs. B. Why opens not the earth to swallow such a monster? Be conscience, then, his punisher, till Heaven, in mercy, gives him penitence, or dooms him in his justice.

Re-enter Lucy.

Come to my chamber, Lucy; I have a tale to tell thee, shall make thee weep for thy poor mistress.

Yet Heaven the guiltless sufferer regards;
And whom it most afflicts it most rewards.

[*Exeunt.*

END of the THIRD ACT.

A C T   IV.

SCENE, Beverley's *Lodgings.*

Enter Mrs. Beverley, Charlotte, *and* Lewson.

CHARLOTTE.

THE smooth-tongu'd hypocrite!

Lew. But we have found him, and will requite him——Be chearful, Madam; [*To* Mrs. B.] and for the insults of this ruffian you shall have ample retribution.

Mrs. B. But not by violence——Remember you have sworn it; I had been silent else.

Lew. You need not doubt me; I shall be cool as patience.

Mrs. B. See him to-morrow, then.

Lew. And why not now? By Heaven, the veriest worm that crawls is made of braver spirit than this Stukely——Yet, for my promise, I'll deal gently with him—I mean to watch his looks—From those, and from his answers to my charge, much may be learnt. Next I'll to Bates, and sift him to the bottom: if I fail there, the gang is numerous, and for a bribe will each betray the other——Good night; I'll lose no time. [*Exit.*

Mrs. B. These boisterous spirits, how they wound me! But reasoning is in vain. Come, Charlotte, we'll to our usual watch. The night grows late.

Char. I am fearful of events; yet pleased—To-morrow may relieve us. [*Going.*

Enter Jarvis.

How now, good Jarvis?

Jar.

Jar. I have heard ill news, Madam.

Mrs. B. What news? Speak quickly.

Jar. Men are not what they seem. I fear me Mr. Stukely is dishonest.

Char. We know it, Jarvis. But what's your news?

Jar. That there's an action against my master, at his friend's suit.

Mrs. B. Oh, villain, villain! 'twas this he threatened then. Run to that den of robbers, Wilson's——Your master may be there. Entreat him home, good Jarvis. Say I have business with him—But tell him not of Stukely—It may provoke him to revenge—Haste, haste, good Jarvis.   [*Exit* Jar.

Char. This minister of hell! Oh, I could tear him piece-meal!——

Mrs. B. I am sick of such a world——Yet Heaven is just; and, in its own good time, will hurl destruction on such monsters.   [*Exeunt.*

SCENE *changes to* Stukely's *Lodgings*

Enter Stukely *and* Bates *meeting.*

Bates. Where have you been?

Stu. Fooling my time away; playing my tricks, like a tame monkey, to entertain a woman—No matter where—I have been vexed and disappointed. Tell me of Beverley; how bore he his last shock?

Bates. Like one (so Dawson says) whose senses had been numb'd with misery. When all was lost, he fixed his eyes upon the ground, and stood some time, with folded arms, stupid and motionless; then snatching his sword, that hung against the wainscot, he sat him down, and with a look of fix'd attention, drew figures on the floor. At last, he started up, look'd wild, and trembled; and, like a woman seized with her sex's fits, laughed out aloud, while the tears trickled down his face—so left the room.

Stu. Why, this was madness.

Bates. The madness of despair.

Stu. We must confine him then. A prison would do well. [*A knocking at the door.*] Hark! that knocking may be his. Go that way down. [*Exit* Bates.]——Who's there?

Enter

Enter Lewfon.

Lew. An enemy——an open and avowed one.

Stu. Why am I thus broke in upon? This houfe is mine, Sir; and fhould protect me from infult and ill-manners.

Lew. Guilt has no place of fanctuary; wherever found, 'tis virtue's lawful game. The fox's hold and tyger's den are no fecurity againft the hunter.

Stu. Your bufinefs, Sir?

Lew. To tell you that I know you——Why this confufion? That look of guilt and terror? Is Beverley awake; or has his wife told tales? The man that dares like you, fhould have a foul to juftify his deeds, and courage to confront accufers: not, with a coward's fear, to fhrink beneath reproof.

Stu. Who waits there?   [*Aloud, and in confufion.*

Lew. By Heaven, he dies that interrupts us. [*Shutting the door.*] You fhould have weighed your ftrength, Sir; and then, inftead of climbing to high fortune, the world had marked you for what you are, a little paltry villain.

Stu. You think I fear you.

Lew. I know you fear me. This is to prove it. [*Pulls him by the fleeve.*] You wanted privacy—A lady's prefence took up your attention—Now we are alone, Sir. Why, what a wretch! [*Flings him from him.*]. The vileft infect in creation will turn when trampled on; yet has this thing undone a man—by cunning and mean arts undone him. But we have found you, Sir; trac'd you through all your labyrinths. If you would fave yourfelf, fall to confeffion: no mercy will be fhewn elfe.

Stu. Firft prove me what you think me—till then, your threatenings are in vain—And for this infult, vengeance may yet be mine.

Lew. Infamous coward! why, take it now then—— [*Draws, and* Stukely *retires.*] Alas, I pity thee!——Yet that a wretch like this fhould overcome a Beverley! It fills me with aftonifhment!——A wretch, fo mean of foul, that even defperation cannot animate him to look upon an enemy. You fhould not have thus foar'd, Sir, unlefs, like others of your black profeffion, you had a fword to keep the fools in awe, your villainy has ruin'd.

Stu. Villainy! 'Twere beft to curb this licence of your
tongue;

tongue; for know, Sir, while there are laws, this outrage on my reputation will not be borne with.

Lew. Laws! Dar'ft thou feek fhelter from the laws, thofe laws which thou and thy infernal crew live in the conftant violation of? Talk'ft thou of reputation too, when, under friendfhip's facred name, thou haft betrayed, robbed, and deftroyed?

Stu. Ay, rail at gaming; 'tis a rich topic, and affords noble declamation——Go, preach againft it in the city: you'll find a congregation in every tavern. If they fhould laugh at you, fly to my Lord, and fermonize it there: he'll thank you, and reform.

Lew. And will example fanctify a vice? No, wretch; the cuftom of my Lord, or of the cit that apes him, cannot excufe a breach of law, or make the gamefter's calling reputable.

Stu. Rail on, I fay——But is this zeal for beggared Beverley? Is it for him that I am treated thus? No; he and his wife might both have groaned in prifon, had but the fifter's fortune efcaped the wreck, to have rewarded the difinterefted love of honeft Mr. Lewfon.

Lew. How I deteft thee for the thought! But thou art loft to every human feeling. Yet let me tell thee, and may it wring thy heart, that tho' my friend is ruined by thy fnares, thou haft unknowingly been kind to me.

Stu. Have I? It was, indeed, unknowingly.

Lew. Thou haft affifted me in love; given me the merit that I wanted; fince, but for thee, my Charlotte had not known 'twas her dear felf I figh'd for, and not her fortune.

Stu. Thank me, and take her then.

Lew. And, as a brother to poor Beverley, I will purfue the robber that has ftripped him, and fnatch him from his gripe.

Stu. Then know, imprudent man, he is within my gripe; and fhould my friendfhip for him be flandered once again, the hand that has fupplied him, fhall fall and crufh him.

Lew. Why, now there's a fpirit in thee! This is indeed to be a villain! But I fhall reach thee yet——Fly where thou wilt, my vengeance fhall purfue thee—And

Beverley

Beverley shall yet be sav'd; be sav'd from thee, thou monster! nor owe his rescue to his wife's dishonour.   [*Exit.*

Stu. [*Pausing.*] Then ruin has enclosed me. Curse
on my coward heart! I would be bravely villainous; but
'tis my nature to shrink at danger, and he has found me.
Yet fear brings caution, and that security——More mischief must be done to hide the past——Look to yourself,
officious Lewson—there may be danger stirring——How
now, Bates?

Enter Bates.

Bates. What is the matter? 'Twas Lewson, and not
Beverley, that left you—I heard him loud——You seem
alarmed too.

Stu. Ay, and with reason——We are discovered.

Bates. I feared as much; and therefore cautioned you.
But you were peremptory.

Stu. Thus fools talk ever; spending their idle breath
on what is past, and trembling at the future. We must
be active. Beverley, at worst, is but suspicious; but
Lewson's genius, and his hate to me, will lay all open.
Means must be found to stop him.

Bates. What means?

Stu. Dispatch him——Nay, start not——Desperate
occasions call for desperate deeds——We live but by his
death.

Bates. You cannot mean it?

Stu. I do, by Heaven.

Bates. Good night, then.   [*Going.*

Stu. Stay. I must be heard, then answered. Perhaps
the motion was too sudden; and human weakness starts
at murder, tho' strong necessity compels it. I have thought
long of this; and my first feelings were like yours; a
foolish conscience awed me, which soon I conquered.
The man that would undo me, Nature cries out, undo.
Brutes know their foes by instinct; and where superior
force is given, they use it for destruction. Shall man do
less? Lewson pursues us to our ruin; and shall we, with
the means to crush him, fly from our hunter, or turn and
tear him? 'Tis folly even to hesitate.

Bates. He has obliged me, and I dare not.

Stu. Why, live to shame, then, to beggary and punishment. You would be privy to the deed, yet want the
soul

foul to act it. Nay, more, had my designs been levelled at his fortune, you had stepped in the foremost——And what is life without its comforts? Those you would rob him of, and by a lingering death, add cruelty to murder. Henceforth adieu to half-made villains—There's danger in them. What you have got is yours; keep it, and hide with it——I'll deal my future bounty to those that merit it.

Bates. What's the reward?

Stu. Equal division of our gains. I swear it, and will be just.

Bates. Think of the means then.

Stu. He's gone to Beverley's——Wait for him in the street—'Tis a dark night, and fit for mischief. A dagger would be useful.

Bates. He sleeps no more.

Stu. Consider the reward. When the deed's done, I have farther business with you. Send Dawson to me.

Bates. Think it already done—and so, farewel. [*Exit.*

Stu. Why, farewel Lewson, then; and farewel to my fears. This night secures me. I'll wait the event within. [*Exit.*

SCENE *changes to the Street. Stage darkened.*

Enter Beverley.

Bev. How like an out-cast do I wander? Loaded with every curse that drives the soul to desperation——The midnight robber, as he walks his rounds, sees by the glimmering lamp my frantic looks, and dreads to meet me. Whither am I going? My home lies there; all that is dear on earth it holds too; yet are the gates of death more welcome to me——I'll enter it no more—— Who passes there? 'Tis Lewson——He meets me in a gloomy hour; and memory tells me he has been meddling with my fame.

Enter Lewson.

Lew. Beverley! Well met. I have been busy in your affairs.

Bev. So I have heard, Sir; and now must thank you as I ought.

Lew. To-morrow I may deserve your thanks. Late

as it is, I go to Bates. Difcoveries are making that an arch villain trembles at.

Bev. Difcoveries are made, Sir, that you fhall tremble at. Where is this boafted fpirit, this high demeanor, that was to call me to account? You fay I have wrong'd my fifter——Now fay as much. But firft be ready for defence, as I am for refentment.   [*Draws.*

Lew. What mean you? I underftand you not.

Bev. The coward's ftale acquittance! who, when he fpreads foul calumny abroad, and dreads juft vengeance on him, cries out, What mean you? I underftand you not.

Lew. Coward and calumny! Whence are thofe words? But I forgive, and pity you.

Bev. Your pity had been kinder to my fame. But you have traduced it; told a vile ftory to the public ear, that I have wronged my fifter.

Lew. 'Tis falfe. Shew me the man that dares ac-cufe me.

Bev. I thought you brave, and of a foul fuperior to low malice; but I have found you, and will have ven-geance. This is no place for argument.

Lew. Nor fhall it be for violence. Imprudent man! who, in revenge for fancied injuries, would pierce the heart that loves him. But honeft friendfhip acts from it-felf, unmoved by flander ' or ingratitude. The life you ' thirft for, fhall be employed to ferve you.

' *Bev.* 'Tis thus you would compound then——Firft ' do a wrong beyond forgivenefs, and, to redrefs it, load ' me with kindnefles unfolicited. I'll not receive it. ' Your zeal is troublefome.

' *Lew.* No matter. It fhall be ufeful.

' *Bev.* It will not be accepted.

' *Lew.* It muft.' You know me not.

Bev. Yes, for the flanderer of my fame; who, under fhew of friendfhip, arraigns me of injuftice; buzzing in every ear foul breach of truft, and family difhonour.

Lew. Have I done this? Who told you fo?

Bev. The world——'Tis talked of every where. It pleafed you to add threats, too. You were to call me to account——Why, do it now, then: I fhall be proud of fuch an arbiter.

Lew. Put up your sword, and know me better. I never injured you. The base suggestion comes from Stukely: I see him and his aims.

Bev. What aims? I'll not conceal it; 'twas Stukely that accused you.

Lew. To rid him of an enemy——Perhaps of two——He fears discovery, and frames a tale of falshood, to ground revenge and murder on.

Bev. I must have proof of this.

Lew. Wait till to-morrow then.

Bev. I will.

Lew. Good night——I go to serve you——Forget what's past, as I do; and cheer your family with smiles. To-morrow may confirm them; and make all happy.

[*Exit.*

Bev. [*Pausing.*] How vile, and how absurd is man! His boasted honour is but another name for pride, which easier bears the conscioufnefs of guilt, than the world's just reproofs. But 'tis the fashion of the times; and in defence of falfehood and falfe honour men die martyrs: I knew not that my nature was so bad.   [*Stands musing.*

Enter Bates *and* Jarvis.

Jar. This way the noise was; and yonder's my poor master.

Bates. I heard him at high words with Lewfon. The cause I know not.

Jar. I heard him too. Misfortunes vex him.

Bates. Go to him, and lead him home. But he comes this way—— I'll not be seen by him.   [*Exit.*

Bev. [*Starting.*] What fellow's that? [*Seeing* Jarvis.] Art thou a murderer, friend?-Come, lead the way; I have a hand as mischievous as thine; a heart as desperate too——Jarvis!——To bed, old man; the cold will chill thee.

Jar. Why are you wandering at this late hour? Your sword drawn too?—For Heaven's fake, sheath it, Sir—— the sight distracts me.

Bev. Whose voice was that?   [*Wildly.*

Jar. 'Twas mine, Sir. Let me intreat you to give the sword to me.

Bev. Ay, take it—quickly take it—Perhaps I am not

E

so

fo curs'd, but Heaven may have fent thee at this moment to fnatch me from perdition.

Jar. Then I am blefs'd.

Bev. Continue fo, and leave me : my forrows are con-tagious.　No one is blefs'd that's near me.

Jar. I came to feek you, Sir.

Bev. And now thou haft found me, leave me——My thoughts are wild, and will not be difturbed.

Jar. Such thoughts are beft difturbed.

Bev. I tell thee that they will not.　Who fent thee hither ?

Jar. My weeping miftrefs.

Bev. Am I fo meek a hufband then, that a command-ing wife prefcribes my hours, and fends to chide me for my abfence ?——Tell her I'll not return.

Jar. Thofe words would kill her.

Bev. Kill her ! Would they not be kind, then ? But fhe fhall live to curfe me——I have deferved it of her. Does fhe not hate me Jarvis ?

Jar. Alas, Sir, forget your griefs, and let me lead you to her ! The ftreets are dangerous.

Bev. Be wife, and leave me then.　The night's black horrors are fuited to my thoughts—Thefe ftones fhall be my refting-place. [*Lies down.*] Here fhall my foul brood o'er its miferies, till, with the fiends of hell, and guilty of the earth, I ftart and tremble at the morning's light.

Jar. For pity's fake, Sir—Upon my knees, I beg you to quit this place, and thefe fad thoughts　Let patience, not defpair, poffefs you——Rife, I befeech you—There's not a moment of your abfence, that my poor miftrefs does not groan for.

Bev. Have I undone her, and is fhe ftill fo kind; [*Starting up.*] It is too much – My brain can't hold it—— Oh, Jarvis, how defperate is that wretch's ftate, which only death or madnefs can relieve.

Jar. Appeafe his mind, good Heaven, and give him re-fignation ! Alas, Sir, could beings in the other world per-ceive the events of this, how would your parents bleffed fpirits grieve for you even in Heaven !—Let me conjure you, by their honoured memories; by the fweet inno-cence of your yet helplefs child, and by the ceafelefs for-

rows

rows of my poor miſtreſs, to rouſe your manhood, and
ſtruggle with theſe griefs.

Bev. Thou virtuous, good old man ! thy tears and thy
intreaties have reached my heart, thro' all its miſeries.

Jar. Be but reſigned, Sir, and happineſs may yet be
yours.

' *Bev.* Pr'ythee, be honeſt, and do not flatter miſery.

' *Jar.* I do not, Sir.'—Hark ! I hear voices—Come
this way ; we may reach home unnoticed.

Bev. ' Well, lead me then.'——Unnoticed, didſt thou
ſay ? Alas, I dread no looks but of thoſe wretches I have
made at home ! Oh, had I liſtened to thy honeſt war-
nings, no earthly bleſſing had been wanting to me !——
I was ſo happy, that even a wiſh for more than I poſſeſſed,
was arrogant preſumption. But I have warred againſt
the power that bleſſed me ; and now am forced to the hell
I merit.   *[Exeunt.*

S C E N E *changes to* Stukely's.

Enter Stukely *and* Dawſon.

Stu. Come hither, Dawſon. My limbs are on the rack,
and my ſoul ſhivers in me, till this night's buſineſs be
complete. Tell me thy thoughts ; is Bates determined,
or does he waver ?

Daw. At firſt he ſeemed irreſolute ; wiſhed the employment had been mine ; and muttered curſes on his
coward hand, that trembled at the deed.

Stu. And did he leave you ſo ?

Daw. No ; we walked together, and, ſheltered by the
darkneſs, ſaw Beverley and Lewſon in warm debate. But
ſoon they cooled, and then I left them to haſten hither ;
but not till 'twas reſolved Lewſon ſhould die.

Stu. Thy words have given me life. That quarrel,
too, was fortunate ; for, if my hopes deceive me not, it
promiſes a grave to Beverley.

Daw. You miſconceive me. Lewſon and he were
friends.

Stu. But my prolific brain ſhall make them enemies.
If Lewſon falls, he falls by Beverley. An upright jury
ſhall decree it. Aſk me no queſtion ; but do as I direct.
This writ, [*Takes out a pocket-book.*] for ſome days paſt,
I have treaſured here, till a convenient time called for its

                                            uſe.

uſe. That time is come. Take it, and give it to an officer. It muſt be ſerved this inſtant. [*Gives a paper.*

Daw. On Beverley!

Stu. Look at it. 'Tis for the ſums that I have lent
him.

Daw. Muſt he to priſon then ?

Stu. I aſked obedience, not replies. This night a jail
muſt be his lodging. 'Tis probable he's not gone home
yet. Wait at his door, and ſee it executed.

Daw. Upon a beggar ? He has no means of payment.

Stu. Dull and inſenſible! If Lewſon dies, who was it
killed him ? Why, he that was ſeen quarrelling with him:
and I, that knew of Beverley's intents, arreſted him in
friendſhip——A little late, perhaps; but 'twas a virtuous act, and men will thank me for it. Now, Sir, you
underſtand me ?

Daw. Moſt perfectly; and will about it.

Stu. Haſte, then; and when 'tis done, come back and
tell me.

Daw. Till then, farewel. [*Exit.*

Stu. Now tell thy tale, fond wife! And, Lewſon, if
again thou canſt inſult me, ' I'll kneel, and own thee for
' my maſter.'

Not avarice now, but vengeance fires my breaſt,

And one ſhort hour muſt make me curs'd or bleſs'd.

[*Exeunt.*

END of the FOURTH ACT.

A C T V.

S C E N E continues.

Enter Stukely, Bates, *and* Dawſon.

BATES.

POOR Lewſon!——But I told you enough laſt night.
The thought of him is horrible to me.

Stu. In the ſtreet, did you ſay ? And no one near him ?

Bates. By his own door; he was leading me to his
houſe. I pretended buſineſs with him, and ſtabbed him
to the heart, while he was reaching at the bell.

Stu. And did he fall ſo ſuddenly ?

Bates.

Bates. The repetition pleafes you, I 'fee. I told you he fell without a groan.

Stu. What heard you of him this morning ?

Bates. That the watch found him in their rounds, and alarmed the fervants. I mingled with the crowd juft now, and faw him dead in his own houfe——The fight terrified me.

Stu. Away with terrors, till his ghoft rife and accufe us. We have no living enemy to fear, unlefs 'tis Beverley ; and him we have lodged fafe in prifon.

Bates. Muft he be murdered too ?

Stu. No ; I have a fcheme to make the law his murderer. At what hour did Lewfon fall ?

Bates. The clock ftruck twelve as I turned to leave him. 'Twas a melancholy bell, I thought, tolling for his death.

Stu. The time was lucky for us——Beverley was arrefted at one, you fay ?.   [*To* Dawfon.

Daw. Exactly.

Stu. Good. We'll talk of this prefently. The women were with him, I think ?

Daw. And old Jarvis. I would have told you of them laft night, but your thoughts were too bufy. 'Tis well you have a heart of ftone ; the tale would melt it elfe.

Stu. Out with it then.

Daw. I traced him to his lodgings ; and, pretending pity for his misfortunes, kept the door open, while the officers feized him. 'Twas a damn'd deed——but no matter——I followed my inftructions.

Stu. And what faid he ?

Daw. He upbraided me with treachery, called you a villain, acknowledged the fums you had lent him, and fubmitted to his fortune.

Stu. And the women——

Daw. For a few minutes aftonifhment kept them filent. They looked wildly at one another, while the tears ftreamed down their cheeks. But rage and fury foon gave them words ; and then, in the very bitternefs of defpair, they curfed me, and the monfter that had employed me.

Stu. And you bore it with philofophy ?

Daw. 'Till the fcene changed, and then I melted. I ordered the officers to take away their prifoner. The

 women

women fhrieked, and would have followed-him ; but we forbade them.   'Twas then they fell upon their knees, the wife fainted, the fifter raving, and both, with all the eloquence of mifery, endeavouring to foften us.   I never felt compaffion till that moment ; and had the officers been moved like me, we had left the bufinefs undone, and fled with curfes on ourfelves.   But their hearts were fteeled by cuftom.   The tears of beauty and the pangs of affection were beneath their pity. They tore him from their arms, and lodged him in prifon, with only Jarvis to comfort him.

Stu. There let him lie, 'till we have farther bufinefs with him——' And for you, Sir, let me hear no more
' of your compaffion——A fellow nurfed in villainy, and
' employed from childhood in the bufinefs of hell, fhould
' have no dealings with compaffion.

' *Daw.* Say you fo, Sir?—You fhould have named
. ' the devil that tempted me——

' *Stu.* 'Tis falfe.   I found you a villain, and there-
' fore employed you——but no more of this——We
' have embarked too far in mifchief to recede.   Lew-
' fon is dead, and we are all principals in his murder.
' Think of that——There's time enough for pity when
' ourfelves are out of danger——Beverley ftill lives,
' though in a gaol——His ruin will fit heavy on him ;
' and difcoveries may be made to undo us all.   Some-
' thing muft be done, and fpeedily—You faw him quar-
' relling with Lewfon in the ftreet laft night. [*To* Bates.

' *Bat.* I did ; his fteward, Jarvis, faw him too.

' *Stu.* And fhall atteft it.   Here's matter to work upon
' ——An unwilling evidence carries weight with him.'
Something of my defign I have hinted t'you before---
Beverley muft be the author of this murder ; and we the parties to convict him——But how to proceed will require time and thought—Come along with me ; the room within is fitted for privacy---But no compaffion, Sir——
[*To* Dawfon.] We wan't leifure for't——This way.

[*Exeunt.

SCENE *changes to* Beverley's *Lodgings.*

Enter Mrs. Beverley *and* Charlotte.

Mrs. Bev. No news of Lewfon yet?

Char.

Char. None. He went out early, and knows not what has happened.

Mrs. B. The clock ſtrikes eight——I'll wait no longer.

Char. Stay but 'till Jarvis comes. He has ſent twice to ſtop us 'till we ſee him.

Mrs. B. I have no life in this ſeparation——Oh, what a night was laſt night! I would not paſs another ſuch to purchaſe worlds by it——My poor *Beverley* too? What muſt he have felt! The very thought diſtracts me ——To have him torn at midnight from me!—A loathſome priſon his habitation! A cold damp room his lodging! The bleak winds perhaps blowing upon his pillow! No fond wife to lull him to his reſt! and no reflections but to wound and tear him !——'Tis too horrible—I wanted love for him, or they had not forced him from me. They ſhould have parted ſoul and body firſt—I was too tame.

Char. You muſt not talk ſo. All that we could we did; and *Jarvis* did the reſt—The faithful creature will give him comfort. Why does he delay coming!

Mrs. B. And there's another fear. His poor maſter may be claiming the laſt kind office from him—His heart perhaps is breaking.

Char. See where he comes---His looks are chearful too.

Enter Jarvis.

Mrs. B. Are tears then chearful? Alas, he weeps! Speak to him, *Charlotte*——I have no tongue to aſk him queſtions.

Char. How does your maſter, *Jarvis?*

Jar. I am old and fooliſh, Madam ; and tears will come before my words—But don't you weep ; [*To Mrs.* Bev.] I have a tale of joy for you.

Mrs. B. What tale?---Say but he's well, and I have joy enough.

Jar. His mind too ſhall be well--all ſhall be well---I have news for him, that will make his poor heart bound again—Fie upon old age---How childiſh it makes me ! I have a tale of joy for you, and my tears drown it.

Char. Shed them in ſhowers then, and make haſte to tell it.

Mrs. B. What is it, *Jarvis?*

Jar.

Jar. Yet why fhould I rejoice when a good man dies ? Your uncle, Madam, died yefterday.

Mrs. B. My uncle!——Oh, heavens!

Char. How heard you of his death ?

Jar. His fteward came exprefs, Madam ?---I met him in the ftreet, enquiring for your lodgings——I fhould not rejoice perhaps---but he was old, and my poor mafter a prifoner——Now he fhall live again——Oh, 'tis a brave fortune ! and 'twas death to me to fee him a prifoner.

Char. Where left you the fteward ?

Jar. I would not bring him hither, to be a witnefs of your diftreffes ; and befides, I wanted, once before I die, to be the meffenger of joy t'you. My good mafter will be a man again.

Mrs. B. Hafte, hafte then ; and let us fly to him !--- We are delaying our own happinefs.

Jar. I had forgot a coach, Madam, and Lucy has or- dered one.

Mrs. B. Where was the need of that ? The news has given me wings.

Char. I have no joy, 'till my poor brother fhares it with me. How did he pafs the night, Jarvis ?

Jar. Why now, Madam, I can tell you. Like a man dreaming of death and horrors. When they led him to his cell---For 'twas a poor apartment for my mafter--- He flung himfelf upon a wretched bed, and lay fpeechlefs 'till day-break. A figh now and then, and a few tears that followed thofe fighs, were all that told me he was alive. I fpoke to him, but he would not hear me ; and when I perfifted, he raifed his hand at me, and knit his brow fo ——I thought he would have ftruck me.

Mrs. B. Oh, miferable ! But what faid he, Jarvis ? Or was he filent all night ?

Jar. At day-break he ftarted from the bed, and look- ing wildly at me, afked who I was. I told him, and bid him be of comfort---Begone, old wretch, fays he——I have fworn never to know comfort---My wife ! my child ! my fifter ! I have undone them all, and will know no comfort---Then falling upon his knees, he imprecated curfes upon himfelf.

Mrs. B. This is too horrible !---But you did not leave him fo ?

Char.

Char. No, I am sure he did not.

Jar. I had not the heart, Madam. By degrees I brought him to himself. A shower of tears came to his relief; and he called me his kindest friend, and begged forgiveness of me, like a child. My heart throbbed so, I could not speak to him. He turned from me for a minute or two, and suppressing a few bitter sighs, enquired after his wretched family---' Wretched was his word, Madam ' —Asked how you bore the misery of last night—If you ' had the goodness to see him in prison : and then begged ' me to hasten to you. I told him he must be more ' himself first---He promised me he would; and bating ' a few sudden intervals, he became composed and easy ' ---And then I left him ; but not without an attendant ' ---a servant in the prison, whom I hired to wait upon ' him—'Tis an hour since we parted—I was prevented ' in my haste to be the messenger of joy to you.'

Mrs. B. What a tale is this ?—But we have staid too long—' A coach is needless.

' *Char.* Hark ! I hear one at the door.'

Jar. '—And Lucy comes to tell us'——We'll away this moment.

Mrs. B. To comfort him or die with him.　　[*Exeunt.*

' SCENE *changes to* Stukely's *Lodgings.*

' *Enter* Stukely, Bates, *and* Dawson.

' *Stu.* Here's presumptive evidence at least---or if we ' want more, why we must swear more: But all un- ' willingly---We gain credit by reluctance---I have told ' you how to proceed. Beverley must die ——We hunt ' him in view now, and must not slacken in the chace. ' 'Tis either death for him, or shame and punishment for ' us. Think of that, and remember your instructions— ' You, Bates, must to the prison immediately. I would ' be there but a few minutes before you; and you, Daw- ' son, must follow in a few minutes after. So here we ' divide—But answer me ; are you resolved upon this ' business like men ?

' *Bates.* Like villains rather—But you may depend ' upon us.

' *Stu.* Like what we are then—You make no answer, ' Dawson——Compassion, I suppose, has seised you.

' *Daw*

' *Daw.* No; I have difclaimed it——My anfwer is
' Bates's——You may depend upon me.
' *Stu.* Confider the reward! Riches and fecurity! I
' have fworn to divide with you to the laft fhilling——So
' here we feparate 'till we meet in prifon——Remember
' your inftructions and be men.   [*Exeunt.*

SCENE *changes to a prifon.*

Beverley *is difcovered fitting. After a fhort paufe, he ftarts
up, and comes forward.*

Bev. Why, there's an end then. I have judged delibe-
rately, and the refult is death. How the felf-murderer's
account may ftand, I know not. But this I know—the
load of hateful life opprefles me too much—The horrors
of my foul are more than I can bear—[*Offers to kneel.*]
Father of mercy!——I cannot pray,——Defpair has laid
his iron hand upon me, and fealed me for perdition——
Confcience! Confcience! thy clamours are too loud——
Here's that fhall filence thee. [*Takes a vial out of his pocket, and looks at it.*] Thou art moft friendly to the miferable. Come then, thou cordial for fick minds——Come
to my heart. [*Drinks.*] Oh, that the grave would bury
memory as well as body! For if the foul fees and feels
the fufferings of thofe dear ones it leaves behind, the
Everlafting has no vengeance to torment it deeper——
I'll think no more on't——Reflection comes too late——
Once there was a time for't——but now 'tis paft.——
Who's there?

Enter Jarvis.

Jar. One that hoped to fee you with better looks——
Why d'you turn fo from me? I have brought comfort
with me. And fee who comes to give it welcome.

Bev. My wife and fifter! Why, 'tis but one pang more
then, and farewel world.   [*Afide.*

Enter Mrs. Beverley *and* Charlotte.

Mrs. B. Where is he? [*Runs and embraces him.*] Oh,
I have him! I have him! And now they fhall never part
us more—I have news, love, to make you happy for ever
——' But don't look coldy on me.

' *Char.* How is it, brother?

' *Mrs. B.*' Alas! he hears us not——Speak to me,
love. I have no heart to fee you thus.

                                          Bev.

Bev. ' Nor I to bear the fenfe of fo much fhame'—This is a fad place !

Mrs. B. We came to take you from it. To tell you the world goes well again. That Providence has feen our forrows, and fent the means to help them—Your uncle died yefterday.

Bev. My uncle!—No, do not fay fo!—Oh, I am fick at heart !

Mrs. B. Indeed !——I meant to bring you comfort.

Bev. Tell me he lives then——If you would bring me comfort, tell me he lives.

Mrs. B. And if I did——I have no power to raife the dead——He died yefterday.

Bev. And I am heir to him ?

Jar. To his whole eftate, Sir——But bear it patiently—pray bear it patiently.

Bev. Well, well---[*Paufing.*] Why fame fays I am rich then ?

Mrs. B. And truly fo---Why do you look fo wildly ?

Bev. Do I ? The news was unexpected. But has he left me all ?

Jar. All, all, Sir---He could not leave it from you.

Bev. I am forry for it.

' *Char.* Sorry ! Why forry ?

' *Bev.* Your uncle's dead, Charlotte.

' *Char.* Peace be with his foul then—Is it fo terrible ' that an old man fhould die ?

' *Bev.* He fhould have been immortal.'

Mrs. B. ' Heaven knows I wifhed not for his death. ' 'Twas the will of Providence that he fhould die'—— Why are you difturbed fo ?

Bev. Has death no terrors in it ?

Mrs. B. Not an old man's death. Yet if it troubles you, I wifh him living.

Bev. And I, with all my heart.

' *Char.* Why, what's the matter ?

' *Bev.* Nothing---How heard you of his death ?

' *Mrs. B.* His fteward came exprefs. Would I had ' never known it !'

Bev. ' Or had heard it one day fooner'---For I have a tale to tell, fhall turn you into ftone ; or, if the power of fpeech remain, you fhall kneel down and curfe me.

Mrs. B. Alas! What tale is this? And why are we to curfe you---I'll blefs you for ever.

Bev. No; I have deferved no bleffings. The world holds not fuch another wretch. All this large fortune, this fecond bounty of heaven, that might have healed our forrows, and fatisfied our utmoft hopes, in a curfed hour I fold laft night.

Char. Sold! How fold?

Mrs. B. Impoffible!---It cannot be!

Bev. That devil Stukely, with all hell to aid him, tempted me to the deed. To pay falfe debts of honour, and to redeem paft errors, I fold the reverfion——Sold it for a fcanty fum, and loft it among villains.

Char. Why, farewel all then.

Bev. Liberty and life---Come kneel and curfe me.

Mrs. B. Then hear me, Heaven! [*Kneels.*] Look down with mercy on his forrows! Give foftnefs to his looks, and quiet to his heart! Take from his memory the fenfe of what is paft, and cure him of defpair! On me! on me! if mifery muft be the lot of either, multiply mis-fortunes! I'll bear them patiently, fo he is happy! Thefe hands fhall toil for his fupport! Thefe eyes be lifted up for hourly bleffings on him! And every duty of a fond and faithful wife be doubly done to chear and comfort him!---So hear me! So reward me! [*Rifes.*

Bev. I would kneel too, but that offended heaven would turn my prayers into curfes. ' What have I to ' afk for! I, who have fhook hands with hope? Is it for ' length of days that I fhould kneel? No; my time is ' limited. Or is it for this world's bleffings upon you ' and yours? To pour out my heart in wifhes for a ruined ' wife, a child and fifter? Oh, no!' for I have done a deed to make life horrible to you---

' *Mrs. B.* Why horrible? Is poverty fo horrible?--- ' The real wants of life are few. A little induftry will ' fupply them all---And chearfulnefs will follow---It is ' the privilege of honeft induftry, and we'll enjoy it ' fully.

' *Bev.* Never, never---Oh, I have told you but in ' part. The irrevocable deed is done.'

Mrs. B. What deed?---' And why do you look fo at ' me?

' *Bev.*

' *Bev.* A deed that dooms my foul to vengeance---
' That feals your mifery here, and mine hereafter.

' *Mrs. B.* No, no; you have a heart too good for't---
' Alas! he raves, Charlotté---His looks too terrify me
' ---Speak comfort to him---He can have done no deed
' of wickednefs.

' *Char.* And yet I fear the worft---What is it, bro-
' ther?'

Bev. A deed of horror.

Jar. Afk him no queftions, Madam---This laft misfortune has hurt his brain. A little time will give him
patience.

Enter Stukely.

Bev. Why is this villain here?

Stu. To give you liberty and fafety. There, Madam's,
his difcharge. [*Giving a paper to Mrs.* Beverley.] Let
him fly this moment. The arreft laft night was meant
in friendfhip; but came too late.

Char. What mean you, Sir?

Stu. The arreft was too late, I fay; I would have kept
his hands from blood, but was too late.

Mrs. B. His hands from blood!---Whofe blood?---Oh,
wretch! wretch!

Stu. From Lewfon's blood.

Char. No, villain! Yet what of Lewfon? Speak
quickly.

Stu. You are ignorant then! I thought I heard the
murderer at confeffion.

Char. What murderer?---And who is murdered? Not
Lewfon?---Say he lives, and I'll kneel and worfhip you.

Stu. In pity, fo I would; but that the tongues of all
cry murder. I came in pity, not in malice; to fave the
brother, not kill the fifter. Your Lewfon's dead.

Char. O horrible! ' Why who has killed him? And
' yet it cannot be. What crime had he committed that
' he fhould die? Villain! he lives! he lives! and fhall
' revenge thefe pangs.

' *Mrs. B.* Patience, fweet Charlotte.

' *Char.* O, 'tis too much for patience!

' *Mrs. B.* He comes in pity, he fays! O, execrable
' villain! The friend is killed then, and this the mur-
' derer?'

F

Bev.

Bev. Silence, I charge you.——Proceed, Sir.

Stu. No. Juftice may ftop the tale——and here's an evidence.

Enter Bates.

Bates. The news, I fee, has reached you. But take comfort, Madam. [*To* Char.] There's one without enquiring for you.——Go to him, and lofe no time.

Char. O mifery! mifery!   [*Exit.*

Mrs. B. Follow her, Jarvis. If it be true that Lewfon's dead, her grief may kill her.

Bates. Jarvis muft ftay here, Madam. I have fome queftions for him.

Stu. Rather let him fly. His evidence may crufh his mafter.

Bev. Why ay; this looks like management.

Bates. He found you quarrelling with Lewfon in the ftreet laft night.   [*To* Bev.

Mrs. B. No; I am fure he did not.

Jar. Or if I did——

Mrs. B. 'Tis falfe, old man——They had no quarrel; there was no caufe for quarrel.

Bev. Let him proceed, I fay——O! I am fick! fick! ——Reach a chair.   [*He fits down.*

Mrs. B. You droop and tremble, love.——Your eyes are fixed too——Yet you are innocent. If Lewfon's dead, you killed him not.

Enter Dawfon.

Stu. Who fent for Dawfon?

Bates. 'Twas I——We have a witnefs too, you little think of——Without there!

Stu. What witnefs?

Bates. A right one. Look at him.

Enter Lewfon *and* Charlotte.

Stu. Lewfon! O villains! villains!

[*To* Bates *and* Dawfon.

Mrs. B. Rifen from the dead! Why, this is unexpected happinefs!

Char. Or is't his ghoft? [*To* Stukely.] That fight would pleafe you, Sir.

Jar. What riddle's this?

Bev. Be quick and tell it——My minutes are but few.

4

Mrs. B.

Mrs. B. Alas! why so ? You shall live long and happily.

Lew. While shame and punishment shall rack that viper. [*Pointing to* Stukely.] The tale is short——I was too busy in his secrets, and therefore doomed to die. Bates, to prevent the murder, undertook it——I kept aloof to give it credit.——

Char. And give me pangs unutterable.

Lew. I felt 'em all, and would have told you——But vegeance wanted ripening. The villain's scheme was but half executed. The arrest by Dawson followed the supposed murder——And now, depending on his once wicked associates, he comes to fix the guilt on Beverley.

Mrs. B. O! execrable wretch !

Bates. Dawson and I are witnesses of this.

Lew. And of a thousand frauds. His fortune ruined by sharpers and false dice ; and Stukely sole contriver and possessor of all.

Daw. Had he but stopped on this side murder, we had been villains still.

Mrs. B. Thus Heaven turns evil into good: and by permitting sin, warns men to virtue.

Lew. Yet punishes the instrument. So shall our laws ; tho' not with death. But death were mercy. Shame, beggary, and imprisonment, unpitied misery, the stings of conscience, and the curses of mankind shall make life hateful to him——till at last, his own hand end him.—— How does my friend ?   [*To* Bev.

Bev. Why well. Who's he that asks me ?

Mrs. B. 'Tis Lewson, love——Why do you look so at him ?

Bev. They told me he was murdered.   [*Wildly.*

Mrs. B. Ay ; but he lives to save us.

Bev. Lend me you hand——The room turns round.

Mrs. B. O Heaven !

Lew. This villain here disturbs him. Remove him from his sight——And for your lives see that you guard him. [Stukely *is taken off by* Dawson *and* Bates.] How is it, Sir ?

Bev. 'Tis here——and here [*Pointing to his head and heart.*] And now it tears me !

Mrs. B. You feel convulſed too——What is't diſturbs you ?

' *Lew.* This ſudden turn of joy perhaps——He
' wants reſt too——Laſt night was dreadful to him. His
' brain is giddy.

' *Char.* Ay, never to be cured——Why, brother !—
' O ! I fear ! I fear !

' *Mrs. B.* Preſerve him, Heaven !'———My love !
my life ! look at me !——How his eyes flame !

Bev. A furnace rages in this heart——' I have been
' too haſty.

' *Mrs. B.* Indeed !——O me ! O me !———Help,
' Jarvis ! Fly, fly for help ! Your maſter dies elſe.——
' Weep not, but fly ! [*Exit* Jar.] What is this haſty
' deed ?——Yet do not anſwer me——My fears have
' gueſſed.

' *Bev.* Call back the meſſenger————'Tis not in me-
' dicine's power to help me.

' *Mrs. B.* Is it then ſo ?

' *Bev.*' Down, reſtleſs flames !———[*Laying his hand
on his heart.*] down to your native hell—There you ſhall
rack me———O ! for a pauſe from pain !

' *Mrs. B.* Help, Charlotte ! Support him, Sir ! [*To
' Lewſon.*] This is a killing ſight !

' *Bev.* That pang was well—It has numbed my ſen-
' ſes.'———Where's my wife ?——Can you forgive me, love ?

Mrs. B. Alas ! for what ?

' *Bev.* [*Starting again.*] And there's another pang—
' Now all is quiet—Will you forgive me ?

' *Mrs. B.* I will——tell me for what ?'

Bev. For meanly dying.

Mrs B. No———do not ſay it.

Bev. As truly as my ſoul muſt anſwer it.———Had
Jarvis ſtaid this morning, all had been well. But preſſed
by ſhame——pent in a priſon——tormented with my
pangs for you——driven to deſpair and madneſs———I
took the advantage of his abſence, corrupted the poor
wretch he left to guard me, and——ſwallowed poiſon.

Mrs. B. O fatal deed !

Char. Dreadful and cruel !

Bev.

Bev. Ay, moft accurfed——And now I go to my account. ' This reft from pain brings death ; yet 'tis
' Heaven's kindnefs to me. I wifhed for eafe, a mo-
' ment's eafe, that cool repentance and contrition might
' foften vengeance.'——Bend me, and let me kneel.
[*They lift him from his chair, and fupport him on his knees.*]
I'll pray for you too. Thou Power that madeft me, hear
me! If for a life of frailty, and this too hafty deed of
death, thy juftice dooms me, here I acquit the fentence.
But if enthroned in mercy where thou fitteft, thy pity
has beheld me, fend me a gleam of hope; that in thefe
laft and bitter moments my foul may tafte of comfort!
and for thefe mourners here, O! let their lives be peaceful, and their deaths happy !——' Now raife me.'

[*They lift him to the chair.*

Mrs. B. Reftore him, Heaven ! Stretch forth thy arm
omnipotent, and fnatch him from the grave !——O fave
him ! fave him ! *or let me die too.*

' *Bev.* Alas ! that prayer is fruitlefs. Already death
' has feized me——Yet Heaven is gracious——I afked
' for hope, as the bright prefage of forgivenefs, and like
' a light, blazing thro darknefs, it came and cheared me
' ——'Twas all I lived for,' and now I die.

' *Mrs. B.* Not yet !——Not yet !——Stay but a
' little and I'll die too.'

Bev. No ; live, I charge you.——We have a little
one. Tho' I have left him, you will not leave him. To
Lewfon's kindnefs I bequeath him.——Is not this Charlotte ? We have lived in love, tho' I have wronged you.
Can you forgive me, Charlotte?

Char. Forgive you !——O my poor brother !

Bev. ' Lend me your hand, love.——So——raife me
' ——No——'twill not be——My life is finifhed——'
O! for a few fhort moments, to tell you how my heart
bleeds for you——That even now, thus dying as I am,
dubious and fearful of hereafter, my bofom pang is for
your miferies, Support her, Heaven !——And now I go
——O, mercy ! mercy ! [*Dies.*

Lew. Then all is over——How is it, Madam ?——
My poor Charlotte too !

Enter

' *Enter* Jarvis.

' *Jar.* How does my mafter, Madam ? Here's help
' at hand——— Am I too late then ?   ' [*Seeing* Bev.'

' *Char.* ' Tears ! tears ! why fall you not ?———O
' wretched fifter !———Speak to her, Lewfon———'
Her grief is fpeechlefs.

Lew. ' Remove her from this fight—Go to her, Jar-
' vis—Lead and fupport her.' Sorrow like hers forbids
complaint—Words are for lighter griefs—Some mi-
niftring angel bring her peace ! [Jar. *and* Char. *lead her
off.*] And thou, poor breathlefs corpfe, may thy departed foul have found the reft it prayed for ! Save but one
error, and this laft fatal deed, thy life was lovely. Let
frailer minds take warning ; and from example learn,
that want of prudence is want of virtue.

Follies, if uncontroul'd, of every kind,
Grow into paffions, and fubdue the mind ;
With fenfe and reafon hold fuperior ftrife,
And conquer honour, nature, fame and life.

                        [*Exeunt.*

END of the FIFTH ACT.

EPILOGUE.

Written by a FRIEND.

ON ev'ry gamefter in th' Arabian nation,
  'Tis faid that Mahomet denounc'd damnation:
But in return for wicked cards and dice,
He gave 'em black-ey'd girls in Paradife.
Should he thus preach, good countrymen, to you,
His converts would, I fear, be mighty few,
So much your hearts are fet on fordid gain,
The brighteft eyes around you fhine in vain.
Should the moft Heav'nly beauty bid you take her,
You'd rather hold——two aces and a maker.
By your example, our poor fex drawn in,
Is guilty of the fame unnat'ral fin;
The ftudy now of ev'ry girl of parts,
Is how to win your money, not your hearts.
O! in what fweet, what ravifhing delights
Our beaux and belles together pafs their nights!
By ardent perturbations kept awake,
Each views with longing eyes the other's—ftake.
The fmiles and graces are from Britain flown,
Our Cupid is an errant fharper grown,
And Fortune fits on Cytherea's throne.
In all thefe things, tho' women may be blam'd,
Sure men, the wifer men, fhould be afham'd!
And 'tis a horrid fcandal, I declare,
That four ftrange queens fhould rival all the fair;
Four jilts with neither beauty, wit, nor parts,
O fhame! have got poffeffion of their hearts:
And thofe bold fluts, for all their queenly pride,
Have play'd loofe tricks, or elfe they're much bely'd.
Cards were at firft for benefits defign'd,
Sent to amufe, and not enflave the mind.
From good to bad how eafy the tranfition!
For what was pleafure once, is now perdition.
Fair ladies, then, thefe wicked gamefters fhun,
Whoever weds one, is, you fee, undone.

M^{rs}. HARTLEY in the Character of ALMEYDA

Now if thou dar'st behold Almeyda's face

DON SEBASTIAN,

KING of PORTUGAL.

A TRAGEDY,

As written by D R Y D E N:

DISTINGUISHING ALSO THE

VARIATIONS OF THE THEATRE,

AS PERFORMED AT THE

𝕿𝖍𝖊𝖆𝖙𝖗𝖊-𝕽𝖔𝖞𝖆𝖑 𝖎𝖓 𝕯𝖗𝖚𝖗𝖞-𝕷𝖆𝖓𝖊.

Regulated from the Prompt-Book.

By PERMISSION *of the* MANAGERS.

By Mr. H O P K I N S, Prompter.

———————*Nec tarda senectus*
Debilitat vires animi, mutatque vigorem.   VIRG.

LONDON:

Printed for JOHN BELL, near Exeter-Exchange, in the *Strand.*

MDCCLXXVII.

PHILIP,

Earl of *Leicester*, &c.

FAR be it from me (my moſt noble Lord) to think, that any thing which my meanneſs can produce, ſhould be worthy to be offered to your patronage ; or that ought which I can ſay of you ſhould recommend you farther, to the eſteem of good men in this preſent age, or to the veneration which will certainly be paid you by poſterity. On the other ſide, I muſt acknowledge it a great preſumption in me, to make you this addreſs ; and ſo much the greater, becauſe by the common ſuffrage even of contrary parties, you have been always regarded as one of the firſt perſons of the age, and yet no one writer has dared to tell you ſo : whether we have been all conſcious to ourſelves that it was a needleſs labour to give this notice to mankind, as all men are aſhamed to tell ſtale news ; or that we were juſtly diffident of our own performances, as even Cicero is obſerved to be in awe when he writes to Atticus ; where knowing himſelf overmatched in good ſenſe, and truth of knowledge, he drops the gaudy train of words, and is no longer the vain-glorious orator. From whatever reaſon it may be, I am the firſt bold offender of this kind : I have broken down the fence, and ventured into the holy grove : how I may be puniſhed for my profane attempt, I know not ; but I wiſh it may not be of ill omen to your Lordſhip ; and that a croud of bad writers do not ruſh into the quiet of your receſſes after me. Every man in all changes of government, which have been, or may poſſibly arrive, will agree, that I could not have offered my incenſe, where it could be ſo well deſerved. For you, my Lord, are ſecure in your own merit ; and all parties, as they riſe uppermoſt, are ſure to court you in their turns ; 'tis a tribute which has ever been paid your virtue : the leading men ſtill bring their bullion to your mint, to receive the ſtamp of their intrinſic value, that they may afterwards hope to paſs with human-kind. They riſe and fall in the variety of revolutions ; and are ſometimes great, and therefore wiſe in men's opinions, who muſt court them for their intereſt : but the reputation of their parts moſt commonly follows their ſucceſs ; few of them are wiſe, but as they are in power : becauſe indeed, they have no ſphere of their own, but like the moon in the Copernican ſyſtem of the world, are whirled about by the motion of a greater planet. This it is to be ever buſy ; neither to give reſt to their fellow-creatures, nor, which is more wretchedly ridiculous, to themſelves : tho' truly, the latter is a kind of juſtice, and giving mankind a due revenge, that they will

A 2

not

not permit their own hearts to be at quiet, who difturb the repofe of all befide them. Ambitious meteors ! how willing they are to fet themfelves upon the wing ; taking every occafion of drawing upward to the fun : not confidering that they have no more time allowed them for their mounting, than the fhort revolution of a day ; and that when the light goes from them, they are of necef-fity to fall. How much happier is he (and who he is I need not fay, for there is but one phœnix in an age) who centering on him-felf, remains immoveable, and fmiles at the madnefs of the dance about him ? He poffeffes the midft, which is the portion of fafety and content : he will not be higher, becaufe he needs it not; but by the prudence of that choice, he puts it out of Fortune's power to throw him down. 'Tis confeft, that if he had not fo been born, he might have been too high for happinefs; but not endeavouring to afcend, he fecures the native height of his ftation from envy ; and cannot defcend from what he is, becaufe he depends not on ano-ther. What a glorious character was this once in Rome ! I fhould fay in Athens, when in the difturbances of a ftate as mad as ours, the wife Pomponius tranfported all the remaining wifdom and virtue of his country, into the fanctuary of peace and learning. But I would afk the world (for you, my Lord, are too nearly concerned to judge this caufe) whether there may not yet be found a character of a noble Englifhman equally fhining with that illuftrious Roman ? Whether I need to name a fecond Atticus ; or whether the world has not already prevented me, and fixed it there without my naming ? Not a fecond with a *longo fed proximus intervallo*, not a young Mar-cellus, flattered by a poet into the refemblance of the firft, with a *frons læta parum, & dejecto lumina vultu,* and the reft that follows, *fi qua fata afpera rumpas, Tu Marcellus eris :* but a perfon of the fame ftamp and magnitude ; who owes nothing to the former, be-fides the word Roman, and the fuperftition of reverence, devolving on him by the precedency of eighteen hundred years : one who walks by him with equal paces, and fhares the eyes of beholders with him : one who had been firft, had he firft lived ; and in fpite of doating veneration is ftill his equal. Both of them born of no-ble families, in unhappy ages of change and tumult : both of them retiring from affairs of ftate ; yet not leaving the commonwealth, till it had left itfelf : but never returning to public bufinefs when they had once quitted it, tho' courted by the heads of either party. But who would truft the quiet of their lives with the extravagan-cies of their countrymen, when they were juft in the giddinefs of their turning ; when the ground was tottering under them at every moment ; and none could guefs whether the next heave of the earthquake would fettle them on the firft foundation, or fwallow it ? Both of them knew mankind exactly well ; for both of them began that ftudy in themfelves ; and there they found the beft part of human compofition, the worft they learned by long experience of the folly, ignorance, and immorality of moft befide them ; their philofophy on both fides, was not wholly fpeculative, for that is barren, and produces nothing but vain ideas of things which cannot poffibly be known, or if they could, yet would only terminate in the

un-

underſtanding; but it was a noble, vigorous, and practical philoſophy, which exerted itſelf in all the offices of pity, to thoſe who
were unfortunate, and deſerved not ſo to be. The friend was always
more conſidered by them than the cauſe: and an Octavius, or an
Antony in diſtreſs, were relieved by them, as well as a Brutus or a
Caſſius. For the lowermoſt party, to a noble mind, is ever the fitteſt
object of good-will. The eldeſt of them, I will ſuppoſe for his honour, to have been of the academic ſect, neither dogmatiſt nor ſtoic;
if he were not, I am ſure he ought in common juſtice, to yield the
precedency to his younger brother. For ſtiffneſs of opinion is the effect of pride, and not of philoſophy: 'tis a miſerable preſumption
of that knowledge which human nature is too narrow to contain.
And the ruggedneſs of a ſtoic is only a ſilly affectation of being a
god: to wind himſelf up by pullies to an inſenſibility of ſuffering;
and at the ſame time to give the lie to his own experience, by ſaying
he ſuffers not, what he knows he feels. True philoſophy is certainly of a more pliant nature, and more accommodated to human
uſe: *Homo ſum, humani a me nihil alienum puto.* A wiſe man will
never attempt an impoſſibility; and ſuch it is to ſtrain himſelf beyond the nature of his being: either to become a deity, by being
above ſuffering, or to debaſe himſelf into a ſtock or ſtone, by pretending not to feel it. To find in ourſelves the weakneſſes and im-
perfections of our wretched kind, is ſurely the moſt reaſonable ſtep
we can make towards the compaſſion of our fellow-creatures. I
could give examples of this kind in the ſecond Atticus. In every
turn of ſtate, without meddling on either ſide, he has always been fa-
vourable and aſſiſting to oppreſſed merit. The praiſes which were
given by a great poet to the late Queen mother on her rebuilding So-
merſet palace, one part of which was fronting to the mean houſes on
the other ſide of the water, are as juſtly his:

> *For, the diſtreſs'd, and the afflicted lie*
> *Moſt in his thoughts, and always in his eye.*

Neither has he ſo far forgot a poor inhabitant of his ſuburbs, whoſe
beſt proſpect is on the garden of Leiceſter Houſe; but that more than
once he has been offering him his patronage, to reconcile him to a
world, of which his misfortunes have made him weary. There is
another Sidney ſtill remaining, though there can never be another
Spenſer to deſerve the favour. But one Sidney gave his patronage
to the applications of a poet; the other offered it unaſked. Thus,
whether as a ſecond Atticus, or a ſecond Sir Philip Sidney, the latter in all reſpects will not have the worſe of the compariſon; and if
he will take up with the ſecond place, the world will not ſo far flatter his modeſty, as to ſeat him there, unleſs it be out of a deference of
manners, that he may place himſelf where he pleaſes at his own table.

I may therefore ſafely conclude, that he, who by the conſent of all
men, bears ſo eminent a character, will out of his inborn nobleneſs
forgive the preſumption of this addreſs. 'Tis an unfiniſhed picture,
I confeſs, but the lines and features are ſo like, that it cannot be
miſtaken for any other; and without writing any name under it,
every beholder muſt cry out, at the firſt ſight, This was deſigned for

A 3

Atticus.

Atticus; but the bad artist has cast too much of him into shades. But I have this excuse, that even the greatest masters commonly fall short of the best faces. They may flatter an indifferent beauty; but the excellencies of nature can have no right done to them: For there both the pencil and the pen are overcome by the dignity of the subject; as our admirable Waller has expressed it,

The heroe's race transcends the poet's thought.

There are few in any age who can bear the load of a dedication; for where praise is undeserved, it is satire: though satire on folly is now no longer a scandal to any one person, where a whole age is dipt together; yet I had rather undertake a multitude one way, than a single Atticus the other; for 'tis easier to descend than 'tis to climb. I should have gone ashamed out of the world, if I had not at least attempted this address, which I have long thought owing: and if I had never attempted, I might have been vain enough to think I might have succeeded in it. Now I have made the experiment, and have failed, through my unworthiness, I may rest satisfied, that either the adventure is not to be atchieved, or that it is reserved for some other hand.

Be pleased, therefore, since the family of Attici is and ought to be above the common forms of concluding letters, that I may take my leave in the words of Cicero to the first of them: *Me, O Pomponi, valdè pœnitet vivere: tantum te oro, ut quoniam me ipse semper amâsti, ut eodem amore sis; ego nimirum idem sum. Inimici mei vica mihi, non me ipsum ademerunt. Cura, Attice, ut valeas.*

Dabam Cal.
Jan. 1690.

PREFACE.

WHETHER it happened thro' a long difuse of writing, that I forgot the ufual compafs of a play; or that by crouding it with characters and incidents, I put a neceffity upon myfelf of lengthening the main action, I know not: but the firft day's audience fufficiently convinced me of my error; and that the poem was infupportably too long. 'Tis an ill ambition of poets, to pleafe an audience with more than they can bear: and, fuppofing that we wrote as well as vainly we imagine ourfelves to write, yet we ought to confider, that no man can bear to be long tickled. There is a naufeoufnefs in a city-feaft, when we are to fit four hours after we are cloyed. I am therefore in the firft place to acknowledge, with all manner of gratitude, their civility, who were pleafed to endure it with fo much patience, to be weary with fo much good-nature and filence, and not to explode an entertainment, which was defigned to pleafe them; or difcourage an author, whofe misfortunes have once more brought him, againft his will, upon the ftage. While I continue in thefe bad circumftances (and truly I fee very little probability of coming out) I muft be obliged to write; and if I may ftill hope for the fame kind ufage, I fhall the lefs repent of. that hard neceffity. I write not this out of any expectation to be pitied; for I have enemies enough to wifh me yet in a worfe condition: but give me leave to fay, that if I can pleafe by writing, as I fhall endeavour it, the town may be fomewhat obliged to my misfortunes, for a part of their diverfion. Having been longer acquainted with the ftage, than any poet now living, and having obferved how difficult it was to pleafe; that the humours of comedy were almoft fpent, that love and honour (the miftaken topicks of tragedy) were quite worn out, that the theatres could not fupport their charges, that the audience forfook them, that young men without learning fet up for judges, and that they talked loudeft who underftood the leaft: all thefe difcouragements had not only weaned me from the ftage, but had alfo given me a loathing of it. But enough of this: the difficulties continue; they increafe, and I am ftill condemned to dig in thofe exhaufted mines. Whatever fault I next commit, reft affured it fhall not be that of too much length. Above twelve hundred lines have been cut off from this tragedy fince it was firft delivered to the actors. They were indeed fo judicioufly lopped by Mr. Betterton, to whofe care and excellent action I am equally obliged, that the connexion of the ftory was not loft; but on the other fide, it was Impoffible to prevent fome part of the action from being precipitated and coming on without that due preparation, which is required to all great events; as in particular, that of raifing the mobile in the beginning of the fourth act; which a man of Benducar's cool character, could not naturally attempt, without taking all thofe precautions, which he forefaw

would

3

would be neceſſary to render his deſign ſuccefsful. On this conſideration I have replaced thoſe lines through the whole poem ; and
thereby reſtored it to that clearneſs of conception, and (if I may
dare to ſay) that luſtre and maſculine vigour in which it was firſt
written. 'Tis obvious to every underſtanding reader, that the moſt
poetical parts, which are deſcription, images, ſimilitudes, and moral ſentences, are thoſe which of neceſſity were to be pared away,
when the body was ſwollen into too large a bulk for the repreſenta-
tion of the ſtage. But there is a vaſt difference betwixt a public
entertainment on the theatre, and a private reading in the cloſet :
in the firſt we are confined to time, and though we talk not by the
hour-glaſs, yet the watch often drawn out of the pocket warns the
actors that their audience is weary : in the laſt every reader is judge
of his own convenience ; he can take up the book and lay it down
at his pleaſure ; and find out thoſe beauties of propriety in thought
and writing, which eſcaped him in the tumult and hurry of repre-
ſenting. And I dare boldly promiſe for this play, that in the
roughneſs of the numbers and cadences (which I aſſure was not ca-
ſual, but ſo deſigned) you will ſee ſomewhat more maſterly ariſing
to your view, than in moſt, if not any of my former tragedies.
There is a more noble daring in the figures, and more ſuitable to
the loftineſs of the ſubject ; and beſides this, ſome newneſſes of En-
gliſh, tranſlated from the beauties of modern tongues, as well as
from the elegancies of the Latin ; and here and there ſome old
words are ſprinkled, which for their ſignificance and ſound deſerved
not to be antiquated, ſuch as we often find in Salluſt amongſt the Roman authors, and in Milton's Paradiſe amongſt ours ; tho' perhaps
the latter, inſtead of ſprinkling, has dealt them with too free a hand,
even ſometimes to the obſcuring of his ſenſe.

As for the ſtory or plot of the tragedy, 'tis purely fiction ; for I
take it up where the hiſtory has laid it down. We are aſſured by
all writers of thoſe times, that Sebaſtian, a young prince of great
courage and expectation, undertook that war partly upon a religious
account, partly at the ſolicitation of Muley-Mahomet, who had
been driven out of his dominions by Abdelmelech, or as others call
him, Muley-Moluch, his nigh kinſman, who deſcended from the
ſame family of the Xeriffs, whoſe fathers, Hamet and Mahomet
had conquered that empire with joint forces, and ſhared it betwixt
them after their victory : that the body of Don Sebaſtian was never found in the field of battle ; which gave occaſion for many to
believe, that he was not ſlain : that ſome years after, when the
Spaniards, with a pretended title, by force of arms, had uſurped
the crown of Portugal from the houſe of Braganza, a certain perſon, who called himſelf Don Sebaſtian, and had all the marks of
his body and features of his face, appeared at Venice, where he was
owned by ſome of his countrymen ; but being ſeized by the Spaniards, was firſt impriſoned, then ſent to the gallies, and at laſt
put to death in private. 'Tis moſt certain, that the Portngueſe expected his return for almoſt an age together after that battle ; which
is at leaſt a proof of their extream love to his memory : and the
uſage which they had from their new conquerors, might poſſibly
make

make them fo extravagant in their hopes and wifhes for their old mafter.

This ground-work the hiftory afforded me, and I defire no better to build a play upon it ; for where the event of a great action is left doubtful, there the poet is left mafter : he may raife what he pleafes on that foundation, provided he makes it of a piece, and according to the rule of probability. From hence I was only obliged that Sebaftian fhould return to Portugal no more ; but at the fame time I had him at my own difpofal, whether to beftow him in Africk, or in any other corner of the world, or to have clofed the tragedy with his death ; and the laft of thefe was certainly the moft eafy, but for the fame reafon, the leaft artful ; becaufe, as I have fomewhere faid, the poifon and the dagger are ftill at hand to butcher a hero, when a poet wants the brains to fave him. It being therefore only neceffary, according to the laws of the *Drama*, that Sebaftian fhould no more be feen upon the throne, I leave it for the world to judge, whether or no I have difpofed of him according to art, or have bungled up the conclufion of his adventure. In the drawing of his character I forgot not piety, which any one may obferve to be one principal ingredient of it ; even fo far as to be a habit in him ; though I fhew him once to be tranfported from it by the violence of a fudden paffion, to endeavour a felf-murder. This being pre-fuppofed, that he was religious, the horror of his inceft, though innocently committed, was the beft reafon which the ftage could give for hindering his return. 'Tis true, I have no right to blaft his memory with fuch a crime : but declaring it to be fiction, I defire my audience to think it no longer true, than while they are feeing it reprefented : for that once ended, he may be a faint for ought I know ; and we have reafon to prefume he is. On this fuppofition, it was unreafonable to have killed him : for the learned Mr. Rymer has well obferved, that in all punifhments we are to regulate ourfelves by poetical juftice ; and according to thofe meafures an involuntary fin deferves not death : from whence it follows, that to divorce himfelf from the beloved object, to retire into a defart, and deprive himfelf of a throne, was the utmoft punifhment which a poet could inflict, as it was alfo the utmoft reparation which Sebaftian could make. For what relates to Almeyda, her part is wholly fictitious : I know it is the firname of a noble famil; in Portugal, which was very inftrumental in the reftoration of Don John de Braganza, father to the moft illuftrious and moft pious princefs our Queen Dowager. The French author of a novel called Don Sebaftian, has given that name to an African lady of his own invention, and makes her fifter to Muley-Mahomet. But I have wholly changed the accidents, and borrowed nothing but the fuppofition, that fhe was beloved by the King of Portugal. Though if I had taken the whole ftory, and wrought it up into a play, I might have done it exactly according to the practice of almoft all the ancients ; who were never accufed of being plagiaries, for building their tragedies on known fables. Thus Auguftus Cæfar wrote an Ajax, which was not the lefs his own, becaufe Euripides had written a play before him on that fubject. Thus of late years Corneille writ an OEdipus after Sophocles ; and I have defigned one after him, which I wrote with Mr. Lee : yet neither the French poet ftole from the

Greek,

Greek, nor we from the Frenchman. 'Tis the contrivance, the new turn, and new characters, which alter the property, and make it ours. The *Materia Poetica* is as common to all writers, as the *Materia Medica* to all phyficians. Thus in our Chronicles, Daniel's hiftory is ftill his own, though Matthew Paris, Stow, and Hollingfhed writ before him ; otherwife we muft have been content with their dull relations, if a better pen had not been allowed to come after them, and writ his own account after a new and better manner.

I muft further declare freely, that I have not exactly kept to the three mechanic rules of unity : I knew them, and had them in my eye, but followed them only at a diftance : for the genius of the Englifh cannot bear too regular a play, we are given to variety, even to a debauchery of pleafure. My fcenes are therefore fometimes broken, becaufe my under-plot required them fo to be: though the general fc ne remains of the fame caftle ; and I have taken the time of two days, becaufe the variety of accidents, which are here reprefented, could not naturally be fuppofed to arrive in one : But to gain a greater beauty, 'tis lawful for a poet to fuperfede a lefs.

I muft likewife own, that I have fomewhat deviated from the known hiftory, in the dearh of Muley-Moluch, who, by all relations, died of a fever in the battle, before his army had wholly won the field : but if I have allowed him another day of life, it was becaufe I ftood in need of fo fhining a character of brutality, as I have given him ; which is indeed the fame with that of the prefent emperor Muley-Ifhmael, as fome of our Englifh officers, who have been in his court, have credibly informed me.

I have been liftening what objections had been made againft the conduct of the play, but found them all fo trivial, that if I fhould name them, a true critic would imagine that I played booty, and only raifed up fantoms for myfelf to conquer. Some are pleafed to fay the writing is dull : but *ætatem habet, de fe loquatur*. Others, that the double poifon is unnatural; let the common received opinion, and Aufonius's famous epigram anfwer that. Laftly, a more ignorant fort of creatures than either of the former, maintain that the character of Dorax is not only unnatural, but inconfiftent with itfelf ; let them read the play and think again ; and if yet they are not fatisfied, caft their eyes on that chapter of the wife Montaigne, which is intitled, *de l'Inconftance des Actions humaines*. A longer reply is what thofe cavillers deferve not ; but I will give them and their fellows to underftand, that the earl of Dorfet was pleafed to read the tragedy twice over before it was acted ; and did me the favour to fend me word, that I had written beyond any of my former plays ; and that he was difpleafed any thing fhould be cut away. If I have not reafon to prefer his fingle judgment to a whole faction, let the world be judge ; for the oppofition is the fame with that of Lucan's hero againft an army ; *concurrere bellum, atque virum*. I think I may modeftly conclude, that whatever errors there may be, either in the defign, or writing of this play, they are not thofe which have been objected to it. I think alfo, that I am not yet arrived to the age of doting ; and that I have given fo much application to this poem, that I could not probably let it run into many grofs abfurdities, which may caution my enemies from too rafh a cenfure ; and

may

may alfo encourage my friends, who are many more than I could reafonably have expected, to believe their kindnefs has not been very undefervedly beftowed on me. This is not a play that was huddled up in hafte: and to fhew it was not, I will own, that befides the general moral of it, which is given in the four laft lines, there is alfo another moral, couched under under every one of the principal parts and characters ; which a judicious critic will obferve, though I point not to in this preface. And there may be alfo fome fecret beauties in the decorum of parts, and uniformity of defign, which my puny judges will not eafily find out : let them confider in the laft fcene of the fourth act, whether I have not preferved the rule of decency, in giving all the advantage to the royal character, and in making Dorax firft fubmit : perhaps too they may have thought, that it was thro' indigence of characters, I have given the fame to Sebaftian and Almeyda ; and confequently made them alike in all things but their fex. But let them look a little deeper into the matter, and they will find that this identity of character in the greatnefs of their fouls, was intended for a preparation of the final difcovery, and that the likenefs of their nature, was a fair hint to the proximity of their blood.

To avoid the imputation of too much vanity (for all writers, and efpecially poets, will have fome) I will give but one other inftance, in relation to the uniformity of the defign. I have obferved, that the Englifh will not bear a thorough tragedy ; but are pleafed, that it fhould be lightened with under-parts of mirth. It had been eafy for me to have given my audience a better courfe of comedy, I mean a more diverting, than that of Antonio and Morayma. But I dare appeal even to my enemies, if I, or any man, could have invented one which had been more of a piece, and more depending on the ferious part of the defign. For what could be more uniform, than to draw from out of the members of a captive court, the fubject of a comical entertainment? To prepare this epifode, you fee Dorax giving the character of Antonio, in the beginning of the play, upon his firft fight of him at the lottery ; and to make the dependance, Antonio is engaged in the fourth act for the deliverance of Almeyda ; which is alfo prepared by his being firft made a flave to the captain of the rabble.

I fhould beg pardon for thefe inftances ; but perhaps they may be of ufe to future poets, in the conduct of their plays : At leaft if I appear too pofitive, I am growing old, and thereby in poffeffion of fome experience, which men in years will always affume for a right of talking. Certainly if a man can ever have reafon to fet a value on himfelf, 'tis when his ungenerous enemies are taking the advantage of the times upon him, to ruin him in his reputation. And therefore for once, I will make bold to take the counfel of my old mafter, Virgil.

Tu ne cede malis, fed contra audentior ito.

PROLOGUE.

Sent to the Author by an unknown Hand, and propofed to be
Spoken by Mrs. *Mountford,* drefled like an Officer.

*B*RIGHT *beauties who in awful circle fit,*
 And you grave fynod of the dreadful pit,
And you the upper-tire of popgun wit,

Pray eafe me of my wonder, if you may:
Is all this croud barely to fee the play,
Or is't the pœt's execution-day ?

His breath is in your hands I will prefume,
But I advife you to defer his doom,
Till you have got a better in his room ;

And don't malicioufly combine together,
As if in fpight and fpleen you were come hither ;
For he has kept the pen, tho' loft the feather.

And on my honour, ladies, I avow,
This play was writ in charity to you :
For fuch a dearth of wit who ever knew ?

Sure 'tis a judgment on this finful nation,
For the abufe of fo great difpenfation :
And therefore I refolve to change vocation.

For want of petty-coat I've put on buff,
To try what may be got by lying rough :
How think you, Sirs, is it not well enough !

Of bully-critics I a troop would lead ;
But one reply'd, Thank you, there's no fuch need,
I at Groom-Porter's, Sir, can fafer bleed.

Another, who the name of danger loaths,
Vow'd he wou'd go, and fwore me forty oaths,
But that his horfes were in body-clothes.

A third cry'd, Damn my blood, I'd be content
To pufh my fortune, if the parliament
Wou'd but recall Claret from banifhment.

A fourth (and I have done) made this excufe,
I'd draw my fword in Ireland, Sir, to chufe ;
Had not their women gouty legs and wore no fhoes.

Well, I may march, thought I, and fight, and trudge,
But of thefe blades the devil a man will budge ;
They there would fight, e'en juft as here they judge.

Here they will pay for leave to find a fault,
But when their honour calls, they can't be bought ;
Honour in danger, blood and wounds is fought.

Loft

Lost Virtue, whither fled, or where's thy dwelling
Who can reveal? at least 'tis past my telling,
Unless thou art embark'd for Iniskilling.

On carrion-tits those sparks denounce their rage,
In boot of wisp and Leinster frise engage:
What would you do in such an equipage?

The siege of Derry does you gallants threaten;
Not out of errant shame of being beaten,
As fear of wanting meat, or being eaten.

Were wit like honour to be won by fighting,
How few just judges would there be of writing.
Then you would leave this villainous back-biting.

Your talents lie how to express your spight,
But where is he knows how to praise aright?
You praise like cowards, but like critics fight.

Ladies, be wise, and wean these yearling calves,
Who in your service too are mere faux-braves,
They judge and write, and fight, and——love by halves.

PROLOGUE.

Spoken by a Woman.

THE judge remov'd, tho' he's no more my Lord,
*   May plead at bar, or at the council-board:*
So may cast poets write; there's no pretension
To argue loss of wit, from loss of pension.
Your looks are chearful; and in all this place
I see not one, that wears a damning face.
The British nation is too brave, to shew
Ignoble vengeance on a vanquish'd foe.
At least be civil to the wretch imploring;
And lay your paws upon him, without roaring:
Suppose our poet was your foe before;
Yet now, the bus'ness of the field is o'er;
'Tis time to let your civil-wars alone,
When troops are into winter-quarters gone.
Jove was alike to Latian and to Phrygian;
And you well know, a play's of no religion.
Take good advice and please yourselves this day;
No matter from what hands you have the play.
Among good fellows every health will pass,
That serves to carry round another glass:
When with full bowls of Burgundy you dine,
Tho' at the mighty monarch you repine,
You grant him still most Christian in his wine.
*   Thus far the poet: but his brains grow addle,*
And all the rest is purely from my noddle;

B   You've

[14]

You've seen young ladies at the senate-door,
Prefer petitions, and your grace implore:
However grave the legiflators were,
Their caufe went ne'er the worfe for being fair.
Reafons as weak as theirs, perhaps, I bring;
But I could bribe you with as good a thing.
I heard him make advances of good nature;
That he, for once, wou'd fheath his cutting fatire:
Sign but his peace, be vows he'll ne'er again
The facred names of fops, and beaus profane,
Strike up the bargain quickly; for I fwear,
As times go now, he offers very fair.
Be not too hard on him with ftatutes neither,
Be kind; and do not fet your teeth together,
To ftretch the laws, as coblers do their leather.
Horfes by papifts are not to be ridden;
But fure the Mufe's horfe was ne'er forbidden.
For in no rate-book it was ever found
That Pegafus was valued at five pound:
Fine him to daily drudging and inditing:
And let him pay his taxes out in writing.

DRAMATIS PERSONÆ.

MEN.

		Covent-Garden.
Don *Sebaftian*, king of *Portugal*,	——	Mr. Smith.
Muley Moluch, emperor of *Barbary*,	——	Mr. Gardner.
Dorax, a noble *Portuguefe*, now a renegade, formerly Don *Alonzo de Sylvera*, Alcade, or Governor of *Alcazar*,	——	Mr. Benfley.
Benducar, chief minifter and favourite of the Emperor,	—— ——	Mr. Thompfon.
The Mufti *Abdallah*,	——	Mr. Quick.
Muley Zeydan, brother to the Emperor,		Mr. Owenfon.
Don *Antonio*, a young, noble, amorous, *Portuguefe*, now a flave,	—— ——	Mr. Lewis.
Don *Alvarez*, an old counfellor to Don *Sebaftian*, now a flave alfo,	—— ——	Mr. Hull.
Muftapha, captain of the rabble,	——	Mr. Dunftall.
Orchan,	—— ——	Mr. Bates.

WOMEN.

Almeyda, a captive Queen of *Barbary*,		Mrs. Hartley.
Morayma, daughter to the Mufti,	——	Mrs. Mattocks.
Jobayma, chief wife to the Mufti,	——	Mrs. Green.
Two Merchants.		
Rabble.		
A Servant to *Benducar*.		
A Servant to the Mufti.		

SCENE in the caftle of *Alcazar*.

DON SEBASTIAN.

₊ *The lines marked with inverted commas, 'thus,' are omitted in the representation.*

ACT I.

The SCENE *at Alcazar, representing a Market-place under the Castle.*

Enter Muley-Zeydan, *and* Benducar.

MULEY-ZEYDAN.

NOW Africa's long wars are at an end,
⠀⠀And our parch'd earth is drench'd in Christian
My conquering brother will have slaves enow⠀⠀[blood;
To pay his cruel vows for victory.
What hear you of Sebastian, king of Portugal?
⠀⠀*Ben.* He fell among a heap of slaughter'd Moors;
Tho' yet his mangled carcase is not found.
The rival of our threaten'd empire, Mahomet,
Was hot pursu'd; and in the general rout,
Mistook a swelling current for a ford,
' And in Mucazar's flood was seen to rise:'
Thrice was he seen; at length, his courser plung'd,
And threw him off; the waves whelm'd over him,
And, helpless in his heavy arms, he drown'd.
⠀⠀*M. Zeyd.* Thus then, a doubtful title is extinguish'd;
Thus Moluch, still the favourite of fate,
Swims in a sanguine torrent to the throne;
As if our prophet only work'd for him,
The heavens and all the stars his hired servants,
As Muley-Zeydan were not worth their care,
And younger brothers but the draff of nature.
⠀⠀*Ben.* Be still, and learn the soothing arts of courts;
Adore his fortune, mix with flattering crowds,
And when they praise him most, be you the loudest:

B 3

Your

Your brother is luxurious, close, and cruel,
Generous by fits, but permanent in mischief.
The shadow of a discontent would ruin us ;
We must be safe before we can be great :
These things obferv'd, leave me to shape the rest.

    ' *M. Zeyd.* You have the key ; he opens inward to you.

    ' *Ben.* So often try'd, and ever found so true,
' Has given me truft, and truft has given me means
' Once to be falfe for all. I truft not him ;
' For now his ends are ferv'd, and he grown abfolute,
' How am I fure to ftand, who ferv'd thofe ends ?
' I know your nature open, mild and grateful ;
' In fuch a prince the people may be blefs'd,
' And I be fafe.

    ' *M. Zeyd.* My father !   [*Embracing him.*

    ' *Ben.* My future king, aufpicious Muley-Zeydan,
' Shall I adore you ? No, the place is public ;
' I worfhip you within, the outward act
' Shall be referv'd till nations follow me,
' And Heav'n fhall envy you the kneeling world.'
You know th' alcade of Alcazar, Dorax ?

    M. Zeyd. The gallant renegade you mean ?

    Ben. The fame :
' That gloomy outfide, like a rufty cheft,
' Contains the fhining treafure of a foul
' Refolv'd and brave ; he has the foldiers' hearts,
' And time fhall make him ours.'

    M. Zeyd. He's juft upon us.

    Ben. I know him ' from afar,'
By the long ftride, and by the fudden port.
Retire, my Lord :
Wait on your brother's triumph, yours is next ;
His growth is but a wild and fruitlefs plant ;
I'll cut his barren branches to the ftock,
And graft you on to bear.

    M. Zeyd. My oracle !   [*Exit M. Zeyd.*

    Ben. Yes, to delude your hopes, poor credulous fool,
To think that I would give away the fruit
Of fo much toil, fuch guilt, and fuch perdition :
' If I am damn'd, it fhall be for myfelf ;
' This eafy fool muft be my ftale, fet up
' To catch the people's eyes ; he's tame and merciful ;'
                               ' Him

' Him I can manage, till I make him odious
' By some unpopular act, and then dethrone him.'
                    Enter Dorax.

Now, Dorax——
  Dor. Well, Benducar!
  Ben. Bare Benducar!
  Dor. Thou wouldst have titles; take them then, chief
First hangman of the state.   [minister,
  Ben. Some call me favourite.
  Dor. ' What's that, his favourite?
' Thou art too old to be a catamite.'
Now, pr'ythee, tell me, and abate thy pride,
Is not Benducar, bare, a better name
In a friend's mouth, than all those gaudy titles,
Which I disdain to give the man I love.
  Ben. But always out of humour——
  Dor. I have cause;
Though all mankind is cause enough for satire.
  Ben. Why then thou hast reveng'd thee on mankind:
They say, in fight thou hadst a thirsty sword,
And well 'twas glutted there.
  Dor. I spitted frogs, I crush'd a heap of emmets,
A hundred of them to a single soul,
And that but scanty weight too.   The great devil
Scarce thank'd me for my pains; ' he swallows vulgar
' Like whipp'd cream, feels them not in going down.'
  Ben. Brave renegade! couldst thou not meet Sebastian?
Thy master had been worthy of thy sword.
  Dor. My master! By what title?
Because I happen'd to be born where he
Happen'd to be king? And yet I serv'd him;
Nay, I was fool enough to love him too.
You know my story, how I was rewarded
For fifteen hard campaigns, still hoop'd in iron,
And why I turn'd Mahometan.   I'm grateful;
But whosoever dares to injure me,
Let that man know, I dare to be reveng'd.
  Ben. Still you run off from bias; say, what moves
Your present spleen?
  Dor. You mark'd not what I told you;
I kill'd not one that was his Maker's image;
I met with none but vulgar two-legg'd brutes;
                    B 3   Sebastian

Sebaſtian was my aim; he was a man:
Nay, though he hated me, and I hate him,
Yet I muſt do him right; ' he was a man,'
Above man's height, ev'n tow'ring to divinity;
Brave, pious, generous, great, and liberal;
Juſt, as the ſcales of heaven that weigh the ſeaſons.
He lov'd his people; him they idoliz'd;
And thence proceeds my mortal hatred to him,
That thus unblameable to all beſides,
He err'd to me alone.
His goodneſs was diffus'd to human kind,
And all his cruelty confin'd to me.

   Ben. You could not meet him then?
   Dor. No, though I ſought
Where ranks fell thickeſt; 'twas, indeed, the place
To ſeek Sebaſtian.   Through a track of death
I follow'd him, by groans of dying foes;
But ſtill I came too late; for he was flown,
Like lightning, ſwift before me to new ſlaughters.
I mow'd a-croſs, and made irregular harveſt,
Defac'd the pomp of battle; but in vain;
For he was ſtill ſupplying death elſewhere.
This mads me, that, perhaps, ignoble hands
Have overlaid him; for they could not conquer.
Murder'd by multitudes, whom I alone
Had right to ſlay.   I too would have been ſlain,
That, catching hold upon his flitting ghoſt,
I might have robb'd him of his opening heaven,
And dragg'd him down with me, ſpite of predeſtination.

   Ben. 'Tis of as much import as Afric's worth,
To know what came of him, and of Almeyda,
' The ſiſter of the vanquiſh'd Mahomet,
' Whoſe fatal beauty to her brother drew
' The land's third part, as Lucifer did Heaven's.'

   Dor. ' I hope ſhe dy'd in her own female calling,
' Choak'd up with man, and gorg'd with circumciſion.'
As for Sebaſtian, we muſt ſearch the field,
And where we ſee a mountain of the ſlain,
Send one to climb, and looking down below,
There he ſhall find him at his manly length,
With his face up to heaven, in the red monument
Which his true ſword has digg'd.

Ben.

Ben. Yet we may possibly hear farther news;
For while our Africans pursu'd the chace,
The captain of the rabble issued out,
With a black, shirtless train, to spoil the dead,
And seize the living.

Dor. Each of them an host,
A million strong of vermin, every villain:
No part of government, but lords of anarchy,
Chaos of power, and privileg'd destruction.

Ben. Yet I must tell you, friend, the great must use
Sometimes as necessary tools of tumult.   [them

Dor. I would use them
Like dogs in time of plague, out-laws of nature,
Fit to be shot and brain'd without a process,
To stop infection; that's their proper death.

Ben. No more.
Behold the emperor coming to survey
The slaves, in order to perform his vow.

Enter Muley-Moluch *the Emperor, with Attendants.*
The Mufti, *and* Muley-Zeydan.

Emp. Our armours now may rust, our idle scymiters
Hang by our sides for ornament, not use;
Children shall beat our atabals and drums,
And all the noisy trades of war no more
Shall wake the peaceful morn. ' The Xeriffs blood
' No longer in divided channels runs,
' The younger house took end in Mahomet;'
Nor shall Sebastian's formidable name
Be longer us'd to lull the crying babe.

Muf. For this victorious day, our mighty prophet
Expects your gratitude, the sacrifice
Of Christian slaves, devoted, if you won.

Emp. The purple present shall be richly paid:
That vow perform'd, fasting shall be abolish'd;
None ever serv'd Heaven well with a starv'd face:
Preach abstinence no more.   I tell thee, Mufti,
Good feasting is devout; and thou, our head,
Hast a religious, ruddy countenance.
' We will have learned luxury; our lean faith
' Gives scandal to the Christians; they feed high.
' Then

' Then look for shoals of converts, when thou haft
" Reform'd us into feasting.'-

   Muf. Fasting is but the letter of the law;
Yet it shews well to preach it to the vulgar.
Wine is against our law, that's literal too;
But not deny'd to kings, and to their guides.
Wine is a holy liquor for the great.

   Dor. [*Aside.*] This Mufti, in my conscience, is some
English renegado, he talks so savourily of toping.

   Emp Bring forth th' unhappy relicks of the war.

*Enter Mustapha, Captain of the rabble, with his followers
   of the black-guard, &c. and other Moors; with them a
   company of Portuguese slaves, without any of the chief
   persons.*

These are not fit to pay an emperor's vow;
Our bulls and rams had been more noble victims;
These are but garbage, not a sacrifice.

   Muf. The prophet must not pick and chuse his offerings;
Now he has given the day, 'tis past recalling;
And he must be content with such as these.

   Emp. But are these all? Speak you that are their masters.

   Must. All, upon mine honour. If you'll take them as
their fathers got them, so; if not, you must stay till they
get a better generation. These Christians are mere bung-
lers; they procreate nothing but out of their own wives,
and these have all the looks of eldest sons.

   Emp. Pain of your lives, let none conceal a slave.

   Must. Let every man look to his own conscience; I am
sure mine shall never hang me.

   Ben. Thou speak'st as if thou wert privy to conceal-
ments. Then thou art an accomplice.

   Must. Nay, if accomplices must suffer, it may go hard
with me. But here's the devil on't, there's a great man
and a holy man too concerned with me. Now, if I confess, he'll be sure to escape between his greatness and his
holiness, and I shall be murdered because of my poverty
and rascality.

   Muf. [*Winking at him.*] Then if thy silence save the
      great and holy,
'Tis sure thou shalt go straight to Paradise.

   Must. 'Tis a fine place, they say; but, Doctor, I am
not worthy on't: I am contented with this homely world;

'tis

'tis good enough for such a poor rascally Mussulman as I am. Besides, I have learnt so much good manners, Doctor, as to let my betters be served before me.

Emp. Thou talkest as if the Mufti were concerned.

Must. Your majesty may lay your soul on't. But for my part, though I am a plain fellow, yet I scorn to be tricked into Paradise, I would he should know it. The truth on't is, an't like you, his reverence bought of me the flower of all the market—These—these are but dogs-meat to them: and a round price he paid me too, I'll say that for him; but not enough for me to venture my neck for. ' If I get Paradise when my time comes, I can't ' help myself; but I'll venture nothing beforehand, ' upon a blind bargain.'

Emp. Where are those slaves ? Produce them.

Muf. They are not what he says.

Emp. No more excuses. [*One goes out to fetch them.* Know, thou mayst better dally
With a dead prophet, than a living king.

Muf. I but reserv'd them to present thy greatness,
An offering worthy thee.

Must. By the same token there was a dainty virgin, (virgin, said I ? But I won't be too positive of that nei-ther) with a roguish leering eye: he paid me down upon the nail a thousand golden sultanins, or he had never had her, I can tell him that. Now, is it very likely he would pay so dear for such a delicious morsel, and give it away out of his own mouth, when it had such a farewel with it too ?

Enter Sebastian, *conducted in mean habit, with* Alvarez,
Antonio, *and* Almeyda, *her face veiled with a barnus.*

Emp. Ay, these look like the workmanship of Heaven;
This is the porcelain clay of human kind,
And therefore cast into these noble molds.

Dor. [*Aside, while the Emperor whispers* Benducar.] By
all my wrongs,
'Tis he! ' Damnation seize me, but 'tis he!'
My heart heaves up and swells; he's poison to me;
My injur'd honour, and my ravish'd love,
Bleed at their murd'rer's sight.

Ben. [*To Dor. aside.*] The Emperor would learn these
You know them. [pris'ners names;
Dor.

Dor. Tell him, no;
And trouble me no more——I will not know them.
' Shall I truſt Heav'n, that Heav'n which I renounc'd,
' With my revenge ? Then, where's my ſatisfaction ?
' No, it muſt be my own ; I ſcorn a proxy.   [*Aſide.*

    Emp. 'Tis decreed,
Theſe of a better aſpect, with the reſt
Shall ſhare one common doom, and lots decide it.
For every number'd captive put a ball
Into an urn, three only black be there,
The reſt, all white, are ſafe.

    Muf. Hold, Sir, the woman muſt not draw.

    Emp. Oh, Mufti,
We know your reaſon ! let her ſhare the danger.

    Muf. Our law ſays plainly women have no ſouls.

    Emp. 'Tis true ; their ſouls are mortal : ſet her by :
Yet were Almeyda here, tho' Fame reports her
The faireſt of her ſex, ſo much, unſeen,
I hate the ſiſter of our rival houſe,
Ten thouſand ſuch dry notions of our Alcoran
Should not protect her life, if not immortal.
' Die as ſhe could, all of a piece, the better,
' That none of her remain.'

Here an urn is brought in ; the priſoners approach with great
    concernment, and amongſt the reſt Sebaſtian, Alvarez, *and*
    Antonio, *who come more chearfully.*

    Dor. Poor abject creatures, how they fear to die ! [*Aſide.*
Theſe never knew one happy hour in life ;
Yet ſhake to lay it down.   Is load ſo pleaſant ?
' Or has Heav'n hid the happineſs of death,
' That men may dare to live ?'——Now for our heroes.
                                  [*The three approach.*
Oh, theſe come up with ſpirits more reſolv'd !
Old, venerable Alvarez ; well I know him ;
The fav'rite once of this Sebaſtian's father ;
Now miniſter—(too honeſt for his trade.)
Religion bears him out, a thing taught young,
In age ill practis'd, yet his prop in death.
Oh, he has drawn a black, and ſmiles upon't,
As who ſhould ſay, my faith and ſoul are white,
Tho' my lot ſwarthy ! Now, if there be hereafter,
He's bleſs'd ; if not, well cheated, and dies pleas'd.

                                  Anton.

Anton. [*Holding his lot in his clench'd hand.*] Here I have
Be what thou wilt.   I will not look too foon.   thee,
Thou haft a colour ; if thou prov'ft not right,
I have a minute good ere I behold thee.
Now let me rowl and grubble thee.
Blind men fay white feels fmooth, and black feels rough :
Thou haft a rugged fkin ; I do not like thee.

   Dor. There's the amorous, airy fpark, Antonio ;
The wittiest woman's toy in Portugal.
Lord what a lofs of treats and ferenades !
The whole fhe nation will be in mourning for him.

   Anton. I have a moift, fweaty palm ; the more's my fin.
If it be black, yet only dy'd, not odious
Damn'd natural ebony, there's hopes, in rubbing,
To wafh this Ethiop white. [*Looks.*] Pox of the proverb !
As black as hell—' another lucky faying !
' I think the devil's in me—good again !
' I cannot fpeak one fyllable, but tends
' To death, or to damnation.'   [*Holds up his ball.*

   Dor. He looks uneafy at his future journey ;   [*Afide.*
And wifhes his boots off again, for fear
Of a bad road, and a worfe inn at night.
Go to bed, fool, and take fecure repofe ;
For thou fhalt wake no more. [*Sebaftian comes up to draw.*

   Emp. (*To* Ben.] Mark him who now approaches to the
He looks fecure of death ; fuperior greatnefs,   [lott'ry :
Like Jove when he made Fate, and faid, Thou art
The flave of my creation——I admire him.

   Ben. He looks as man was made, with face erect,
That fcorns his brittle corpfe, and feems afham'd
He's not all fpirit ; his eyes, with a dumb pride,
Accufing Fortune, that he fell not warm ;
Yet now difdains to live.   [*Sebaft. draws a black.*

   Emp. He has his wifh ;
And I have fail'd of mine.

   Dor. Robb'd of my vengeance by a trivial chance ! [*Afide.*
Fine work above, ' that their anointed care
' Should die fuch little death ! Or did his genius
' Know mine the ftronger dæmon, fear'd the grapple,
' And looking round him, found this nook of fate
' To fkulk behind my fword ? Shall I difcover him ?
' Still he would not die mine ; no thanks to my
                         ' Revenge :

' Revenge; referv'd but to more royal fhambles.
' 'Twere bafe, too, and below thofe vulgar fouls
' That fhar'd his danger, yet not one difclos'd him;
' But, ftruck with reverence, kept an awful filence.'
I'll fee no more of this—Dog of a prophet! [*Exit* Dor.
   Emp. One of thefe three is a whole hecatomb;
And therefore only one of them fhall die.
' The reft are but mute cattle; and when Death
' Comes like a rufhing lion, couch like fpaniels,
' With lolling tongues, and tremble at the paw.'
Let lots again decide it.
        [*The three draw again, and the lot falls on* Sebaftian.
   Sebaft. Then there's no more to manage.   If I fall,
It fhall be like myfelf: a fetting fun
Should leave a track of glory in the fky.
Behold Sebaftian, King of Portugal.
   Emp. Sebaftian! Ha! it muft be he; no other
Could reprefent fuch fuffering majefty.
I faw him, as he terms himfelf, a fun
Struggling in dark eclipfe, and fhooting day
On either fide of the black orb that veil'd him.
   Sebaft. Not lefs, ev'n in this defpicable now,
Than when my name fill'd Afric with affrights,
And froze your hearts beneath your torrid zone.
   Ben. [*To the Emp.*] Extravagantly brave! even to an
Of greatnefs.   [impudence
   Sebaft. Here fatiate all your fury;
Let Fortune empty her whole quiver on me;
I have a foul, that, like an ample fhield,
Can take in all, and verge enough for more.
' I would have conquer'd you; and ventur'd only
' A narrow neck of land for a third world,
' To give my fubjects room to play.
' Fate was not mine,
' Nor am I Fate's.   Now I have pleas'd my longing,
' And trod the ground which I beheld from far.
' I beg no pity for this mould'ring clay;
' For if you give it burial, there it takes
' Poffeffion of your earth;
' If burnt and fcatter'd in the air, the winds
' That ftrow my duft, diffufe my royalty,
                    2   ' And

‘ And fpread me o'er your clime ; for where one atom
‘ Of mine fhall light, know, there Sebaftian reigns.’
   Emp. What fhall I do to conquer thee ?
   Sebaft. Impoffible ——
Souls know no conquerors.
   Emp. I'll fhew thee for a monkey thro' my Afric.
   Sebaft. No, thou canft only fhew me for a man.
Afric is ftor'd with monfters ; man's a prodigy
Thy fubjects have not feen.
   Emp. Thou talk'ft as if
Still at the head of battle.
   Seb. Thou miftak'ft ;
For then I would not talk.
   Ben. Sure he would fleep.
   Seb. Till doomfday, when the trumpet founds to rife ;
For that's a foldier's call.
   Emp. Thour't brave too late ;
Thou fhouldft have dy'd in battle like a foldier.
   Seb. I fought and fell like one ; but death deceiv'd me :
I wanted weight of feeble Moors upon me,
To crufh my foul out.
   Emp. Still untameable !
In what a ruin has thy headftrong pride,
And boundlefs thirft of empire, plung'd thy people !
   Seb. What fay'ft thou ? Ha ! No more of that.
   Emp. Behold,
What carcafes of thine thy crimes have ftrew'd,
And left our Afric vultures to devour.
   ‘ *Ben.* Thofe fouls were thofe thy god intrufted with
‘ To cherifh, not deftroy.’   [thee,
   Seb. Witnefs, Oh, Heaven, how much
This fight concerns me ! Would I had a foul
For each of thefe ; how gladly would I pay
The ranfom down ! But fince I have but one,
'Tis a king's life, and freely 'tis beftow'd.
Not your falfe prophet, but eternal juftice,
Has deftin'd me the lot to die for thefe.
'Tis fit a fovereign fo fhould pay fuch fubjects ;
For fubjects, fuch as they, are feldom feen,
Who not forfook me at my greateft need,
‘ Nor for bafe lucre fold their loyalty,
‘ But fhar'd my dangers to the laft event,

C

                                                    ‘ And

' And fenc'd them with their own :' thefe thanks I pay
  you: *[Wipes his eyes.*
And know, that when Sebaftian weeps, his tears
Come harder than his blood.

 Emp. They plead too ftrongly
To be withftood: my clouds are gathering too,
In kindly mixture with his royal fhow'r:
Be fafe and owe thy life, not to my gift,
But to the greatnefs of thy mind, Sebaftian :
Thy fubjects too fhall live ; a due reward
For their untainted faith, in thy concealment.

 Muf. Remember, Sir, your vow. *[A general fhout.*
 Emp. Do thou remember.
Thy function, Mercy, and provoke not blood.

 ' *M. Zeyd.* One of his generous fits, too ftrong to laft.
         ' [*Afide to* Benducar.

 ' *Ben.* The Mufti reddens, mark that holy cheek.
         ' [*To him.*

' He frets within, froths treafon at his mouth,
' And churns it through his teeth ; leave me to work him.'
 Seb. A mercy unexpected, undefir'd,
Surprizes more : you've learn'd the art to vanquifh :
You could not (give me leave to tell you, Sir)
Have giv'n me life but in my fubjects fafety :
Kings, who are fathers, live but in their people.

 Emp. Still great, and grateful, that's thy character.
Unveil the woman ; I would view the face
That warm'd our Mufti's zeal :
Thefe pious parrots peck the faireft fruit :
Such taflers are for kings.
    [*Officers go to* Almeyda *to unveil her.*
 Alm. Stand off, ye flaves, I will not be unveil'd.
 Emp. Slave is thy title: force her.
 Seb. On your lives approach her not.
 Emp. How's this ?
 Seb. Sir, pardon me,
And hear me fpeak.————
 Alm. Hear me; I will be heard :
I am no flave ; the nobleft blood of Afric
Runs in my veins ; a purer ftream than thine ;
For, though deriv'd from the fame fource, thy current
Is puddled and defil'd with tyranny.

   4   ' *Emp.*

' *Emp.* What female fury have we here ?
' *Alm.* I fhould be one,
' Becaufe of kin to thee :' Wouldft thou be touch'd
By the prefuming hands of faucy grooms ?
The fame refpect, nay, more, is due to me :
More for my fex ; the fame for my defcent.
Thefe hands are only fit to draw the curtain.
Now, if thou dar'ft, behold Almeyda's face.

[Unveils herfelf.

' *Ben.* Would I had never feen it !'   [*Afide.*
Alm. She whom thy Mufti tax'd to have no foul ;
Let Afric now be judge ;
Perhaps thou think'ft I meanly hope to 'fcape,
As did Sebaftian when he own'd his greatnefs.
But to remove that fcruple, know, bafe man,
My murder'd father, and my brother's ghoft
Still haunt this breaft, and prompt it to revenge.
Think not I could forgive, nor dare thou pardon.
' *Emp.* Wouldft thou revenge thee, trait'refs, hadft
        thou power ?
' *Alm.* Traitor, I would ! the name's more juftly thine :
' Thy father was not more than mine the heir
' Of this large empire ; but with arms united
' They fought their way, and feiz'd the crown by force :
' And equal as their danger was their fhare :
' For where was elderfhip, where none had right
' But that which conqueft gave ? 'Twas thy ambition
' Pull'd from my peaceful father what his fword
' Help'd thine to gain : furpriz'd him and his kingdom,
' No provocation given, no war declar'd.
' *Emp.* I'll hear no more.
' *Alm.* This is the living coal, that burning in me,
' Would flame to vengeance, could it find a vent :
' My brother too, that lies yet fcarcely cold
' In his deep wat'ry bed : my wand'ring mother,
' Who in exile died.
' Oh, that I had the fruitful heads of Hydra,
' That one might bourgeon where another fell !
' Still would I give thee work ; ftill, ftill, thou tyrant,
' And hifs thee with the laft.'
Emp. Somewhat, I know not what, comes over me :
Whether the toils of battle, unrepair'd

C 2.   With

With due repofe, or other fudden qualm.
Benducar, do the reft.   [*Goes off, the court follows him.*
   Ben. Strange ! in full health ! This pang is of the foul :
The body's unconcern'd : I'll think hereafter.
Conduct thefe royal captives to the caftle ;
Bid Dorax ufe them well, till further order.

                              [*Going off, ftops.*
The inferior captives their firft owners take,
To fell, or to difpofe---You, Muftapha,
Set ope the market for the fale of flaves.   [*Exit* Bend.
   [*The mafters and flaves come forward, and buyers of feve-
      ral qualities come in and chaffer about the feveral
      owners, who make their flaves do tricks.*
   Muft. My chattels are come into my hands again, and
my confcience will ferve me to fell them twice over ; any
price now, before the Mufti comes to claim them.
   1ft Mer. [*To* Muft.] What doft hold that old fellow at ?
[*Pointing to* Alvarez.] He's tough, and has no fervice in
his limbs.
   Muft. I confefs he's fomewhat tough ; but, I fuppofe,
you would not boil him. I afk for him a thoufand
crowns.
   1ft Mer. Thou meaneft a thoufand maravedi's.
   Muft. Pr'ythee, friend, give me leave to know my own
meaning.
   1ft Mer. What virtues has he to deferve that price ?
   Muft. Marry come up, Sir ! Virtues quoth-a ! I took
him in the king's company ; he's of a great family, and
rich ; what other virtues wouldft thou have in a nobleman ?
   1ft Mer. I buy him with another man's purfe, that's
my comfort. My Lord Dorax, the governor, will have
him at any rate :——There's handfel. Come, old fellow,
to the caftle.
   Alv. To what is miferable age referv'd !   [*Afide.*
But, Oh, the king ! and, Oh, the fatal fecret !
Which I have kept thus long to time it better,
And now I would difclofe, 'tis paft my power.
                              [*Exit with his mafter.*
   Muft. Something of a fecret, and of the king I heard
him mutter: a pimp I'll warraht him, for I am fure he
                                                       is

is an old courtier. . Now to put off t'other remnant of
my merchandize.---' Stir up, firrah.   [*To* Antonio.

' *Ant.* Dog, what wouldſt thou have ?

' *Muſt.* Learn better manners, or I ſhall ſerve you a
' dog-trick; come down upon all four immediately; I'll
' make you know your rider.

' *Ant.* Thou wilt not make a horſe of me ?

' *Muſt.* Horſe or aſs, that's as thy mother made thee:
' ----but take earneſt in the firſt place for thy ſaucineſs.
' [*Laſhes him with his whip.*] Be adviſed, friend, and
' buckle to thy geers : behold my enſign of royalty diſ-
' played over thee.

' *Ant.* I hope one day to uſe thee worſe in Portugal.

' *Muſt.* Ay, and good reaſon, friend : if thou catcheſt
' me conquering on thy ſide of the water, lay me on
' luſtily, I'll take it as kindly as thou doſt this.

                              ' [*Holds up his whip.*

' *Ant.* [*Lying down.*] Hold, my dear thrum-cap :: I
' obey thee cheerfully. I ſee the doctrine of non-re-
' ſiſtance is never practiſed thoroughly, but when a man
' can't help himſelf.

                    ' *Enter a ſecond Merchant:*

' 2d *Mer.* You, friend, I would ſee that fellow do his
' poſtures.

' *Muſt.* [*Bridling* Ant.] Now, ſirrah, follow, for you
' have rode enough : to your paces, villain, amble, trot,
' and gallop :——Quick about there.——Yeap, the,
' more money's bidden for you, the more your credit.

     ' [Antonio *follows at the end of the bridle on his hands*
        ' *and feet, and does all his poſtures.*]

' 2d *Mer.* He's well chined, and has a tolerable good
' back ; that's half in half. [*To* Muſtapha.] I would ſee
' him ſtrip, has he no diſeaſes about him ?

' *Muſt.* He's the beſt piece of man's fleſh in the mar-
' ket, not an eye-ſore in his whole body. Feel his legs,
' maſter, neither ſplint, ſpaven, nor wind-gall.

                    ' [*Claps him on the ſhoulder.*]

' *Mer.* [*Feeling about him, and then putting his hand on*
' *his ſide.*] Out upon him, how his flank heaves ! The
' whorſon's broken-winded.

' *Muſt.* Thick-breathed a little ; nothing but a ſorry
' cold with lying out a nights in trenches ; but ſound .

                    C 3   ' wind

' wind and limb, I warrant him.   Try him at a loose
' trot a little. [*Puts the bridle into his hand, he strokes him.*

' *Ant.* For heaven's fake, owner, fpare me : you know
' I am but new broken.'

2d Mer. ' 'Tis but a wafhy jade, I fee.'   What do you
afk for this bauble ?

Muft. Bauble do you call him ? he's a fubftantial true-
bred beaft ; bravely forehanded : mark but the cleannefs
of his fhapes too : his dam may be a Spanifh gennet, but
a true barb by the fire, or I have no fkill in horfe-flefh—
Marry, I afk fix hundred xerifs for him.

Enter Mufti.

Muf. What's that you are afking, firrah ?

Muft. Marry I afk your reverence fix hundred par-
dons ; I was doing you a fmall piece of fervice here,
putting off your cattle for you.

Muf. And putting the money into your own pocket ?

Muft. Upon vulgar reputation, no my Lord, it was
for your profit and emolument. ' What, wrong the head
' of my religion ? I was fenfible you would have damned
' me, or any man that fhould have injured you in a fingle
' farthing ; for I knew that was facrifice.

' *Muf.* Sacrilege you mean, firrah,—and damning
' fhall be the leaft part of your punifhment : I have taken
' you in the manner, and will have the law upon you.

' *Muft.* Good my Lord, take pity upon a poor man in
' this world, and damn me in the next.

' *Muf.* No, firrah, fo you may repent, and fcape
' punifhment : Did not you fell this very flave amongft
' the reft to me, and take money for him ?

' *Muft.* Right, my Lord.

' *Muf.* And felling him again, take money twice for
' the fame commodity ? Oh, villain ! But did you not
' know him to be my flave, firrah ?

' *Muft.* Why fhould I lie to your honour ? I did know
' him ; and thereupon feeing him wander about, took
' him up for a ftray, and impounded him, with intention
' to reftore him to the right owner.

' *Muf.* And yet at the fame time was felling him to
' another : how rarely the ftory hangs together !

' *Muft.* Patience, my Lord.   I took him up, as your
' herriot, with intention to have made the beft of him,
' and

' and then have brought the whole product of him in a
' purfe to you; for I know you would have fpent half
' of it upon your pious pleafures,' have hoarded up the
other half, and given the remainder in charities to the
poor.

Muf. And what's become of my other flave? Thou
haft fold him too, I have a villainous fufpicion.

Muft. I know you have, my Lord; but while I was
managing this young robuftious fellow, that old fpark,
who was nothing but fkin and bone, and by confequence
very nimble, flipt through my fingers like an eel, for
there was no hold-faft of him, and ran away to buy himfelf a new mafter.

Muf. [*To* Ant.] Follow me home, firrah. [*To* Muft.]
I fhall remember you fome other time.

[*Exeunt* Muf. *with* Ant.

Muft. I never doubted your Lordfhip's memory, for an
ill turn: and I fhall remember him too in the next rifing
of the mobile, for this act of refumption; ' and more ef-
' pecially for the ghoftly counfel he gave me before the
' emperor, to have hanged myfelf in filence, to have
' faved his reverence.' The beft on't is, I am before-
hand with him, for felling one of his flaves twice over.
——And if he had not come juft in the nick, I might
have pocketted up t'other: for what fhould a poor man
do that gets his living by hard labour, but pray for bad
times when he may get it eafily? Oh, for fome incom-
parable tumult! Then fhould I naturally wifh that the
beaten party might prevail; becaufe we have plundered
t'other fide already, and there's nothing more to get of
them.

Both rich and poor for their own intereft pray,
'Tis ours to make our fortune while we may;
For kingdoms are not conquer'd every day.   [*Ex.*

END of the FIRST ACT.

ACT

ACT II.

SCENE, *suppofed to be a terrace walk, on the fide of the caftle of* Alcazar.

Enter Emperor *and* Benducar.

EMPEROR.

AND think'ft thou not it was difcover'd?
   Ben. No:
' The thoughts of kings are like religious groves,
' The walks of muffled gods : facred retreat,.
' Where none but whom they pleafe t'admit, approach.
  ' *Em.* Did not my confcious eyes flafh out a flame
' To lighten thofe brown horrors, and difclofe
' The fecret path I trod?
  ' *Ben.* I could not find it, 'till you lent a clue
' To that clofe labyrinth ; how then fhould they?'
  Emp. I would be loth they fhould : it breeds contempt
For herds to liften, or prefume to pry,
When the hurt lion groans within his den :.
But is't not ftrange?
  Ben. To love? not more than 'tis to live ;. a tax
Impos'd on all by Nature, paid in kind,.
Familiar as our being.
  Emp. Still 'tis ftrange
' To me : I know my foul as wild as wind,
' That fweeps the defarts of our moving plains ;.
' Love might as well be fow'd upon our fands,.
' As in a breaft fo barren.'
To love an enemy, ' the only one
' Remaining too, whom yefter fun beheld,
' Muft'ring her charms, and rolling as fhe paft
' By every fquadron her alluring eyes ;
' To edge her champions fwords, and urge my ruin.
' The fhouts of foldiers, and the burft of cannon,.
' Maintain even ftill a deaf and murm'ring noife ;
' Nor is heav'n yet recover'd of the found
' Her battle rous'd : yet fpite of me, I love..
  ' *Ben.* What then controuls you?
' Her perfon is as proftrate as her party.
  ' *Emp.* A thoufand things controul this conqueror:

' My

' My native pride to own th' unworthy paſſion,
' Hazard of intereſt, and my people's love.
' To what a ſtorm of fate am I expoſed !
' What if I had her murder'd ? 'tis but what
' My ſubjects all expect, and ſhe deſerves.
' Would not the impoſſibility
' Of ever, ever ſeeing, or poſſeſſing,
' Calm all this rage, this hurricane of ſoul ?
   ' *Ben.* That ever, ever,
' I mark'd the double, ſhows extreme reluctance
' To part with her for ever.
   ' *Emp.* Right, thou haſt me.
' I would, but cannot kill, I muſt enjoy her:
' I muſt, and what I muſt, be ſure I will.
' What's royalty, but power to pleaſe myſelf !
' And if I dare not, then am I the ſlave,
' And my own ſlaves the ſovereigns,— 'tis reſolv'd !
' Weak princes flatter when they want the power
' To curb their people.: tender plants muſt bend :
' But when a government is grown to ſtrength,
' Like ſome old oak, rough with its armed bark,
' It yields not to the tug, but only nods,
' And turns to ſullen ſtate.'
   Ben. Then you reſolve
T' implore her pity, and to beg relief ?
   Emp. Death ! muſt I beg the pity of my ſlave ?
Muſt a king beg ? Yes, love's a greater king ;
' A tyrant, nay, a devil that poſſeſſes me :'
He tunes the organs of my voice, and ſpeaks
Unknown to me within me ; puſhes me,
And drives me on by force,——
Say I ſhould wed her, would not my wife ſubjects
Take check, and think it ſtrange ? perhaps revolt ?
   Ben. I hope they would not.
   ' *Emp.* Then thou doubt'ſt they would ?
   Ben. To whom ?
   Emp. To her
Perhaps, or to my brother, or to thee.
   Ben. [*In diſorder.*] To me ! Me did you mention ?
     How I tremble !
The name of treaſon ſhakes my honeſt ſoul.

If I am doubted, Sir,
Secure yourſelf this moment, take my life.
   Emp. No ' more :' if I ſuſpeƈted thee——I would.
   Ben. I thank your kindneſs : guilt had almoſt loſt me.
                                              [*Aſide.*
   Emp. But clear my doubts : think'ſt thou they may
       rebel ?
   Ben. ' This goes as I would wiſh——'   [*Aſide.*
'Tis poſſible :
A ſecret party ſtill remains, that lurks
Like embers rak'd in aſhes——wanting but
A breath to blow aſide th' involving duſt,
And then they blaze abroad.
   Emp. They muſt be trampled out.
   Ben. But firſt be known.
   Emp. Torture ſhall force it from them.
   Ben. You would not put a nation to the rack ?
   Emp. Yes, the whole world ; ſo I be ſafe, I care not.
   Ben. Our limbs and lives
Are yours, but mixing friends with foes is hard.
   Emp. All may be foes ; or how to to be diſtinguiſh'd,
If ſome be friends ?
   Ben. They may with eaſe be winnow'd ;
Suppoſe ſome one who has deſerv'd your truſt,
Some one who knows mankind, ſhould be employ'd
To mix among 'em, ſeem a malecontent,
And dive into their breaſts, to try how far
They dare oppoſe your love ?
   Emp. I like this well ; 'tis wholeſome wickedneſs.
   Ben. Whomever he ſuſpeƈts, he faſtens there,
And leaves no cranny of his ſoul unſearch'd :
' Then like a bee bagg'd with his honey'd venom,
' He brings it to your hive :' if ſuch a man
So able and ſo honeſt may be found ;
If not, my projeƈt dies.——
   Emp. By all my hopes thou haſt deſcrib'd thyſelf :—
Thou, thou alone art fit to play that engine
Thou only couldſt contrive.
   Ben. Sure I could ſerve you ;
I think I could :——but here's the difficulty,
I'm ſo intirely yours,

                                       That

That I fhould fcurvily diffemble hate;
The cheat would be too grofs.
   Emp. Art thou a ftatefman,
And canft not be a hypocrite? Impoffible:
Do not diftruft thy virtues.
   Ben. If I muft perfonate this feeming villain,
Remember 'tis to ferve you.
   Emp. No more words:
Love goads me to Almeyda, all affairs
Are troublefome but that; and yet that moft.   *[Going.*
Bid Dorax treat Sebaftian like a king;
I had forgot him;——' but this love mars all,
' And takes up my whole breaft.'   *[Exit Emperor.*
   Ben. [*To the Emp.*] Be fure I'll tell him——
With all the aggravating circumftances
I can, to make him fwell at that command.
' The tyrant firft fufpected me:
' Then with a fudden guft he whirl'd about,
' And trufted me too far: madnefs of pow'r!
' Now, by his own confent I ruin him.
' For, fhould fome feeble foul, for fear or gain,
' Bolt out t'accufe me, ev'n the king is cozen'd,
' And thinks he's in the fecret.
' How fweet is treafon when the traitor's fafe!'
       Enter Mufti *and* Dorax, *feeming to confer.*
The Mufti, and with him my fullen Dorax:
The firft is mine already.
'Twas eafy work to gain a covetous mind,
Whom rage to lofe his pris'ners had prepar'd:
Now, caught himfelf.
He would feduce another; I muft help him:
For churchmen, though they itch to govern all,
Are filly, woeful, aukward politicians:
' They make lame mifchief, though they mean it well:
' Their int'reft is not finely drawn, and hid,
' But feams are coarfely bungled up, and feen.'
   Muf. He'll tell you more.
   Dor. I've heard enough already
To make me loath thy morals.
   Ben. [*To* Dor.] You feem warm;
The good man's zeal perhaps has gone too far.

Dor.

Dor. Not very far ; not farther than zeal goes
Of courfe ; a fmall day's journey fhort of treafon.

   Muf. By all that's holy, treafon was not nam'd :
' I fpar'd the emperor's broken vows, to fave
' The flaves from death : tho' it was cheating heav'n,
' But I forgave him that.

    ' *Dor.* And flighted o'er   [*Scornfully.*
' The wrongs himfelf fuftain'd in property :
' When his bought flaves were feiz'd by force, no lofs
' Of his confider'd, and no coft repaid.

    ' *Muf.* Not wholly flighted o'er, not abfolutely :
' Some modeft hints of private wrongs I urg'd.'

   Dor. Two thirds of all he faid : ' there he began
' To fhew the fulnefs of his heart ; there ended :
' Some fhort excurfions of a broken vow
' He made indeed, but flat infipid ftuff :
' But when he made his lofs the theme, he flourifh'd,
' Reliev'd his fainting rhetoric with new figures,
' And thunder'd at oppreffing tyranny.'

   Muf. Why not, when facrilegious pow'r would feize
My property ? 'tis an affront to heav'n,
Whofe perfon, though unworthy, I fuftain.

   Dor. ' You've made fuch ftrong alliances above,
' That 'twere profanenefs in us laiety
' To offer earthly aid.'
I tell thee, Mufti, if the world were wife,
They would not wag one finger in your quarrels.
Your heav'n you promife, but our earth you covet:
The Phaetons of mankind, who fire that world,
Which you were fent by preaching but to warm.

   Ben. This goes beyond the mark.

   Muf. No, let him rail :
His prophet works within him ;
He's a rare convert.

   Dor. ' Now his zeal yearns
' To fee me burnt ; he damns me from his church,
' Becaufe I would reftrain him to his duty :'
Is not the care of fouls a load fufficient ?
Are not your holy ftipends paid for this ?
Were you not bred apart from worldly noife,
To ftudy fouls, their cures, and their difeafes ?
If this be fo, we afk you but our own :

Give

Give us your whole employment, all your care :
The province of the soul is large enough
To fill up every cranny of your time,
And leave you much to answer, if one wretch
Be damn'd by your neglect.

    Ben. [*To the* Mufti.] He speaks but reason.

    ' *Dor.* Why then these foreign thoughts of state-
        employments,
' Abhorrent to your function and your breeding ?
' Poor droaning truants of unpractis'd cells,
' Bred in the fellowship of bearded boys,
' What wonder is it if you know not men ?
' Yet there you live demure, with down-cast eyes,
' And humble as your discipline requires :
' But, when let loose from thence to live at large,
' Your little tincture of devotion dies ;
' Then luxury succeeds, and sets agog
' With a new scene of yet untasted joys,
' You fall with greedy hunger to the feast.
' Of all your college virtues, nothing now
' But your original ignorance remains ;
' Bloated with pride, ambition, avarice,
' You swell, to counsel kings, and govern kingdoms.

    ' *Muf.* He prates as if kings had not consciences,
' And none requir'd directors but the crowd.

    ' *Dor.* As private men they want you, not as kings ;
' Nor would you care t'inspect their public conscience,
' But that it draws dependencies of pow'r,
' And earthly interest, which you long to sway :
' Content you with monopolizing heav'n,
' And let this little hanging ball alone ;
' For give you but a foot of conscience there,
' And you, like Archimedes, toss the globe.
' We know your thoughts of us that laymen are,
' Lag souls, and rubbish of remaining clay,
' Which heav'n, grown weary of more perfect work,
' Set upright with a little puff of breath,
' And bid us pass for men.'

    Muf. I will not answer,
Base foul-mouth'd renegade ; but I'll pray for thee,
To shew my charity.   [*Exit* Mufti.

    Dor. Do ; but forget not him who needs it most :

D

Allow

Allow thyfelf fome fhare : ' he's gone too
' I had to tell him of his holy jugglings ;
' Things that would ftartle faith, and mak
' Not this, or that, but all religions falfe.'
   Ben. Our holy orator has loft the caufe :
But I fhall yet redeem it.—[To Dorax.]]
For I have fecret orders from the emperoi
Which none but you muft hear : I muft (
I could have wifh'd fome other hand had b
When did you fee your pris'ner, great Se
   Dor. You might as well have afk'd me,
A crefted dragon, or a bafilifk ;
Both are lefs poifon to my eyes and naturi
He knows not I am I ; nor fhall he fee mi
Till time has perfected a lab'ring thought,
That rowls within my breaft.
   Ben. 'Twas my miftake :
I guefs'd indeed that time, and his misfori
And your returning duty, had effac'd
The mem'ry of paft wrongs ; they would
And I judg'd you as tame, and as forgivii
   Dor. Forgive him ! No ; I left my foo
Becaufe it would oblige me to forgivenefs.
   Ben. I can't but grieve to find you obft
For you muft fee him ; 'tis our emp'ror's
And ftrict command.
   Dor. I laugh at that command.
   Ben. You muft do more than fee ; fei
   Dor. See, ferve him, and refpect, and i
My yet uncancell'd wrongs, I muft do thi
But I forget myfelf.
   Ben. Indeed you do.
   Dor. The emp'ror is a ftranger to my '
I need but tell my ftory, to revoke
This hard commiffion.
   Ben. Can you call me friend,
And think I could neglect to fpeak, at ful
Th' affronts you had from your ungratefu
   Dor. And yet enjoin'd my fervice and i
   Ben. And yet enjoin'd them both : wou
He fkrew'd his face into a harden'd fmile,
And faid Sebaftian knew to govern flaves.

Dor. Slaves are the growth of Afric, not of Europe:
By Heav'n, I will not lay down my commiffion;
Not at his foot, I will not ftoop fo low.:
But if there be a part in all his face
More facred than the reft, I'll throw it there.

Ben. You may: but then you lofe all future means
Of vengeance on Sebaftian, ' when no more
' Alcade of this fort.'

Dor. That thought efcap'd me.

Ben. Keep your command, and be reveng'd on both:
' Nor footh yourfelf; you have no pow'r t'affront him;
' The emp'ror's love protects him from infults.
' And he who fpoke that proud, ill-natur'd word,
' Following the bent of his impetuous temper,
' May force your reconcilement to Sebaftian:
' Nay, bid you kneel, and kifs the offending foot,
' That kick'd you from his prefence.'
But think not to divide their punifhment;
You cannot touch a hair of loath'd Sebaftian,
While Muley-Moluch lives.

Dor. What means this riddle?

Ben. 'Tis out: there no needs to Œdipus to folve it.
Our emp'ror is a tyrant, fear'd and hated;
I fcarce remember in his reign, one day
Pafs guiltlefs o'er his execrable head.
He thinks the fun is loft that fees no blood:
When none is fhed we count it holiday.
We, who are moft in favour, cannot call
This hour our own:—you know the younger brother,
Mild Muley-Zeydan?——

Dor. Hold, and let me think.

Ben. The foldiers idolize you,
He trufts you with the caftle,
The key of all his kingdom.

Dor. Well; and he trufts you too.

Ben. Elfe I were mad,
To hazard fuch a daring enterprize.

Dor. He trufts us both; mark that, fhall we betray
' A mafter, who repofes life and empire   [him:
' On our fidelity? I grant he is a tyrant,
' That hated name my nature moft abhors;
' More, as you fay, has loaded me with fcorn,

                                    ' Ev'n

' Ev'n with the laſt contempt, to ſerve Sebaſtian.
' Yet more I know he vacates my revenge:
' Which but by this revolt I cannot compaſs:
' But, while he truſts me, 'twere ſo baſe a part
' To fawn, and yet betray; I ſhould be hiſs'd
' And whoop'd in hell for that ingratitude.'
    Ben. Conſider well what I have done for you.
    Dor. Conſider thou what thou would'ſt have me do.
    Ben. You've too much honour for a renegade.
    Dor. And thou too little faith to be a fav'rite.
' Is not the bread thou eat'ſt, the robe thou wear'ſt,
' Thy wealth and honours, all the pure indulgence
' Of him thou would'ſt deſtroy?
' And would his creature, nay, his friend, betray him:
' Why then no bond is left on human kind:
' Diſtruſts, debates, immortal ſtrifes enſue;
' Children may murder parents, wives their huſbands;
' All muſt be rapine, wars and deſolation,
' When truſt and gratitude no longer bind.'
    Ben. Well have you argued in your own defence;
You, who have burſt aſunder all thoſe bonds,
And turn'd a rebel to your native prince.
    Dor. True, I rebell'd: but when did I betray?
Indignities, which man could not ſupport,
Provok'd my vengeance to this noble crime:
But he had ſtripp'd me firſt of my command,
Diſmiſs'd my ſervice, and abſolv'd my faith;
And, with diſdainful language, dar'd my worſt.
I but accepted war, which he denounc'd.
Elſe had you ſeen, not Dorax, but Alonzo,
With his couch'd lance againſt your foremoſt Moors,
Perhaps too turn'd the fortuue of the day;
Made Afric mourn, and Portugal triumph.
    Ben. Let me embrace thee.
    Dor. Stand off, ſycophant,
And keep infection diſtant.
    Bend. Brave and honeſt.
    Dor. In ſpite of thy temptations.
    Ben. Call them trials:
There were no more: ' thy faith was held in balance,
' And nicely weigh'd by jealouſy of pow'r;
' Vaſt was the truſt of ſuch a royal charge,

' And

‘ And our wife emperor might juftly fear
‘ Sebaftian might be freed and reconcil'd,
‘ By new obligements, to thy former love.’
   Dor. I doubt thee ftill; thy reafons were too ftrong,
And driven too near the head, to be but artifice:
And after all, I know thou art a ftatefman,
Where truth is rarely found.
   Ben. Behold the emperor;
Afk him, I beg thee, to be juftify'd,
If he employ'd me not to ford thy foul,
And try the footing whether falfe or firm.
   Dor. Death to my eyes, I fee Sebaftian with him!
Muft he be ferv'd! Avoid him; if we meet,
It muft be like the crufh of heav'n and earth,
T'involve us both in ruin.   [*Exit.*
   Ben. 'Twas a bare faving game I made with Dorax,
But better fo than loft: he cannot hurt me,
That I precautioned; I muft ruin him.
But now this love; ay, there's the gath'ring ftorm!
The tyrant muft not wed Almeyda; no;
That ruins all the fabric I am raifing.
Yet feeming to approve it gave me time,
And gaining time gains all.
       [Benducar *goes and waits behind the Emperor.*
Enter Emperor, Sebaftian, *and* Almeyda, *advancing to the*
    front of the ftage; guards and attendants.
   Emp. [*To* Seb.] I bade them ferve you, and if they
      obey not,
I keep my lions keen within their dens,
To ftop their maws with difobedient flaves.
   Seb. If I had conquer'd,
They could not have with more obfervance waited:
‘ Their eyes, hands, feet,
‘ Are all fo quick, they feem t'have but one motion,
‘ To catch my flying words.’ Only the Alcade
Shuns me, and with a grim civility
Bows, and declines my walks.
   Emp. A renegade!
I know no more of him: but that he's brave,
And hates your Chriftian fect. If you can frame
A farther wifh, give wing to your defires,
And name the thing you want.
        D 3   *Seb.*

Seb. My liberty;
For were ev'n Paradise itself my prison,
Still I should long to leap the cryſtal walls.
  Emp. Sure our two souls have somewhere been acquaint-
In former beings: or ſtruck out together,   [ed
One ſpark to Afric flew, and one to Portugal.
Expeƈt a quick deliverance: [*Turning to* Almey.] Here's
                third,
Of kindred ſoul to both: pity our ſtars
Have made us foes! I ſhould not wiſh her death.
  Alm. I aſk no pity; if I thought my ſoul
Of kin to thine, ſoon would I rend my heart-ſtrings,
And tear out that alliance: but thou, viper,
Haſt cancell'd kindred, made a rent in nature,
And through her holy bowels gnaw'd thy way,
Through thy own blood to empire.
  Emp. This again:
And yet ſhe lives, and only lives t'upbraid me.
  Seb. What honour is there in a woman's death!
Wrong'd as ſhe ſays, but helpleſs to revenge;
‘ Strong in her paſſion, impotent of reaſon,’
Too weak to hurt, too fair to be deſtroy'd.
Mark her majeſtic fabrick; ſhe's a temple
Sacred by birth, and built by hands divine;
Her ſoul's the deity that lodges there:
Nor is the pile unworthy of the god.
  Emp. She's all that thou canſt ſay, or I can think.
But the perverſeneſs of her clam'rous tongue
Strikes pity deaf.
  Seb. Then only hear her eyes;
Tho' they are mute, they plead; nay more, command;
For beauteous eyes have arbitrary power.
‘ All females have prerogative of ſex,
‘ The ſhees even of the ſavage herd are ſafe:
‘ All, when they ſnarl or bite, have no return
‘ But courtſhip from the male.’
  Emp. Were ſhe not ſhe, and I not Muley-Moluch,
She's miſtreſs of inevitable charms,
For all but me; nor am I ſo exempt,
But that——I know not what I was to ſay——
But I am too obnoxious to my friends,
And ſway'd by your advice.

                                            Seb.

Seb. Sir, I advis'd not ;
By Heav'n, I never counsell'd love, but pity.
 Emp. By Heav'n thou didst : deny it not, thou didst :
For what was all that prodigality
Of praise, but to enslave me !——
 Seb. Sir——
 Emp. No more :
Thou hast convinc'd me, that she's worth my love.
 Seb. Was ever man so ruin'd by himself ? [*Aside.*
 Alm. ' Thy love ! that odious mouth was never fram'd
' To speak a word so soft.'
Name death again, for that thou canst pronounce
With horrid grace, becoming of a tyrant.
Love is for human hearts, and not for thine,
Where the brute beast extinguishes the man.
 Emp. Such if I were, yet rugged lions love,
And grapple, and compel their savage dames.——
Mark, my Sebastian, how that sullen frown, [*She frowns.*
Like flashing lightning, opens angry heaven ;
And while it kills, delights. But yet, insult not
Too soon, proud beauty, I confess no love.
 Seb. No, Sir, I said so, and I witness for you :
Not love, but noble pity mov'd your mind :
Int'rest might urge you too to save her life ;
For those who wish her party lost, might murmur
At shedding royal blood.
 Emp. Right, thou instruct'st me :
Interest of state requires not death, but marriage,
T' unite the jarring titles of our line,
 Seb. Let me dumb for ever, all I plead, [*Aside.*
Like wildfire thrown against the winds, returns
With double force to burn me.
 Emp. Could I but bend, to make my beauteous foe
The partner of my throne, and of my bed——
 Alm. Still thou dissemblest ; but I read thy heart,
And know the power of my own charms ; thou lov'st,
And I am pleas'd, for my revenge, thou dost.
 Emp. And thou hast cause.
 Alm. I have, for I have power to make thee wretched.
Be sure I will, and yet despair of freedom.
 Emp. Well then, I love,——
And 'tis below my greatness to disown it :

2 Love

Love thee implacably, yet hate thee too:
Would hunt thee bare-foot, in the mid-day fun,
' Through the parch'd defarts, and the fcorching fands,'
T' enjoy thy love, and once enjoy'd, to kill thee.

   Alm. 'Tis a falfe courage, when thou threatneft me;
Thou canft not ftir a hand to touch my life:
Do not I fee thee tremble while thou fpeak'ft?
Lay by thy lion's hide, vain conqueror,
And take the diftaff; for thy foul's my flave.

   Emp. Confufion! How thou view'ft my very heart!
' I could as foon
' Stop a fpring tide, blown in, with my bare hand,
' As this impetuous love:'——Yes, I will wed thee:
In fpite of thee, and of myfelf, I will.

   Alm. For what? to people Africa with monfters,
Which that unnatural mixture muft produce?
' No, were we join'd, ev'n though it were in death,
' Our bodies burning in one funeral pile,
' The prodigy of Thebes would be renew'd,
' And my divided flame fhould break from thine.

   ' *Emp.* Serpent, I will engender poifon with thee;
' Join hate with hate, add venom to the birth;
' Our off-fpring, like the feed of dragon teeth,
' Shall iffue arm'd, and fight themfelves to death.'

   Alm. I'm calm again, thou canft not marry me.

   ' *Emp.* As gleams of funfhine foften ftorms to fhowers,
' So if you fmile, the loudnefs of my rage
' In gentle whifpers fhall return, but this——
' That nothing can divert my love but death.

   ' *Alm.* See how thou art deceiv'd,' I am a Chriftian;
' 'Tis true, unpractis'd in my new belief,
' Wrongs I refent, nor pardon yet with eafe;
' Thofe fruits come late, and are of flow increafe,
' In haughty hearts, like mine:' now, tell thyfelf
If this one word deftroy not thy defign;
Thy law permits thee not to marry me.

   ' *Emp.* 'Tis but a fpecious tale, to blaft my hopes,
' And baffle my pretenfions. Speak, Sebaftian,
' And as a king, fpeak true.

   ' *Seb.* Then, thus adjur'd
' On a king's word 'tis truth, but truth ill-tim'd;
' For her dear life is now expos'd anew;
                          ' Unlefs.

' Unless you wholly can put on divinity,
' And graciously forgive.
     ' *Alm*. Now learn by this,
' The little value I have left for life,
' And trouble me no more.'
     Emp. I thank thee, woman ;
Thou haft restor'd me to my native rage ;
And I will seize my happiness by force.
     Seb. Know, Muley-Moluch, when thou dar'st attempt—
     Emp. Beware, I would not be provok'd to use
A conqueror's right, and therefore charge thy silence,
If thou would'st merit to be thought my friend,
I leave thee to persuade her to compliance ;
If not, there's a new gust in ravishment,
Which I have ne'er yet try'd.
     ' *Ben*. They must be watch'd ;   [*Aside*.
' For something I observ'd creates a doubt.'
                                   [*Exit* Emp. *and* Bend.
     Seb. I've been too tame, have basely borne my wrongs,
And not exerted all the king within me :
I heard him, Oh, sweet heav'ns, he threat'ned rape ;
Nay, insolently urg'd me to persuade thee,
Ev'n thee, thou idol of my soul and eyes ;
For whom I suffer life, and drag this being.
     ' *Alm*. You turn my prison to a Paradise ;
' But I have turn'd your empire to a prison :
' In all your wars good fortune flew before you ;
' Sublime you sat in triumph on her wheel ;
' Till in my fatal cause your sword was drawn,
' The weight of my misfortunes dragg'd you down.
     ' *Seb*. And is't not strange, that heav'n should bless my
' In common causes, and desert the best ?   [arms
' Now in your greatest, last extremity,
' When I would aid you most, and most desire it,
' I bring but sighs, the succours of a slave.'
     Alm. ' Leave then the luggage of your fate behind,
' To make your flight more easy, leave Almeyda :
' Nor think me left a base ignoble prey,
' Expos'd to this inhuman tyrant's lust ;'
My virtue is a guard beyond my strength,
And death, my last defence, within my call.
     ' *Seb*. Death may be call'd in vain, and cannot come ;
                                             ' Ty-

'Tyrants can tie him up from your relief:
'Nor has a Christian privilege to die.
'Alas, thou art too young in thy new faith;
'Brutus and Cato might discharge their souls,
'And give them furlo's for another world:
'But we, like centries, are oblig'd to stand
'In starless nights, and wait th' appointed hour.
  'Alm. If shunning ill be good
'To those who cannot shun it but by death,
'Divines but peep on undiscover'd worlds,
'And draw the distant landscape as they please:
'But who has e'er return'd from those bright regions,
'To tell their manners, and relate their laws?
'I'll venture landing on that happy shore
'With an unsully'd body and white mind;
'If I have err'd, some kind inhabitant
'Will pity a stray'd soul, and take me home.'
  Seb. Beware of death, thou canst not die unperjur'd,
And leave an unaccomplish'd love behind.
Thy vows are mine; nor will I quit my claim:
The tie of minds are but imperfect bonds,
Unless the bodies join to seal the contract.
  Alm. What joys can you possess, or can I give,
Where groans of death succeed the sighs of love?
Our Hymen has not on his saffron robe;
But muffled up in mourning, downward holds
His drooping torch, extinguish'd with his tears.
  Seb. The God of Love stands ready to revive it
With his ætherial breath.
  'Alm. 'Tis late to join, when we must part so soon.
  'Seb. Nay, rather let us haste it, ere we part:
'Our souls for want of that acquaintance here,
'May wander in the starry walks above,
'And, forc'd on worse companions, miss ourselves.
  'Alm. The tyrant will not long be absent hence;
'And soon I shall be ravish'd from your arms.
  'Seb. Wilt thou thyself become the greater tyrant,
'And give not love, while thou hast love to give?
'In dangerous days, when riches are a crime,
'The wise betimes make over their estates;
'Make o'er thy honour, by a deed of trust,
'And give me seizure of the mighty wealth.'

Alm.

Alm. What shall I do ? Oh, teach me to refuse !
‘ I would, and yet I tremble at the grant :
‘ For dire presages fright my soul by day,
‘ And boding visions haunt my nightly dreams ;
‘ Sometimes, methinks, I hear the groans of ghosts,
‘ Thin, hollow sounds, and lamentable screams ;
‘ Then, like a dying echo, from afar,
‘ My mother’s voice, that cries, Wed not, Almeyda !
‘ Forewarn’d Almeyda, marriage is thy crime.
    ‘ *Seb.* Some envious dæmon, to delude our joys——
‘ Love is not sin, but where ’tis sinful love.
    ‘ *Alm.* Mine is a flame so holy and so clear,
‘ That the white taper leaves no soot behind,
‘ No smoke of lust : but chaste as sister’s love,
‘ When coldly they return a brother’s kiss,
‘ Without the zeal that meets at lovers mouths.
    ‘ *Seb.* Laugh, then, at fond presages ; I had some :
‘ Fam’d Nostrodamus, when he took my horoscope,
‘ Foretold my father, I should wed with incest.
‘ Ere this unhappy war my mother dy’d,
‘ And sisters I had none : vain augury !
‘ A long religious life, a holy age,
‘ My stars assign’d me too—impossible ;
‘ For how can incest suit with holiness,
‘ Or priestly orders with a princely state ?’
    Alm. Old venerable Alvarez !———   [*Sighing.*
    Seb. But why that sigh in naming that good man ?
    ‘ *Alm.* Your father’s counsellor and confident——
    ‘ *Seb.* He was ; and, if he lives, my second father.’
    Alm. Mark’d our farewel, when, going to the fight,
You gave Almeyda for the word of battle :
’Twas in that fatal moment he discover’d
The love that long we labour’d to conceal.
‘ I know it ; tho’ my eyes stood full of tears,
‘ Yet thro’ the mist I saw him stedfast gaze ;’
Then knock’d his aged breast, and inward groan’d,
Like some sad prophet, that foresaw the doom
Of those whom best he lov’d, and could not save.
    Seb. It startles me, and brings to my remembrance,
That, when the shock of battle was begun,
‘ He would have much complain’d (but had not time)
‘ Of our hid passion ; then, with lifted hands,’

He

He begg'd me, by my father's sacred soul,
Not to espouse you, if he dy'd in fight:
For, if he liv'd, and we were conquerors,
He had such things to urge against our marriage,
As, now declar'd, would blunt my sword in battle,
And dastardize my courage.
  ' *Alm.* My blood curdles,
' And cakes about my heart.
   ' *Seb.* I'll breathe a sigh so warm into thy bosom,
' Shall make it flow again.   My love, he knows not
' Thou art a Christian : that produc'd his fear,
' Lest thou should sooth my soul with charms so strong,
' That Heav'n might prove too weak.'
  Alm. There must be more;
This could not blunt your sword.
  Seb. Yes, if I drew it with a curs'd intent
To take a misbeliever to my bed :
It must be so.
  Alm. Yet——
  Seb. No, thou shalt not plead,
With that fair mouth, against the cause of love.
Within this castle is a captive priest,
My holy confessor, whose free access
Not ev'n the barb'rous victors have refus'd :
This happy hour his hands shall make us one.
  Alm. I go, with Love and Fortune, two blind guides,
To lead my way, half loth, and half consenting.
If, as my soul forebodes, some dire event
Pursue this union, or some crime unknown,
Forgive me, Heav'n; and all ye bless'd above,
Excuse the frailty of unbounded love.   [*Exeunt.*

SCENE, *supposed a Garden, with Lodging Rooms behind
it, or on the Side.*

Enter Mufti, Antonio *as a slave, and* Johayma, *the*
Mufti's *wife.*

  Muf. And how do you like him? Look upon him well ;
he's a personable fellow, of a Christian dog.   Now I
think you are fitted for a gardener. Ha, what say'st thou,
Johayma ?
  Joh. He may make a shift to sow lettice, raise melons,
and water a garden-plat ; ' but otherwise, a very filthy
                                       ' fellow.

‘ fellow.   How odioufly he fmells of his country gar-
‘ lick!—Fugh, how he ftinks of Spain!’

  Muf. Why, honey-bird, I bought him on purpofe for
thee.   Didft thou not fay thou long’dft for a Chriftian
flave?

  Joh. Ay, but ‘ the fight of that loathfome creature has
‘ almoft cured me; and’ how can I tell that he’s a Chriftian? ‘ An he were well fearched, he may prove a Jew,’
‘ for ought I know.’   And befides, I have always longed
for an eunuch; for they fay that’s a civil creature, and
almoft as harmlefs as yourfelf, hufband.   Speak, fellow,
are not you fuch a kind of peaceable thing?

  Ant. I never was taken for one in my own country;
and not very peaceable neither, when I am well provoked.

  ‘ *Muf.* To your occupation, dog; bind up the jeffa-
‘ mines in yonder arbour, and handle your pruning-knife
‘ with dexterity; tightly, I fay, go tightly to your bufi-
‘ nefs.   You have coft me much, and muft earn it in your
‘ work: here’s plentiful provifion for you, rafcal, fal-
‘ lading in the garden, and water in the tanck, and, on
‘ holydays, the licking of a platter of rice, when you de-
‘ ferve it.’

  Joh. What have you been bred up to, firrah? And
what can you perform, to recommend you to my fervice?

  Ant. [*Making legs.*] Why, Madam, I can perform as
much as any man, in a fair lady’s fervice.   I can play
upon the flute, and fing; I can carry an umbrella, and
fan your ladyfhip, and cool you when you are too hot;
in fine, no fervice, either by day or by night, fhall come
amifs to me; and befides, am of fo quick an apprehenfion, that you need but wink upon me at any time, to
make me underftand my duty. [*She winks at him.*] ‘ Very
‘ fine; fhe has tipt the wink already.   [*Afide.*

  ‘ *Joh.* The whelp may come to fomething in time,
‘ when I have entered him into his bufinefs.

  ‘ *Muf.* A very malapert cur, I can tell him that; I do
‘ not like his fawning.   You muft be taught your diftance,
‘ firrah.   [*Strikes him.*

  ‘ *Joh.* Hold, hold—He has deferved it, I confefs; but,
‘ for once, let his ignorance plead his pardon; we muft
‘ not difcourage a beginner.   Your reverence has taught
                          E   ‘ us

' us charity, even to birds and beasts.   Here, you filthy
' brute you, take this little alms to buy you plaisters.

       ' [*Gives him a piece of money.*

' *Ant.* Money, and a love-pinch in the inside of my
' palm into the bargain !   -   [*Aside.*

     Enter a Servant.

Serv. Sir, my Lord Benducar is coming to wait on you,
and is already at the palace-gate.

Muf. Come in, Johayma; regulate the rest of my
wives and concubines, and leave this fellow to his work.

' *Joh.* How stupidly he stares about him, like a calf
' new come into the world ! I shall teach you, sirrah, to
' know your business a little better——This way, you
' awkward rascal ; here lies the arbour : must I be shew-
' ing you eternally ?   [*Turning him about.*

' *Muf.* Come away, minion ; you shall shew him no-
' thing.

' *Joh.* I'll bring him into the arbour, where a rose-
' tree and a myrtle-tree are just falling, for want of a
' prop : if they were bound together, they would help to
' keep up one another.   He's a raw gardener ; and 'tis
' but charity to teach him.

' *Muf.* No more deeds of charity to-day.   Come in,
' or I shall think you a little better disposed than I could
' wish you.

' *Joh.* Well, go before ; I will follow my pastor.

' *Muf.* So, you may cast a sheep's eye behind you.
' In before me.' And you, sauciness, mind your pruning-
knife ; or I may chance to use it for you.

     [*Exeunt* Mufti *and* Johayma.

—— *Ant.* I thank you for that ; but I am in no such haste
to be made a Mussulman.   For his wedlock, for all her
haughtiness, I find her coming.   How far a Christian
should resist, I partly know ; but how far a lewd young
Christian can resist, is another question.   ' She's tolerable,
' and I am a poor stranger, far from better friends, and
' in a bodily necessity.'   Now have I a strange temptation to try what other females are belonging to this family—I am not far from the women's apartment, I am sure ;
and if these birds are within distance, here's that will
chuckle them together. [*Pulls out his flute.*] ' If there
' be variety of Moor's flesh in this holy market, 'twere

         ' madness

' madnefs to lay out all my money upon the firft bargain.
[*He plays. A grate opens, and* Morayma, *the* Mufti's
daughter, appears at it.]——Ay, there's an apparition!
This is a morfel worthy of a Mufti; ' this is a relifhing
' bit in fecret; this is the myftery of his Alcoran, that
' muft be referved from the knowledge of the profane
' vulgar;' this is the holiday devotion. See, fhe beckons
too.   [*She beckons to him.*

Mor. Come a little nearer, and fpeak foftly.

Ant. I come, I come; I warrant thee, the leaft twinkle
had brought me to thee: fuch another kind fyllable or
two, would turn me to a meteor, and draw me up to
thee.

Mor. I dare not fpeak, for fear of being overheard;
but if you think my perfon worth your hazard, and can
deferve my love——the reft this note fhall tell you——
' [*Throws down a handkerchief.*]' No more; my heart
goes with you.   [*Exit from the grate.*

Ant. ' Oh, thou pretty little heart! art thou flown
' hither? I'll keep it warm, I warrant it, and brood upon
' it in the new neft. But now upon my treafure trove,
' that's wrapped up in the handkerchief--No peeping here;
' tho' I long to be fpelling her Arabic fcrawls and pot-
' hooks—But I muft carry off my prize, as robbers do,
' and not think of fharing the booty, before I am free
' from danger, and out of eye-fhot from the other win-
' dows.' If her wit be as poignant as her eyes, I am a
double flave. Our northern beauties are mere dough to
thefe; infipid white earth, mere tobacco-pipe clay; with
no more foul and motion in them, than a fly in winter.

Here the warm planet ripens and fublimes
The well-bak'd beauties of the fouthern climes:
Our Cupid's but a bungler in his trade;
His keeneft arrows are in Afric made.

                                                      [*Exit.*

End of the Second Act.

ACT III.

SCENE, *a Terrace-walk, or some other publick Place in the Castle of Alcazar.*

Enter the Emperor, *and* Benducar.

EMPEROR.

MARRY'D! I'll not believe it; 'tis imposture;
' Improbable they should presume t' attempt:
' Impossible they should effect their wish.'
Ben. Have patience, till I clear it.
Emp. I have none:
Go bid our moving plains of sand lie still,
' And stir not, when the stormy south blows high.
' From top to bottom thou hast toss'd my soul;
' And now 'tis in the madness of the whirl,
' Requir'st a sudden stop. Unsay thy lie,
' That may, in time, do somewhat.
  ' *Ben.* I have done;
' For, since it pleases you it should be forg'd,
' 'Tis fit it should. Far be it from your slave,
' To raise disturbance in your sacred breast.
  ' *Emp.* Sebastian is my slave as well as thou;
' Nor durst offend my love by that presumption.
  ' *Ben.* Most sure he ought not.
  ' *Emp.* Then all means are wanting;
' No priest, no ceremonies of their sex:
' Or, grant we these defects could be supply'd,
' How could our prophet do an act so base,
' So to resume his gifts, and curse my conquests,
' By making me unhappy.' No, the slave
That told thee so absurd a story, lied.
  Ben. Yet till this moment I have found him faithful:
He said he saw it too.
  Emp. Dispatch; what saw he?
  Ben. ' Truth is, considering with what earnestness
' Sebastian pleaded for Almeyda's life,
' Inhanc'd her beauty, dwelt upon her praise——
  ' *Emp.* Oh, stupid and unthinking as I was!
' I might have mark'd it too; 'twas gross and palpable.
  ' *Ben.* Methought I trac'd a love but ill disguis'd;
' And sent my spy, a sharp observing slave,

' T' in-

' T' inform me better, if I guess'd aright.'
He told me, that he saw Sebastian's page
Run cross the marble square, who soon return'd,
And after him there lagg'd a puffing friar;
Close wrapp'd he bore some secret instrument
Of Christian superstition in his hand.
My servant follow'd fast, and, thro' a chink,
Perceiv'd the royal captives hand in hand,
And heard the hooded father mumbling charms,
That make those misbelievers man and wife;
Which done, the spouses kiss'd with such a fervour,
And gave such furious earnest of their flames,
That their eyes sparkled, and their mantling blood
Flew flushing o'er their faces.   *You may guess the rest.*
   ' *Emp.* Hell confound them !
   ' *Ben.* The reverend father, with a holy leer,
' Saw he might well be spar'd, and soon withdrew:
' This forc'd my servant to a quick retreat,
' For fear to be discover'd.   Guess the rest.'
   Emp. I do.   My fancy is too exquisite,
And tortures me with their imagin'd bliss.
Some earthquake should have risen, and rent the ground,
Have swallow'd him, and left the longing bride
In agony of unaccomplish'd love.   [*Walks disorderly.*
            Enter the Mufti.

   Ben. In an unlucky hour   [*Aside.*
That fool intrudes, raw in this great affair,
And uninstructed how to stem the tide.
                    [*Coming up to the* Mufti *aside.*
The Emp'ror must not marry, nor enjoy;
Keep to that point, stand firm; for all's at stake.
   Emp. [*Seeing him.*] You druggerman of Heav'n, must
      I attend
Your drowning prayers ? Why came ye not before ?
Dost thou not know the captive King has dar'd
To wed Almeyda ? Cancel me that marriage,
And make her mine.   About thy business, quick ;
Expound thy Mahomet, make him speak my sense,
Or he's no prophet here, and thou no Mufti,
' Unless thou know'st the trick of thy vocation,
' To wrest and rend the law to please thy prince.'
   Muf. Why, verily, the law is monstrous plain :

There's not one doubtful text in all the Alcoran,
Which can be wrench'd in favour to your project.
——— *Emp.* Forge one, and foist it into some bye-place
Of some old rotten roll : do't, I command thee :
Must I teach thee thy trade ?
    Muf. It cannot be ;
For matrimony being the dearest point
Of law, the people have it all by heart :
A cheat on procreation will not pass.
' Besides, th' offence is so exorbitant,   [*In a higher tone.*
' To mingle with a misbelieving race,
' That speedy vengeance would pursue your crime,
' And holy Mahomet launch himself from Heav'n
' Before th' unready thunderbolt were form'd.'
    Emp. [*Taking him by the throat with one hand, snatching
out his sword with the other, and pointing it to his breast.*]
Slave ! have I rais'd thee to this pomp and pow'r,
To preach against my will ? Know, I am law ;
And thou not Mahomet's messenger, but mine :
Make it, I charge thee, make my pleasures lawful ;
' Or first I'll strip thee of thy ghostly greatness,
' Then send thee post to tell thy tale above,
' And bring thy vain memorials to thy prophet,
' Of justice done below for disobedience.'
    Muf. For Heaven's sake hold ; the respite of a moment,
To think for you———
    Emp. And for thyself———
    Muf. For both.
    Ben. Disgrace, and death, and avarice have lost him !
                        [*Aside.*
Muf. 'Tis true, our law forbids to wed a Christian ;
But it forbids you not to ravish her.
You have a conqueror's right upon your slave :
And then, the more despite you do a Christian,
You serve the prophet more, who loaths that sect.
    Emp. Oh, now it mends, and you talk reason, Mufti !
But stay ; I promis'd freedom to Sebastian ;
Now, should I grant it, his revengeful soul
Would ne'er forgive his violated bed.
    Muf. Kill him ; for then you give him liberty :
His soul is from his earthly prison freed.
                                   Emp.

Emp. How happy is the prince who has a churchman
So learn'd and pliant to expound his laws !
  Ben. Two things I humbly offer to your prudence.
  Emp. Be brief ; but let not either thwart my love.
  Ben. Firſt, ſince our holy man has made rape lawful,
Fright her with that ; proceed not yet to force :
Why ſhould you pluck the green diſtaſteful fruit
From the unwilling bough,
When it may ripen of itſelf, and fall ?
  Emp. Grant her a day ; tho' that's too much to give
Out of a life which I devote to love.
  Ben. Then next, to bar
All future hopes of her deſir'd Sebaſtian,
Let Dorax be enjoin'd to bring his head.
  Emp. [*To the* Mufti.] Go, Mufti, call him to receive
        his orders.   [*Exit* Mufti.
' I taſte thy counſel ; her deſires, new rous'd,
' And yet unſlak'd, will kindle in her fancy,
' And make her eager to renew the feaſt.'
  Ben. [*Aſide.*] Dorax, I know before, will diſobey ;
There's a foe's head well cropp'd——
But this hot love precipitates my plot,
And brings it to projection ere its time.
Enter Sebaſtian *and* Almeyda, *hand in hand ; upon ſight*
      of the Emperor *they ſeparate, and ſeem diſturbed.*
  Alm. He breaks at unawares upon our walks ;
And, like a midnight wolf, invades the fold.
' Make ſpeedy preparation of your ſoul,
' And bid it arm apace.   He comes for anſwer ;
' And brutal miſchief ſits upon his brow.'
  Seb. Not the laſt ſounding could ſurpriſe me more,
' That ſummons drouſy mortals to their doom :
' When call'd in haſte, they fumble for their limbs,
' And tremble, unprovided for their charge.
' My ſenſe has been ſo deeply plung'd in joys,
' The ſoul out-ſlept her hour ; and, ſcarce awake,
' Would think, too late, and cannot.   But brave minds,
' At worſt, can dare their fate.'
  Emp. [*Coming up to them.*] Have you perform'd
Your embaſſy, and treated with ſucceſs ?
  Seb. I had not time.

Emp.

Emp. No, not for my affairs;
But for your own too much.

Seb. You talk in clouds. Explain your meaning, Sir.

Emp. Explain yours firſt. What meant you hand in
And when you ſaw me, with a guilty ſtart,   [hand;
You loos'd your hold, affrighted at my preſence?

Seb. Affrighted!

Emp. Yes, aſtoniſh'd and confounded.

Seb. What mak'ſt thou of thyſelf, and what of me?
‘ Art thou ſome ghoſt, ſome dæmon, or ſome god,’
That I ſhould ſtand aſtoniſh'd at thy fight?
If thou couldſt deem ſo meanly of my courage,
Why didſt thou not engage me man for man,
And try the virtue of that Gorgon face,
To ſtare me into ſtatue?

Emp. Oh, thou art now recover'd! but, by Heav'n,
Thou wert amaz'd at firſt, as if ſurpriz'd
At unexpected baſeneſs brought to light:
For, know, ungrateful man, that kings, like gods,
Are every where; walk in th' abyſs of minds,
And view the dark receſſes of the ſoul.

Seb. Baſe and ungrateful never was I thought;
Nor, till this turn of fate, durſt thou have call'd me.
But, ſince thou boaſt'ſt th' omniſcience of a god,
Say, in what cranny of Sebaſtian's ſoul,
Unknown to me, ſo loath'd a crime is lodg'd?

Emp. Thou haſt not broke my truſt repos'd in thee?

Seb. Impos'd, but not receiv'd. Take back that falſhood.

Emp. Thou art not marry'd to Almeyda?

Seb. Yes.

Emp. And own'ſt the uſurpation of my love?

Seb. I own it, in the face of Heav'n, and thee;
No uſurpation, but a lawful claim,
Of which I ſtand poſſeſs'd.

Emp. Sh' has choſen well,
Betwixt a captive and a conqueror.

Alm. Betwixt a monſter and the beſt of men.
‘ He was the envy of his neighb'ring kings;
‘ For him their ſighing queens deſpis'd their lords,
‘ And virgin daughters bluſh'd when he was nam'd.’
To ſhare his noble chains is more to me,
Than all the ſavage greatneſs of thy throne.

Seb.

Seb. Were I to chufe again, and knew my fate,
For fuch a night, I would be what I am.
The joys I have poffefs'd are ever mine;
Out of thy reach, behind eternity,
Hid in the facred treafure of the paft;
But blefs'd remembrance brings them hourly back.

Emp. Hourly indeed, who haft but hours to live!
Oh, mighty purchafe of a boafted blifs!
To dream of what thou hadft one fugitive night,
And never fhalt have more.

' *Seb.* Barbarian, thou canft part us but a moment—
' We fhall be one again in thy defpite.
' Life is but air,
' That yields a paffage to the whiftling fword,
' And clofes when 'tis gone.

' *Alm.* How can we better die, than clofe embrac'd,
' Sucking each others fouls while we expire;
' Which, fo transfus'd, and mounting both at once,
' The faints, deceiv'd, fhall by a fweet miftake,
' Hand up thy foul for mine, and mine for thine.

' *Emp.* No, I'll untwift you;
' I have occafion for your ftay on earth:
' Let him mount firft, and beat upon the wing,
' And wait an age for what I here detain;
' Or ficken at immortal joys above,
' And languifh for the Heav'n he left below.'   [join'd?

Alm. Thou wilt not dare to break what Heav'n has

Emp. Not break the chain; but change a rotten link,
And rivet one to laft.
Think'ft thou I come to argue right and wrong?
Why lingers Dorax thus? Where are my guards,
   [Benducar *goes out for the guards, and returns.*
To drag that flave to death? [*Pointing to* Sebaftian.
Now ftorm and rage;
Call vainly on thy prophet, then defy him,
For wanting power to fave thee.

Seb. That were to gratify thy pride. I'll fhew thee
How a man fhould, and how a king dare die:
So even, that my foul fhall walk with eafe
Out of its flefh, and fhut out life as calmly
As it does words; without a figh to note
One ftruggle in the fmooth diffolving frame.

Alm.

Alm. [*To the* Emp.] Expect revenge from Heav'n, inhu-
Nor hope t' afcend Sebaftian's holy bed.   [man wretch!
Flames, daggers, poifons, guard the facred fteps;
Thofe are the promis'd pleafures of my love.

Emp. And thefe might fright another, but not me :
Or me, if I defign, to give you pleafure.
I feek my own ; and while that lafts, you live.

Enter two of the guards.

Go, bear the captive to a fpeedy death,
And fet my foul at eafe.

Alm. I charge you, hold, ye minifters of death !
Speak, my Sebaftian,
Plead for thy life ; Oh, afk it of the tyrant !
'Tis no difhonour ; truft me, love, 'tis none.
I would die for thee, but I cannot plead :
My haughty heart difdains it, ev'n for thee.
Still filent ! Will the King of Portugal
Go to his death like a dumb facrifice ?
Beg him to fave my life, in faving thine.

Seb. Farewel ; my life's not worth another word.

Emp. [*To the guards.*] Perform your orders.

Alm. Stay, take my farewel too.
Farewel the greatnefs of Almeyda's foul !
Look, tyrant, what excefs of love can do ;
It pulls me down, thus low, as to thy feet ;   [*Kneels to him.*
Nay, to embrace thy knees with loathing hands,
Which blifter when they touch thee.   Yet ev'n thus,
Thus far I can, to fave Sebaftian's life.

Emp. A fecret pleafure trickles through my veins ;
It works about the inlets of my foul,
To feel thy touch ; and pity tempts the pafs :
But the tough metal of my heart refifts ;
'Tis warm'd with the foft fire, not melted down.

' *Alm.* A flood of fcalding tears will make it run.
' Spare him, Oh, fpare ! Can you pretend to love,
' And have no pity ? Love and that are twins.
' Here will I grow ;
' Thus compafs you with thefe fupplanting cords,
' And pull fo long till the proud fabric falls.'

Emp. Still kneel, and ftill embrace ; 'tis double pleafure
So to be hugg'd, and fee Sebaftian die.

Alm. Look, tyrant, when thou nam'ft Sebaftian's death,
                                                        Thy

Thy very executioners turn pale.
Rough as they are, and harden'd in their trade
Of death, they ſtart at an anointed head,
And tremble to approach——He hears me not,
‘ Nor minds th' impreſſion of a god on kings ;
‘ Becauſe no ſtamp of Heav'n was on his ſoul ;
‘ But the reſiſting maſs drove back the ſeal.
‘ Say, tho' thy heart be rock of adamant,
‘ Yet rocks are not impregnable to bribes :
‘ Inſtruct me how to bribe thee—Name thy price ;’
Lo, I reſign my title to the crown ;
Send me to exile with the man I love,
And baniſhment is empire.
    Emp. ‘ Here's my claim ;
                        ‘ [*Clapping his hand to his ſword.*
‘ And this extinguiſh'd thine—thou giv'ſt me nothing.
    ‘ *Alm.* My father's, mother's, brother's deaths I pardon:
‘ That's ſomewhat, ſure ; a mighty ſum of murder,
‘ Of innocent and kindred blood ſtruck off.
‘ My prayers and penance ſhall diſcount for theſe,
‘ And beg of Heav'n to charge the bill on me.
‘ Behold what price I offer, and how dear,
‘ To buy Sebaſtian's life.
    Emp. Let after-reck'nings trouble fearful fools ;
‘ I'll ſtand the trial of thoſe trivial crimes.
‘ But, ſince thou begg'ſt me to preſcribe my terms,
‘ The only I can offer are thy love ;
‘ And this one day of reſpite to reſolve.’
Grant or deny ; for thy next word is fate,
And fate is deaf to pray'r.
    Alm. May Heav'n be ſo,   [*Riſing up.*
At thy laſt breath, to thine.   ‘ I curſe thee not ;
‘ For who can better curſe the plague or devil,
‘ Than to be what they are ? That curſe be thine.’
Now, do not ſpeak, Sebaſtian ; for you need not :
But die ; for I reſign your life.   Look, Heav'n,
Almeyda dooms her dear Sebaſtian's death !
‘ But is there Heav'n ? For I begin to doubt :
‘ The ſkies are huſh'd, no grumbling thunders roll.
‘ Now take your ſwing, ye impious ; ſin unpuniſh'd,
‘ Eternal Providence ſeems over-watch'd,
‘ And with a ſlumb'ring nod aſſents to murder.’
                                            Enter

Enter Dorax, *attended by three soldiers.*

Emp. Thou mov'st a tortoise-pace to my relief.
Take hence that once-a-king, that sullen pride
That swells to dumbness, lay him in the dungeon,
And sink him deep with irons; ' that, when he would,
' He shall not groan to hearing.   When I send,'
The next commands are death.

Alm. Then prayers are vain as curses.

Emp. Much at one
In a slave's mouth, against a monarch's pow'r.
This day thou hast to think;
At night, if thou wilt curse, thou shalt curse kindly.
' Then I'll provoke thy lips, lay siege so close,
' That all thy sallying breath shall turn to blessings.'
Make haste, seize, force her, bear her hence.

Alm. Farewel, my lost Sebastian!
I do not beg, I challenge justice now.
Oh, Pow'rs! if kings be your peculiar care,
Why plays this wretch with your prerogative?
Now flash him dead, now crumble him to ashes;
' Or henceforth live confin'd in your own palace,
' And look not idly out upon a world
' That is no longer yours.'

[*She is carried off struggling:* Emp. *and* Ben. *follow.*
[Sebastian *struggles in his Guards arms, and shakes off one
  of them; but two others come in and hold him; he speaks
  not all the while.*

Dor. I find I'm but a half-strain'd villain yet;   [*Aside.*
But mongrel-mischievous; for my blood boil'd
To view this brutal act, and my stern soul
Tugg'd at my arm to draw in her defence.
Down thou rebelling Christian in my heart;
Redeem thy fame on this Sebastian first;   [*Walks a turn.*
Then think on others wrongs, when thine are righted.
But how to right them? On a slave, disarm'd,
Defenceless, and submitted to my rage?
A base revenge is vengeance on myself —— [*Walks again.*
I have it—and I thank thee, honest head,
Thus present to me at my great necessity——
                         [*Comes up to* Sebastian.

You know me not?

Seb. I hear men call thee Dorax.

                                        Dor.

Dor. 'Tis well; you know enough for once; you fpeak,
You were ftruck mute before.   [too:
    Seb. Silence became me then.
    Dor. Yet we may talk hereafter.
    Seb. Hereafter is not mine——
Difpatch thy work, good executioner.   [falfhood
    Dor. None of my blood were hangmen. Add that
To a long bill that yet remains unreckoned.
    Seb. A king and thou can never have a reck'ning.
    Dor. A greater fum, perhaps, than you can pay.
Mean time, I fhall make bold t' increafe your debt.
                                    [*Gives him his fword.*
Take this, and ufe it at your greateft need.
    Seb. This hand and this have been acquainted well.
[*Looks on it.*] It fhould have come before into my grafp,
To kill the ravifher.
    Dor. Thou heard'ft the tyrant's orders; guard thy life,
When 'tis attack'd, and guard it like a man.
    Seb. I'm ftill without thy meaning; but I thank thee.
    Dor. Thank me when I afk thanks; thank me with
    Seb. Such furly kindnefs did I never fee.   [that.
    Dor. [*To the Captain of his Guards.*] Muza, draw out
        a file, pick man by man,
Such who dare die, and dear will fell their deaths.
Guard him to th' utmoft——Now, conduct him hence,
And treat him as my perfon.
    Seb. Something like
That voice, methinks, I fhould have fomewhere heard;
But floods of woes have hurry'd it far off,
Beyond my ken of foul.   [*Exit Seb. with the foldiers.*
    Dor. But I fhall bring him back, ungrateful man!
I fhall, and fet him full before thy fight,
When I fhall front thee, like fome ftaring ghoft,
With all my wrongs about me——What, fo foon
Return'd? This hafte is boding.
        Enter to him Emperor, Benducar, *and* Mufti.
    Emp. She's ftill inexorable, ftill imperious,
And loud, as if, like Bacchus, born in thunder.
Be quick, ye falfe phyficians of my mind,
Bring fpeedy death, or cure.
    Ben. What can be counfell'd while Sebaftian lives?
The vine will cling, while the tall poplar ftands;
                        F   But

down, creeps to the next support,
es as closely there.

Emp. That's done with ease; I speak him dead. Proceed.

Muf. Proclaim your marriage with Almeyda next,
That civil wars may cease.   This gains the crowd:
Then you may safely force her to your will:
' For people side with violence and injustice,
' When done for public good.'

Emp. Preach thou that doctrine.

Ben. Th' unreasonable fool has broach'd a truth [*Aside.*
That blasts my hopes: but since 'tis gone so far,
He shall divulge Almeyda is a Christian.
If that produce no tumult, I despair.

Emp. Why speaks not Dorax?

Dor. Because my soul abhors to mix with him.
Sir, let me bluntly say, you went too far,
To trust the preaching pow'r on state affairs
To him, or any heav'nly demagogue.
'Tis a limb lopp'd from your prerogative;
And so much of Heaven's image blotted from you.

' *Muf.* Sure thou hast never heard of holy men
'. (So Christians call them) fam'd in state affairs;
' Such as in Spain, Ximenes, Albornez,
' In England, Wolsey: match me these with laymen.

' *Dor.* How you triumph in one or two of these,
' Born to be statesmen, happ'ning to be churchmen!
' Thou call'st them holy; so their function was:
' But, tell me, Mufti, which of them were saints?
' Next, Sir, to you; the sum of all is this,
' Since he claims pow'r from Heaven, and not from kings,
' When 'tis his int'rest, he can int'rest Heav'n
' To preach you down; and ages oft depend
' On hours, uninterrupted, in the chair.

' *Emp.* I'll trust his preaching, while I rule his pay;
' And I dare trust my Africans to hear
' Whatever he dare preach.

' *Dor.* You know them not.
' The genius of your Moors is mutiny;
' They scarcely want a guide to move their madness.
' Prompt to rebel on every weak pretence;
' Blustering when courted, crouching when oppress'd;
' Wise to themselves, and fools to all the world;

' Restless

' Reſtleſs in change, and perjur'd to a proverb:
' They love religion ſweeten'd to the ſenſe;
' A good, luxurious, palatable faith.
' Thus Vice and Godlineſs, prepoſt'rous pair!
' Ride cheek by jowl: but churchmen hold the reins.
' And whenc'er kings would lower clergy greatneſs,
' They learn, too late, what power the preachers have,
' And whoſe the ſubjects are. The Mufti knows it;
' Nor dares deny what paſs'd betwixt us two.'
    Emp. No more; whate'er he ſaid was my command.
    Dor. Why, then, no more, ſince you will hear no more.
Some kings are reſolute to their own ruin.
    Emp. Without your meddling where you are not aſk'd,
Obey your orders, and diſpatch Sebaſtian.
    Dor. Truſt my revenge; be ſure I wiſh him dead.
    Emp. What mean'ſt thou? What's thy wiſhing to my
Diſpatch him: rid me of the man I loath.   [will?
    Dor. I hear you, Sir: I'll take my time, and do't.
    Emp. Thy time! what's all thy time? What's thy
To my one hour of eaſe? No more replies; [whole life,
But ſee thou doſt it; or——
    Dor. Choak in that threat. I can ſay Or, as loud.
    Emp. 'Tis well; I ſee my words have no effect.
But I may ſend a meſſage to diſpoſe you.   [*Is going off.*
    Dor. Expect an anſwer worthy of that meſſage.
    Muf. The Prophet ow'd him this: [*Aſide.*
And, thank'd be Heaven, he has it.
    Ben. By holy Alha, I conjure you, ſtay,
And judge not raſhly of ſo brave a man.
          [*Draws the* Emperor *aſide, and whiſpers him.*
I'll give you reaſons why he cannot execute
Your orders now, and why he will hereafter.
    Muf. Benducar is a fool to bring him off: [*Aſide.*
I'll work my own revenge, and ſpeedily.
    Ben. The fort is his, the ſoldiers hearts are his;
A thouſand Chriſtian ſlaves are in the caſtle,
Which he can free to reinforce his pow'r;
' Your troops far off, beleaguering Larache,
' Yet in the Chriſtian hands.'
    Emp. I grant all this;
But grant me he muſt die.
    Ben. He ſhall, by poiſon;

F 2

'Tis

'Tis here, the deadly drug prepar'd in powder,
Hot as hell fire—then, to prevent his soldiers
From rising to revenge their general's death;
While he is struggling with his mortal pangs,
The rabble on the sudden may be rais'd
To seize the castle.

Emp. Do't; 'tis left to thee.

Ben. Yet more—but clear your brow; for he observes.

[*They whisper again.*

Dor. What, will the fav'rite prop my falling fortunes?
Oh, prodigy of court!   [*Aside.*

[*Emp. and* Ben. *return to* Dor.

Emp. Your friend has fully clear'd your innocence:
I was too hasty to condemn unheard;
And you, perhaps, too prompt in your replies.
As far as fits the majesty of kings,
I ask excuse.

Dor. I'm sure I meant it well.

Emp. I know you did ——this to our love renew'd.

[*Emp. drinks.*

Benducar, fill to Dorax.

[Ben. *turns, and mixes a powder in it.*

Dor. Let it go round; for all of us have need
To quench our heats: 'tis the King's health, Benducar,

[*He drinks.*

And I would pledge it, tho' I knew 'twere poison.

Ben. Another bowl; for what the King has touch'd,
And you have pledg'd, is sacred to your loves.

[*Drinks out of another bowl.*

Muf. Since charity becomes my calling, thus
Let me provoke your friendship: and Heaven bless it,
As I intend it well——

[Drinks, *and, turning aside, pours some drops out of a little
vial into the bowl, then presents it to* Dorax.

Dor. Heav'n make thee honest:
On that condition we'shall soon be friends.   [*Drinks.*

Muf. Yes, at our meeting in another world;   [*Aside.*
For thou hast drunk thy passport out of this.
' Not the Nonacrian sont, nor Lethe's lake,
' Could sooner numb thy nimble faculties
' Than this, to sleep eternal.'

                                              Emp.

Emp. Now, farewel, Dorax; this was our firſt quarrel;
And I dare prophecy, will prove our laſt.

[*Exit* Emp. *with* Ben. *and the* Mufti.

Dor. It may be ſo—I'm ſtrangely diſcompos'd;
Quick ſhootings thro' my limbs, and pricking pains,
Qualms at my heart, convulſions in my nerves,
Shiv'rings of cold, and burnings of my entrails,
Within my little world make medley-war:
Loſe and regain, beat, and are beaten back,
' As momentary victors quit their ground.
' Can it be poiſon? Poiſon's of one tenour,'
Or hot, or cold; this neither, and yet both.
Some deadly draught, ſome enemy of life
Boils in my bowels, and works out my ſoul.
Ingratitude's the growth of every crime;
Afric, the ſcene remov'd, is Portugal.
Of all court-ſervice learn the common lot;
To-day 'tis done, to-morrow 'tis forgot.
Oh, were that all!—my honeſt corpſe muſt lie
Expos'd to ſcorn and public infamy:
My ſhameful death will be divulg'd alone;
The worth and honour of my ſoul unknown.   [*Exit.*

A NIGHT-SCENE, *of the* Mufti's *Garden, where an
Arbour is diſcovered.*

Enter Antonio.

Ant. She names herſelf Morayma, the Mufti's only
daughter, and a virgin. This is the time and place that
ſhe appointed in her letter, yet ſhe comes not. ' Why,
' thou ſweet, delicious creature, why to torture me with
' thy delay? Dar'ſt thou be falſe to thy aſſignation?
' What, in the cool and ſilence of the night, and to a
' new lover? Pox on the hypocrite, thy father, for in-
' ſtructing thee ſo little in the ſweeteſt point of his reli-
' gion. Hark! I hear the ruſtling of her ſilk mantle.'
' Now ſhe comes! now ſhe comes!—No, hang it, that
' was but the whiſtling of the wind through the orange-
' trees. Now again, I hear the pit-a-pat of a pretty
' foot thro' the dark alley—No, 'tis the ſon of a mare
' that's broken looſe, and munching upon the melons.'—
Oh, the miſery of an expecting lover! Well, I'll e'en

                    deſpair,

defpair, go into my arbour, and try to fleep; in a dream
I fhall enjoy her in defpight of her.

[Goes to the arbour, and lies down.

Enter Johayma, wrapt up in a Moorifh Mantle.

Joh. Thus far my love has carried me, almoft without
my knowledge whither I was going: ‘ fhall I go on, fhall
‘ I difcover myfelf?——What an injury am I doing to
‘ my old hufband!——Yet what injury, fince he’s old
‘ and has three wives, and fix concubines befides me! ’tis
‘ but ftealing my own tythe from’ him.’

[She comes a little nearer the arbour.

Ant. [*Raifing himfelf a little, and looking.*] At laft ’tis
fhe, this is no illufion I am fure; ’tis a true fhe-devil of
flefh and blood; and fhe could never have taken a fitter
time to tempt me——

Joh. He’s young and handfome————

‘ *Ant.* Yes, well enough, I thank nature.　　[*Afide.*’

Joh. And I am yet neither old nor ugly: fure he will
not refufe me.

Ant. No, thou may’ft pawn thy maidenhead upon’t he
wonnot.　　　　　　　　　　　　　　　[*Afide.*

Joh. The Mufti would feaft himfelf upon other women, and keep me fafting.

Ant. Oh, the holy curmudgeon!　　　　　[*Afide.*

‘ *Joh.* Would preach abftinence, and practife luxury;
‘ but I thank my ftars, I have edified more by his exam-
‘ ple than his precept.

‘ *Ant.* Moft divinely argued: fhe’s the beft cafuift in
‘ all Afric.　　　　　　　　　　　　　　[*Afide.*’

[*He rufhes out and embraces her.*] I can hold no longer from
embracing thee, my dear Morayma; ‘ the old uncon-
‘ fcionable whorefon thy father, could he expect cold
‘ chaftity from a child of his begetting?’

‘ *Joh.* What nonfenfe do you talk? Do you take me
‘ for the Mufti’s daughter?

‘ *Ant.* Why are you not, Madam?’

[Throwing off her barnus.

Joh. I find you had an appointment with Morayma.

Ant. By all that’s good, the naufeous wife.　　[*Afide.*

Joh. What, you are confounded, and ftand mute?

Ant. Somewhat nonpluft I confefs, to hear you deny
your name fo pofitively: why, are not you Morayma,

the

the Mufti's daughter ? Did not I fee you with him, did not he prefent me to you ? ' Were you not fo charitable
' as to give me money ? Ay, and to tread upon my foot,
' and fqueeze my hand too, if I may be fo bold to re-
' member you of paft favours ?"

' *Joh.* And you fee I am come to make them good; but
' I am neither Morayma nor the Mufti's daughter.

' *Ant.* Nay, I know not that : but I am fure he is old
' enough to be your father; and either father, or reve-
' rend father I heard you call him.

' *Joh.* Once again, how came you to name Morayma ?

' *Ant.* Another damned miftake of mine : for afking
' one of my fellow-flaves, who were the chief ladies
' about the houfe, he anfwered me, Morayma and Jo-
' hayma; but fhe, it feems, is his daughter, with a pox
' to her, and you are his beloved wife.'

Joh. ' Say your beloved miftrefs, if you pleafe; for
' that's the title I defire.' This moon-fhine grows offenfive to my eyes : come, fhall we walk into the arbour ?
there we may rectify all miftakes.

' *Ant.* That's clofe and dark.

' *Joh.* And are thofe faults to lovers ?

' *Ant.* But there I cannot pleafe myfelf with the fight
' of your beauty.

' *Joh.* Perhaps you may do better.

' *Ant.* But there's not a breath of air ftirring.

' *Joh.* The breath of lovers is the fweeteft air; but
' you are fearful.

' *Ant.* I am confidering indeed, that if am taken with
' you——

' *Joh.* The beft way to avoid it, is to retire, where we
' may not be difcovered.

' *Ant.* Where lodges your hufband ?

' *Joh.* Juft againft the face of this open walk.

' *Ant.* Then he has feen us already, for ought I know.

' *Joh.* You make fo many difficulties, I fear I am dif-
' pleafing to you.'

Ant. [*Afide.*] If Morayma comes, and takes me in the arbour with her, I have made a fine exchange of that diamond for this pebble.

Joh. You are much fallen off, let me tell you, from the fury of your firft embrace.

Ant.

Ant. I confess, I was somewhat too furious at first, but you will forgive the transport of my passion ; now I have considered it better, I have a qualm of conscience.

Joh. Of conscience ! why, what has conscience to do with two young lovers that have opportunity ?

' *Ant.* Why truly, conscience is something to blame for
' interposing in our matters : but how can I help it, if I
' have a scruple to betray my master ?

' *Joh.* There must be something more in't ? for your
' conscience was very quiet when you took me for Mo-
' rayma.

' *Ant.* I grant you, Madam, when I took you for his
' daughter ; for then I might have made you an honou-
' rable amends by marriage.

' *Joh.* You, Christians, are such peeking sinners, you
' tremble at a shadow in the moonshine.

' *Ant.* And you, Africans, are such termagants, you stop
' at nothing. I must be plain with you, you are married,
' and to a holy man, the head of your religion. Go back
' to your chamber, go back, I say, and consider of it for
' this night ; as I will do on my part : I will be true to
' you ; and invent all the arguments I can to comply with
' you ; and who knows, but at our next meeting, the
' sweet devil may have more power over me ? I am true
' flesh and blood, I can tell you that for your comfort.'

Joh. ' Flesh without blood I think thou art ; or if any,
' 'tis as cold as that of fishes.' But I'll teach thee, to thy cost, what vengeance is in store for refusing a lady, who has offered thee her love——Help, help, there ! will nobody come to my assistance ?

Ant. What do you mean, Madam ? for heaven's sake peace ; your husband will hear you ; think of your own danger, if you will not think of mine.

Joh. Ingrateful wretch, thou deservest no pity : help, help, husband, or I shall be ravished : the villain will be too strong for me. Help, help, for pity of a poor distressed creature.

Ant. Then I have nothing but impudence to assist me : I must drown her clamour, whate'er comes on't.

     [*He takes out his flute, and plays as loud as he can
      possibly, and she continues crying out.*

                             Enter

Enter the Mufti *in his night-gown, and two servants.*

Muf. Oh, thou villain, what horrible impiety art thou committing? What! ravishing the wife of my bosom? Take him away, ganch him, impale him, rid the world of such a monster.   [*Servants seize him.*

Ant. Mercy, dear master, mercy: hear me first, and after, if I have deserved hanging, spare me not. What have you seen to provoke you to this cruelty?

Muf. I have heard the outcries of my wife; the bleatings of the poor innocent lamb: ' seen nothing ' sayest thou? If I see the lamb lie bleeding, and the ' butcher by her with his knife drawn, and bloody,' is not that evidence sufficient of the murder? I come too late, and the execution is already done.

Ant. Pray think in reason, Sir, is a man to be put to death for a similitude? ' No violence has been commit- ' ted; none intended: the lamb's alive; and if I durst ' tell you so, no more a lamb than I am a butcher.

' *Joh.* How's that, villain, darest thou accuse me?'

Ant. Be patient, Madam, and speak but truth, and I'll do any thing to serve you: ' I say again, and swear ' it too, I'll do any thing to serve you.'

Joh. [*Aside.*] I understand him; but, I fear, 'tis now too late to save him.——Pray hear him speak, husband; perhaps he may say something for himself; I know not.

Muf. Speak thou, has he not violated my bed, and thy honour?

Joh. I forgive him freely, for he has done nothing. What he will do hereafter, to make me satisfaction, him- self best knows.

Ant. Any thing, any thing, sweet Madam: I shall re- fuse no drudgery.

Muf. But did he mean no mischief? Was he endea- vouring nothing?

Joh. In my conscience, I begin to doubt he did not.

Muf. 'Tis impossible; then what meant all these out- cries?

Joh. I heard music in the garden, and at an unseason- able time of night, and I stole softly out of my bed, as imagining it might be he.

' *Muf.* How's that, Johayma? Imagining it was he, ' and yet you went?

                                      ' *Joh.*

' *Joh.* Why not, my Lord, am not I the miſtreſs of
' the family? and is it not my place to ſee good orders
' kept in it? I thought he might have allured ſome of
' the ſhe-ſlaves to him; and was reſolved to prevent what
' might have been betwixt him and them:' when, on the
ſudden, he ruſhed out upon me, caught me in his arms
with ſuch a fury——

' *Muf.* I have heard enough, away with him.

' *Joh.* Miſtaking me, no doubt, for one of his fellow-
' ſlaves: with that, affrighted as I was, I diſcovered my-
' ſelf, and cried aloud:' but as ſoon as ever he knew me,
the villain let me go, and I muſt needs ſay, he ſtarted
back, as if I were ſome ſerpent; and was more afraid
of me than I of him.

Muf. Oh, thou corrupter of my family, that's cauſe
enough of death; once again, away with him.

Joh. What, for an intended treſpaſs? No harm has
been done, whate'er may be. He coſt you five hundred
crowns, I take it.

Muf. Thou ſayeſt true, a very conſiderable ſum: he
ſhall not die, though he had committed folly with a ſlave;
'tis too much to loſe by him.

Ant. My only fault has ever been to love playing in
the dark, and the more ſhe cried, the more I played; that
it might be ſeen I intended nothing to her.

Muf. To your kennel, ſirrah, mortify your fleſh, and
conſider in whoſe family you are.

Joh. And one thing more, remember from henceforth
to obey better.

Muf. [*Aſide.*] For all her ſmoothneſs, I am not quite
cured of my jealouſy; but I have thought of a way
that will clear my doubts.

[*Exit* Mufti *with* Joh. *and ſervants.*

Ant. I am mortified ſufficiently already, without the
help of his ghoſtly counſel. Fear of death has gone
farther with me in two minutes, than my conſcience
would have gone in two months. I find myſelf in a very
dejected condition, all over me; poor ſin lies dormant;
' concupiſence is retired to his winter quarters;' and if
Morayma ſhould now appear, I ſay no more, but, alas,
for her and me!

[Morayma comes out of the arbour, ſhe ſteals behind
him, and claps him on the back.

Mor.

Mor. And if Morayma fhould appear, as fhe does appear, alas, you fay for her and you !

Ant. Art thou there, my fweet temptation ! my eyes, my life, my foul, my all !

Mor. A mighty compliment, when all thefe, by your own confeffion, are juft nothing.

Ant. Nothing, till thou cameft to new create me; thou doft not know the power of thy own charms : let me embrace thee, and thou fhalt fee how quickly I can turn wicked.

' *Mor.* [*Stepping back.*] Nay, if you are fo dangerous,
' 'tis beft keeping you at a diftance ; I have no mind to
' warm a frozen fnake in my bofom ; he may chance to
' recover, and fting me for my pains.

' *Ant.* Confider what I have fuffered for thy fake al-
' ready; and make me fome amends : two difappoint-
' ments in a night! Oh, cruel creature !

' *Mor.* And you may thank yourfelf for both : I came
' eagerly to the charge, before my time, thro' the back-
' walk behind the arbour; and you, like a frefh-water
' foldier, ftood guarding the pafs before : if you miffed
' the enemy, you may thank your own dulnefs.

' *Ant.* Nay, if you will be ufing ftratagems, you fhall
' give me leave to make ufe of my advantages, now I have
' you in my power : we are fairly met ; I'll try it out,
' and give no quarter.

' *Mor.* By your favour, Sir, we meet upon treaty now
' and not upon defiance.

' ' *Ant.* If that be all, you fhall have *carte blanche* im-
' mediately ; for I long to be ratifying.'

Mor. No, now I think on't, you are already entered into articles with my enemy Johayma : any thing to ferve you, Madam ; I fhall refufe no drudgery : whofe words were thofe, gentleman ? Was that like a cavalier of honour ?

' *Ant.* Not very heroic ; but felf-prefervation is a point
' above honour and religion too—Antonio was a rogue, I
' muft confefs ; but you muft give me leave to love him.

' *Mor.* To beg your life fo bafely ; and to prefent
' your fword to your enemy : Oh, recreant !

' *Ant.* If I had died honourably, my fame indeed would
' have founded loud, but I fhould never have heard the

' blaſt. Come, don't make yourſelf worſe-natured than
' you are ; to ſave my life, you would be content I ſhould
' promiſe any thing.

' *Mor.* Yes, if I were ſure you would perform nothing.'

Ant. Can you ſuſpect I would leave you for Johayma ?

Mor. No, but I can expect you would have both of
us : love is covetous, I muſt have all of you ; heart for
heart is an equal truck : in ſhort, I am younger ; I think
handſomer, and am ſure I love you better ; ſhe has been
my ſtep-mother theſe fifteen years ; you think that's her
face you ſee, but 'tis only a daubed vizard : ſhe wears
an armour of proof upon't ; an inch thick of paint, beſides ' the waſh : her face is ſo fortified, that you can
' make no approaches to it, without a ſhovel. But for
' her conſtancy, I can tell you for your comfort, ſhe
' will love till death, I mean till yours ; for when ſhe
' has worn out, ſhe will certainly diſpatch you to another
' world, for fear of telling tales ; as ſhe has already
' ſerved three ſlaves, your predeceſſors of happy me-
' mory in her favours.' She has made my pious father
a three-piled cuckold to my knowledge ; and now ſhe
would be robbing me of my ſingle ſheep too.

Ant. Pr'ythee prevent her then ; and at leaſt take the
ſhearing of me firſt.

' *Mor.* No, I'll have a butcher's pen'worth of you ;
' firſt ſecure the carcaſs, and then take the fleece into the
' bargain.

' *Ant.* Why ſure, you did not put yourſelf and me to
' all this trouble, for a dry come-off :' by this hand—
                                        [*Taking it.*

Mor. Which you ſhall never touch, but upon better
aſſurances than you imagine.   [*Pulling her hand away.*

Ant. I'll marry thee, and make a Chriſtian of thee,
thou pretty damned infidel.

Mor. I mean you ſhall ; but no earneſt, till the bargain
be made before witneſs ; there's love enough to be had,
and as much as you can turn you to, never doubt, but
all upon honourable terms.

Ant. I vow and ſwear by Love ; and he's a deity in
all religions.

Mor. But never to be truſted in any : he has another
name too, of a worſe ſound. Shall I truſt an oath, when
                                        I ſee

I fee your eyes languishing, your cheeks flushing, and
can hear your heart throbbing? No, I'll not come near
you: he's a foolish physician who will feel the pulse of
a patient, that has the plague spots upon him.

Ant. Did one ever hear a little moppet argue fo per-
verfly againft fo good a caufe! Come, pr'ythee let me
anticipate a little of my revenue.

'*Mor.* You would fain be fingering your rents before-
' hand; but that makes a man an ill hufband ever after.
' Confider, marriage is a painful vocation, as you fhall
' prove it : manage your incomes as thriftily as you can,
' you fhall find a hard tafk on't to make even at the
' year's end, and yet to live decently.

'*Ant.* I came with a Chriftian intention to revenge
' myfelf upon thy father, for being the head of a falfe
' religion.'

Mor. And fo you fhall; I offer you his daughter for
your fecond: but fince you are fo preffing, meet me
under my window to-morrow night, body for body, about
this hour; I'll flip down out of my lodging, and bring
my father in my hand.

Ant. How! thy father!

Mor. I mean, all that's good of him; his pearls, and
jewels, his whole contents, his heart and foul; as much
as ever I can carry! I'll leave him his Alcoran; that's
revenue enough for him : every page of it is gold and
diamonds. ' He has the turn of an eye, a demure finile,
' and a godly cant, that are worth millions to him. I
' forgot to tell you, that' I will have a flave prepared at
the poftern gate, with two horfes ready faddled : no more,
for I fear I may be miffed; and think I hear them calling
for me——if you have conftancy and courage——

Ant. Never doubt it: and love in abundance, to wander with thee all the world over.

Mor. The value of twelve hundred thoufand crowns
in a cafket!

Ant. A heavy burden, heaven knows! but we muft
pray for patience to fupport it.

Mor. Befides a willing tit that will venture her corps
with you :——come, I know you long to have a parting
blow with me; and therefore to fhew I am in charity—

[He kiffes her.
Ant.

G

Ant. Once more for pity ; that I may keep the flavour upon my lips till we meet again.

Mor. No : frequent charities make bold beggars : and. besides, I have learned of a falconer, never to feed up a hawk when I would have him fly : that's enough——but if you would be nibbling, here's a hand to stay your stomach.   [*Kiffing her hand.*

Ant. Thus conquered infidels, that wars may ceafe, Are forc'd to give their hands, and fign the peace.

Mor. Thus Chriftians are outwitted by the foe ; You had her in your pow'r, and let her go. If you releafe my hand, the fault's not mine ; You fhou'd have made me feal as well as fign.
   [*She runs off, he follows her to the door ; then comes back again, and goes out at the other.*

END of the THIRD ACT.

A C T   IV.

SCENE, Benducar's *Palace in the Caftle of* Alcazar.

Enter Benducar.

BENDUCAR.

MY future fate, the colour of my life, My all depends on this important hour : This hour my lot is weighing in the fcales, And heav'n, perhaps, is doubting what to do. Almeyda and a crown have puſh'd me forward : 'Tis fix'd, the tyrant muft not ravifh her ; He and Sebaftian ftand betwixt my hopes ; He moft ; and therefore firft to be difpatch'd. Thefe and a thoufand things are to be done In the fhort compafs of this rowling night, And nothing yet perform'd, ' None of my emiffaries yet return'd.
          ' *Enter* Haly, *firft fervant.*
' Oh, Haly, thou haft held me long in pain.
' What haft thou learn'd of Dorax ? Is he dead ?
   ' *Haly.* Two hours I warily have watch'd his palace ;
' All doors are fhut, no fervant peeps abroad ;
                              ' Some

' Some officers with striding haste pass'd in,
' While others outward went on quick dispatch;
' Sometimes hush'd silence seem'd to reign within;
' Then cries confus'd, and a joint clamour follow'd;
' Then lights went gliding by, from room to room,
' And shot like thwarting meteors crofs the house.
' Not daring further to enquire, I came
' With speed, to bring you this imperfect news.
 ' *Bend.* Hence I conclude him either dead or dying:
' His mournful friends, summon'd to take their leaves,
' Are throng'd about his couch, and fit in council.
' What those caballing captains may defign,
' I must prevent, by being first in action.
' To Muley Zeydan fly with speed; defire him
' To take my last inftructions; tell the importance,
' And haste his prefence here.   [*Exit* Haly.
' How has this poifon loft its wonted way?
' It should have burnt its paffage, not have linger'd
' In the blind labyrinths and crooked turnings
' Of human compofition; now it moves
' Like a flow fire that works againft the wind,
' As if his ftronger ftars had interpos'd.
   ' *Enter* Hamet.
' Well, Hamet, are our friends the rabble rais'd?
' From Muftapha what meffage?
 ' *Ham.* What you wifb:
' The ftreets are thicker in this noon of night,
' Than at the mid-day fun: a drouzy horror
' Sits on their eyes, like Fear, not well awake:
' All croud in heaps, as at a night-alarm
' The bees drive out upon each others backs,
' T' imbofs their hives in clufters: all afk news:
' Their bufy captain runs the weary round
' To whifper orders, and commanding fllence,
' Makes not noife ceafe but deafens it to murmurs.
 ' *Bend.* Night waftes apace: when, when will he ap-
 ' *Ham.* He only waits your fummons.   [pear?
 ' *Bend.* Hafte their coming.
' Let fecrecy and filence be enjoin'd
' In their clofe march. What news from the lieutenant?
 ' *Ham.* I left him at the gate firm to your intereft,
' T' admit the townfmen at their firft appearance.
     ' *Bend.*

' *Bend.* Thus far 'tis well. Go haſten Muſtapha.

[*Exit* Hamet.

Enter Orchan, *the third ſervant.*

' O. Orchan, did I think thy diligence
' Would lag behind the reſt ? What from the Mufti ?
   ' *Orc.* I ſought him round his palace ;   made enquiry
' Of all the ſlaves : in ſhort I uſed your name,
' And urg'd the importance home ; but had for anſwer,
' That ſince the ſhut of evening none had ſeen him.
   Bend. O the curſt fate of all conſpiracies !
' They move on many ſprings ; if one but fail,
' The reſtiff machine ſtops—In an ill hour he's abſent ;
' 'Tis the firſt time, and ſure will be the laſt
' That e'er a Mufti was not in the way,
' When tumults and rebellion ſhould be broach'd.
' Stay by me : thou art reſolute and faithful ;
' I have employment worthy of thy arm.   [*Walks.*

Enter Muley-Zeydan.

   M. Zeyd. You ſee me come impatient of my hopes,
And eager as the courſer for the race.
Is all in readineſs ?
   Bend. All but the Mufti.
   M. Zeyd. We muſt go on without him.
   Bend. True, we muſt ;
For 'tis ill ſtopping in the full career,
Howe'er the leap be dangerous and wide.
   Orc. [*Looking out.*] I ſee the blaze of torches from afar ;
And hear the trampling of thick-beating feet ;
This way they move.
   Bend. No doubt, the Emperor.
We muſt not be ſurpriz'd in conference.
'Truſt to my management the tyrant's death ;
And haſte yourſelf to join with Muſtapha.
' The officer who guards the gate is yours ;
' When you have gain'd that paſs, divide your force ;
' Yourſelf in perſon head one choſen half,
' And march t' oppreſs the faction in conſult
' With dying Dorax : Fate has driven 'em all
' Into the net : you muſt be bold and ſudden :
' Spare none, and if you find him ſtruggling yet
' With pangs of death, truſt not his rowling eyes

' And

' And heavy gafps ; for poifon may be falfe,
' The home thruft of a friendly fword is fure.'
   M. Zeyd. Doubt not my conduct : they fhall be fur-
Mercy may wait without the gate one night,   [priz'd ;
At morn I'll take her in——
   Bend. Here lies your way,
You meet your brother there.
   M. Zeyd. May we ne'er meet :
For like the twins of Leda, when I mount,
He gallops down the fkies——   [*Exit* M. Zeyd.
   Bend. He comes ; now heart
Be ribb'd with iron for this one attempt ;
' Set ope thy fluices, fend thy vigorous blood
' Through every active limb for my relief ;'
Then take thy reft within thy quiet cell,
For thou fhalt drum no more.
          Enter Emperor, *and guards attending him.*
   Emp. What news of our affairs, and what of Dorax ?
Is he no more ? Say that, and make me happy.
   Bend. May all your enemies be like that dog,
Whofe parting foul is labouring at the lips.
   Emp. The people, are they rais'd ?
   Bend. And marfhall'd too ;
Juft ready for the march.
   Emp. Then I'm at eafe.
   Bend. The night is yours, the glittering hoft of Heav'n
Shines but for you ; but moft the ftar of love,
That twinkles you to fair Almeyda's bed.
Oh ! there's a joy, to melt in her embrace,
Diffolve in pleafure,
And make the gods curfe immortality,
That fo they could not die.
But hafte and make 'em yours.
   Emp. I will ; and yet
A kind of weight hangs heavy at my heart ;
My flagging foul flies under her own pitch ;
Like fowl in air too damp, and lugs along,
As if fhe were a body in a body,
And not a mounting fubftance made of fire.
' My fenfes too are dull and ftupify'd,
' Their edge rebated ;' fure fome ill approaches,

G 3   And

And fome kind fpirit knocks foftly at my foul,
To tell me Fate's at hand.
    Bend. Mere fancies all.
' Your foul has been before-hand with your body,
' And drunk fo deep a draught of promis'd blifs,
' She flumbers o'er the cup;' no danger's near,
But of a furfeit at too full a feaft.
    Emp. It may be fo; ' it looks fo like the dream
' That overtook me at my waking hour
' This morn; and dreams they fay are then divine,
' When all the balmy vapours are exhal'd,
' And fome o'erpow'ring god continues fleep.
' 'Twas then methought Almeyda, fmiling, came
' Attended with a train of all her race,
' Whom in the rage of empire I had murder'd.
' But now, no longer foes, they gave me joy
' Of my new conqueft, and with helping hands
' Heav'd me into our holy prophet's arms,
' Who bore me in a purple cloud to Heav'n.
    ' *Bend.* Good omen, Sir; I wifh you in that heav'n
' Your dreams portend you,
' Which prefages death——   [*Afide.*
    ' *Emp.* Thou too wert there;
' And thou methought didft pufh me from below,
' With thy full force to Paradife.
    ' *Bend.* Yet better.
    ' *Emp.* Ha! what's that grizly fellow that attends thee?
    ' *Bend.* Why afk you, Sir?
    ' *Emp.* For he was in my dream;
' And help'd to heave me up.
    ' *Bend.* With prayers and wifhes;
' For I dare fwear him honeft.
    ' *Emp.* That may be;
' But yet he looks damnation.
    ' *Bend.* You forget
The face would pleafe you better: do you love,
And can you thus forbear?'
    Emp. I'll head my people;
Then think of dalliance when the danger's o'er,
' My warlike fpirits work now another way;
' And my foul's tun'd to trumpets.'

                                        Ben.

Bend. You debafe yourfelf,
To think of mixing with th' ignoble herd.
Let fuch perform the fervile work of war,
Such who have no Almeyda to enjoy.
' What, fhall the people know their god-like prince
' Skulk'd in a nightly fkirmifh ? Stole a conqueft,
' Headed a rabble, and profan'd his perfon,
' Shoulder'd with filth, borne in a tide of ordure,
' And ftifled with their rank offenfive fweat ?
  ' *Emp.* I am off again : I will not proftitute
' The regal dignity fo far, to head 'em.'
  Bend. ' There fpoke a king.'
Difmifs your guards to be employ'd elfewhere
In ruder combats : you will want no feconds
' In thofe alarms you feek.' -
  Emp. Go join the crowd.   [*To the Guards.*
Benducar, thou fhalt lead 'em in my place. [*Ex. Guards.*
The god of love once more has fhot his fires
Into my foul ; and my whole heart receives him.
Almeyda now returns with all her charms ;
I feel her as fhe glides along my veins,
And dances in my blood.   So when our prophet
Had long been hamm'ring in his lonely cell,
Some dull, infipid, tedious Paradife,
A brifk Arabian girl came tripping by ;
Paffing, fhe caft at him a fide-long glance,
And look'd behind in hopes to be purfu'd :
He took the hint, embrac'd the flying fair :
And having found his heav'n, he fix'd it there.   [*Exit.*
  Bend. That Paradife thou never fhalt poffes.
His death is eafy now, his guards are gone ;
And I can fin but once to feize the throne.
' All after-acts are fanctify'd by power.
  ' *Orc.* Command my fword and life.
  ' *Bend.* I thank thee, Orchan,
' And fhall reward thy faith : this mafter-key
' Frees every lock, and leads us to his perfon :
' And fhould we mifs our blow, as Heav'n forbid,
' Secures retreat : leave open all behind us ;
' And firft fet wide the Mufti's garden gate,
' Which is his private paffage to the palace :
' For there our mutineers appoint to meet,
                              ' And

ence we may have aid.' Now fleep ye ftars,
....tly o'erwatch the fate of kings;
Be all propitious influences barr'd,
And none but murd'rous planets mount the guard.

[*Exeunt.*

A NIGHT-SCENE *of the* Mufti's *Garden.*

Enter the Mufti *alone, in a Slave's Habit, like that of*
Antonio's.

Muf. This 'tis to have a found head-piece; by this I
have got to be chief of my religion; that is, honeftly
fpeaking, to teach others what I neither know nor believe myfelf. For what's Mahomet to me, but that I
get by him? Now for my policy of this night: I have
mew'd up my fufpected fpoufe in her chamber. No
more embaffies to that lufty young ftallion of a gard'ner.
Next, my habit of a flave; I have made myfelf as like
him as I can, all but his youth and vigour; which when
I had, I pafs'd my time as well as any of my holy pre-
deceffors. Now, walking under the windows of my fe-
raglio -- if Johayma look out, fhe will certainly take me
for Antonio, and call to me; and by that I fhall know
what concupifcence is working in her; fhe cannot come
down to commit iniquity, there's my fafety; but if fhe
peep, if fhe put her nofe abroad, there's demonftration
of her pious will: and I'll not make the firft precedent
for a churchman to forgive injuries.

Enter Morayma *running to him with a cafket in her hand,*
and embracing him.

Mor. Now I can embrace you with a good confcience;
here are the pearls and jewels, here's my father.

Muf. I am indeed thy father; but how th'e devil didft
thou know me in this difguife? And what pearls and
jewels doft thou mean?

Mor. [*Going back.*] What have I done, and what will
now become of me!

Muf. Art thou mad, Morayma?

Mor. I think you'll make me fo.

Muf. Why, what have I done to thee? Recollect thyfelf, and fpeak fenfe to me.

Mor. Then give me leave to tell you, you are the worft
of fathers.

Muf.

Muf. Did I think I had begotten such a monster? Proceed, my dutiful child, proceed, proceed.

Mor. You have been raking together a mass of wealth, by indirect and wicked means : the spoils of orphans are in these jewels, and the tears of widows in these pearls.

Muf. Thou amazest me!

Mor. I would do so. This casket is loaded with your sins; 'tis the cargo of rapines, simony, and exortions; the iniquity of thirty years Muftiship converted into diamonds.

' *Muf.* Would some rich, railing rogue would say as
' much to me, that I might squeeze his purse for scan-
' dal.

' *Mor.* No, Sir; you get more by pious fools than
' railers, when you infinuate into their families, manage
' their fortunes whilst they live, and beggar their heirs
' by getting legacies when they die. And do you think
' I'll be the receiver of your theft? I discharge my
' conscience of it : here, take again your filthy mam-
' mon, and restore it, you had best, to the true owners.

' *Muf.* I am finely documented by my own daughter.

' *Mor.* And a great credit for me to be so. Do but
' think how decent a habit you have on, and how be-
' coming your function to be disguised like a slave, and
' eves-dropping under the women's windows, to be sa-
' luted, as you deserve it richly, with a pifs-pot. If I
' had not known you casually by your shambling gait,
' and a certain reverend aukwardness that is natural to
' all of your function, here you had been exposed to the
' laughter of your own servants ; who have been in
' search of you thro' the whole Seraglio, peeping under
' every petticoat to find you.

' *Muf.* Pr'ythee, child, reproach me no more of hu-
' man failings ; they are but a little of the pitch and
' spots of the world that are still sticking on me ; but I
' hope to scour 'em out in time : I am better at bottom
' than thou thinkest ; I am not the man thou takest me
' for.

' *Mor.* No, to my sorrow, Sir, you are not.

' *Muf.* It was a very odd beginning tho' methought,
' to see thee come running in upon me with such a warm

embrace :

‘ embrace: pr’ythee what was the meaning of that vio-
‘ lent hot hug?

‘ *Mor.* I am fure I meant nothing by it, but the zeal
‘ and affection which I bear to the man of the world
‘ whom I may love lawfully.

‘ *Muf.* But thou wilt not teach me at this age the na-
‘ ture of a clofe embrace?

‘ *Mor.* No indeed: for my mother-in-law complains,
‘ you are paft teaching: but if you miftook my innocent
‘ embrace for fin, I wifh heartily it had been given where
‘ it fhould have been more acceptable.

‘ *Muf.* Why this is as it fhould be now: take the trea-
‘ fure again, it can never be put into better hands.

‘ *Mor.* Yes to my knowledge but it might. I have
‘ confeffed my foul to you, if you can underftand me
‘ rightly; I never difobeyed you till this night; and
‘ now fince thro’ the violence of my paffion, I have been
‘ fo unfortunate, I humbly beg your pardon, your blef-
‘ fing, and your leave, that upon the firft opportunity I
‘ may go for ever from your fight; for Heav’n knows,
‘ I never defire to fee you more.

‘ *Muf.* [*Wiping his eyes.*] Thou makeft me weep at thy
‘ unkindnefs; indeed, dear daughter, we will not part.

‘ *Mor.* Indeed, dear daddy, but we will.’

Muf. Why, if I have been a little pilfering or fo, I
take it bitterly of thee to tell me of it, fince it was to
make thee rich; and I hope a man may make bold with
his own foul, without offence to his own child: here,
take the jewels again, take ’em I charge thee upon thy
obedience.

Mor. Well then, in virtue of obedience I will take
’em; but on my foul, I had rather they were in a better
hand.

Muf. Meaning mine, I know it.

Mor. Meaning his whom I love better than my life.

Muf. That’s me again.

Mor. I would have you think fo.

Muf. How thy good-nature works upon me; ‘ well, I
‘ can do no lefs than venture damning for thee, and I
‘ may put fair for it, if the rabble be ordered to raife to-
‘ night.’

Enter

Enter Antonio *in an African rich habit.*

Ant. What do you mean, my dear, to stand talking in this suspicious place, just underneath Johayma's window? [*To the* Mufti.] You are well met, comrade, I know you are the friend of our flight; are the horses ready at the Postern Gate ;

Muf. Antonio, and in disguise ? Now I begin to smell a rat.

Ant. And I another, that out-stinks it; false Morayma, hast thou thus betrayed me to thy father ?

Mor. Alas ! I was betrayed myself : he came disguised like you, and I, poor innocent, ran into his hands !

Muf. In a good time you did so; ' I laid a trap for a ' bitch-fox, and a worse vermin has caught himself in ' it :' you would fain break loose now, though you left a limb behind you ; but I am yet in my own territories and in call of company, that's my comfort.

Ant. [*Taking him by the throat.*] No ; I have a trick left to put thee past thy squeeking : I have given thee the quinzey ; that ungracious tongue shall preach no more false doctrine.

Mor. What do you mean ? You will not throttle him ? Consider he's my father.

Ant. Pr'ythee let us provide first for our own safety : if I do not consider him, he will consider us with a vengeance afterwards.

' *Mor.* You may threaten him for crying out, but for ' my sake give him back a little cranny of his windpipe, ' and some part of speech.

' *Ant.* Not so much as one single interjection. Come ' away, father-in-law, this is no place for dialogues; ' when you are in the Mosque you talk by hours, and ' there no man must interrupt you ; this is but like for ' like, good father-in-law ; now I am in the pulpit, 'tis ' your turn to hold your tongue.' [*He struggles.*] ' Nay, ' if you will be hanging back, I shall take care you shall ' hang forward.'

[*Pulls him along the stage with his sword at his reins.*

Mor. T'other way to the arbour with him ; and make haste before we are discovered.

' *Ant.* If I only bind and gag him there, he may com- ' mend me hereafter for civil usage ; he deserves not so ' much favour by any action of his life.

' *Mor.*

' *Mor.* Yes, pray bate him one, for begetting your
' miſtreſs.'

· *Ant.* ' I would, if he had not thought more of thy mo-
' ther than of thee : once more' come along in ſilence,
my Pythagorean father-in-law.

Joh. [*At the balcony.*]————A bird in a cage may
peep at leaſt, tho' ſhe muſt not fly. What buſtle's there
beneath my window? Antonio, by all my hopes! I
know him by his habit; but what makes that woman
with him, and a friend, a ſword drawn, and haſtening
hence? This is no time for ſilence : who's within call
there? where are the ſervants? Why, Omar, Abedin,
Haſſan, and the reſt, make haſte and run into the garden;
there are thieves and villains; arm all the family, and
ſtop 'em.

Ant. [*Turning back.*] O that ſcriech owl at the window! we ſhall be purſued immediately; which way ſhall
we take?

Mor. [*Giving him the caſket.*] 'Tis impoſſible to eſcape
them : for the way to our horſes lies back again by the
houſe; and then we ſhall meet 'em full in the teeth.
Here, take theſe jewels; thou mayeſt leap the walls and
get away.

Ant. And what will become of thee then, poor kind
foul?

Mor. I muſt take my fortune. ' When you have got
' fafe into your own country, I hope you will beſtow a
' figh on the memory of her who loved you.

' *Ant.* It makes me mad, to think how many a good
' night will be loſt betwixt us! Take back thy jewels;
' 'tis an empty caſket without thee; beſides, I ſhould
' never leap well with the weight of all thy father's ſins
' about me; thou and they had been a bargain.

' *Mor.* Pr'ythee take 'em, 'twill help me to be re-
' venged on him.

' *Ant.* No; they'll ſerve to make thy peace with
' him.

Mor. I hear 'em coming : ſhift for yourſelf at leaſt;
remember I am yours for ever.

Servants crying, This way, this way, *behind the ſcenes.*

' *Ant.* And but the empty ſhadow of myſelf without
' thee! Farewel, father-in-law, that ſhould have been, '

' if

' if I had not been curfed in my mother's belly—Now,
' which way, Fortune?'——

    [*Runs amazedly backwards and forwards.*
Servants. [*Within.*] Follow, follow! yonder are the
villains.

 Ant. Oh, here's a gate open! but it leads into the
caftle; yet I muft venture it. [*Going out. A fhout behind
the fcenes.*] There's the rabble in a mutiny—What, is
the devil up at midnight?——However, 'tis good herding
in a crowd.   [*Runs out.*

' [*Mufti runs to* Morayma, *and lays hold on her, then
 ' fnatches away the cafket.*

 ' *Muf.* Now, to do things in order, firft I feize upon
' the bag, and then upon the baggage: for thou art but
— my flefh and blood; but thefe are my life and foul.

 ' *Mor.* Then let me follow my flefh and blood, and
' keep to yourfelf your life and foul.

 ' *Muf.* Both or none—Come away to durance.

 ' *Mor.* Well, if it muft be fo, agreed; for I have ano-
' ther trick to play you, and thank yourfelf for what
' fhall follow.

    ' *Enter Servants.*

 ' *Joh.* [*From above.*] One of them took through the
' private way into the caftle. Follow him, be fure: for
' thefe are yours already.

 ' *Mor.* Help here, quickly! Omar, Abedin! I have
' hold on the villain that ftole my jewels; but 'tis a lufty
' rogue, and he will prove too ftrong for me. What,
' help, I fay! Do you not know your mafter's daughter?

 ' *Muf.* Now, if I cry out, they will know my voice,
' and then I am difgraced for ever. Oh, thou art a ve-
' nomous cockatrice!

 ' *Mor.* Of your own begetting. [*The Servants feize him.*

 ' 1 *Serv.* What a glorious deliverance have you had,
' Madam, from this bloody-minded Chriftian!

 ' *Mor.* Give me back my jewels, and carry this noto-
' rious malefactor to be punifh'd by my father. I'll hunt
' the other dry-foot.

 ' [*Takes the jewels, and runs out after* Antonio *at the fame
 ' paffage.*

 ' 1 *Serv.* I long to be handfelling his hide, before we
' bring him to my mafter.

      H   ' 2 *Serv.*

' *2 Serv.* Hang him for an old covetous hypocrite, he
' deserves a worse punishment himself, for keeping us so
' hardly.

' *1 Serv.* Ay, would he were in this villain's place :
' thus would I lay him on, and thus.   [*Beats him.*

' *2 Serv.* And thus would I revenge myself of my last
' beating.   [*He beats him too, and then the rest.*

' *Muf.* Oh, ho, ho !

' *1 Serv.* Now, supposing you were the Mufti, Sir—
'   ' [*Beats him again.*

' *Muf.* The devil's in that supposing rascal : I can
' bear no more ; and I am the Mufti. Now, suppose
' yourselves my servants, and hold your hands : an
' anointed halter take you all.

' *1 Serv.* My master ! You will pardon the excess of
' our zeal for you, Sir : indeed we all took you for a
' villain ; and so we used you.'

Muf. ' Ay, so I feel you did ; my back and sides are
' abundant testimonies of your zeal.' Run, rogues, and
bring me back my jewels, and my fugitive daughter :
run, I say.

' [*They run to the gate, and the first Servant runs back again.*

' *1 Serv.* Sir, the castle is in a most terrible combustion ;
' you may hear them hither.

' *Muf.* 'Tis a laudable commotion : the voice of the
' mobile is the voice of Heaven, I must retire a little,
' to strip me of the slave, and to assume the Mufti ; and
' then I will return : for the piety of the people must
' be encouraged, that they may help me to recover my
' jewels and my daughter. [*Exeunt* Mufti *and Servants.*'

SCENE *changes to the Castle-Yard,*

And discovers Antonio, Muftapha, *and the Rabble shouting.*
           They come forward.

Ant. And so, at length, as I informed you, I escaped
out of his covetrous clutches; and now fly to your illustrious feet for my protection.

Muft. Thou shalt have it : and now defy the Mufti.
'Tis the first petition that has been made to me since my
exaltation to tumult—' In this second night of the month
' Abib, and in the year of the Hegira—the lord knows
' what year : but 'tis no matter ; for when I am settled,

2   ' the

' the learned are always bound to find it out for me ; for
' I am resolved to date my authority over the rabble
' like other monarchs,'

Ant. I have always had a longing to be yours again,
tho' I could not compass it before : and had defigned you
a cafket of my mafter's jewels too ; ' for I knew the cuf-
' tom, and would not have appeared before a great per-
' fon, as you are, without a prefent ;' but he has de-
frauded my good intentions, and bafely robbed you of
them. ' 'Tis a prize worth a million of crowns ; and you
' carry your letters of marque about you.'

Muft. I fhall make bold with his treafure, for the fupport of my new government. [*The people gather about him.*]
' What do thefe vile raggamuffins fo near our perfon ?'
Your favour is offenfive to us—Bear back, there, and
make room for honeft men to approach us. Thefe fools
and knaves are always impudently crowding next to
princes, and keeping off the more deferving—Bear back,
I fay. [*They make a wider circle.*] That's dutifully done.
Now, fhout to fhew your loyalty. [*A great fhout.*] Hear'ft
thou that, flave Antonio ? Thefe obftreperous villains
fhout, and know not for what they make a noife. You
fhall fee me manage them, that you may judge what ignorant beafts they are. For whom do you fhout now ?
Who's to live and reign ? Tell me that, the wifeft of you.

1 Rabble. Even who you pleafe, Captain.

Muft. La you there ! I told you fo.

2 Rabble. We are not bound to know who is to live
and reign ; our bufinefs is only to rife upon command,
and plunder.

3 Rabble. Ay, the richeft of both parties ; for they are
our enemies.

Muft. This laft fellow is a little more fenfible than the
reft ; he has entered fomewhat into the merits of the
caufe.

1 Rabble. If a poor man may fpeak his mind, I think,
Captain, that yourfelf are the fitteft to live and reign, ' I
' mean not over, but next, and immediately under the
' people :' and thereupon I fay, a Muftapha, a Muftapha !

All. A Muftapha, a Muftapha !

Muft. I muft confefs the found is pleafing, and tickles
the ears of my ambition : ' but, alas, good people, it muft

' not be! I am contented to be a poor simple viceroy;
' but Prince Muley-Zeydan is to be the man—I shall
' take care to instruct him in the arts of government, and
' in his duty to us all; and therefore, mark my cry—A
' Muley-Zeydan, a Muley-Zeydan!
  ' *All.* A Muley-Zeydan, a Muley-Zeydan!
  ' *Muft.* You see, slave Antonio, what I might have
' been.
  ' *Ant.* I observe your modesty.
  ' *Muft.* But for a foolish promise I made once to my
' Lord Benducar, to set up any one he pleased.'

    Re-enter the Mufti, *with his Servants.*

Ant. Here's the old hypocrite again. Now, stand your
ground, and bate him not an inch. Remember the jewels,
the rich and glorious jewels; they are designed to be
yours by virtue of prerogative.

Muft. Let me alone to pick a quarrel; I have an old
grudge to him upon thy account.

Muf. [*Making up to the Mobile.*] Good people, here
you are met together.

1 *Rabble.* Ay, we know that without your telling; but
why are we met together, Doctor? For that's it which
nobody here can tell.

2 *Rabble.* Why, to see one another in the dark, and to
make holiday at midnight.

Muf. You are met, as becomes good Muffulmen, to
settle the nation; for I muft tell you, that tho' your tyrant is a lawful emperor, yet your lawful emperor is but a
tyrant.

Ant. What stuff he talks!

Muft. ' This is excellent fine matter, indeed, slave An-
' tonio.' He has a rare tongue. Oh, he would move a
rock or elephant!

Ant. [*Afide.*] What a block have I to work upon!
' But still remember the jewels, Sir, the jewels. [*To him.*

' *Muft.* Nay that's true on the other side; the jewels
' must be mine; but he has a pure fine way of talking;
' my confcience goes along with him; but the jewels
' have set my heart against him.

' *Muf.* That your emperor is a tyrant, is most mani-
' fest; for you were born to be Turks, but he has played
' the Turk with you, and is taking your religion away.

          ' 2 *Rabble.*

' 2 *Rabble.* We find that in our decay of trade : I
' have feen, for thefe hundred years, that religion and
' trade always go together.'

Muf. He is now upon the point of marrying himfelf,
without your fovereign confent; and what are the effects
of marriage?

3 *Rabble.* A fcolding domineering wife, if fhe prove
honeft ; and if a whore, a fine gaudy minx, that robs our
counters every night, and then goes out, and fpends it
upon our cuckold-makers.

' *Muf.* No, the natural effects of marriage are children.
' Now, on whom would he beget thefe children ? Even
' upon a Chriftian ! Oh, horrible ! how can you believe
' me, tho' I am ready to fwear it upon the Alcoran ? Yes,
' true believers, you may believe, that he is going to be-
' get a race of mifbelievers.

' *Muft.* That's fine, in earneft : I cannot forbear hear-
' kening to his enchanting tongue.

' *Ant.* But yet remember——

' *Muft.* Ay, ay, the jewels—Now again I hate him ;
' but yet my confcience makes me liften to him.'

Muf. Therefore, to conclude all, believers, pluck up
your hearts, and pluck down the tyrant. ' Remember
' the courage of your anceftors ; remember the majefty
' of the people ; remember yourfelves, your wives and
' children ; and laftly, above all, remember your religion,
' and our holy Mahomet ; all thefe require your timous
' affiftance ; fhall I fay, they beg it ? No, they claim it
' of you, by all the neareft and deareft ties of thefe three
' P's, felf-prefervation, our property, and our prophet.
' Now, anfwer me with an unanimous, chearful cry, and'
follow me, who am your leader, to a glorious deliverance,
[*All cry,* A Mufti, A Mufti ! *and are following him off
the ftage.*

' *Ant.* Now you fee what comes of your foolifh qualms
' of confcience : the jewels are loft, and they are all
' leaving you.'

Muft. What, am I forfaken of my fubjects? Would
the rogue purloin my liege people from me ? I charge
you, in my own name, come back, ye deferters, and hear
me fpeak.

1 Rabble. What, will he come with his balderdash, after the Mufti's eloquent oration?

2 Rabble. He's our Captain, lawfully picked up, and elected upon a stall; we will hear him.

Omnes. Speak, Captain; for we will hear you.

Muft. Do you remember the glorious rapines and robberies you have committed; your breaking open and gutting of houses, your rummaging of cellars, ‘ your de-‘ molishing of Christian temples, and bearing off in tri-‘ umph the superstitious plate and pictures, the ornaments ‘ of their wicked altars, when all rich moveables were ‘ sentenced for idolatrous, and all that was idolatrous was ‘ seized? Answer first for your remembrance of all these ‘ sweetnesses of mutiny; for upon those grounds I shall ‘ proceed.’

Omnes. Yes, we do remember, we do remember.

Muft. Then make much of your retentive faculties. And who led you to those honey-combs? Your Mufti? No, believers, he only preached you up to it, but durst not lead you; he was but your counsellor, but I was your captain; he only loo'd you, but 'twas I that led you.

Omnes. That's true, that's true.

Ant. There you were with him for his figures.

Muft. I think I was, slave Antonio. Alas, I was ignorant of my own talent!—Say, then, believers, will you have a Captain for your Mufti, or a Mufti for your Captain? And further, to instruct you how to cry, will you have a Mufti, or no Mufti?

Omnes. No, Mufti, no Mufti.

‘ *Muft.* That I laid in for them, slave Antonio—Do I ‘ then spit upon your faces? Do I discourage rebellion, ‘ mutiny, rapine, and plundering? You may think I do, ‘ believers; but, Heaven forbid! No, I encourage you ‘ to all these laudable undertakings; you shall plunder, ‘ you shall pull down the government; but you shall do ‘ this upon my authority, and not by his wicked insti-‘ gation.

‘ *3 Rabble.* Nay, when his turn is served, he may ‘ preach up loyalty again, and restitution, that he might ‘ have another smack among us.

‘ *1 Rabble.* He may, indeed; for 'tis but his saying ‘ 'tis sin, and then we must restore: and therefore I
‘ would

would have a new religion, where half the command-
‘ ments fhould be taken away, the reft mollified, and there
‘ fhould be little or no fin remaining.
‘ *Omnes.* Another religion, a new religion, another
‘ religion.
‘ *Muft.* And that may eafily be done, with the help
‘ of a little infpiration: for I muft tell you I have a
‘ pigeon at home, of Mahomet’s own breed; and when I
‘ have learned her to pick peafe out of my ear, reft fatis-
‘ fied till then, and you fhall have another. But now I
‘ think on’t, I am infpired already, that ’tis no fin to de-
‘ pofe the Mufti.
‘ *Ant.* And good reafon; for when kings and queens
‘ are to be difcarded, what fhould knaves do any longer
‘ in the pack?
‘ *Omnes.* He is depofed, he is depofed, he is depofed!
‘ *Muft.* Nay, if he and his clergy will needs be preach-
‘ ing up rebellion, and giving us their blefling, ’tis but
‘ juftice they fhould have the firft-fruits of it—Slave An-
‘ tonio, take him into cuftody; and, doft thou hear, boy?
‘ be fure to fecure the little tranfitory box of jewels—If
‘ he be obftinate, put a civil queftion to him upon the
‘ rack, and he fqueeks, I warrant him.
‘ *Ant.* [*Seizing the* Mufti.] Come, my quondam ma-
‘ fter; you and I muft change qualities.
‘ *Muf.* I hope you will not be fo barbarous to torture
‘ me; we may preach fuffering to others; but, alas,
‘ holy flefh is too well pampered to endure martyrdom!’
Muft. Now, late Mufti, not forgetting my firft quarrel to you, we will enter ourfelves with the plunder of
your palace. ‘ ’Tis good to fanctify a work, and begin
‘ a God’s name.
‘ 1 *Rabble.* Our prophet let the devil alone with the
‘ laft mob.
‘ *Mob.* But he takes care of this himfelf.’
As they are going out, enter Benducar *leading* Almeyda;
he with a fword in one hand; Benducar’s *flave follows,
with* Muley-Moluch’s *head upon a fpear.*
Muft. ‘ Not fo much hafte, mafters; come back again.
‘ You are fo bent upon mifchief, that you take a man
‘ upon the firft word for plunder.’ Here’s a fight for
you! the Emperor is come upon his head to vifit you.
[Bowing.]

[*Bowing.*] Moſt noble Emperor, now I hope you will
not hit us in the teeth, that we have pulled you down ;
for we can tell you to your face, that we have exalted
you.   [*They all ſhout.*

   Ben. [*To* Almeyda, *apart.*] Think what I am, and
        what yourſelf may be
In being mine : refuſe not proffer'd love
That brings a crown.
   Alm. [*To him.*] I have reſolv'd ;
And theſe ſhall know my thoughts.
   Ben. [*To her.*] On that I build——
                           [*He comes up to the Rabble.*
Joy to the people for the tyrant's death !
' Oppreſſion, rapine, baniſhment, and blood
' Are now no more ; but ſpeechleſs as that tongue,
' That lies for ever ſtill.
' How is my grief divided with my joy,
' When I muſt own I kill'd him ! Bid me ſpeak ;
' For not to bid me, is to diſallow
' What for your ſakes is done.'
   Muſt. In the name of the people, we command you
ſpeak.   But that pretty lady ſhall ſpeak firſt ; for we have
taken ſomewhat of a liking to her perſon.   Be not afraid,
lady, to ſpeak to theſe rude raggamuffins : there's nothing
ſhall offend you, unleſs it be their ſtink, an't pleaſe you.
                                   [*Making a leg.*
   Alm. Why ſhould I fear to ſpeak, who am your queen ?
My peaceful father ſway'd the ſceptre long ;
And you enjoy'd the bleſſings of his reign,
While you deſerv'd the name of Africans.
Then, not commanded, but commanding you,
Fearleſs I ſpeak—Know me for what I am.
   ' *Ben.* How ſhe aſſumes ! I like not this beginning.
                                   ' [*Aſide.*

   ' *Alm.* I was not born ſo baſe to flatter crowds,
' And move your pity by a whining tale.
' Your tyrant would have forc'd me to his bed ;
' But in th' attempt of that foul brutal act,
' Theſe loyal ſlaves ſecur'd me by his death.
                                   ' [*Pointing to* Ben.
   ' *Ben.* Makes ſhe no more of me than of a ſlave ! [*Aſide.*
' Madam, I thought I had inſtructed you·   [*To* Alm.
                                   ' To

‘ To frame a speech more suiting to the times :
‘ The circumstances of that dire design,
‘ Your own despair, my unexpected aid,
‘ My life endanger’d by his bold defence,
‘ And after all, his death, and your deliverance,
‘ Were themes that ought not to be slighted o’er.
   ‘ *Muft.* She might have passed over all your petty
‘ bufineffes, and no great matter—But the raifing of my
‘ rabble is an exploit of confequence, and not to be mum-
‘ bled up in filence, for all her pertnefs.
   ‘ *Alm.* When force invades the gift of nature, life,
‘ The eldeft law of nature, bids defend ;
‘ And if, in that defence, a tyrant fall,
‘ His death’s his crime, not ours.
‘ Suffices that he’s dead ; all wrongs die with him ;
‘ When he can wrong no more, I pardon him :
‘ Thus I abfolve myfelf, and him excufe
‘ Who fav’d my life and honour ; but praife neither.
   ‘ *Ben.* ’Tis cheap to pardon whom you would not pay,
‘ But what fpeak I of payment or reward ?
‘ Ungrateful woman ! you are yet no queen ;
‘ Nor more than a proud, haughty Chriftian flave :
‘ As fuch I feize my right.   [*Going to lay hold of her.*
   ‘ *Alm.* [*Drawing a dagger.*] Dare not to approach me.
‘ Now, Africans,
‘ He fhows himfelf to you ; to me he ftood
‘ Confefs’d before, and own’d his infolence
‘ T’ efpoufe my perfon, and affume the crown,
‘ Claim’d in my right.   For this he flew your tyrant :
‘ Oh, no, he only chang’d him for a worfe ;
‘ Embas’d your flavery by his own vilenefs,
‘ And loaded you with more ignoble bonds.
‘ Then think me not ungrateful, not to fhare
‘ Th’ imperial crown with a prefuming traitor.
‘ He fays I am a Chriftian : true, I am ;
‘ But yet no flave. If Chriftians can be thought
‘ Unfit to govern thofe of other faith,
‘ ’Tis left for you to judge.
   ‘ *Ben.* I have no patience ; fhe confumes the time
‘ In idle talk, and owns her falfe belief.
‘ Seize her by force, and bear her hence unheard.’

                                            Alm.

Alm. [*To the people.*] ' No, let me rather die your facri-
' Than live his triumph.'   [fice,
I throw myfelf into my people's arms :
As you are men, compaffionate my wrongs,
And as good men, protect me.
  ' *Ant.* Something muft be done to fave her.——[*Afide*
' *to* Muft.] This is all addreffed to you, Sir : fhe fingled
' you out with her eye, as commander in chief of the
' mobility.
  ' *Muft.* Think'ft thou fo, flave Antonio ?
  ' *Ant.* Moft certainly, Sir ; and you cannot in honour
' but protect her.   Now, look to your hits, and make
' your fortune.
  ' *Muft.* Methought, indeed, fhe caft a kind leer to-
' wards me.   Our prophet was but juft fuch another
' fcoundrel as I am, till he raifed himfelf to power, and
' confequently to holinefs, by marrying his mafter's
' widow.   I am refolved I'll put forward for myfelf;
' for why fhould I be my Lord Benducar's fool and flave,
' when I may be my own fool, and his mafter ?'
  Ben. Take her into poffeffion, Muftapha.
  Muft. That's better counfel than you meant it.   Yes,
I do take her into poffeffion, and into protection too——
What fay you, mafters, will you ftand by me ?
  Omnes. One and all, one and all !
  ' *Ben.* Haft thou betray'd me, traitor ? Mufti, fpeak,
' And mind them of religion.   [Mufti *fhakes his head.*
  ' *Muft.* Alas, poor gentleman ! he has gotten a cold,
' with a fermon of two hours long, and a prayer of
' four ; and, befides, if he durft fpeak, mankind is grown
' wifer, at this time of day, than to cut one another's
' throats about religion.   Our Mufti's is a green coat, and
' the Chriftian's is a black coat ; and we muft wifely go to-
' gether by the ears, whether green or black fhall fweep
' our fpoils.'   [*Drums within, and fhouts.*
  Ben. Now we fhall fee whofe numbers will prevail :
The conquering troops of Muley-Zeydan come,
To crufh rebellion, and efpoufe my caufe.
  Muft. We will have a fair trial of fkill for it, I can
tell him that.   When we have difpatched with Muley-
Zeydan, your Lordfhip fhall march in equal proportions
                                                          of

of your body, to the four gates of the city, and every tower shall have a quarter of you.

[*Antonio draws them up, and takes* Alm. *by the hand. Shouts again, and drums.*

Enter Dorax *and* Sebaftian, *attended by* African Soldiers *and* Portuguefes. Almeyda *and* Sebaftian *run into each other's Arms, and both fpeak together.*

Seb. and *Alm.* My Sebaftian! My Almeyda?

Alm. Do you then live?

Seb. And live to love thee ever.

Ben. How! Dorax and Sebaftian ftill alive!
The Moors and Chriftians join'd! I thank thee, prophet.

Dor. The citadel is ours; and Muley-Zeydan
Safe under guard, but as becomes a prince.
Lay down your arms: fuch bafe plebeian blood
Would only ftain the brightnefs of my fword,
And blunt it for fome nobler work behind.

Muft. I fuppofe you may put it up without offence to
any man here prefent. For my part, I have been loyal to
my fovereign lady; though that villain, Benducar, and
that hypocrite, the Mufti, would have corrupted me;
but if thofe two 'fcape public juftice, then I, and all my
lateft honeft fubjects here, deferve hanging.

Ben. [*To* Dor.] I'm fure I did my part to poifon thee,
What faint foe'er has fodder'd thee again:
A dofe lefs hot had burft through ribs of iron.

Muf. Not knowing that, I poifon'd him once more,
And drench'd him with a draught fo deadly cold,
That, had'ft not thou prevented, had congeal'd
The channel of his blood, and froze him dry.

Ben. Thou interpofing fool, to mangle mifchief,
And think to mend the perfect work of hell.

Dor. Thus, when heav'n pleafes, double poifons cure.
I will not tax thee of ingratitude
To me thy friend, who haft betray'd thy prince:
Death he deferv'd indeed, but not from thee.
But Fate, it feems, referv'd the worft of men
To end the worft of tyrants.
Go, bear him to his fate,
And fend him to attend his mafter's ghoft.

Let fome fecure my other poifoning friend,
Whofe double dil·gence preferv'd my life.
     ' *Ant.* You are fallen into good hands, father-in-law ;
' your fparkling jewels, and Morayma's eyes may prove
' a better bail than you deferve.
     ' *Muf.* The beft that can come of me, in this condi-
' tion, is to have my life begged firft, and then to be
' begged for a fool afterwards.'
          [*Exit* Antonio *with the* Mufti, *and at the fame time*
               Benducar *is carried off.*
     ' *Dor.* [*To* Muft.] You and your hungry herd depart
' For juftice cannot ftoop fo low, to reach   [untouch'd ;
' The groveling fin of crouds ; but curft be they
' Who truft revenge with fuch mad inftruments,
' Whofe blindfold bufinefs is but to deftroy ;
' And like the fire commiffion'd by the winds,
' Begins on fheds, but rowling in a round,
' On palaces returns.   Away, ye fkum,
' That ftill rife upmoft when the nation boils :
' Ye mongrel work of heav'n, with human fhapes,
' Not to be damn'd or fav'd, but breathe and perifh,
' That have but juft enough of fenfe, to know
' The mafter's voice when rated, to depart.
                    ' [*Exeunt* Muftapha *and rabble.*'
Alm. With gratitude as low, as knees can pay
                         [*Kneeling to him.*
To thofe bleft holy fires, our guardian angels,
Receive thefe thanks ; till altars can be rais'd.
     Dor. Arife, fair excellence, and pay no thanks,
                         [*Raifing her up.*
Till time difcover what I have deferv'd.
     Seb. More than reward can anfwer.
' If Portugal and Spain were join'd to Africa,
' And the main ocean crufted into land,'
If univerfal monarchy were mine,
Here fhould the gift be plac'd.
     Dor. And from fome hands I fhould refufe that gift :
Be not too prodigal of promifes ;
But ftint your bounty to one only grant,
Which I can afk with honour.
     Seb. What I am

Is but thy gift, make what thou canst of me,
Se.ure of no repulfe.

    Dor. [*To* Seb.] Difmifs your train.

[*To* Alm.] You, Madam, pleafe one moment to retire.

[Sebaftian *figns to the* Portguefes *to go off :* Almeyda *bowing to him, goes off alfo : the* Africans *follow her.*

    Dor. [*To the Captain of the Guard.*] With you one word in private.   [*Goes out with the Captain.*

    Seb, [*Solus.*] Referv'd behaviour, open noblenefs,
A long myfterious track of ftern bounty.
But now the hand of Fate is on the curtain,
And draws the fcene to fight.

Re-enter Dorax, *having taken off his turbant, and put on a peruke, hat, and cravat.*

    Dor. Now do you know me ?

    Seb. Thou fhould'ft be Alonzo.

    Dor. So you fhould be Sebaftian :
But when Sebaftian ceas'd to be himfelf,
I ceas'd to be Alonzo.

    Seb. As in a dream
I fee thee here, and fcarce believe mine eyes.

    Dor. Is it fo ftrange to find me where my wrongs,
And your inhuman tyranny have fent me ?
' Think not you dream : or, if you did, my injuries
' Shall call fo loud, that lethargy fhould wake ;
' And death fhould give you back to anfwer me.
' A thoufand nights have brufh'd their balmy wings
' Over thefe eyes, but ever when they clos'd,
' Your tyrant image forc'd them ope again,
' And dry'd the dews they brought.
' The long-expected hour is come at length,
' By manly vengeance to redeem my fame :
' And that once clear'd, eternal fleep is welcome.

    ' *Seb.* I have not yet forgot I am a king;
' Whofe royal office is redrefs of wrongs :
' If I have wrong'd thee, charge me face to face ;
' I have not yet forgot I am a foldier.

    ' *Dor.* 'Tis the firft juftice thou haft ever done me ;
' Then though I loath this woman's war of tongues,'
Yet fhall my caufe of vengeance firft be clear ;
And, Honour, be thou judge.

    Seb. ' Honour befriend us both.'

I

Beware,

Beware, I warn thee yet, to tell thy griefs
In terms becoming majesty to hear:
‘ I warn thee thus, becaufe I know thy temper
‘ Is infolent and haughty to fuperiors:
‘ How often haft thou brav’d my peaceful court,
‘ Fill’d it with noify brawls, and windy boafts;
‘ And, with paft fervice, naufeoufly repeated,
‘ Reproach’d ev’n me thy prince ?’
　　Dor. ‘ And well I might, when you forgot reward,
‘ The part of heav’n in kings: for punifhment
‘ Is hangman’s work, and drudgery for devils.’
I muft, and will reproach thee with my fervice,
Tyrant (it irks me fo to call my prince)
But juft refentment and hard ufage coin’d
Th’ unwilling word; and grating as it is,
Take it, for ’tis thy due.
　　Seb. How, tyrant!
　　Dor. Tyrant.
　　Seb. Traitor; that name thou can’ft not echo back:
That robe of infamy, that circumcifion
Ill hid beneath that robe, proclaim the traitor:
And, if a name
More foul than traitor be, ’tis renegade.
　　Dor. If I’m a traitor, think, and blufh, thou tyrant,
Whofe injuries betray’d me into treafon,
Effac’d my loyalty, unhing’d my faith,
And hurry’d me from hopes of heaven to hell,
‘ All thefe, and all my yet unfinifh’d crimes,
‘ When I fhall rife to plead before the faints,
‘ I charge on thee, to make thy damning fure.’
　　Seb. Thy old prefumptuous arrogance again,
That bred my firft diflike, and then my loathing.
Once more be warn’d, and know me for thy king.
　　Dor. Too well I know thee, but for king no more:
This is not Lifbon, nor the circle this,
Where, like a ftatue, thou haft ftood befieg’d
By fycophants, and fools, the growth of courts;
Where thy gull’d eyes, in all the gaudy round,
Met nothing but a lie in every face;
‘ And the grofs flattery of a gaping croud,
‘ Envious who firft fhould catch, and firft applaud
‘ The ftuff or royal nonfenfe: when I fpoke,’

My

My honeſt homely words were carp'd, and cenſur'd,
For want of courtly ſtile: related actions,
Though modeſtly reported, paſs'd for boaſts:
Secure of merit, if I aſk'd reward,
Thy hungry minions thought their rights invaded,
' And the bread ſnatch'd from pimps and paraſites.'
Henriquez anſwer'd, with a ready lie,
To ſave his king's, the boon was begg'd before.

  Seb. ' What ſay'ſt thou of Henriquez ?' Now by heav'n,
Thou mov'ſt me more by barely naming him,
Than all thy foul unmanner'd ſcurril taunts.

  Dor. And therefore 'twas to gaul thee, that I nam'd
That thing, that nothing, but a cringe and ſmile; [him,
That woman, but more daub'd; or, if a man,
Corrupted to a woman; thy man miſtreſs.

  Seb. All falſe as hell or thou.

  Dor. Yes; full as falſe
As that I ſerv'd thee fifteen hard campaigns,
And pitch'd thy ſtandard in theſe foreign fields:
By me thy greatneſs grew, thy years grew with it,
But thy ingratitude outgrew them both.

  Seb. I ſee to what thou tend'ſt, but tell me firſt,
If thoſe great acts were done alone for me;
If love produc'd not ſome, and pride the reſt ?

  Dor. Why, love does all that's noble here below:
But all th' advantage of that love was thine:
For, coming fraughted back, in either hand
With palm and olive, victory and peace,
I was indeed prepar'd to aſk my own,
(For Violante's vows were mine before:)
Thy malice had prevention, ere I ſpoke;
And aſk'd me Violante for Henriquez.

  ' *Seb.* I meant thee a reward of greater worth.

  ' *Dor.* Where juſtice wanted, could reward be hop'd ?
' Could the robb'd paſſenger expect a bounty
' From thoſe rapacious hands who ſtripp'd him firſt ?
  ' *Seb.* He had my promiſe, ere I knew thy love.
  ' *Dor.* My ſervices deſerv'd thou ſhould'ſt revoke it.'

  Seb. Thy inſolence had cancell'd all thy ſervice;
To violate my laws, even in my court,
Sacred to peace, and ſafe from all affronts;
Ev'n to my face, and done in my deſpight,

L 2   Under

Under the wing of awful majefty
To ftrike the man I lov'd!
    Dor. Ev'n in the face of heav'n, a place more facred,
Would I have ftruck the man, who, prompt by power,
Would feize my right, and rob me of my love:
But, for a blow provoked by thy injuftice,
The hafty product of a juft defpair,
When he refus'd to meet me in the field,
That thou fhould'ft make a coward's caufe thy own?
    Seb. He durft: nay, more, defir'd and begg'd with tears,
To meet thy challenge fairly: 'twas thy fault
To make it public; but my duty, then
To interpofe, on pain of my difpleafure,
Betwixt your fwords.
    Dor. On pain of infamy
He fhould have difobey'd.
    Seb. Th' indignity thou didft was meant to me:
' Thy gloomy eyes were caft on me with fcorn,
' As who fhould fay, the blow was there intended;'
But that thou did'ft not dare to lift thy hands
Againft anointed power:——fo was I forc'd
To do a fovereign juftice to myfelf,
And fpurn thee from my prefence.
    Dor. Thou haft dar'd
To tell me, what I durft not tell myfelf:
I durft not think that I was fpurn'd, and live;
' And live to hear it boafted to my face.
' All my long avarice of honour loft,
' Heap'd up in youth, and hoarded up for age;
' Has honour's fountain then fuck'd back the ftream?
' He has; and hooting boys may dry-fhod pafs,
' And gather pebbles from the naked ford.'
Give me my love, my honour; give them back——
Give me revenge, while I have breath to afk it——
    Seb. Now by this honour'd order which I wear,
More gladly would I give, than thou dar'ft afk it——
' Nor fhall the facred character of king
' Be urg'd to fhield me from thy bold appeal.
' If I have injur'd thee, that makes us equal:
' The wrong, if done, debas'd me down to thee.'
But thou haft charg'd me with ingratitude;
Haft thou not charg'd me? Speak.

Dor.

Dor. Thou know'ſt I have :
If thou diſown'ſt that imputation, draw,
And prove my charge a lie.

Seb. No ; to diſprove that lie I muſt not draw :
Be conſcious to thy worth, and tell thy ſoul
What thou haſt done this day in my defence :
To fight thee, after this, what were it elſe
Than owning that ingratitude thou urgeſt ?
That Iſthmus ſtands between two ruſhing ſeas ;
Which mounting, view each other from afar :
And ſtrive in vain to meet.

Dor. I'll cut that Iſthmus,
Thou know'ſt I meant not to preſerve thy life,
But to reprieve it, for my own revenge.
' I ſav'd thee out of honourable malice :'
Now draw ; I ſhould be loth to think thou dar'ſt not :
Beware of ſuch another vile excuſe.

Seb. Oh, patience, heav'n ?

Dor. Beware of patience too ;
That's a ſuſpicious word : ' it had been proper,
' Before thy foot had ſpurn'd me ; now 'tis baſe :
' Yet to diſarm thee of thy laſt defence,'
I have thy oath for my ſecurity :
The only boon I begg'd was this fair combat :
Fight or be perjur'd now ; that's all thy choice.

Seb. Now can I thank thee as thou would'ſt be thank'd :
[*Drawing.*

Never was vow of honour better paid,
If my true ſword but hold, than this ſhall be.
' The ſprightly bridegroom on his wedding night,
' More gladly enters not the liſts of love.
' Why 'tis enjoyment to be ſummon'd thus.'
Go ; bear my meſſage to Henriquez' ghoſt ;
And ſay his maſter and his friend reveng'd him.

Dor. His ghoſt ! then is my hated rival dead ?

Seb. The queſtion is beſide our preſent purpoſe ;
Thou ſeeſt me ready ; we delay too long.

Dor. A minute is not much in either's life,
When there's but one betwixt us ; ' throw it in,
' And give it him of us who is to fall.

' *Seb.* He's dead : make haſte, and thou may'ſt yet
o'ertake him.

I 3

' *Dor.*

' *Dor.* When I was hasty, thou delay'd'st me longer.
' I pr'ythee let me hedge one moment more
' Into thy promise :' for thy life preserv'd,
Be kind ; and tell me how that rival dy'd,
Whose death next thine I wish'd.

  Seb. ' If it would please thee, thou should'st never
' But thou, like jealousy, enquir'st a truth,   [know :
' Which found will torture thee : he dy'd in fight :
Fought next my person ; as in consort fought :
Kept pace for pace, and blow for every blow ;
Save when he heav'd his shield in my defence ;
And on his naked side receiv'd my wound :
Then when he could no more, he fell at once,
But rowl'd his falling body cross their way ;
And made a bulwark of it for his prince.

  Dor. I never can forgive him such a death !

  Seb. I prophesy'd thy proud soul could not bear it.
Now judge thyself, who best deserv'd my love.
I knew you both ; and (durst I say) as heav'n
Foreknew among the shining angel host
Who should stand firm, who fall.

  Dor. Had he been tempted so, so had he fall'n ;
And so, had I been favour'd, had I stood.

  ' *Seb.* What had been, is unknown ; what is, appears ;
' Confess he justly was preferr'd to thee.

  ' *Dor.* Had I been born with his indulgent stars,
' My fortune had been his, and his been mine,'
Oh, worse than hell ! what glory have I lost,
And what has he acquir'd by such a death !
I should have fallen by Sebastian's side,
My corps had been the bulwark of my king,
His glorious end was a patch'd work of Fate,
Ill sorted with a soft effeminate life :
It suited better with my life than his
So to have dy'd : mine had been of a piece,
Spent in your service dying at your feet.

  Seb. The more effeminate and soft his life,
The more his fame, to struggle to the field,
And meet his glorious fate : confess, proud spirit,
(For I will have it from thy very mouth)
That better he deserv'd my love than thou.

  Dor. Oh, whither would you drive me ! I must grant,

Yes, I muſt grant, but with a ſwelling ſoul,
Henriquez had your love with more deſert :
For you he fought and dy'd ; I fought againſt you;
Through all the mazes of the bloody field,
Hunted your ſacred life ; which that I miſs'd
Was the propitious error of my fate,
Not of my ſoul ; my ſoul's a regicide.
   Seb. Thou might'ſt have given it a more gentle name :
Thou meant'ſt to kill a tyrant, not a king.   [*More calmly.*
Speak, did'ſt thou not, Alonzo ?
   Dor. Can I ſpeak !
Alas, I cannot anſwer to Alonzo :
No, Dorax cannot anſwer to Alonzo :
Alonzo was too kind a name for me.
‘ Then, when I fought and conquer'd with your arms,
‘ In that bleſt age I was the man you nam'd :
‘ Till rage and pride debas'd me into Dorax ;
‘ And loſt, like Lucifer, my name above.'
   Seb. Yet twice this day I ow'd my life to Dorax.
   Dor. I ſav'd you but to kill you : there's my grief.
   Seb. Nay, if thou canſt be griev'd, thou canſt repent :
Thou couldſt not be a villain, though thou wouldſt :
Thou own'ſt too much in owning thou haſt err'd ;
And I too little, who provok'd thy crime.
   Dor. Oh, ſtop this headlong torrent of your goodneſs :
It comes too faſt upon a feeble ſoul,
Half drown'd in tears before ; ſpare my confuſion :
For pity ſpare, and ſay not, firſt you err'd.
For yet I have not dar'd, through guilt and ſhame,
To throw myſelf beneath your royal feet.
                                          [*Falls at his feet.*
Now ſpurn this rebel, this proud renegade :
'Tis juſt you ſhould, nor will I more complain.
   Seb. Indeed thou ſhouldſt not aſk forgiveneſs firſt,
But thou prevent'ſt me ſtill, in all that's noble.
                                          [*Taking him up.*
Yes, I will raiſe thee up with better news :
Thy Violante's heart was ever thine ;
Compell'd to wed, becauſe ſhe was my ward,
Her ſoul was abſent when ſhe gave her hand :
Nor could my threats, or his purſuing courtſhip,
Effect the conſummation of his love ;

                                          So,

So, ſtill indulging tears, ſhe pines for thee,
A widow and a maid.
　　Dor. Have I been curſing Heav'n, while Heaven bleſt
‘ I ſhall run mad with extaſy of joy :’　　　　　　me !
What, in one moment, to be reconcil'd
To Heav'n, and to my king, and to my love !
But pity is my friend, and ſtops me ſhort,
For my unhappy rival. Poor Henriquez !
　　Seb. Art thou ſo generous too, to pity him ?
Nay, then I was unjuſt to love him better.
Here let me ever hold thee in my arms ; [*Embracing him.*
And all our quarrels be but ſuch as theſe,
Who ſhall love beſt, and cloſeſt ſhall embrace :
Be what Henriquez was : be my Alonzo.
　　Dor. What, my Alonzo, ſaid you ? My Alonzo !
Let my tears thank you ; for I cannot ſpeak ;
‘ And if I could,
‘ Words were not made to vent ſuch thoughts as mine.’
　　Seb. ‘ Thou can'ſt not ſpeak, and I can ne'er be ſilent.’
Some ſtrange reverſe of Fate muſt ſure attend
This vaſt profuſion, this extravagance
Of Heav'n to bleſs me thus.　’Tis gold ſo pure,
It cannot bear the ſtamp, without allay.
Be kind, ye pow'rs, and take but half away ：
With eaſe the gifts of fortune I reſign ;
But, let my love, and friend, be ever mine.　　[*Exeunt.*

END of the FOURTH ACT.

A C T　V.

‘ *The* SCENE *is a Room of State.*

‘ *Enter* Dorax *and* Antonio.

‘ DORAX.

‘　JOY is on every face, without a cloud ：
‘　　As, in the ſcene of opening Paradiſe,
‘ The whole creation danc'd at their new being ;
‘ Pleas'd to be what they were ; pleas'd with each other.
‘ Such joy have I, both in myſelf, and friends ;
‘ And double joy that I have made them happy.
　　　　　　　　　　　　　　　　　‘ *Ant.*

' *Ant.* Pleasure has been the business of my life;
' And every change of fortune easy to me,
' Because I still was easy to myself.
' The loss of her I lov'd wou'd touch me nearest;
' Yet, if I found her, I might love too much,
' And that's uneasy pleasure.
    ' *Dor.* If she be fated
' To be your wife, your fate will find her for you:
' Predestinated ills are never lost.
    ' *Ant.* I had forgot
' T' enquire before, but long to be inform'd;
' How, poison'd and betray'd, and round beset,
' You could unwind yourself from all these dangers;
' And move so speedily to our relief!
    ' *Dor.* The double poisons, after a short combat,
' Expell'd each other in their civil war,
' By nature's benefit; and rous'd my though
' To guard that life which now I found attack'd.
' I summon'd all my officers in haste,
' On whose experienc'd faith I might rely:
' All came resolv'd to die in my defence,
' Save that one villain who betray'd the gate.
' Our diligence prevented the surprize
' We justly fear'd: So Muley-Zeydan found us
' Drawn up in battle, to receive the charge,
    ' *Ant.* But how the Moors and Christian slaves were
' You have not yet unfolded.   [join'd,
    ' *Dor.* That remains.
' We knew their interest was the same with ours:
' And though I hated more than death, Sebastian;
' I could not see him die by vulgar hands;
' But prompted by my angel, or by his,
' Freed all the slaves, and plac'd him next myself,
' Because I would not have his person known.
' I need not tell the rest, th' event declares it.
    ' *Ant.* Your conquests came of course; their men
                    were raw,
' And yours were disciplin'd: one doubt remains,
' Why you industriously conceal'd the king,
' Who, known, had added courage to his men?
    ' *Dor.* I would not hazard civil broils betwixt
' His friends and mine; which might prevent our combat.
' Yet, had he fall'n, I had dismiss'd his troops;
                                        ' Or,

‘ Or, if victorious, order'd his escape.
‘ But I forgot a new increase of Joy,
‘ To feast him with surprize ; I must about it :
‘ Expect my swift return.   . [*Exit* Dorax.’

Enter a Servant to Antonio.

Ser. Here's a lady at the door, that bids me tell you, she is come to make an end of the game, that was broken off betwixt you.

Ant. What manner of woman is she ? Does she not want two of the four elements ? Has she any thing about her but air and fire ?

‘ *Ser.* Truly, she flies about the room, as if she had
‘ wings instead of legs ; I believe she's just turning into
‘ a bird : a house-bird, I warrant her : and so hasty to fly
‘ to you, that rather than fail of entrance, she would
‘ come tumbling down the chimney, like a swallow.’

Enter Morayma.

Ant. [*Running to her, and embracing her.*] Look if she be not here already ! What, no denial, it seems, will serve your turn ? Why, thou little dun, is thy debt so pressing ?

Mor. Little devil, if you please, your lease is out, good Mr. Conjurer ; and I am come to fetch your soul and body ; not an hour of leudness longer in this world for you.

Ant. Where the devil hast thou been ? and how the devil didst thou find me here ?

Mor. I followed you into the castle-yard : but there was nothing but tumult and confusion ; and I was bodily afraid of being picked up by some of the rabble : considering I had a double charge about me——my jewels, and my maiden-head.

‘ *Ant.* Both of them intended for my worship's sole
‘ use and property.

‘ *Mor.* And what was poor little I among them all ?

‘ *Ant.* Not a mouthful a-piece : 'twas too much odds
‘ in conscience.

‘ *Mor.* So seeking for shelter, I naturally ran to the
‘ old place of assignation, the garden-house ; where, for
‘ want of instinct, you did not follow me.’

Ant. Well, for thy comfort, I have secured thy father ; and, I hope, thou hast secured his effects for us.

‘ *Mor.*

' *Mor.* Yes, truly, I had the prudent forefight to con-
' fider, that when we grow old, and weary of folacing one
' another, we might have, at leaft, wherewithal to make
' merry with the world; and take up with a worfe plea-
' fure of eating and drinking, when we were difabled
' for a better.

' *Ant.* Thy fortune will be even too good for thee:
' for thou art going into the country of ferenades and
' gallantries; where thy ftreet will be haunted every
' night with thy foolifh lovers, and my rivals; who
' will be fighing, and finging under thy inexorable win-
' dows, lamentable ditties, and call thee cruel, and god-
' defs, and moon, and ftars, and all the poetical names
' of wicked rhyme. While thou and I are minding our
' bufinefs, and jogging on, and laughing at them, at lei-
' fure minutes; which will be very few, take that by
' way of threatening.

' *Mor.* I am afraid you are not very valiant, that you
' huff fo much beforehand. But they fay, your churches
' are fine places for love-devotion; many a fhe faint is
' there worfhipped.

' *Ant.* Temples are there as they are in all other coun-
' tries, good conveniences for dumb interviews: I hear
' the Proteftants are not much reformed in that point nei-
' ther; for their fectaries call their churches by the na-
' tural name of meeting-houfes. Therefore I warn thee
' in good time, not more of devotion than needs muft,
' good future fpoufe; and always in a veil; for thofe
' eyes of thine are damned enemies to mortificat on.'

Mor. The beft thing I have heard of Chriftendom, is,
that we women are allowed the privilege of having fouls;
and I affure you, I fhall make bold to beftow mine upon
fome lover, whenever you begin to go aftray; ' and if
' I find no convenience in a church, a private chamber
' will ferve the turn.'

Ant. When that day comes, I muft take my revenge,
and turn gardener again: for, I find, I am much given
to planting.

Mor. But take heed in the mean time, that fome young
Antonio does not fpring up in your own family; as falfe
as his father, though of another man's planting.

Re-

Re-enter Dorax *with* Sebaſtian *and* Almeyda. Sebaſtian
enters ſpeaking to Dorax, *while in the mean time* Antonio *preſents* Moraynia *to* Almeyda.

Seb. How fares our royal priſ'ner, Muley-Zeydan?

Dor. Diſpos'd to grant whatever I deſire,
To gain a crown, and freedom : ' well I know him,
' Of eaſy temper, naturally good,
' And faithful to his word.'

Seb. Yet one thing wants,
To fill the meaſure of my happineſs ;
I'm ſtill in pain for poor Alvarez' life.

Dor. Releaſe that fear, the good old man is ſafe ;
I paid his ranſom ;
And have already order'd his attendance.

Seb. Oh, bid him enter, for I long to ſee him.

Enter Alvarez *with a Servant, who departs when* Alvarez
is entered.

Alv. Now by my ſoul, and by theſe hoary hairs,
　　　[*Falling down, and embracing the* King's knees.
I'm ſo o'er-whelm'd with pleaſure, that I feel
A latter ſpring within my with'ring limbs,
That ſhoots me out again.

Seb. Thou good old man ! 　　　　　　[*Raiſing him.*
Thou haſt deceiv'd me into more, more joys;
Who ſtood brim-full before.

' *Alv.* Oh, my dear child !
' I love thee ſo, I cannot call thee king,
' Whom I ſo oft have dandled in theſe arms !
' What, when I gave thee loſt, to find thee living !
' 'Tis like a father who himſelf had ſcap'd
' A falling houſe, and after anxious ſearch,
' Hears from afar, his only ſon within ;
' And digs through rubbiſh, till he drags him out.
' To ſee the friendly light.
' Such is my haſte, ſo trembling is my joy,
' To draw thee forth from underneath thy fate.'

Seb. The tempeſt is o'er-blown ; the ſkies are clear,
And the ſea charm'd into a calm ſo ſtill,
That not a wrinkle ruffles her ſmooth face.

Alv. Juſt ſuch ſhe ſhows before a riſing ſtorm :
And therefore am I come with timely ſpeed,
To warn you into port.

　　　　　　　　　　　　　　　　　　　Ant.

Alm. My foul forbodes   [*Afide.*
Some dire event involv'd in thofe dark words;
And juft difclofing in a birth of fate.
  Alv. Is there not yet an heir of this vaft empire,
Who ftill furvives, of Muley-Moluch's branch?
  Dor. Yes, fuch a one there is, a captive here,
And brother to the dead.
  Alv. The Pow'rs above
Be prais'd for that: my prayers for my good mafter
I hope are heard.
  Seb. ' Thou haft a right in heav'n;'
And why thefe prayers for me?
  Alv. A door is open yet for your deliverance.
Now you, my countrymen, and you, Almeyda,
Now all of us, and you (my all in one)
May yet be happy in that captive's life.
  Seb. We have him here an honourable hoftage
For terms of peace: what more he can contribute
To make me bleft, I know not.
  Alv. Vaftly more:
Almeyda may be fettled in the throne;
And you revew your native clime with fame:
A firm alliance, and eternal peace,
(The glorious crown of honourable war)
Are all included in that prince's life:
Let this fair queen be given to Muley-Zeydan:
And make her love the fanction of your league.
  Seb. No more of that; his life's in my difpofe;
And pris'ners are not to infift on terms,
Or if they were, yet he demands not thefe.
  Alv. You fhould exact them.
  Alm. Better may be made;
Thefe cannot; I abhor the tyrant's race;
My parents' murderers, my throne's ufurpers.
But, at one blow, to cut off all difpute,
Know this, thou bufy, old, officious man,
I am a Chriftian. Now be wife no more;
Or if thou wouldft be ftill thought wife, be filent.
  Alv. Oh, I perceive you think your int'reft touch'd:
'Tis what before the battle I obferv'd:
But I muft fpeak, and will.
                    K   *Seb.*

Seb. I pr'ythee peace:
Perhaps she thinks they are too near of blood.
   Alv. I wish she may not wed to blood more near.
   Seb. What if I make her mine?
   Alv. Now Heav'n forbid!
   ' *Seb.* Wish rather Heav'n may grant.
' For, if I could deserve, I have deserv'd her:
' My toils, my hazards, and my subjects lives,
' (Provided she consent) may claim her love;
' And, that once granted, I appeal to these,
' If better I could chuse a beauteous bride.
   ' *Ant.* The fairest of her sex.
   ' *Mor.* The pride of nature.
   ' *Dor.* He only merits her; she only him.
' So pair'd, so suited in their minds and persons,
' That they were fram'd the tallies for each other.
' If any alien love had interpos'd,'
It must have been an eye-sore to beholders,
And to themselves a curse.
   Alv. And to themselves
The greatest curse that can be, were to join.
   Seb. Did not I love thee, past a change to hate,
That word had been thy ruin; but no more,
I charge thee, on thy life, perverse old man.
   Alv. Know, Sir, I would be silent if I durst:
But, if on shipboard, I should see my friend
Grown frantic in a raging calenture,
And he, imagining vain flow'ry fields,
Would headlong plunge himself into the deep;
Should I not hold him from that mad attempt,
Till his sick fancy were by reason cur'd?
   Seb. I pardon thee th' effects of doting age;
Vain doubts, and idle cares, and over-caution;
The second non-age of a soul, more wise;
But now decay'd, and sunk into the socket,
Peeping by fits, and giving feeble light.
   Alv. Have you forgot?
   Seb. Thou mean'st my father's will,
In bar of marriage to Almeyda's bed:
' Thou seest my faculties are still entire,
' Though thine are much impair'd. I weigh'd that will,
' And found 'twas grounded on our diff'rent faiths;
                                          ' But,

‘ But, had he liv’d to fee her happy change,
‘ He would have cancell’d that harſh interdict,
‘ And join’d our hands himſelf.
‘ *Alv.* Still had he liv’d and feen this change,
‘ He ſtill had been the fame.
‘ *Seb.* I have a dark remembrance of my father ;
‘ His reas’nings and his actions both were juſt ;
‘ And, granting that, he muſt have chang’d his meaſures.
‘ *Alv.* Yes, he was juſt, and therefore could not change.
‘ *Seb.* ’Tis a bafe wrong thou offer’ſt to the dead.
‘ *Alv.* Now Heav’n forbid,
‘ That I ſhould blaſt his pious memory :
‘ No, I am tender of his holy fame :
‘ For dying he bequeath’d it to my charge.
‘ Believe, I am ; and feek to know no more,
‘ But pay a blind obedience to his will.
‘ For to preferve his fame I would be filent.
‘ *Seb.* Craz’d fool, who would’ſt be though an oracle,
‘ Come down from off the tripos, and ſpeak plain :
‘ My father ſhall be juſtify’d, he ſhall :
‘ ’Tis a fon’s part to rife in his defence ;
‘ And to confound thy malice, or thy dotage.’
Alv. ‘ It does not grieve me that you hold me craz’d :
‘ But, to be clear’d at my dead maſter’s coſt,
‘ Oh, there’s the wound ! but let me firſt adjure you,’
I do ; and
By all you owe that dear departed foul,
No more to think of marriage with Almeyda.
Seb. Not heav’n and earth combin’d can hinder it.
Alv. Then witnefs heav’n and earth, how loth I am
To fay, you muſt not, nay you cannot wed.
And fince not only a dead father’s fame,
But more, a lady’s honour muſt be touch’d,
Which nice as ermines will not bear a foil ;
Let all retire ; that you alone may hear
What ev’n in whiſpers I would tell you ear.
                       [*All are going out.*
Alm. Not one of you depart ; I charge you ſtay.
‘ And were my voice a trumpet loud as fame,
‘ To reach the round of heav’n, and earth, and fea,
‘ All nations ſhould be fummon’d to this place.
K 2

                                             ‘ So

‘ So little do I fear that fellow's charge :
‘ So fhould my honour, like a rifing fwan,
‘ Brufh with her wings the falling drops away,
‘ And proudly plough the waves.
    ‘ *Seb.* This noble pride becomes thy innocence:
‘ And I dare truft my father's memory,
‘ To ftand the charge of that foul forging tongue.’
    Alv. ‘ It will foon be difcover'd if I forge.’
Have you not heard your father in his youth,
When newly marry’d, travell'd into Spain,
And made a long abode in Philip's court?
    Seb. Why fo remote a queftion ? ‘ which thyfelf
‘ Can anfwer to thyfelf, for thou wert with him,
‘ His fav’rite, as I oft have heard thee boaft,
‘ And neareft to his foul.
    Alv. ‘ Too near indeed ; forgive me, gracious Heav'n,
‘ That ever I fhould boaft I was fo near :
‘ The confident of all his young amours.’
And have not you, unhappy beauty, heard,   [*To* Alm
Have you not often heard, your exil'd parents
Were refug’d in that court, and at that time ?
    Alm. ’Tis true : and often fince, my mother own'd
How kind that prince was, to efpoufe her caufe ;
She counfell'd, nay, enjoin’d me on her blefling,
To feek the fanctuary of your court :
Which gave me firft encouragement to come,
And with my brother, beg Sebaftian's aid.
    Seb. Thou help’ft me well, to juftify my war.
‘ [*To* Alm] My dying father fwore me, then a boy,
‘ And made me kifs the crofs upon his fword,
‘ Never to fheath it, till that exil'd queen
‘ Were by my arms reftor'd.’
    Alv. And can you find
No myft’ry couch'd in this excefs of kindnefs ?
‘ Were kings e'er known, in this degenerate age,
‘ So paffionately fond of noble acts,
‘ Where intereft fhar'd not more than half with honour ?
    ‘ *Seb.* Bafe groveling foul, who know’ft not honour's
‘ But weigh’ft it out in mercenary fcales ;   [worth,
‘ The fecret pleafure of a generous act,
‘ Is the great mind's great bribe.
                          ‘ *Alv.*

' *Alv.* Shew me that king, and I'll believe the phœnix.
' But knock at your own breaſt, and aſk your ſoul,
' If thoſe fair fatal eyes edg'd not your ſword,
' More than your father's charge, and all your vows ?
' If ſo, and ſo your ſilence grants it is,
' Know, King, your father had, like you, a ſoul ;
' And love is your inheritance from him.
' Almeyda's mother too had eyes, like her,
' And not leſs charming ; and were charm'd no leſs
' Than yours are now with her, and hers with you.
 ' *Alm.* Thou ly'ſt, impoſtor ; perjur'd fiend, thou ly'ſt.
 ' *Seb.* Was't not enough to brand my father's fame,
' But thou muſt load a lady's memory ?
' O infamous, O baſe, beyond repair !
' And to what end this ill-concerted lie,
' Which palpable and groſs, yet granted true,
' It bars not my inviolable vows ?'
 Alv. Take heed, and double not your father's crimes ;
To his adult'ry do not add your inceſt.
Know, ſhe's the product of unlawful love,
And 'tis your carnal ſiſter you would wed.
 Seb. Thou ſhalt not ſay thou wert condemn'd unheard ;
Elſe, by my ſoul, this moment were thy laſt.
 ' *Alm.* But think not oaths ſhall juſtify thy charge ;
' Nor imprecations on thy curſed head.
' For who dares lie to Heav'n, thinks Heaven a jeſt.
' Thou haſt confeſs'd thyſelf the conſcious pandar
' Of that pretended paſſion ;
' A ſingle witneſs, infamouſly known,
' Againſt two perſons of unqueſtion'd fame.'
 Alv. What intereſt can I have, or what delight
To blaze their ſhame, or to divulge my own ?
' If prov'd, you hate me ; if unprov'd condemn.
' Not racks or tortures could have forc'd this ſecret,
' But too much care to ſave you from a crime,
' Which would have ſunk you both ? for let me ſay,
Almeyda's beauty well deſerves your love.
 Alm. Out, baſe impoſtor ! I abhor thy praiſe.
 Dor. It looks not like impoſtor ; but a truth,
On utmoſt need reveal'd.
 Seb. Did I expect from Dorax this return ?
Is this the love renew'd ?

K 3

Dor.

Dor. Sir, I am silent ;
Pray Heaven my fears prove false.

Seb. Away ; you all combine to make me wretched.

Alv. But hear the story of that fatal love ;
Where every circumstance shall prove another :
And Truth so shine by her own native light,
That if a lie were mixt, it must be seen.

Seb. No ; all may still be forg'd and of a piece.
No ; I can credit nothing thou canst say.

Alv. One proof remains ; and that's your father's hand :
Firm'd with his signet ; both so fully known,
That plainer evidence can hardly be,
' Unless his soul would want her heav'n a while,
' And come on earth to swear.'

Seb. Produce that writing.

Alv. [*To* Dor.] Alonzo has it in his custody.
The same, which when his nobleness redeem'd me,
And in a friendly visit own'd himself
For what he is, I then deposited ;
And had his faith to give it to the King.

Dor. Untouch'd, and seal'd, as when intrusted with me.
                     [*Giving a sealed paper to* Seb.
Such I restore it with a trembling hand,
Lest ought within disturb your peace of soul.

Seb. Draw near, Almeyda ; thou art most concern'd :
                     [*Tearing open the seals.*
For I am most in thee.
Alonzo, mark the characters :
Thou know'st my father's hand, observe it well :
And if th' impostor's pen have made one slip,
That shews it counterfeit, mark that and save me.

Dor. It looks indeed too like my master's hand :
So does the signet : more I cannot say ;
But wish 'twere not so like.

Seb. Methinks it owns
The black adult'ry, and Almeyda's birth :
But such a mist of grief comes o'er my eyes,
I cannot, or I would not read it plain.

Alm. Heav'n cannot be more true, than this is false.

Seb. O couldst thou prove it with the same assurance !
Speak, hast thou ever seen thy father's hand ?

Alm. No ; but my mother's honour has been read
By me, and by the world, in all her acts,

In

In characters more plain and legible
Than this dumb evidence, this blotted lie.
Oh! that I were a man, as my foul's one,
To prove thee traitor and affaffinate
Of her fame: thus mov'd I'd tear thee, thus:——
                              [*Tearing the paper.*

And fcatter o'er the field thy coward limbs,
Like this foul off-fpring of thy forging brain.
                              [*Scattering the paper.*

  Alv. Juft fo fhalt thou be torn from all thy hopes.
For know, proud woman, know in thy defpite,
The moft authentic proof is yet behind ;
Thou wear'ft it on thy finger ; 'tis that ring,
Which match'd to that on his, fhall clear the doubt.
'Tis no dumb forgery : for that fhall fpeak ;
And found a rattling peal to either's confcience.

  Seb. This ring indeed, my father, with a cold
And fhaking hand, juft in the pangs of death,
Put on my finger ; with a parting figh,
And would have fpoke ; but falter'd in his fpeech
With undiftinguifh'd found.

  Alv. I know it well ;
For I was prefent.   Now, Almeyda, fpeak :
And truly tell us, how you came by yours.

  Alm. My mother, when I parted from her fight
To go to Portugal, bequeath'd it to me,
Prefaging fhe fhould never fee me more :
She pull'd it from her finger, fhed fome tears,
Kifs'd it, and told me 'twas a pledge of love,
And hid a myftery of great importance
Relating to my fortunes.

  Alv. Mark me now,
While I difclofe that fatal myftery.
Thofe rings, when you were born and thought another's,
Your parent glowing yet in finful love,
Bid me befpeak : a curious artift wrought 'em,
With joints fo clofe; as not to be perceiv'd ;
Yet are they both each other's counterpart :
Her part had Juan infcrib'd, and his had Zayda,
(You know thofe names are theirs) and in the midft,
A heart divided in two halves was plac'd.
Now if the rivets of thofe rings inclos'd,

Fit not each other, I have forg'd this lie:
But if they join, you muſt for ever part.
[Sebaſtian *pulling off his ring* ; Almeyda *does the ſame, and
gives it to* Alvarez, *who unſcrues both the rings, and fits
one half on the other.*
Seb. Now life or death.
Alm. And either thine or ours.
I'm loſt for ever.——   [*Swoons.*
[*The women and* Morayma *take her up, and carry her off.*
[Sebaſtian *here ſtands amazed without motion, his eyes fixed
upwards.*
Seb. Look to the queen my wife ; for I am paſt
All pow'r of aid to her or to myſelf.
Alv. His wife, ſaid he, his wife ! O fatal ſound !
For, had I known it, this unwelcome news
Had never reach'd their ears.
So they had ſtill been bleſt in ignorance,
And I alone unhappy.
Dor. I knew it but too late, and durſt not ſpeak.
Seb. [*Starting out of his amazement.*] I will not live;
no not a moment more ;
I will not add one moment more to inceſt ;
I'll cut it off, and end a wretched being,
‘ For, ſhould I live, my ſoul's ſo little mine,
‘ And ſo much hers, that I ſhould ſtill enjoy.
‘ Ye cruel powers,
‘ Take me as you have made me, miſerable ;
‘ You cannot make me guilty ; 'twas my fate,
‘ And you made that, not I.   [*Draws his ſword.*
‘ [Ant. *and* Alv. *lay hold on him, and* Dorax *wreſts the
ſword out of his hand.*
 ‘ *Ant.* For Heav'n's ſake hold, and recollect your
mind.
  ‘ *Alv.* Conſider whom you puniſh, and for what ;
‘ Yourſelf unjuſtly : you have charg'd the fault
‘ On Heav'n, that beſt may bear it.
‘ Tho' inceſt is indeed a deadly crime,
‘ You are not guilty, ſince unknown 'twas done,
‘ And known, had been abhorr'd.
 ‘ *Seb.* By Heav'n you're traitors all that hold my
‘ If death be but ceſſation of our thought,   [hands.
‘ Then let me die, for I would think no more.
‘ I'll boaſt my innocence above ;
                                            ‘ And

‘ And let ’em fee a foul they could not fully :
‘ I fhall be there before my father’s ghoft ;
‘ That yet may languifh long in frofts and fires,
‘ For making me unhappy by his crime.
                                        ‘ [*Struggling again.*
‘ Stand off, and let met ake my fill of death :
‘ For I can hold my breath in you defpite,
‘ And fwell my heaving foul out when I pleafe.
   ‘ *Alv.* Heav’n comfort you !
   ‘ *Seb.* What, art thou giving comfort !
‘ Wouldft thou give comfort, who haft giv’n defpair ?
‘ Thou feeft Alonzo filent ; he’s a man.
‘ He knows, that men abandon’d of their hopes,
‘ Should afk no leave, nor ftay for fuing out
‘ A tedious writ of eafe from ling’ring Heav’n ;
‘ But help themfelves, as timely as they could,
‘ And teach the Fates their duty.
   ‘ *Dor.* [*To* Alv. *and* Ant.] Let him go.
‘ He is our king ; and he fhall be obey’d.
   ‘ *Alv.* What, to deftroy himfelf ? O parricide !
   ‘ *Dor.* Be not injurious in your foolifh zeal,
‘ But leave him free ; or, by my fword I fwear,
‘ To hew that arm away, that ftops the paffage
‘ To his eternal reft.
   ‘ *Ant.* [*Letting go his hold.*] Let him be guilty of his
‘ own death if he pleafes ; for I’ll not be guilty of mine
‘ by holding him.   [Seb. *fhakes off* Alv.
   ‘ *Alv.* [*To* Dor.] Infernal fiend,
‘ Is this a fubject’s part ?
   ‘ *Dor.* ’Tis a friend’s office.
‘ He has convinc’d me that he ought to die ;
‘ And rather than he fhould not, here’s my fword
‘ To help him on his journey.
   ‘ *Seb.* My laft, my only friend, how kind art thou,
‘ And how inhuman thefe !
   ‘ *Dor.* To make the trifle death a thing of moment !‘
   ‘ *Seb.* And not to weigh th’ important caufe I had
‘ To rid myfelf of life !
   ‘ *Dor.* True ; for a crime
‘ So horrid in the face of men and angels,
‘ As wilful inceft is !
   ‘ *Seb.* Not wilful neither.
                                        ‘ *Dor.*

' *Dor.* Yes, if you liv'd, and with repeated acts
' Refresh'd your fin, and loaded crimes with crimes,
' To fwell your fcores of guilt.
   ' *Seb.* True ; if I liv'd.
   ' *Dor.* I faid fo, if you liv'd.
   ' *Seb.* For hitherto was fatal ignorance,
' And no intended crime.
   ' *Dor.* That you beft know :
' But the malicious world will judge the worft.
   ' *Alv.* Oh, what a fophifter has hell procur'd,
' To argue for damnation !
   ' *Dor.* Peace, old dotard !
' Mankind, that always judge of kings with malice,
' Will think he knew this inceft, and purfu'd it.
' His only way to rectify miftakes,
' And to redeem her honour, is to die.
   ' *Seb.* Thou haft it right, my dear, my beft Alonzo !
' And that but petty reparation too ;
' But all I have to give.
   ' *Dor.* Your pardon, Sir ;
' You may do more, and ought.
   ' *Seb.* What, more than death ?
   ' *Dor.* Death ! why, that's children's fport ; a ftage-
' We act it every night we go to bed.   [play, death.
' Death to a man in mifery is fleep.
' Would you, who perpetrated fuch a crime
' As frighten'd nature, made the faints above
' Shake heaven's eternal pavement with their trembling
' To view that act, would you but barely die ?
' But ftretch your limbs, and turn on t'other fide,
' To lengthen out a black voluptuous flumber,
' And dream you had your fifter in your arms ?
   ' *Seb.* To expiate this, can I do more than die ?
   ' *Dor.* Oh, yes, you muft do more ; you muft be
' You muft be damn'd to all eternity ;   [damn'd &
' And fure felf-murder is the readieft way.
   ' *Seb.* How, damn'd !
   ' *Dor.* Why, is that news ?
   ' *Alv.* Oh, horror, horror !
   ' *Dor.* What, thou a ftatefman,
' And make a bufinefs of damnation
' In fuch a world as this ! Why, 'tis a trade :
' The fcrivener, ufurer, lawyer, fhopkeeper,

' And

' And foldier, cannot live but by damnation.
' The politician does it by advance,
' And gives all gone before-hand.
  ' *Seb.* Oh, thou haft giv'n me fuch a glimpfe of hell,
' So pufh'd me forward, even to the brink
' Of that irremeable burning gulf,
' That, looking in th' abyfs, I dare not leap.
' And now I fee what good thou mean'ft my foul,
' And thank thy pious fraud.   Thou haft, indeed,
' Appear'd a devil, but didft an angel's work.'
  Dor. ' 'Twas the laft remedy, to give you leifure:
' For,' if you could but think, I knew you fafe.
  Sed. I thank thee, my Alonzo.   I will live;
But never more to Portugal return:
For to go back and reign, that were to fliew
Triumphant inceft, and pollute the throne.
  ' *Alv.* Since ignorance———
  ' *Seb.* Oh, palliate not my wound!
' When you have argu'd all you can, 'tis inceft.
' No, 'tis refolv'd; I charge you, plead no more:
' I cannot live without Almeyda's fight,
' Nor can I fee Almeyda, but I fin.
' Heav'n has infpir'd me with a facred thought,
' To live alone to Heav'n, and die to her.
  ' *Dor.* Mean you to turn an anchoret?
  ' *Seb.* What elfe?
' The world was once too narrow for my mind;
' But one poor little nook will ferve me now,
' To hide me from the reft of human kind.
' Afric has defarts wide enough to hold
' Millions of monfters, and I am, fure, the greateft.
  Dor. You may repent, and wifh your crown too late.
  ' *Seb.* Oh, never, never! I am paft the boy:
' A fceptre's but a play-thing, and a globe
' A bigger bounding ftone.   He who can leave
' Almeyda, may renounce the reft with eafe.'
  Dor. Oh, truly great!
A foul fix'd high, and capable of heav'n.
Old as he is, your uncle Cardinal
Is not fo far enamour'd of a cloyfter,
But he will thank you for the crown you leave him.
  Seb. To pleafe him more, let him believe me dead;
That he may never dream I may return.

Alonzo!

Alonzo, I am now no more thy king,
But ftill thy friend ; and, by that holy name,
Adjure thee, to perform my laft requeft :
Make our conditions with yon captive king :
Secure me but my folitary cell ;
'Tis all I afk him for a crown reftor'd.
   ' *Dor.* I will do more.
' But fear not Muley-Zeydan ; his foft metal
' Melts down with eafy warmth, runs in the mold,
' And needs no further forge.'   [*Exit* Dor.
Re-enter Almeyda, *led by* Morayma, *and followed by
        her Attendants.*
   Seb. ' See where fhe comes again !
' By Heav'n,' when I behold thofe beauteous eyes,
Repentance lags, and fin comes hurrying on.
   Alm. This is too cruel !
   ' *Seb.* Speak'ft thou of love, of fortune, or of death,
' Or double death ; for we muft part, Almeyda ?
   ' *Alm.* I fpeak of all ;
' For all things that belong to us are cruel :
' But what's moft cruel, we muft love no more.
' Oh, 'tis too much that I muft never fee you ;
' But not to love you is impoffible :
' No, I muft love you—Heav'n may bate me that,
' And charge that finful fympathy of fouls
' Upon our parents, when they lov'd too well.
   ' *Seb.* Good Heav'n! thou fpeak'ft my thought, and I
' Nay, then there's inceft in our very fouls ; [*fpeak thine.*
' For we were form'd too like.
   ' *Alm.* Too like, indeed ;
' And yet not for each other.
' Sure, when we part, (for I refolv'd it too,
' Tho' you propos'd it firft) however diftant,
' We fhall be ever thinking of each other ;
' And, the fame moment, for each other pray.
   ' *Seb.* But if a wifh fhould come athwart our prayers—
   ' *Alm.* It would do well to curb it, if we could.
   ' *Seb.* We cannot look upon each other's face ;
' But when we read our love we read our guilt :
' And yet, methinks, I cannot chufe but love.
   ' *Alm.* I would have afk'd you, if I durft, for fhame,
' If ftill you lov'd ? You give it air before me.
' Ah, why were we not born both of a fex ?
' For then we might have lov'd without a crime.
                               ' Wh.

‘ Why was not I your brother ? Tho’ that wifh
‘ Involv’d our parents guilt, we had not parted :
‘ We had been friends, and friendfhip is no inceft.
  ‘ *Seb.* Alas, I know not by what name to call thee !
‘ Sifter and wife are the two deareft names,
‘ And I would call thee both ; and both are fin.
‘ Unhappy we ! that ftill we muft confound
‘ The deareft names into a common curfe.’
  Alm. To love, and be belov’d, and yet be wretched !
  ‘ *Seb.* To have but one poor night of all our lives !
‘ It was, indeed, a glorious, guilty night ;
‘ So happy, that, forgive me, Heaven ! I wifh,
‘ With all its guilt, it were to come again.
‘ Why did we know fo foon, or why at all,
‘ That fin could be conceal’d in fuch a blifs ?
  ‘ *Alm.* Men have a larger privilege of words,
‘ Elfe I fhould fpeak——But we muft part, Sebaftian,
‘ That’s all the name that I have left to call thee.
‘ I muft not call thee by the name I would ;
‘ But when I fay, Sebaftian, dear Sebaftian,
‘ I kifs the name I fpeak.’
  Seb. We muft make hafte, or we fhall never part.
‘ I would fay fomething that’s as dear as this :
‘ Nay, would do more than fay—One moment longer,
‘ And I fhould break thro’ laws divine and human,
‘ And think them cobwebs, fpread for little man,
‘ Which all the bulky herd of nature breaks.
‘ The vigorous young world was ignorant
‘ Of thefe reftrictions ; ’tis decrepit now :
‘ Not more devout, but more decay’d and cold.
‘ All this is impious ; therefore we muft part :
‘ For, gazing thus, I kindle at thy fight,
‘ And once, burnt down to tinder, light again
‘ Much fooner than before.’
           Re-enter Dorax.
  Alm. Here comes the fad denouncer of my fate,
To toll the mournful knell of feparation ;
While I, as on my death-bed, hear the found,
That warns me hence for ever.
  Seb. [*To* Dor.] Now, be brief,
And I will try to liften,
‘ And fhare the minute that remains, betwixt
‘ The care I owe my fubjects, and my love.’
  Dor. Your fate has gratify’d you all fhe can ;

L

Gives

Gives eafy mifery, and makes exile pleafing.
I trufted Muley-Zeydan, as a friend;
But fwore him firft to fecrecy.   He wept
Your fortune, and with tears not fqueez'd by art,
But fhed from nature, like a kindly fhower.
In fhort, he proffer'd more than I demanded,
A fafe retreat, a gentle folitude,
' Unvex'd with noife, and undifturb'd with fears:'
I chofe you one——.
   Alm. Oh, do not tell me where!
For if I knew the place of his abode,
I fhould be tempted to purfue his fteps,
And then we both were loft.
   ' *Seb.* Ev'n paft redemption :
' For, if I knew thou wert on that defign,
' (As I muft know, becaufe our fouls are one)
' I fhould not wander, but by fure inftinct,
' Should meet thee juft half-way in pilgrimage,
' And clofe for ever : for I know my love
' More ftrong than thine, and I more frail than thou.
   ' *Alm.* Tell me not that; for I muft boaft my crime,
' And cannot bear that thou fhouldft better love.'
   Dor. I may inform you both; for you muft go
Where feas, and winds, and defarts will divide you.
Under the ledge of Atlas lies a cave,
Cut in the living rock, by Nature's hands;
The venerable feat of holy hermits,
Who there, fecure in feparated cells,
' Sacred ev'n to the Moors,' enjoy devotion;
And from the purling ftreams, and favage fruits,
Have wholefome bev'rage, and unbloody feafts.
   Seb. 'Tis penance too voluptuous for my crime.
   ' *Dor.* Your fubjects confcious of your life are few;
' But all defirous to partake your exile,
' And to do office to your facred perfon.
' The reft, who think you dead, fhall be difmifs'd,
' Under fafe convoy, till they reach your fleet.'
   Alm. But how am wretched I to be difpos'd?
A vain enquiry, fince I leave my Lord;
For all the world befide is banifhment.
   Dor. I have a fifter, abbefs in Terceras,
Who loft her lover on her bridal day.
   Alm. There fate provided me a fellow-turtle,
To mingle fighs with fighs, and tears with tears.

Dor.

Dor. Laft, for myfelf, if I have well fulfill'd
My fad commiffion, let me beg the boon,
To fhare the forrows of your laft recefs,
And mourn the common loffes of our loves.
  ' *Alv.* And what becomes of me ? Muft I be left
' (As age and time had worn me out of ufe) ?
' Thefe finews are not yet fo much unftrung,
' To fail me when my mafter fhou!d be ferv'd :
' And when they are, then I will fteal to death,
' Silent and unobferv'd, to fave his tears.'
  Seb. ' I've heard you both.   Alvarez, have thy wifh ;
' But thine, Alonzo, thine is too unjuft.'
I charge thee, with my laft commands, return,
And blefs thy Violante with thy vows.
Antonio, be thou happy, too, in thine.
Laft, let me fwear you all to fecrecy ;
And to conceal my fhame, conceal my life,
  ' *Dor. Ant. Mor.* We fwear to keep it fecret.'
  Alm. Now, I would fpeak the laft farewel, I cannot.
' It would be ftill farewel, a thoufand times ;
' And, multiply'd in echo's, ftill farewel.
' I will not fpeak, but think a thoufand thoufand.
' And be thou filent too, my laft Sebaftian ;
' So, let us part in the dumb pomp of grief.'
My heart's too great, or I would die this moment ;
But Death, I thank him, in an hour, has made
A mighty journey, and I hafte to meet him.
                 [*She ftaggers, and her women hold her up.*
  Seb. Help to fupport this feeble, drooping flower,
This tender fweet, fo fhaken by the ftorm ;
For thefe fond arms muft thus be ftretch'd in vain,
And never, never muft embrace her more——
'Tis paft——my foul goes in that word——farewel !
[*Alv. goes with* Seb. *to one end of the ftage ;* Women, *with*
  Alm. *to the other.*
  Dor. [*Coming up to* Ant. *and* Mor. *who ftand on the*
middle of the ftage.] ' Hafte to attend Almeyda.' For
Your father is forgiven ; ' but to Antonio   [your fake,
' He forfeits half his wealth.' Be happy both ;
And let Sebaftian and Almeyda's fate,
This dreadful fentence to the world relate,
That unrepented crimes of parents dead,
Are juftly punifh'd on their children's head.
                                             [*Exeunt.*

END of the FIFTH ACT.

EPILOGUE.

Spoken by ANTONIO and MORAYMA.

MORAYMA.

I *Quak'd at heart, for fear the royal fashion,*
Should have seduc'd us two to separation.
To be drawn in against our own desire,
Poor I to be a nun, poor you a friar.

Ant. I trembled, when the old man's hand was in,
He would have prov'd we were too near of kin :
Discovering old intrigues of love, like t'other,
Betwixt my father and thy sinful mother,
To make us sister Turk, and Christian brother.

Mor. Excuse me there ; that league should have been rather
Betwixt your mother and my Mufti father :
'Tis for my own, and my relations credit.
Your friends should bear the bastard, mine should get it.

Ant. Suppose us two Almeyda and Sebastian,
With incest prov'd upon us——
Mor. Without question
Their conscience was too queazy of digestion.

Ant. Thou wouldst have kept the counsel of thy brother,
And sinn'd till we repented of each other.

Mor. Beast as you are, on nature's laws to trample !
'Twere fitter that we follow'd their example.
And since all marriage in repentance ends,
'Tis good for us to part while we are friends.
To save a maid's remorses and confusions,
E'en leave me now, before we try conclusions.

Ant. To copy their example, first make certain
Of one good hour, like theirs, before our parting ;
Make a debauch, o'er night, of love and madness ;
And marry, when we wake, in sober sadness.

Mor. I'll follow no new sects of your inventing :
One night might cost me nine long months repenting.
First wed, and if you find that life a fetter,
Die when you please, the sooner, Sir the better.
My wealth would get me love ere I could ask it :
Oh, there's a strange temptation in the casket !
All these young sharpers would my grace importune,
And make me thund'ring votes of lives and fortune.

I. Roberts del. Publish'd for Bells British Theatre June 7.th 1776. Reading sc.

Mr SHERIDAN in the Character of OEDIPUS.
What mean these exclamations on my Name?

BELL'S EDITION.

OE D I P U S.

A TRAGEDY,

As written by DRYDEN and LEE.

DISTINGUISHING ALSO THE

VARIATIONS OF THE THEATRE,

AS PERFORMED AT THE

Theatre-Royal in Drury-Lane.

Regulated from the Prompt-Book.

By PERMISSION of the MANAGERS.

By Mr. HOPKINS, Prompter.

Hi proprium decus & partum indignantur honorem,
Ni teneant————————　　　　　　VIRG.

Vos exemplaria Græca
Nocturnâ verfate manu, verfate diurnâ.　　　HORAT.

LONDON:
Printed for JOHN BELL, near *Exeter-Exchange*, in the *Strand*.

MDCCLXXVII.

[illegible]

[illegible]

[illegible]

[illegible]

[illegible]

[illegible]

[illegible]

[illegible]

PREFACE.

THOUGH it be dangerous to raife too great an expectation, efpecially in works of this nature, where we are to pleafe an un-
fatiable audience; yet 'tis reafonable to prepoffefs them in favour of
an author, and, therefore both the prologue and epilogue informed
you that OEdipus was the moft celebrated piece of all antiquity : that
Sophocles, not only the greateft wit, but one of the greateft men in
Athens, made it for the ftage at the public coft, and that it had the
reputation of being his mafter-piece, not only amongft the feven of
his which are ftill remaining, but of the greater number which are
perifhed. Ariftotle has more than once admired it in his book of
poetry; Horace has mentioned it; Lucullus, Julius Cæfar, and other
noble Romans, have written on the fame fubject, though their poems
are wholly loft; but Seneca's is ftill preferved. In our own age,
Corneille has attempted it, and it appears by his preface, with great
fuccefs: but a judicious reader will eafily obferve how much the
copy is inferior to the original. He tells you himfelf, that he owes
a great part of his fuccefs to the happy epifode of Thefeus and Dirce;
which is the fame thing as if we fhould acknowledge, that we were
indebted for our good fortune to the underplot of Adraftus, Eurydice,
and Creon. The truth is, he miferably failed in the character of his
hero. If he defired that OEdipns fhould be pitied, he fhould have
made him a better man. He forgot that Sophocles had taken care to
fhew him in his firft entrance, a juft, a merciful, a fuccefsful, a religious prince: and, in fhort, a father of his country : inftead of thefe,
he has drawn him fufpicious, defigning, more anxious of keeping the
Theban crown, than folicitous for the fafety of his people; hectored
by Thefeus, contemned by Dirce, and fcarce maintaining a fecond
part in his own tragedy. This was an error in the firft concoction:
and therefore never to be mended in the fecond or third. He introduced a greater hero than OEdipus himfelf; for when Thefeus was
once there, that companion of Hercules muft yield to none. The
poet was obliged to furnifh him with bufinefs, to make him an equipage fuitable to his dignity, and, by following him too clofe, to lofe
his other King of Brentford in the crowd. Seneca, on the other fide,
as if there were no fuch thing as nature to be minded in a play, is always running after pompous expreffion, pointed fentences, and philo-
fophical notions, more proper for the ftudy than the ftage. The

 Frenchman

Frenchman followed a wrong scent, and the Roman was absolutely at cold hunting. All we could gather out of Corneille was, that an episode must be, but not his way; and Seneca supplied us with no new hint, but only a relation which he makes of his Tiresias raising the ghost of Laius; which is here performed in view of the audience; the rites and ceremonies so far his, as he agreed with antiquity, and the religion of the Greeks: but he himself was beholden to Homer's Tiresias in the Odysses for some of them, and the rest have been collected from Heliodore's Æthiopiques, and Lucan's Erictho. Sophocles, indeed, is admirable every where; and therefore we have followed him as close as possibly we could. But the Athenian theatre (whether more perfect than ours, is not now disputed) had a perfection differing from ours. You see there in every act a single scene, (or two at most) which manage the business of the play, and after that succeeds the chorus, which commonly takes up more time in singing, than there has been employed in speaking. The principal person appears almost constantly through the play; but the inferior parts seldom above once in the whole tragedy. The conduct of our stage is much more difficult, where we are obliged never to lose any considerable character which we have once presented. Custom likewise has obtained, that we must form an under-plot of second persons, which must be depending on the first, and their bye-walks must be like those in a labyrinth, which all of them lead into the great parterre; or like so many several lodging chambers, which have their outlets into the same gallery. Perhaps, after all, if we could think so, the ancient method, as it is the easiest, is also the most natural, and the best. For variety, as it is managed, is too often subject to breed distraction; and while we would please too many ways, for want of art in the conduct, we please in none. But we have given you more already than was necessary for a preface, and, for ought we know, may gain no more by our instructions, than that politic nation is like to do, who have taught their enemies to fight so long, that at last they are in a condition to invade them.

PROLOGUE.

WHEN Athens all the Grecian states did guide,
And Greece gave laws to all the world beside,
Then Sophocles and Socrates did fit,
Supreme in wifdom one, and one in wit:
And wit from wifdom differ'd not in thofe,
But as 'twas fung in verfe, or faid in profe.
Then OEdipus, on crowded theatres,
Drew all admiring eyes, and lift'ning ears:
The pleas'd fpeƈator fhouted every line,
The nobleft, manlieft, and the beft defign!
And every critick of each learned age,
By this juft model has reform'd the ftage.
Now, fhould it fail, (as Heav'n avert our fear!)
Damn it in filence, left the world fhould hear.
For were it known this poem did not pleafe,
You might fet up for perfeƈt favages:
Your neighbours would not look on you as men;
But think the nation all turn'd Piƈts again.
Faith, as you manage matters, 'tis not fit,
You fhould fufpeƈt yourfelves of too much wit.
Drive not the jeft too far, but fpare this piece:
And, for this once, be not more wife than Greece.
See twice; do not pell-mell to damning fall,
Like true-born Britons, who ne'er think at all.
Pray, be advis'd; and though at Mons yon won,
On pointed cannon do not always run.
With fome refpeƈt to ancient wits proceed:
You take the four firft councils for your creed,
But when you lay tradition wholly by,
And on the private fpirit alone rely,
You turn fanatics in your poetry.
If, notwithftanding all that we can fay,
You needs will have your penn'worths of the play,
And come refolv'd to damn, becaufe you pay,
Record it, in memorial of the faƈt,
The firft play bury'd fince the woollen aƈt.

A 3

DRAMATIS PERSONÆ.

MEN.

OEdipus,	*Diocles,*
Adrastus,	*Pyracmon,*
Creon,	*Phorbas,*
Tiresias,	*Dymas,*
Hæmon,	*Ægeon,*
Alcander,	Ghost of *Laius.*

WOMEN.

Jocasta,
Eurydice,
Manto.

Priests, Citizens, Attendants, &c.

SCENE, *THEBES.*

OEDIPUS.

OE D I P U S.

⁎ *The lines marked with inverted commas, 'thus,' are omitted in the representation.*

ACT I.

The curtain rises to a plaintive tune, representing the miseries of Thebes; dead bodies appear at a distance in the streets; some faintly go over the stage, others drop.

Enter Alcander, Diocles, *and* Pyracmon.

ALCANDER.

METHINKS we stand on ruins; nature shakes
    About us, and the universal frame
So loose, that it but wants another push
To leap from off its hinges.
  Dioc. ' No fun to chear us; but a bloody globe
' That rolls above; a bald and beamless fire;
' His face o'er-grown with scurf.' The Sun's sick too;
Shortly he'll be an earth.
  Pyr. Therefore the seasons
Lie all confus'd; and, by the Heav'ns neglected,
Forget themselves. ' Blind winter meets the summer
' In his mid-way, and, seeing not his livery,
' Has driv'n him headlong back: and the raw damps
' With flaggy wings fly heavily about,
' Scattering their pestilential colds and rheums
' Through all the lazy air.'
  Alc. Hence murrains follow'd
On bleating flocks, and on the lowing herds:
At last, the malady
Grew more domestic, and the faithful dog
Dy'd at his master's feet.
  Dioc. And next his master:
' For all those plagues which earth and air had brooded,
' First on inferior creatures try'd their force;
' And last they seiz'd on man.'

Pyr.

Pyr. ' And then a thoufand deaths at once advanc'd,
' And every dart took place.   All was fo fudden,
' That fcarce a firft man fell—One but began
' To wonder, and ftraight fell a wonder too ;
' A third, who ftoop'd to raife his dying friend,
' Dropp'd in the pious act.'—Heard you that groan ?
                                        [*Groan within.*

Dioc. A troop of ghofts took flight together there :
' Now Death's grown riotous, and will play no more
' For fingle ftakes ; but families and tribes.'
How are we fure we breathe not now our laft,
And that, next minute,
Our bodies, caft into fome common pit,
Shall not be built upon, and overlaid
By half a people ?
  Alc. There's a chain of caufes
Link'd to effects ; invincible neceffity,
That whate'er is, could not but fo have been ;
That's my fecurity.
                    Enter Creon.
  Cre. So had it need, when all our ftreets lie cover'd
With dead and dying men ;
And Earth expofes bodies on the pavements
More than fhe hides in graves.
Betwixt the bride and bridegroom have I feen
The nuptial torch do common offices
Of marriage and of death.
  Dioc. Now OEdipus
(If he returns from war, our other plague)
Will fcarce find half he left, to grace his triumphs.
  Pyr. A feeble Pæan will be fung before him.
  Alc. He would do well to bring the wives and children
Of conquer'd Argians, to renew his Thebes.
  Cre. May funerals meet him at the city gates,
With their detefted omen.
  Dioc. Of his children.
  Cre. Nay, though fhe be my fifter, of his wife.
  Alc. Oh, that our Thebes might once again behold
A monarch Theban born !
  Dioc. We might have had one.
  Pyr. Yes, had the people pleas'd.
  Cre. Come, you're my friends—
The Queen, my fifter, after Laius' death,

Fear'd

Fear'd to lie single, and supply'd his place
With a young succeffor.
   Dioc. He much refembles
Her former hufband too.
   Alc. I always thought fo.
   Pyr. When twenty winters more have grizzl'd his black
He will be very Laius.   [locks,
   Cre. So he will :
Mean time fhe ftands provided of a Laius
More young and vigorous too, by twenty fprings.
Thefe women are fuch cunning purveyors!.
Mark, where their appetites have once been pleas'd,
The fame refemblance in a younger lover
Lies brooding in their fancies the fame pleafures,
And urges their remembrance to defire.
   Dioc. Had merit, not her dotage, been confider'd,
Then Creon had been king : but OEdipus !
A ftranger !———
   Cre. That word, ftranger, I confefs,
Sounds harfhly in my ears.
   Dioc. We are your creatures.
The people prone, as in all general ills,
To fudden change ; the King in wars abroad ;
The Queen a woman weak and unregarded ;
Euridice, the daughter of dead Laius,
A princefs young, and beauteous, and unmarried.
Methinks, from thefe difjointed propofitions
Something might be produc'd.
   Cre. The gods have done
Their part, by fending this commodious plague.
But, Oh, the Princefs ! her hard heart is fhut,
By adamantine locks, againft my love.
   Alc. Your claim to her is ftrong ; you are betroth'd.
   Pyr. True, in her nonage.
   ' *Alc.* But that let's remov'd.'
   Dioc. I heard the Prince of Argos, young Adraftus,
When he was hoftage here——
   Cre. Oh, name him not ! the bane of all my hopes ;
That hot-brain'd, headlong warrior, has the charms
Of youth, and fomewhat of a lucky rafhnefs,
To pleafe a woman yet more fool than he.
That thoughtlefs fex is caught by outward form,
And empty noife, and loves itfelf in man.
                                     Alc.

Alc. But fince the war broke out about our frontiers,
He's now a foe to Thebes.

Cre. But is not fo to her. See, fhe appears ;
Once more I'll prove my fortune: you infinuate
Kind thoughts of me into the multitude ;
Lay load upon the court ; gull them with freedom ;
And you fhall fee them tofs their tails, and gad,
As if the breeze had ftung them.

Dioc. We'll about it.   [*Exeunt* Alc. Dioc. *and* Pyr.

Enter Eurydice.

Cre. Hail, royal maid ; thou bright Eurydice !
A lavifh planet reign'd when thou wert born ;
And made thee of fuch kindred-mold to heav'n,
Thou feem'ft more heav'n's than ours.

Eur. Caft round your eyes ;
Where late the ftreets were fo thick fown with men,
Like Cadmus brood, they juftled for the paffage :
Now look for thofe erected heads, and fee them
Like pebbles paving all our public ways :
When you have thought on this, then anfwer me,
If thefe be hours of courtfhip.

Cre. Yes, they are ;
For when the gods deftroy fo faft, 'tis time
We fhould renew the race.

Eur. What, in the midft of horror ?

Cre. Why not then ?
There's the more need of comfort.

Eur. Impious Creon !

Cre. Unjuft Eurydice ! can you accufe me
Of love, which is Heav'n's precept, and not fear
That vengeance which you fay purfues our crimes,
Should reach your perjuries ?

Eur. Still th' old argument.
I bade you caft your eyes on other men,
Now caft them on your felf: think what you are.

Cre. A man.

Eur. A man !

Cre. Why doubt you ? I'm a man.

Eur. 'Tis well you tell me fo, I fhould miftake you
For any other part o'th' whole creation,
Rather than think you man. Hence from my fight,
Thou poifon to my eyes.

Cre. 'Twas you firft poifon'd mine ; and yet methinks
My face and perfon fhould not make you fport.

                                        Eur.

Eur. You force me, by your importunities,
To shew you what you are.

Cre. A prince, who loves you:
And since your pride provokes me, worth your love,
Ev'n at its higheft value.

Eur. Love from thee!
Why love renounc'd thee ere thou faw'ft the light:
Nature herfelf ftart back when thou wert born;
And cry'd, the work's not mine——
The midwife ftood aghaft; and when fhe faw
Thy mountain back, and thy diftorted legs,
Thy face itfelf,
Half-minted with the royal ftamp of man,
And half o'ercome with beaft, ftood doubting long,
Whofe right in thee were more;
And knew not, if to burn thee in the flames,
Were not the holier work.

Cre. Am I to blame, if Nature threw my body
In fo perverfe a mould? Yet when fhe caft
Her envious hand upon my fupple joints,
Unable to refift, and rumpled them
On heaps in their dark lodging, to revenge
Her bungled work, fhe ftampt my mind more fair;
And as from chaos, huddled and deform'd,
The god ftruck fire, and lighted up the lamps
That beautify the fky, fo he inform'd
This ill-fhap'd body with a daring foul;
And making lefs than man, he made me more.

Eur. No; thou art all one error; foul and body.
The firft young trial of fome unfkill'd pow'r;
Rude in the making art, and ape of Jove.
Thy crooked mind within hunch'd out thy back;
And wander'd in thy limbs: to thy own kind
Make love, if thou can'ft find it in the world;
And feek not from our fex to raife an off-fpring,
Which, mingled with the reft, would tempt the gods
To cut off human kind.

Cre. No; let them leave
The Argian prince for you; that enemy
Of Thebes has made you falfe, and break the vows
You made to me.

Eur. They were my mother's vows,
Made in my nonage.

                                                     Cre.

Cre. But hear me, maid :
This blot of nature, this deform'd, loath'd Creon,
Is master of a sword, to reach the blood
Of your young minion, spoil the gods' fine work,
And stab you in his heart.
    Eur. This when thou dost,
Then may'st thou still be curs'd with loving me ;
And, as thou art, be still unpitied, loath'd ;
And let his ghost—No, let his ghost have rest :
But let the greatest, fiercest, foulest fury,
Let Creon haunt himself.   [*Exit* Eur.
    Cre. 'Tis true, I am
What she has told me, an offence to sight :
My body opens inward to my soul,
And lets in day to make my vices seen
By all discerning eyes, but the blind vulgar.
I must make haste ere OEdipus return,
To snatch the crown and her ; for I still love ;
But love with malice ; as an angry cur
Snarls while he feeds, so will I seize and stanch
The hunger of my love on this proud beauty,
And leave the scraps for slaves.
Enter Tiresias, *leaning on a staff, and led by his daughter*
                Manto.
What makes this blind prophetic fool abroad !
Would his Apollo had him ; he's too holy
For earth and me ; I'll shun his walk ; and seek
My popular friends.   [*Exit* Creon.
    Tir. A little farther ; yet a little farther,
Thou wretched daughter of a dark old man,
Conduct my weary steps : and thou, who feest
For me and for thyself, beware thou tread not
With impious steps upon dead corps ;—now stay ;
Methinks I draw more open, vital air.
Where are we ?
    Man. Under covert of a wall :
The most frequented once, and noisy part
Of Thebes, now midnight silence reigns ev'n here ;
And grass untrodden springs beneath our feet.
    Tir. If there be nigh this place a sunny bank,
There let me rest a-while : a sunny bank !
Alas, how can it be, where no sun shines !
But a dim winking taper in the skies,

That nods, and ſcarce holds up his drowzy head
To glimmer through the damps!
      [*A noiſe within.* Follow, follow, follow! A Creon,
        a Creon, a Creon!
Hark! a tumultuous noiſe, and Creon's name
Thrice echo'd.
    Man. Fly! the tempeſt drives this way.
    Tir. Whither can age and blindneſs take their flight?
If I could fly, what could I ſuffer worſe,
Secure of greater ills!
        [*Noiſe again*, Creon, Creon, Creon!
Enter Creon, Diocles, Alcander, Pyracmon; *followed*
        by the crowd.
    Cre. I thank ye, countrymen; but muſt refuſe
The honours you intend me; they're too great;
And I am too unworthy; think again,
And make a better choice.
    1ſt Cit. Think twice! I ne'er thought twice in all my
life: that's double work.
    2d Cit. My firſt word is always my ſecond; and there-
fore I'll have no ſecond word; and therefore once again,
I ſay, a Creon.
    All. A Creon, a Creon, a Creon!
    Cre. Yet hear me, fellow-citizens.
    Dioc. Fellow-citizens! there was a word of kindneſs.
    Alc. When did OEdipus ſalute you by that familar
    1ſt Cit. Never, never; he was too proud.   [name?
    Cret. Indeed he could not, for he was a ſtranger:
But under him our Thebes is half deſtroy'd.
Forbid it, Heav'n, the reſidue ſhould periſh
Under a Theban born.
'Tis true, the gods might ſend this plague among you,
Becauſe a ſtranger rul'd: but what of that,
Can I redreſs it now?
    3d Cit. Yes, you or none.
'Tis certain that the gods are angry with us,
Becauſe he reigns.
    Cre. OEdipus may return: you may be ruin'd.
    1ſt Cit. Nay, if that be the matter, we are ruined
already.
    2d Cit. Half of us that are here preſent, were living
men but yeſterday, and we that are abſent do but drop
and drop, and no man knows whether he be dead or

B

                                       living.

living.   And therefore while we are found and well, let
us fatisfy our confciences, and make a new king.

3d Cit. Ha, if we were but worthy to fee another coronation, and then, if we muft die, we'll go merrily together.

All. To the queftion, to the queftion.

Dioc. Are you content, Creon fhould be your king?

All. A Creon, a Creon, a Creon!

Tir. Hear me, ye Thebans, and thou, Creon, hear me.

1ft Cit. Who's that would be heard? We'll hear no
man : we can fcarce hear one another.

Tir. I charge you, by the gods, to hear me.

2d Cit. Oh, 'tis Apollo's prieft, we muft hear him;
'tis the old blind prophet that fees all things.

3d Cit. He comes from the gods too, and they are our
betters ; and in good manners we muft hear him. Speak,
prophet.

2d Cit. For coming from the gods that's no great matter, they can all fay that ; but he's a great fcholar ; he
can make almanacks, an he were put to't, and therefore,
I fay, hear him.

Tir. When angry Heav'n fcatters its plaguesamong you,
Is it for nought, ye Thebans? Are the gods
Unjuft for punifhing? Are there no crimes
Which pull this vengeance down?

1ft Cit. Yes, yes, no doubt there are fome fins ftirring,
that are the caufe of all.

3d Cit. Yes, there are fins; or we fhould have no taxes.

2d Cit. For my part, I can fpeak it with a fafe confcience, I ne'er finned in all my life.

1ft Cit. Nor I.

3d Cit. Nor I.

2d Cit. Then we are all juftified, the fin lies not at our

Tir. All juftified alike, and yet all guilty;   [doors.
Were every man's falfe dealing brought to light,
His envy, malice, lying, perjuries,
His weights and meafures, th' other man's extortions,
With what face could you tell offended Heav'n,
You had not finn'd?

2d Cit. Nay, if thefe be fins, the cafe is altered; for
my part I never thought any thing but murder had been
a fin.

Tir. And yet, as if all thefe were lefs than nothing,
                                            You

You add rebellion to them, impious Thebans,!
Have you not fworn before the gods to ferve
And to obey this OEdipus, your King
By public voice elected ? Anfwer me,
If this be true !

　　2d Cit. This is true ; but it's a hard world, neighbours,
If a man's oath muft be his mafter.

　　Cre. Speak, Diocles ; all goes wrong.

　　Dioc. How are you traitors, countrymen of Thebes ?
This holy fire, who preffes you with oaths,
Forgets your firft ; were you not fworn before
To Laius and his blood ?

　　All. We were ; we were,

　　Dioc. While Laius has a lawful fucceffor,
Your firft oath ftill muft bind : Eurydice
Is heir to Laius ; let her marry Creon :
Offended Heav'n will never be appeas'd
While OEdipus pollutes the throne of Laius,
A ftranger to his blood.

　　All. We'll no OEdipus, no OEdipus.

　　1ft Cit. He puts the prophet in a moufe-hole.

　　2d Cit. I knew it would be fo ; the laft man ever fpeaks
the beft reafon.

　　Tir. Can benefits thus die, ungrateful Thebans !
Remember yet, when after Laius' death,
The monfter Sphinx laid your rich country wafte,
Your vineyards fpoil'd, your labouring oxen flew ;
Yourfelves for fear mew'd up within your walls,
She, taller than your gates, o'er-look'd your town ;
But when fhe rais'd her bulk to fail above you,
She drove the air around her like a whirlwind,
And fhaded all beneath ; till ftooping down,
She clapp'd her leathern wing again your tow'rs,
And thruft out her long neck, ev'n to your doors.

　　Dioc. Alc. Pyr. We'll hear no more.

　　Tir. You durft not meet in temples
'T' invoke the gods for aid, the proudeft he
Who leads you now, then cower'd, like a dar'd lark :
This Creon fhook for fear,
The blood of Laius curdled in his veins ;
'Till OEdipus arriv'd.
Call'd by his own high courage and the gods,
Himfelf to you a god : ye offer'd him

B 2

Your

Your queen and crown; (but what was then your crown?)
And Heav'n authoriz'd it by his fuccefs.
Speak then, who is your lawful king?
    All. 'Tis OEdipus.
    Tir. 'Tis OEdipus indeed: your king more lawful
Than yet you dream; for fomething ftill there lies
In heav'n's dark volume, which I read through mifts:
'Tis great, prodigious; 'tis a dreadful birth,
Of wond'rous fate; and now, juft now difclofing.
I fee, I fee, how terrible it dawns:
And my foul fickens with it.
    1ft Cit. How the god fhakes him!   [umph!
    Tir. He comes! he comes! Victory! Conqueft! Tri-
But, Oh, guiltlefs and guilty! Murder! Parricide!
Inceft! Difcovery! Punifhment——'tis ended,
And all your fufferings o'er.
                A trumpet within: enter Hæmon.
    Hæm. Rouze up, you Thebans; tune your Io Pæans!
Your king returns; the Argians are o'ercome;
Their warlike prince in fingle combat taken,
And led in bands by godlike OEdipus.
    All. OEdipus, OEdipus, OEdipus!
    Cre. Furies confound his fortune!——   [*Afide.*
Hafte, all hafte.   [*To them.*
And meet with bleffings our victorious king;
Decree proceffions; bid new holy-days;
Crown all the ftatues of our gods with garlands;
And raife a brazen column, thus infcrib'd:
To OEdipus, now twice a conqueror: deliverer of his
Truft me, I weep for joy to fee this day.   [Thebes.
    Tir. Yes, Heav'n knows how thou weep'ft:—Go, coun-
And, as you ufe to fupplicate your gods——   [trymen,
So meet your king with bayes, and olive-branches:
Bow down, and touch his knees, and beg from him
An end of all your woes; for only he
Can give it you.   [*Exit* Tirefias, *the people following.*
Enter OEdipus *in triumph;* Adraftus *prifoner;* Dymas,
                    train.
    Cre. All hail, great OEdipus;
Thou mighty conqueror, hail; welcome to Thebes;
To thy own Thebes; to all that's left of Thebes;
For half thy citizens are fwept away,
And wanting for thy triumphs:

                                                And

And we, the happy remnant, only live
To welcome thee, and die.
  OEdip. Thus pleafure never comes fincere to man;
But lent by Heav'n upon hard ufury;
And, while Jove holds us out the bowl of joy,
Ere it can reach our lips, it's dafh'd with gall
By fome left-handed god.   Oh, mournful triumph!
Oh, conqueft gain'd abroad, and loft at home!
Oh, Argos! now rejoice, for Thebes lies low;
Thy flaughter'd fons now fmile, and think they won;
When they can count more Theban ghofts than theirs.
  Adr. No; Argos mourns with Thebes; you temper'd fo
Your courage while you fought, that mercy feem'd
The manlier virtue, and much more prevail'd.
While Argos is a people, think your Thebes
Can never want for fubjects.   Every nation
Will crowd to ferve where OEdipus commands.
  Cre. [*To* Hæm.] How mean it fhows to fawn upon the
                  victor!
  Hæm. Had you beheld him fight, you had faid other-
Come, 'tis brave bearing in him, not to envy   [wife:
Superior virtue.
  OEdip. This indeed is conqueft,
To gain a friend like you: why were we foes?
  Adr. 'Caufe we were kings, and each difdain'd an equal.
I fought to have it in my pow'r to do
What thou haft done; and fo to ufe my conqueft.
To fhew thee, honour was my only motive,
Know this, that were my army at thy gates,
And Thebes thus wafte, I would not take the gift,
Which, like a toy dropt from the hands of fortune,
Lay for the next chance-comer.
  OEdip. [*Embracing.*] No more captive,
But brother of the war: 'tis much more pleafant,
And fafer, truft me, thus to meet thy love,
Than when hard gantlets clench'd our warlike hands,
And keep them from foft ufe.
  Adr. My conqueror!
  OEdip. My friend! that other name keeps enmity alive—
But longer to detain thee were a crime:
To love, and to Eurydice, go free:
Such welcome as a ruined town can give,
Expect from me; the reft let her fupply.
B 3

Adr.

Adr. I go without a blush, though conquer'd twice,
By you, and by my princess.   [*Exit* Adrastus.

Cre. [*Aside.*] Then I am conquer'd thrice; by OEdipus,
And her, and ev'n by him, the slave of both :
Gods, I'm beholden to you, for making me your image,
Would I could make you mine !

*Enter the people with branches in their hands, holding them
          up, and kneeling : two priests before them.*

Alas, my people !
What means this speechless sorrow, down-cast eyes,
And lifted hands ? If there be one among you
Whom grief has left a tongue, speak for the rest.

1st Pr. Oh, father of thy country !
To thee these knees are bent, these eyes are lifted,
As to a visible divinity.
A prince on whom heav'n safely might repose
The business of mankind : for Providence
Might on thy ' careful' bosom sleep secure,
And leave her task to thee.
But where's the glory of thy former acts ?
Ev'n that's destroy'd, when none shall live to speak it.
Millions of subjects shalt thou have ; but mute.
A people of the dead ; a crowded desart ;
A midnight silence at the noon of day.

OEdip. Oh, were our gods as ready with their pity,
As I with mine, this presence should be throng'd
With all I left alive ; and my sad eyes
Not search in vain for friends, whose promis'd fight
Flatter'd my toils of war.

1st Pr. Twice our deliverer.

OEdip. Nor are now your vows
Addrefs'd to one who sleeps.
When this unwelcome news first reach'd my ears,
Dymas was sent to Delphos, to enquire
The caufe and cure of this contagious ill :
And is this day return'd ? But since his message
Concerns the public, I refus'd to hear it,
But in this general presence : let him speak.

Dym. A dreadful answer from the hallow'd urn,
And sacred Tripos did the priestess give,
In these mysterious words.

The Oracle. " Shed in a cursed hour, by cursed hand,
Blood-royal unreveng'd has curs'd the land.

                              When

When Laius' death is expiated well,
Your plague fhall ceafe. The reft let Laius tell."
    OEdip. Dreadful indeed! Blood! and a king's blood
And fuch a king's, and by his fubjects fhed!   [too;
(Elfe why this curfe on Thebes?) no wonder then
If monfters, wars, and plagues, revenge fuch crimes!
If Heav'n be juft, its whole artillery,
All muft be empty'd on us: not one bolt
Shall err from Thebes; but more be call'd for, more:
New moulded thunder of a larger fize;
Driv'n by whole Jove.   What, touch anointed pow'r!
Then, gods, beware; Jove would himfelf be next;
Could you but reach him too.
    2d Pr. We mourn the fad remembrance.
    OEdip. Well you may:
Worfe than a plague infects you: y'are devoted
To mother earth, and to th' infernal pow'rs:
Hell has a right in you: I thank you, gods,
That I'm no Theban born. How my blood curdles!
As if this curfe touch'd me, and touch'd me nearer
Than all this prefence!——Yes, 'tis a king's blood,
And I, a king, am ty'd in deeper bonds
To expiate this blood——But where, from whom,
Or how muft I atone it? Tell me, Thebans,
How Laius fell; for a confus'd report
Pafs'd through my ears, when firft I took the crown:
But full of hurry, like a morning dream,
It vanifh'd in the bufinefs of the day.
    1ft Pr. He went in private forth; but thinly follow'd;
And ne'er return'd to Thebes.
    OEdip. Nor any from him? Came there no attendant?
None to bring the news?
    2d Pr. But one; and he fo wounded,
He fcarce drew breath to fpeak fome few faint words.
    OEdip. What were they? Something may be learn'd
            from thence.
    1ft Pr. He faid a band of robbers watch'd their paffage;
Who took advantage of a narrow way
To murder Laius and the reft: himfelf
Left too for dead.
    OEdip. Made you no more enquiry,
But took this bare relation?
    2d Pr. 'Twas neglected:
    3   For

For then the monſter Sphinx began to rage;
And preſent cares ſoon buried the remote;
So was it huſh'd, and never ſince reviv'd.
　　OEdip. Mark, Thebans, mark!
Juſt then, the Sphinx began to rage among you;
The gods took hold ev'n of th' offending minute,
And dated thence your woes: thence will I trace them.
　　1ſt Pr. 'Tis juſt thou ſhould'ſt.
　　OEdip. Hear then this dreadful imprecation; hear it:
'Tis laid on all; not any one exempt:
Bear witneſs, Heav'n, avenge it on the perjur'd.
If any Theban born, if any ſtranger
Reveal this murder, or produce its author,
Ten Attick talents be his juſt reward:
But, if for fear, for favour, or for hire,
The murd'rer he conceal, the curſe of Thebes
Fall heavy on his head: unite our plagues,
Ye gods, and place them there: from fire and water,
Converſe, and all things common, be he baniſh'd.
But for the murderer's ſelf, unfound by man,
Find him, ye pow'rs cœleſtial and infernal;
And the ſame fate or worſe than Laius met,
Let be his lot: his children be accurſt;
His wife and kindred, all of his be curs'd.
　　Both Pr. Confirm it, Heav'n!
　　　　　　　Enter Jocaſta, *attended by women.*
　　Joc. At your devotions! Heav'n ſucceed your wiſhes;
And bring th' effect of theſe your pious pray'rs
On you, on me, and all.
　　Pr. Avert this omen, Heav'n?
　　OEdip. Oh, fatal found, unfortunate Jocaſta!
What haſt thou ſaid? An ill hour haſt thou choſen
For theſe foreboding words! Why, we were curſing!
　　Joc. Then may that curſe fall only where you laid it.
　　OEdip. Speak no more!
For all thou ſay'ſt is ominous: we were curſing;
And that dire imprecation haſt thou faſten'd
On Thebes, and thee and me, and all of us.
　　Joc. Are then my bleſſings turn'd into a curſe?
Oh, unkind OEdipus! My former Lord
Thought me his bleſſing: be thou like my Laius.
　　OEdip. What yet again? The third time haſt thou
　　　　curs'd me:

　　　　　　　　　　　　　　　　　　　This

This imprecation was for Laius' death,
And thou haft wifh'd me like him.

Joc. Horror feizes me!

OEdip. Why doft thou gaze upon me ? Pr'ythee, love,
Take off thy eye ; it burdens me too much.

Joc. The more I look, the more I find of Laius :
His fpeech, his garb, his action ; nay, his frown ;
(For I have feen it ;) but ne'er bent on me.

OEdip. Are we fo like ?

Joc. In all things but his love.

OEdip. I love thee more : fo well I love, words can-
not fpeak how well.
No pious fon e'er lov'd his mother more
Than I my dear Jocafta.

Joc. I love you too
The felf-fame way ; and when you chid, methought
A mother's love ftart up in your defence,
And bade me not be angry : be not you :
For I love Laius ftill, as wives fhould love :
But you more tenderly ; as part of me ;
And when I have you in my arms, methinks
I lull my child afleep.

OEdip. Then we are bleft :
And all thefe curfes fweep along the fkies
Like empty clouds ; but drop not on our heads.

Joc. I have not joy'd an hour fince you departed,
For public miferies, and for private fears ;
But this bleft meeting has o'er-paid 'em all.
Good fortune that comes feldom comes more welcome.
All I can wifh for now, is your confent
To make my brother happy.

OEdip. How, Jocafta ?

Joc. By marriage with his niece, Eurydice ?

OEdip. Uncle and niece ; there are too near, my love :
'Tis too like inceft : 'tis offence to kind :
Had I not promis'd, were there no Adraftus,
No choice but Creon left her of mankind,
They fhould not marry ; fpeak no more of it ;
The thought difturbs me.

Joc. Heav'n can never blefs.
A vow fo broken, which I made to Creon ;
Remember he's my brother.

OEdip. That's the bar ;

And

And she thy daughter : nature would abhor
To be forc'd back again upon herself,
And like a whirlpool swallow her own streams.
   Joc. Be not displeas'd : I'll move the suit no more.
   OEdip. No, do not ; for, I know not why, it shakes me
When I but think on incest ; move we forward
To thank the gods for my success, and pray
To wash the guilt of royal blood away.   [*Ex. omnes.*

END of the FIRST ACT.

ACT II.

SCENE, *an open Gallery. A Royal Bedchamber being supposed behind.*

The Time, Night. Thunder, &c.

Enter Hæmon, Alcander, *and* Pyracmon.

HÆMON.

SURE 'tis the end of all things ; Fate has torn
   The lock of time off, and his head is now
The ghastly ball of round eternity !
Call you these peals of thunder, but the yawn
Of bellowing clouds ? By Jove, they seem to me
The world's last groans ; and those vast sheets of flame
Are its last blaze ! The tapers of the god,
The sun and moon, run down like waxen-globes ;
The shooting stars end all in purple jellies,
And Chaos is at hand.
   Pyr. 'Tis midnight, yet there's not a Theban sleeps,
But such as ne'er must wake. All crowd about
The palace, and implore, as from a god,
Help of the King ; who, from the battlement,
By the red lightning's glare, descry'd afar,
Atones the angry powers.   [*Thunder, &c.*
   Hæm. Ha ! Pyracmon, look ;
Behold, Alcander, from yon' west of heav'n,
The perfect figures of a man and woman :
A scepter bright with gems in each right hand,
Their flowing robes of dazzling purple made,
Distinctly yonder in that point they stand,

Just

Juſt weſt ; a bloody red ſtains all the place ;
And ſee, their faces are quite hid in clouds.
 Pyr. Cluſters of golden ſtars hang o'er their heads,
And ſeem ſo crowded, that they burſt upon them :
All dart at once their baleful influence
In leaking fire.
 Alc. Long-bearded comets ſtick,
Like flaming porcupines, to their left ſides,
 As they would ſhoot their quills into their hearts.
 Hæm. But ſee ! the king, and queen, and all the court !
Did ever day or night ſhew ought like this ?
          [*Thunders again. The Scene draws, and diſcovers*
               the **Prodigies.**
Enter OEdipus, Jocaſta, Eurydice, Adraſtus, *and all*
          coming forward with Amazement.
 OEdip. Anſwer, you Pow'rs divine ; ſpare all this noiſe,
This rack of heav'n, and ſpeak your fatal pleaſure.
Why breaks yon dark and duſky orb away ?
Why from the bleeding womb of monſtrous night,
Burſt forth ſuch myriads of abortive ſtars ?.
Ha ! my Jocaſta, look ! the ſilver moon !
A ſettling crimſon ſtains her beauteous face !
She's all o'er blood ! and look, behold again,
What mean the myſtic heav'ns ſhe journeys on ?
A vaſt eclipſe darkens the labouring planet :
Sound there, ſound all our inſtruments of war ;
Clarions and trumpets, ſilver, braſs, and iron,
And beat a thouſand drums to help her labour.
 Adr. 'Tis vain ; you ſee the prodigies continue ;
Let's gaze no more, the gods are humorous.
 OEdip. Forbear, raſh man——Once more I aſk your
If that the glow worm light of human reaſon [pleaſure !
Might dare to offer at immortal knowledge,
And cope with gods, why all this ſtorm of nature ?
Why do the rocks ſplit, and why rolls the ſea ?
Why theſe portents in heav'n, and plagues on earth ?
Why yon gigantic forms, ethereal monſters ?
Alas ! is all this but to fright the dwarfs
Which your own hands have made ? Then be it ſo.
Or if the fates reſolve ſome expiation
For murder'd Laius : hear me, hear me, gods !
Hear me thus proſtrate : ſpare this groaning land,
Save innocent Thebes, ſtop the tyrant Death ; .
                              Do

Do this, and lo I stand up an oblation
To meet your swiftest and severest anger,
Shoot all at once, and strike me to the centre.
[*The Cloud draws that veil'd the Heads of the Figures of the*
　　sky, and shews them crowned with the Names of OEdipus
　　and Jocasta *written above in great Characters of Gold.*
　　Adr. Either I dream, and all my cooler senses
Are vanish'd with that cloud that fleets away,
Or just above those two majestic heads,
I see, I read distinctly in large gold,
OEdipus and Jocasta.
　　Alc. I read the same.
　　Adr. 'Tis wonderful ; yet ought not man to wade
Too far in the vast deep of destiny.
　　　　　　　　　　[*Thunder, and the Prodigies vanish.*
　　Joc. My Lord, my OEdipus, why gaze you now,
When the whole heav'n is clear, as if the gods
Had some new monsters made ? Will you not turn,
And bless your people, who devour each word
You breathe ?
　　OEdip. It shall be so.
Yes, I will die, Oh, Thebes, to save thee !
Draw from my heart my blood, with more content
Than e'er I wore thy crown. Yet, Oh, Jocasta !
By all th' indearments of miraculous love,
By all our languishings, our fears in pleasure,
Which oft have made us wonder ; here I swear
On thy fair hand, upon thy breast I swear,
I cannot call to mind, from budding childhood
To blooming youth, a crime by me committed,
For which the awful gods should doom my death.
　　Joc. 'Tis not you, my Lord,
But he who murder'd Laius, frees the land :
Were you, which is impossible, the man,
Perhaps my poignard first should drink your blood ;
But you are innocent, as your Jocasta,
From crimes like those. This made me violent
To save your life, which you unjust would lose :
Nor can you comprehend, with deepest thought,
The horrid agony you cast me in,
When you resolv'd to die.
　　OEdip. Is't possible ?
　　Joc. Alas, why start you so ? Her stiff'ning grief,
　　　　　　　　　　　　　　　　　　　　　　Who

Who saw her children slaughter'd all at once,
Was dull to mine : methinks I should have made
My bosom bare against the armed god,
To save my OEdipus !
  OEdip. I pray, no more.
  Joc. You've silenc'd me, my Lord.
  OEdip. Pardon me, dear Jocasta !
Pardon a heart that sinks with sufferings,
And can but vent itself in sobs and murmurs :
Yet to restore my peace, I'll find him out.
Yes, yes, you gods ! you shall have ample vengeance
On Laius' murderer.   O, the traitor's name !
I'll know't, I will ; art shall be conjur'd for it,
And nature all unravell'd.
  Joc. Sacred Sir——
  OEdip. Rage will have way, and 'tis but just ; I'll fetch
Tho' lodg'd in air, upon a dragon's wing,   [him,
Tho' rocks should hide him : nay he shall be dragg'd
From hell, if charms can hurry him along :
His ghost shall be, by sage Tiresias' power,
(Tiresias, that rules all beneath the moon)
Confin'd to flesh, to suffer death once more ;
And then be plung'd in his first fires again.
                    Enter Creon.
  Cre. My Lord,
Tiresias attends your pleasure.
  OEdip. Haste, and bring him in.
O, my Jocasta, Eurydice, Adrastus,
Creon, and all ye Thebans, now the end
Of plagues, of madness, murders, prodigies,
Draws on : this battle of the heav'ns and earth
Shall by his wisdom be reduc'd to peace.
Enter Tiresias, leaning on a staff, led by his daughter Manto,
          followed by other Thebans.
O thou, whose most aspiring mind
Knows all the business of the courts above,
Opens the closets of the gods, and dares
To mix with Jove himself and Fate at council ;
O prophet, answer me, declare aloud
The traitor who conspir'd the death of Laius :
Or be they more, who from malignant stars
Have drawn this plague that blasts unhappy Thebes ?
  Tir. We must no more than Fate commissions us
                    C   To

To tell ; yet fomething and of moment I'll unfold,
If that the god would wake ; I feel him now,
' Like a ftrong fpirit charm'd into a tree,
' That leaps and moves the wood without a wind :
' The rouzed god, as all this while he lay,
' Intomb'd alive, ftarts and dilates himfelf ;'
He ftruggles, and he tears my aged trunk
With holy fury, ' my old arteries buft ;
' My rivel'd fkin,
' Like parchment, crackles at the hallow'd fire ;
' I fhall be young again :' Manto, my daughter,
' Thou haft a voice that might have fav'd the bard
' Of Thrace, and forc'd the raging Bacchanals,
' With lifted prongs, to liften to thy airs :'
O charm this god, this fury in my bofom,
Lull him with tuneful notes, and artful ftrings,
With pow'rful ftrains ; ' Manto, my lovely child,'
Sooth the unruly godhead to be mild.

S O N G *to* A P O L L O.

Phœbus, god belov'd by men,
At thy dawn, every beaft is rouz'd in his den ;
At thy fetting, all the birds of thy abfence complain,
And we die, all die till the morning comes again.
  Phœbus, god belov'd by men !
  Idol of the Eaftern kings,
  Awful as the god who flings
  His thunder round, and the lightning wings ;
  God of fongs, and Orphean ftrings,
  Who to this mortal bofom brings
  All harmonious heav'nly things !
  Thy drouzy prophet to revive,
T'en thoufand thoufand forms before him drive ;
With chariots and horfes all o'fire awake him,
Convulfions, and furies, and prophefies fhake him :
Let him tell it in groans, tho' he bend with the load,
Tho' he burft with the weight of the terrible god.

  Tir. The wretch, who fhed the blood of old Labdaci-
Lives, and is great ;   [des,
But cruel greatnefs ne'er was long :
The firft of Laius' blood his life did feize,

                                                     And

And urg'd his fate,
Which elfe had lafting been and ftrong,
The wretch, who Laius kill'd muft bleed or fly ;
Or Thebes, confum'd with plagues, in ruins lie.
    OEdip. The firft of Laius' blood! pronounce the perfon ;
May the god roar from thy prophetic mouth,
That even the dead may ftart up, to behold.
Name him, I fay, that moft accurfed wretch,
For, by the ftars, he dies !
Speak, I command thee ;
By Phœbus, fpeak ; for fudden death's his doom ;
Here fhall he fall, bleed on this very fpot ;
His name, I charge thee once more, fpeak.
    Tir. 'Tis loft,
Like what we think can never fhun remembrance ;
Yet of a fudden's gone beyond the clouds.
    OEdip. Fetch it from thence ; I'll have it, where-e'er
    Cre. Let me intreat you, facred Sir, be calm,   [it be.
And Creon fhall point out the great offender.
'Tis true, refpect of nature might enjoin
Me filence, at another time ; but, oh,
Much more the pow'r of my eternal love !
That, that fhould ftrike me dumb: yet, Thebes, my coun-
I'll break through all to fuccour thee, poor city.   [try—
O, I muft fpeak.
    OEdip. Speak then, if ought thou know'ft :
As much thou feem'ft to know, delay no longer.
    Cre. O beauty ! O illuftrious royal maid !
To whom my vows were ever paid till now,
And with fuch modeft, chafte and pure affection,
The coldeft nymph might read 'em without blufhing.
Art thou the murd'rels, then, of wretched Laius ?
And I, muft I accufe thee ? Oh, my tears !
Why will you fall in fo abhorr'd a caufe ?
But that thy beauteous, barbarous hand deftroy'd
Thy father (O monftrous act !) both gods
And men at once take notice.
    OEdip. Eurydice !
    Eur. Traitor, go on ; I fcorn thy little malice,
And knowing more my perfect innocence,
Than gods and men, then how much more than thee,
Who art their oppofite, and form'd a liar,

C 2

I thus

I thus difdain thee ! Thou once didft talk of love;
Becaufe I hate thy love,
Thou doft accufe me.

Adr. Villain, inglorious villain,
And traitor, doubly damn'd, who durft blafpheme
The fpotlefs virtue of the brighteft beauty ;
Thou dy'ft : nor fhall the facred majefty

[*Draws and wounds him.*

That guards this place, preferve thee from my rage.

OEdip. Difarm them both. Prince, I fhall make you
That I can tame you twice. Guards, feize him. [know

Adr. Sir,
I muft acknowledge in another caufe
Repentance might abafh me ; but I glory
In this, and fmile to fee the traitor's blood.

OEdip. Creon, you fhall be fatisfy'd at full.

Cre. My hurt is nothing, Sir ; but I appeal
To wife Tirefias, if my accufation
Be not moft true. The firft of Laius' blood
Gave him his death. Is there a prince before her ?
Then fhe is faultlefs, and I afk her pardon.
And may this blood ne'er ceafe to drop, O Thebes,
If pity of thy fufferings did not move me
To fhew the cure which Heav'n itfelf prefcrib'd.

Eur. Yes, Thebans, I will die to fave your lives,
More willingly than you can wifh my fate ;
But let this good, this wife, this holy man,
Pronounce my fentence : for to fall by him,
By the vile breath of that prodigious villain,
Would fink my foul, tho' I fhould die a martyr.

Adr. Unhand me, flaves. O mightieft of kings,
See at your feet a prince not us'd to kneel ;
Touch not Eurydice, by all the gods,
As you would fave your Thebes, but take my life :
For fhould fhe perifh, Heav'n would heap plagues on
Rain fulphur down, hurl kindled bolts [plagues,
Upon your guilty heads.

Cre. You turn to gallantry, what is but juftice :
Proof will be eafy made. Adraftus was
The robber who bereft th' unhappy king
Of life ; becaufe he flatly had deny'd
To make fo poor a prince his fon-in-law :

Therefore

Therefore 'twere fit that both should perish.

1 *Theb.* Both, let both die.

All Theb. Both, both; let them die.

OEdip. Hence you wild herd! For your ring-leader
He shall be made example.   Hæmon, take him.   [here,

1 *Theb.* Mercy! O mercy!

OEdip. Mutiny in my presence!
Hence, let me see that busy face no more.

Tir. Thebans, what madness makes you drunk with
Enough of guilty death's already acted;   [rage ?
Fierce Creon has accused Eurydice,
With prince Adrastus; which the god reproves
By inward checks, and leaves their fates in doubt.

OEdip. Therefore instruct us what remains to do,
Or suffer; for I feel a sleep like death
Upon me, and I sigh to be at rest.

Tir. Since that the pow'rs divine refuse to clear
The mystic deed, I'll to the Grove of Furies;
There I can force the infernal gods to shew
Their horrid forms; each trembling ghost shall rise,
And leave their grizly king without a waiter.
For prince Adrastus and Eurydice,
My life's engag'd, I'll guard them in the fane,
Till the dark mysteries of hell are done.
Follow me, princes. Thebans, all to rest.
O, OEdipus, to-morrow—but no more.
If that thy wakeful genius will permit,
Indulge thy brain this night with softer slumbers :
To-morrow, O to-morrow!——sleep, my son;
And in prophetic dreams thy fate be shewn.
                 [*Exeunt* Tir. Adr. Eur. Man. *and Thebans.*

OEdip. To bed, my fair, my dear, my best Jocasta.
After the toils of war, 'tis wondrous strange
Our loves should thus be dash'd. One moment's thought,
And I'll approach the arms of my belov'd.

Joc. Consume whole years in care, so now and then
I may have leave to feed my famish'd eyes
With one short passing glance, and sigh my vows :
This and no more, my Lord, is all the passion
Of languishing Jocasta.   [*Exit.*

OEdip. Thou softest, sweetest of the world! good night.
                 C 3   Nay,

Nay, she is beauteous too; yet, mighty love!
I never offer'd to obey thy laws,
But an unusual chilness came upon me;
An unknown hand still check'd my forward joy,
Dash'd me with blushes, tho' no light was near;
That even the act became a violation.

    Pyr. He's strangely thoughtful.

    Oedip. Hark! who was that! Ha! Creon, didst thou

    Cre. Not I, my gracious Lord, nor any here.   [call me?

    Oedip. That's strange! methought I heard a doleful
Cry Oedipus—The prophet bad me sleep.   [voice
He talk'd of dreams, of visions, and to-morrow!
I'll muse no more, come what will or can,
My thoughts are clearer than unclouded stars;
And with those thoughts I'll rest.   Creon, good night.

                      [*Exit with* Hæm.

    Cre. Sleep seal your eyes up, Sir, eternal sleep.
But if he sleep and wake again, O all
Tormenting dreams, wild horrors of the night,
And hags of fancy, wing him through the air:
From precipices hurl him headlong down;
Charybd's' roar, and death be set before him.

    Alc. Your curses have already ta'en effect;
For he looks very sad.

    Cre. May he be rooted where he stands for ever;
His eye-balls never move, brows be unbent,
His blood, his entrails, liver, heart and bowels,
Be blacker than the place I wish him, hell.

    Pyr. No more; you tear yourself, but vex not him.
Methinks 'twere brave this night to force the temple,
While blind Tiresias conjures up the fiends,
And pass the time with nice Eurydice.

    Alc. Try promises and threats, and if all fail,
Since hell's broke loose, why should not you be mad?
Ravish, and leave her dead with her Adrastus.

    Cre. Were the globe mine, I'd give a province hourly
For such another thought.   Lust and revenge!
To stab at once the only man I hate,
And to enjoy the woman whom I love!
I ask no more of my auspicious stars,

                                      The

The reſt as Fortune pleaſe; ſo but this night
She play me fair, why, let her turn for ever.
Enter Hæmon.

Hæm. My Lord, the troubled king is gone to reſt ;
Yet, ere he ſlept, commanded me to clear
The antichambers : none muſt dare be near him.

Cre. Hæmon, you do your duty——   [*Thunder.*
And we obey.—The night grows yet more dreadful !
'Tis juſt that all retire to their devotions ;
The gods are angry : but to-morrow's dawn,
If prophets do not lie, will make all clear.
As they go off, OEdipus *enters, walking aſleep in his ſhirt,*
with a dagger in his right-hand, and a taper in his left.

OEdip. O, my Jocaſta ! 'tis for this the wet
Starv'd ſoldier lies on the cold ground ;
For this he bears the ſtorms
Of winter camps, and freezes in his arms :
To be thus circled, to be thus embrac'd ;
That I cou!d hold thee ever !—Ha ! where art thou ?
What means this melancholy light, that ſeems
The gloom of glowing embers ?
The curtain's drawn ; and ſee ſhe's here again !
Jocaſta ! Ha ! what, fall'n aſleep ſo ſoon ?
How fares my love ? This taper will inform me.
Ha ! lightning blaſt me, thunder
Rivet me ever to Prometheus' rock,
And vultures gnaw out my inceſtuous heart.
By all the gods, my mother Merope !
My ſword, a dagger ! Ha, who waits there ? Slaves,
My ſword. What, Hæmon, dar'ſt thou, villain, ſtop me ?
With thy own poignard periſh.   Ha ! who's this ?
Or is't a change of death ? By all my honours,
New murder ; thou haſt ſlain old Polybus :
Inceſt and parricide, thy father's murdered !
Out, thou infernal flame : now all is dark,
All blind and diſmal, moſt triumphant miſchief !
And now, while thus I ſtalk about the room,
I challenge fate to find another wretch
Like OEdipus !   [*Thunder, &c.*
Enter Jocaſta *attended, with lights, in a night-gown.*
Night, horror, death, confuſion, hell, and furies !
Where am I ? O, Jocaſta, let me hold thee :

Thus

Thus to my bofom, ages let me grafp me,
All that the hardeft temper'd weather'd flefh,
With fierceft human fpirit infpir'd, can dare,
Or do, I dare ; but, O you pow'rs, this was
By infinite degrees too much for man.
Methinks my deafen'd ears
Are burft ; my eyes, as if they had been knock'd
By fome tempeftuous hand, fhoot flafhing fire :
That fleep fhould do this !

   Joc. Then my fears were true.
Methought I heard your voice, and yet I doubted,
Now roaring like the ocean, when the winds
Fight with the waves ; now, in a ftill fmall tone
Your dying accents fell, as racking fhips,
After the dreadful yell, fink murm'ring down,
And bubble up a noife.

   OEdip. Truft me, thou faireft, beft of all thy kind,
None e'er in dreams was tortur'd fo before.
Yet what moft fhocks the nicenefs of my temper,
Ev'n far beyond the killing of my father,
And my own death, is that this horrid fleep
Dafh'd my fick fancy with an act of inceft :
I dream'd, Jocafta, that thou wert my mother ;
Which tho' impoffible, fo damps my fpirits,
That I could do a mifchief on myfelf,
Left I fhould fleep and dream the like again.

   Joc. O, OEdipus, too well I underftand you !
I know the wrath of heav'n, the care of Thebes,
The cries of its inhabitants, war's toils,
And thoufand other labours of the ftate,
Are all refer'd to you, and ought to take you
For ever from Jocafta.

   OEdip. Life of my life, and treafure of my foul,
Heav'n knows I love thee.

   Joc. O, you think me vile,
And of an inclination fo ignoble,
That I muft hide me from your eyes for ever.
Be witnefs, gods, and ftrike Jocafta dead,
If an immodeft thought, or low defire
Inflain'd my breaft, fince firft our loves were lighted.

   OEdip. O rife, and add not, by thy cruel kindnefs,
A grief more fenfible than all my torments.

Thou

Thou think'ſt my dreams are forg'd ; but by thyſelf,
The greateſt oath I ſwear, they are moſt true :
But, be they what they will, I here diſmiſs them ;
Begone, chimæras, to your mother clouds.
Is there a fault in us ? Have we not ſearch'd
The womb of Heav'n, examin'd all the entrails
Of birds and beaſts, and tired the prophet's art ?
Yet what avails ? He, and the gods together,
Seem like phyſicians at a loſs to help us ;
Thefore, like wretches that have linger'd long,
We'll ſnatch the ſtrongeſt cordial of our love.——
To bed, my fair.
  Ghoſt within. OEdipus !
  OEdip. Ha ! who calls ?
Didſt thou not hear a voice ?
  Joc. Alas ! 1 did.
  Ghoſt. Jocaſta !
  Joc. O, my love, my Lord, ſupport me !
  OEdip. Call louder, till you burſt your airy forms :
Reſt on my hand. Thus, arm'd with innocence,
I'll face theſe babbling dæmons of the air :
In ſpight of ghoſts, I'll on,
'Tho' round my bed the furies plant their charms ;
I'll break them with Jocaſta in my arms ;
Claſp'd in the folds of love, I'll wait my doom,
 And act my joys, tho' thunder ſhake the room.
                                        [*Excunt.*

END of the SECOND ACT.

A C T II.

SCENE, *a dark Grove.*

Enter Creon *and* Diocles.

CREON.

'TIS better not to be, than be unhappy.
  Dioc. What mean you by theſe words ?
  Cre. 'Tis better not to be, than to be Creon.
A thinking ſoul is puniſhment enough ;
But when 'tis great, like mine, and wretched too,
Then every thought draws blood.
                                        Dioc.

Dioc. You are not wretched.

Cre. I am : my foul's ill-married to my body ;
I would be young, be handfome, be belov'd :
Could I but breathe myfelf into Adraftus——

Dioc. You rave ; call home your thoughts.

Cre. I pr'ythee let my foul take air a while ;
Were fhe in OEdipus, I were a king ;
Then I had kill'd a monfter, gain'd a battle,
And had my rival pris'ner ; brave, brave actions :
Why have not I done thefe ?

Dioc. Your fortune hinder'd.

Cre. There's it.   I have a foul to do them all :
But Fortune will have nothing done that's great
But by young handfome fools : body and brawn
Do all her work : Hercules was a fool,
And ftraight grew famous : a mad boift'rous fool :
Nay worfe, a woman's fool.
Fool is the ftuff, of which Heav'n makes a hero.

Dioc. A ferpent ne'er becomes a flying dragon,
Till he has eat a ferpent.

Cre. Goes it there ?
I underftand thee ; I muft kill Adraftus.

Dioc. Or not enjoy your miftrefs :
Eurydice and he are pris'ners here,
But will not long be fo : this tell-tale ghoft
Perhaps will clear them both.

Cre. Well ; 'tis refolv'd.

Dioc. The princefs walks this way ;
You muft not meet her
Till this be done.

Cre. I muft.

Dioc. She hates your fight ;
And more fince you accus'd her.

Cre. Urge it not.
I cannot ftay to tell thee my defign,
For fhe's too near.

Enter Eurydice.

How, Madam, were your thoughts employ'd ?

Eur. On death and thee.

Cre. Then they were not well forted : life and me
Had been the better match.

Eur. No, I was thinking

On

On two the moſt deteſted things in nature:
And they are death and thee.
    Cre. The thought of death to one near death is dreadful!
O 'tis a fearful thing to be no more.
Or if to be, to wander after death ;
To walk as ſpirits do, in brakes all day ;
And when the darkneſs comes, to glide in paths
That lead to graves ; and in the ſilent vault,
Where lies your own pale ſhrowd, to hover o'er it,
Striving to enter your forbidden corps :
And often, often, vainly breathe your ghoſt
Into your lifeleſs lips :
Then, like a lone benighted traveller
Shut out from lodging, ſhall your groans be anſwer'd
By whiſtling winds, whoſe every blaſt will ſhake
Your tender form to atoms.
    Eur. Muſt I be this thin being, and thus wander
No quiet after death ?
    Cre. None : you muſt leave
This beauteous body ; all this youth and freſhneſs
Muſt be no more the object of deſire,
But a cold lump of clay ;
Which then your diſcontented ghoſt will leave,
And loath its former lodging.
This is the beſt of what comes after death,
Ev'n to the beſt.
    Eur. What then ſhall be thy lot !
Eternal torments, baths of boiling ſulphur ;
Viciſſitudes of fires, and then of froſts :
And an old guardian fiend, ugly as thou art,
To hollow in thy ears at every laſh ;
This for Eurydice ; theſe for her Adraſtus !
    Cre. For her Adraſtus !
    Eur. Yes, for her Adraſtus ;
For death ſhall ne'er divide us. Death ! what's death ?
    ' *Dioc.* You ſeem'd to fear it.
    ' *Eur.* But I more fear Creon :
' To take that hunch-back'd monſter in my arms,
' Th' excreſcence of a man.
    ' *Dioc.* [*To* Cre.] See what you've gain'd.
    ' *Eur.* Death only can be dreadful to the bad :
' To innocence, 'tis like a bug-bear dreſs'd
                                    ' To

‘ To frighten children ; pull but off his mask,
‘ And he’ll appear a friend.’
　Cre. You talk too slightly
Of death and hell.　Let me inform you better.
　Eur. You best can tell the news of your own country.
　Dioc. Nay, now you are too sharp.
　Eur. Can I be so to one who has accus’d me
Of murder and of parricide ?
　Cre. You provok’d me :
And yet I only did thus far accuse you,
As next of blood to Laius : be advis’d,
And you may live.
　Eur. The means ?
　Cre. ’Tis offer’d you ;
The fool Adrastus has accus’d himself.
　Eur. He has indeed, to take the guilt from me.
　Cre. He says he loves you ; if he does, ’tis well :
He ne’er could prove it in a better time.
　Eur. Then death must be his recompence for love !
　Cre. ’Tis a fool’s just reward :
The wife can make a better use of life :
But ’tis the young man’s pleasure ; his ambition :
I grudge him not that favour.
　Eur. When he’s dead,
Where shall I find his equal ?
　Cre. Every where.
Fine empty things, like him,
The court swarms with them.
Fine fighting things ; in camps they are so common,
Crows feed on nothing else ; plenty of fools ;
A glut of them in Thebes.
And Fortune still takes care they should be seen :
She places them aloft, o’ th’ topmost spoke
Of all her wheel : fools are the daily work
Of Nature ; her vocation ; if she form
A man, she loses by’t, ’tis too expensive ;
’Twould make ten fools : a man’s a prodigy.
　Eur. That is, a Creon : O thou black detractor,
‘ Who spitt’st thy venom against gods and men !
‘ Thou enemy of eyes :’
’Thou who lov’st nothing but what nothing loves,
And that’s thyself : who hast conspir’d against

My

My life and fame, to make me loath'd by all,
And only fit for thee.
But for Adraſtus' death, good gods, his death !
What curſe ſhall I invent ?
   Dioc. No more—he's here.
   Eur. He ſhall be ever here.
He who would give his life, give up his fame——
            Enter Adraſtus.
If all the excellence of woman-kind
Were mine——No, 'tis too little all for him :
Were I made up of endleſs, endleſs joys——
   Adr. And ſo thou art :
The man who loves like me,
Would think ev'n infamy, the worſt of ills,
Were cheaply purchas'd, were thy love the price.
Uncrown'd, a captive, nothing left but honour,
'Tis the laſt thing a prince ſhould throw away :
But when the ſtorm grows loud, and threatens love,
Throw ev'n that over-board ; for love's the jewel,
And laſt it muſt be kept. .
   Cre. [*To* Dioc.] Work him, be ſure,
To rage—He's paſſionate ;
Make him th' aggreſſor.
   Dioc. Oh, falſe love ! falſe honour !
   Cre. Diſſembled both, and falſe !
   Adr. Dar'ſt thou ſay this to me ?
   Cre. To you ! why, what are you, that I ſhould fear
I am not Laius.   Hear me, Prince of Argos.   [you ?
You give what's nothing, when you give your honour;
'Tis gone, 'tis loſt in battle.   For your love,
Vows made in wine are not ſo falſe as that :
You kill'd her father ; you confeſs'd you did :
A mighty argument to prove your paſſion to the daughter !
   Adr. [*Aſide.*] Gods, muſt I bear this brand, and not
The lie to his foul throat !   [retort
   Dioc. Baſely you kill'd him.
   Adr. [*Aſide.*] Oh, I burn inward ! my blood's all o'fire !
Alcides, when the poiſon'd ſhirt ſate cloſeſt,
Had but an ague-fit to this my fever.
Yet, for Eurydice, ev'n this I'll ſuffer,
To free my love——Well, then, I kill'd him baſely.
   Cre. Fairly, I'm ſure, you could not.
             D   *Dioc.*

Dioc. Nor alone.

Cre. You had your fellow thieves about you, Prince:
They conquer'd, and you kill'd.

Adr. [*Afide.*] Down, fwelling heart!
'Tis for thy princefs, all—Oh, my Euridice!— [*To her.*

Eur. [*To him.*] Reproach not thus the weaknefs of my
As if I could not bear a fhameful death,　　　　　[fex,
Rather than fee you burden'd with a crime
Of which I know you free.

Cre. You do ill, Madam,
To let your headlong love triumph o'er nature.
Dare you defend your father's murderer?

Eur. You know he kill'd him not.

Cre. Let him fay fo.

Dioc. See, he ftands mute.

Cre. Oh, pow'r of confcience! ev'n in wicked men
It works, it ftings, it will not let him utter
One fyllable, one No, to clear himfelf
From the moft bafe, detefted, horrid act,
That ere could ftain a villain, not a prince.

Adr. Ha! villain!

Cre. Echo to him, groves, cry villain.

Adr. Let me confider—Did I murder Laius,
Thus like a villain?

Cre. Beft revoke your words,
And fay, you kill'd him not.

Adr. Not like a villain; pr'ythee, change me that
For any other lie.

Dioc. No, villain, villain.

Cre. You kill'd him not—Proclaim your innocence,
Accufe the Princefs: fo I knew 'twould be.

Adr. I thank thee; thou inftruct'ft me.
No matter how I kill'd him.

Cre. [*Afide.*] Cool'd again!

Eur. Thou, who ufurp'ft the facred name of confcience,
Did not thy own felf declare him innocent?
To me declare him fo? The King fhall know it.

Cre. You will not be believ'd; for I'll forfwear it.

Eur. What's now thy confcience?

Cre. 'Tis my flave, my drudge, my fupple glove,
My upper garment, to put on, throw off,
As I think beft: 'tis my obedient confcience.

Adr.

Adr. Infamous wretch !

Cre. My confcience fhall not do me the ill office
To fave a rival's life ; when thou art dead,
(As dead thou fhalt be, or be yet more bafe
Than thou think'ft me,
By forfeiting her life, to fave thy own.)
Know this, and let it grate thy very foul,
She fhall be mine : (fhe is, if vows were binding)
Mark me, the fruit of all thy faith and paffion,
Ev'n of thy foolifh death, fhall all be mine.

Adr. Thine, fay'ft thou, monfter ?
Shall my love be thine ?
Oh, I can bear no more !
Thy cunning engines have with labour rais'd
My heavy anger, like a mighty weight,
To fall and ftrike thee dead.
See here thy nuptials ; fee, thou rafh Ixion,   [*Draws.*]
Thy promis'd Juno vanifh'd in a cloud,
And in her room avenging thunder rolls
To blaft thee thus——Come both——   [*Both draw.*

Cre. 'Tis what I wifh'd——
Now fee whofe arm can launch the furer bolt,
And who's the better Jove ——   [*Fight.*

Eur. Help, murder, help !

*Enter Hæmon and Guards, run betwixt them, and beat
down their fwords.*

Hæm. Hold, hold your impious hands ! I think the Furies,
To whom this grove is hallow'd, have infpir'd you.
Now, by my foul, the holieft earth of Thebes
You have profan'd with war. Nor tree, nor plant
Grows here, but what is fed with magic juice,
All full of human fouls, that cleave their barks,
To dance at midnight by the moon's pale beams.
At leaft two hundred years thefe reverend fhades
Have known no blood, but of black fheep and oxen,
Shed by the prieft's own hand to Proferpine.

Adr. Forgive a ftranger's ignorance—I knew not
The honours of the place.

Ham. Thou, Creon, didft.
Not OEdipus, were all his foes here lodg'd,
Durft violate the religion of thefe groves,
To touch one fingle hair ; but muft, unarm'd,

D 2

Parle,

Parle, as in truce, or furlily avoid.
What most he long'd to kill..
   Cre. I drew not first ;
But in my own defence..
   Adr. I was provok'd
Beyond man's patience ; all reproach could urge
Was us'd to kindle one not apt to bear.
   Hæm.. 'Tis OEdipus, not I, muft judge this act.
Lord Creon, you and Diocles retire ;
Tirefias and the brotherhood of priefts
Approach the place.   None at thefe rites affift,
But you th' accus'd, who by the mouth of Laius
Muft be abfolv'd or doom'd.
   Adr. I bear my fortune.
   Eur. And I provoke my trial.
   Hæm. 'Tis at hand :
For fee, the prophet comes with vervain crown'd,
The priefts with yew ; a venerable band.
We leave you to the gods.
            [*Exit* Hæmon, *with* Creon *and* Diocles.
Enter Tirefias, *led by* Manto ; *the priefts follow, all cloathed*
            in long black habits.
   Tir. Approach, ye lovers ;
Ill-fated pair, whom, feeing not, I know.
This day your kindly ftars in heav'n were join'd ;
When lo, an envious planet interpos'd,
And threaten'd both with death.   I fear, I fear.
   Eur. Is there no god fo much a friend to love,
Who can controul the malice of our fate ?
Are they all deaf ? Or have the giants heav'n ?
   Tir. The gods are juft——
But how can finite meafure infinite ?
Reafon ! alas, it does not know itfelf !
Yet man, vain man, would, with this fhort-lin'd plummet,
Fathom the vaft abyfs of heav'nly juftice.
Whatever is, is in its caufes juft ;
Since all things are by fate.   But purblind man
Sees but a part o' th' chain ; the neareft links ;
His eyes not carrying to that equal beam
That poifes all above.
   Eur. Then we muft die !
   Tir. The danger's imminent this day.

                                    Adr.

Adr. ‘ Why then there’s one day lefs for human ills;
‘ And who would moan himfelf for fuffering that
‘ Which in a day muft pafs ? Something or nothing:
‘ I fhall be what I was again, before
‘ I was Adraftus.’
Penurious Heav’n ! canft thou not add a night
To our one day ? Give me a night with her,
And I’ll give all the reft.
    Tir. She broke her vow
Firft made to Creon.   But the time calls on;
And Laius’ death muft now be made more plain.
How loth I am to have recourfe to rites
So full of horror, that I once rejoice
I want the ufe of fight.
    1 *Pr.* The cremonies ftay.
    Tir. Choofe the darkeft part o’ th’ grove,
Such as ghofts at noon-day love.
Dig a trench, and dig it nigh
Where the bones of Laius lie,
Altars rais’d of turf or ftone,
Will th’ infernal pow’rs have none.
Anfwer me if this be done ?
    All Pr. ’Tis done.
    Tir. Is the facrifice made fit ?
Draw her backward to the pit;
Draw the barren heifer back;
Barren let her be, and black.
Cut the curled hair that grows
Full betwixt her horns and brows;
And turn your faces from the fun;
Anfwer me if this be done ?
    All Pr. ’Tis done.
    Tir. Pour in blood, and blood like wine,
To mother Earth and Proferpine;
Mingle milk into the ftream;
Feaft the ghofts that love the fteam;
Snatch a brand from funeral pile,
Tofs it in, to make them boil;
And turn your faces from the fun;
Anfwer me, if all be done ?
    All Pr. All is done.
[*Peals of thunder and flafhes of lightning; then groaning
    below the ftage.*

Man. Oh, what laments are those?   [pain,
   Tir. The groans of ghosts that cleave the earth with
And heave it up; they pant and stick half way.
               [*The stage wholly darkened.*
   Man. And now a sudden darkness covers all;
True, genuine night; night added to the groves;
The fogs are blown full in the face of heav'n.
   Tir. Am I but half obey'd? Infernal gods,
Must you have music too? Then tune your voices,
And let them have such sounds as hell ne'er heard.
Since Orpheus brib'd the shades.
          '*Music first, then sing.*
' 1. Hear, ye sullen pow'rs below;
      ' Hear, ye tafkers of the dead:
' 2. You that boiling cauldrons blow,
     ' You that fcum the molten lead.
' 3. You that pinch with red-hot tongs:
' 1. You that drive the trembling hofts.
    ' Of poor, poor ghofts,
   ' With your sharpen'd prongs.
' 2. You that thruft them off the brim.
' 3. You that plunge them when they fwim,
' 1. Till they drown,
    ' Till they go,
   ' On a row,
  ' Down, down, down,
  ' Ten thoufand, thoufand, thoufand fathoms low.
' *Chorus.* Till they drown, *&c.*
' 1. Mufic for a while:
' Shall your cares beguile,
' Wond'ring how your pains were eas'd;
' 2 And difdaining to be pleas'd,
' 3. Till Alecto free the dead
  ' From their eternal bands;
' Till the fnakes drop from her head,
  ' And whip from out her hands.
' 1. Come away,
  ' Do not ftay,
  ' But obey,
  ' While we play,
  ' For hell's broke up, and ghofts have holiday.
' *Chorus.* Come away, *&c.*
   2   ' [*A flafh*

' [*A flash of lightning : the stage is made bright, and the*
' *ghosts are seen passing betwixt the trees.*
' 1. Laius ! 2. Laius ! 3. Laius !
' 1. Hear ! 2. Hear ! 3. Hear !
' *Tir.* Hear and appear.
' By the Fates that spun thy thread,
' *Cho.* Which are three.
' *Tir.* By the furies fierce and dread,
' *Cho.* Which are three.
' *Tir.* By the Judges of the dead,
' *Cho.* Which are three.
' Three times three.
' *Tir.* By Hell's blue flame ;
' By the Stygian lake ;
' And by Demogorgon's name,
' At which ghosts quake,
' Hear and appear ?'

[*The ghost of* Laius *rises, armed in his chariot, as he was*
slain ; and behind his chariot sit the three who were mur-
dered with him.

Ghost of Laius. Why hast thou drawn me from my pains
To suffer worse above ; to see the day,   [below.
And Thebes more hated ? Hell is heav'n to Thebes.
For pity, send me back, where I may hide,
In willing night, this ignominious head.
In hell I shun the public scorn ; and then
They hunt me for their sport, and hoot me as I fly :
Behold, ev'n now, they grin at my gor'd side,
And chatter at my wounds.
  Tir. I pity thee.
Tell but why Thebes is for thy death accurs'd,
And I'll unbind the charm.
  Ghost. Oh, spare my shame !
  Tir. Are these two innocent ?
  Ghost. Of my death they are.
But he who holds my crown, Oh, must I speak !
Was doom'd to do what nature most abhors.
The gods foresaw it, and forbade his being
Before he yet was born. I broke their laws,
And cloth'd with flesh his pre-existing soul.
Some kinder pow'r, too weak for destiny,

                                        Took

Took pity, and indu'd his new-form'd mafs
With temperance, juftice, prudence, fortitude,
And every kingly virtue. But in vain ;
For Fate, that fent him hoodwink'd to the world,
Perform'd its work by his miftaken hands.
Afk'ft thou who murder'd me ? 'Twas OEdipus.
Who ftains my bed with inceft ? OEdipus.
For whom then are you curs'd, but OEdipus ?
He comes ! the parricide ! I cannot bear him !
My wounds ake at him !   Oh, his murd'rous breath
Venoms my airy fubftance ! Hence with him,
Banifh him, fweep him out ; the plagues he bears
Will blaft your fields, and mark his way with ruin.
From Thebes, my throne, my bed, let him be driven ;
Do you forbid him earth, and I'll forbid him heav'n.

[Ghoft defcends.

Enter OEdipus, Creon, Hæmon, &c.

    OEdip. What's this ? Methought fome peftilential blaft
Struck me juft entering ; and fome unfeen hand
Struggled to pufh me backward.   Tell me why
My hair ftands briftling up, why my flefh trembles ?
You ftare at me ! Then hell has been among ye,
And fome lag fiend yet lingers in the grove.
    Tir. What omen faw'ft thou, ent'ring ?
    OEdip. A young ftork,
That bore his aged parent on his back,
Till, weary with the weight, he fhook him off,
And peck'd out both his eyes.
    Adr. Oh, OEdipus !
    Eur. Oh, wretched OEdipus !
    Tir. Oh, fatal king !
    OEdip. What mean thefe exclamations on my name ?
I thank the gods, no fecret thoughts reproach me.
' No, I dare challenge Heav'n to turn me outward,
' And fhake my foul quite empty in your fight.'
Then wonder not that I can bear unmov'd
Thefe fix'd regards, and filent threats of eyes.
A generous fiercenefs dwells with innocence ;
And confcious virtue is allow'd fome pride.
    Tir. Thou know'ft not what thou fay'ft.
    OEdip. What mutters he ? Tell me, Euridice—
Thou fhak'ft—thy foul's a woman. Speak, Adraftus,

And

And boldly, as thou met'ſt my arm in fight.
Dar'ſt thou not ſpeak ? Why, then 'tis bad indeed.
Tireſias, thee I ſummon by thy prieſthood ;
Tell me what news from hell ; where Laius points,
And who's the guilty head ?
    Tir. Let me not anſwer.
    OEdip. Be dumb, then, and betray thy native ſoil
To farther plagues.
    Tir. I dare not name him to thee.
    OEdip. Dar'ſt thou converſe with hell, and canſt thou
An human name ?   [fear
    Tir. Urge me no more to tell a thing, which, known,
Would make thee more unhappy. 'Twill be found,
Tho' I am ſilent.
    OEdip. Old and obſtinate ! Then thou thyſelf
Art author or accomplice of this murder ;
And ſhun'ſt the juſtice, which, by public ban,
Thou haſt incurr'd.
    Tir. Oh, if the guilt were mine,
It were not half ſo great ! Know, wretched man,
Thou, only thou art guilty ; thy own curſe
Falls heavy on thyſelf.
    OEdip. Speak this again :
But ſpeak it to the winds when they are loudeſt,
Or to the raging ſeas ; they'll hear as ſoon,
And ſooner will believe.
    Tir. Then hear me, Heav'n,
For, bluſhing, thou haſt ſeen it : hear me, Earth,
Whoſe hollow womb could not contain this murder,
But ſent it back to light : and thou, Hell, hear me,
Whoſe own black ſeal has 'firm'd this horrid truth :
OEdipus murder'd Laius.
    OEdip. Rot the tongue,
And blaſted be the mouth that ſpoke that lie.
Thou blind of ſight, but thou more blind of ſoul——
    Tir. Thy parents thought not ſo.
    OEdip. Who were my parents ?
    Tir. Thou ſhalt know too ſoon.
    OEdip. Why ſeek I truth from thee ?
The ſmiles of courtiers, and the harlot's tears,
The tradeſman's oaths, and mourning of an heir,
Are truths to what prieſts tell.

                                                  Ob.

Oh, why has priesthood privilege to lie,
And yet to be believ'd !—Thy age protects thee——

   Tir. Thou canst not kill me; 'tis not in thy fate,
As 'twas to kill thy father, wed thy mother,
And beget sons, thy brothers.

   OEdip. Riddles, riddles !

   Tir. Thou art thyself a riddle, a perplex'd,
Obscure ænigma, which, when thou unty'st,
Thou shalt be found and lost.

   OEd. Impossible !
Adrastus, speak ; and, as thou art a king,
Whose royal word is sacred, clear my fame.

   Adr. Would I could !

   OEdip. Ha ! wilt thou not ? Can that plebeian vice
Of lying mount to kings ? Can they be tainted ?
Then truth is lost on earth.

   Cre. The cheat's too gross.
Adrastus is his oracle, and he,
The pious juggler, but Adrastus' organ.

   OEdip. 'Tis plain ; the priest's suborn'd to free the
   Cre. And turn the guilt on you.   [pris'ner.
   OEdip. Oh, honest Creon, how hast thou been bely'd !
   Eur. Hear me.
   Cre. She's brib'd to save her lover's life.
   Adr. If, OEdipus, thou think'st——
   Cre. Hear him not speak.
   Adr. Then hear these holy men.
   Cre. Priests, priests, all brib'd, all priests !
   OEdip. Adrastus, I have found thee :
The malice of a vanquish'd man has seiz'd thee.

   Adr. If envy, and not truth——
   OEdip. I'll hear no more : away with him.
[*Hæmon takes him off by force*; Creon *and* Eurydice *follow.*
[*To* Tir.] Why stand'st thou here, impostor ?
So old and yet so wicked !—Lie for gain,
And gain so short as age can promise thee !

   Tir. So short a time as I have yet to live
Exceeds thy pointed hour. Remember Laius——
No more—if e'er we meet again, 'twill be
In mutual darkness ; we shall feel before us,
To reach each other's hand—Remember Laius.
               [*Exit* Tiresias; *Priests follow.*
                       Remember

OEdip. Remember Laius! that's the burden ftill.
Murder and inceft ! But to hear them nam'd
My foul ftarts in me : ' the good centinel
' Stands to his weapons, takes the firft alarm,
' To guard me from fuch crimes.'   Did I kill Laius?
Then I walk'd fleeping, in fome frightful dream;
My foul then ftole my body out by night,
And brought me back to bed ere morning-wake.
It cannot be, ev'n this remoteft way;
But fome dark hint would juftle forward now,
And goad my memory——Oh, my Jocafta!

       Enter Jocafta.

Joc. Why are you thus difturb'd?
OEdip. Why, would'ft thou think it?
No lefs than murder.
  Joc. Murder! what of murder?
  OEdip. Is murder then no more? Add parricide
And inceft—bear not thefe a frightful found?
  Joc. Alas!
  OEdip. How poor a pity is alas,
For two fuch crimes!—Was Laius us'd to lie?
  Joc. Oh, no! the moft fincere, plain, honeft man;
One who abhorr'd a lie.
  OEdip. Then he has got that quality in hell.
He charges me——but why accufe I him?
I did not hear him fpeak it. They accufe me,
The Prieft, Adraftus, and Eurydice,
Of murdering Laius——Tell me, while I think on't,
Has old Tirefias practis'd long this trade?
  Joc. What trade?
  OEdip. Why, this foretelling trade.
  Joc. For many years.
  OEdip. Has he before this day accus'd me?
  Joc. Never.
  OEdip. Have you, ere this, enquir'd who did this mur-
  Joc. Often; but ftill in vain.   -[der?
  OEdip. I am fatisfy'd.
Then 'tis an infant-lie; but one day old.
The oracle takes place before the prieft;
The blood of Laius was to murder Laius:
I'm not of Laius' blood.

                      Joc.

Joc. Ev'n oracles.
Are always doubtful, and are often forg'd :
Laius had one, which never was fulfill'd,
Nor ever can be now.

OEdip. And what foretold it ?

Joc. That he ſhould have a ſon by me, fore-doom'd
The murderer of his father.   True, indeed,
A ſon was born; but, to prevent that crime,
The wretched infant of a guilty fate,
Bor'd through his untry'd feet, and bound with cords,
On a bleak mountain naked was expos'd.
The King himſelf liv'd many, many years,
And found a different fate ; by robbers murder'd,
Where three ways meet.   Yet theſe are oracles ;
And this the faith we owe them.

OEdip. Say'ſt thou, woman ?
By Heav'n, thou haſt awaken'd ſomewhat in me,
That ſhakes my very ſoul !

Joc. What new diſturbance ?——

OEdip. Methought thou ſaid'ſt, or do I dream thou
This murder was on Laius' perſon done   [ſaid'ſt it ?
Where three ways meet.

Joc. So common fame reports.

OEdip. Would it had lied !

Joc. Why, good my Lord ?

OEdip. No queſtions.
'Tis buſy time with me; diſpatch mine firſt.
Say, where, where was it done ?

Joc. Mean you the murder ?

OEdip. Could'ſt thou not anſwer without naming murder ?

Joc. They ſay in Phocide; on the verge that parts it
From Dalia, and from Delphos.

OEdip. So——How long ? When happen'd this ?

Joc. Some little time before you came to Thebes.

OEdip. What will the gods do with me ?

Joc. What means that thought ?

OEdip. Something—But 'tis not yet your turn to aſk.
How old was Laius, what his ſhape, his ſtature,
His action, and his mien ? Quick, quick, your anſwer—

Joc. Big made he was, and tall; his port was fierce,
Erect his countenance ; manly majeſty
Sate in his front, and darted from his eyes,

Com-

Commanding all he viewed; his hair juſt grizzled,
As in a green old age.   Bate but his years,
You are his picture.
   OEdip. [*Aſide.*] Pray Heav'n he drew me not! Am I
   Joc. So I have often told you.   [his picture?
   OEdip. True, you have:
Add that unto the reſt.   How was the King
Attended when he travell'd?
   Joc. By four ſervants.
He went out privately.
   OEdip. Well counted ſtill!
One 'ſcap'd, I hear.   What ſince became of him?
   Joc. When he beheld you firſt, as King in Thebes,
He kneel'd, and, trembling, begg'd I would diſmiſs him.
He had my leave; and now he lives retir'd.
   OEdip. This man muſt be produc'd; he muſt, Jocaſta.
   Joc. He ſhall—Yet have I leave to aſk you why?
   OEdip. Yes, you ſhall know; for where ſhould I repoſe
The anguiſh of my ſoul, but in your breaſt?
I need not tell you Corinth claims my birth;
My parents, Polybus and Merope,
Two royal names; their only child am I.
It happen'd once, 'twas at a bridal feaſt,
One, warm with wine, told me I was a foundling,
Not the King's ſon: I, ſtung with this reproach,
Struck him; my father heard of it; the man
Was made aſk pardon, and the buſineſs huſh'd.
   Joc. 'Twas ſomewhat odd.
   OEdip. And ſtrangely it perplex'd me.
I ſtole away to Delphos, and implor'd
The god, to tell my certain parentage.
He bade me ſeek no farther; 'twas my fate
To kill my father, and pollute his bed,
By marrying her who bore me.
   Joc. Vain, vain oracles!
   OEdip. But yet they frighted me.
I look'd on Corinth as a place accurs'd;
Reſolv'd my deſtiny ſhould wait in vain,
And never catch me there.
   Joc. Too nice a fear.
   OEdip. Suſpend your thoughts, and flatter not too ſoon.
Juſt in the place you nam'd, where three ways meet,
E

And

And near that time, five perfons I encounter'd ;
One was too like (Heav'n grant it prove not him !)
The perfon you defcribe for Laius: infolent
And fierce they were, as men who liv'd on fpoil ;
I judg'd them robbers, and by force repell'd
The force they us'd.   In fhort, four men I flew ;
The fifth, upon his knees, demanding life,
My mercy gave it——Bring me comfort now.
If I flew Laius, what can be more wretched ?
From Thebes and you my curfe has banifh'd me ;
From Corinth, Fate.

   Joc. Perplex not thus your mind.
My hufband fell by multitudes opprefs'd ;
So Phorbas faid.   This band you chanc'd to meet ;
And murder'd not my Laius, but reveng'd him.

   OEd. There's all my hope : let Phorbas tell me this,
And I fhall live again.
To you, good gods, I make my laft appeal ;
Or clear my virtue, or my crime reveal.
If wandering in the maze of fate I run,
And backward trod the paths I fought to fhun,
Impute my errors to your own decree ;
My hands are guilty, but my heart is free.

                                               [*Exeunt.*

END of the THIRD ACT.

A C T   IV.

Enter Pyracmon *and* Creon.

PYRACMON.

SOME bufinefs of import, that triumph wears,
  You feem to go with ; nor is it hard to guefs
When you are pleas'd, ' by a malicious joy,
' Whofe red and fiery beams caft through your vifage
' A glowing pleafure.   Sure' you fmile revenge,
And I could gladly hear.
   Cre. Wouldft thou believe,
This giddy, hair-brain'd King, whom old Tirefias
Has thunderftruck with heavy accufation,
Tho' confcious of no inward guilt, yet fears ?

He

He fears Jocasta, fears himself, his shadow;
He fears the multitude; and, which is worth
An age of laughter, out of all mankind,
He chufes me to be his orator:
Swears that Adraftus and the lean-look'd prophet
Are joint confpirators; and wish'd me to
Appeafe the raving Thebans; which I fwore
To do.

   Pyr. A dangerous undertaking;
Directly oppofite to your own intereft.

   Cre. No, dull Pyracmon; when I left his prefence,
With all the wings with which revenge could imp
My flight, I gain'd the midft o' the city;
There, ftanding on a pile of dead and dying,
I to the mad and fickly multitude,
With interrupting fobs, cry'd out, Oh, Thebes!
Oh, wretched Thebes, thy king, thy OEdipus,
This barbarous ftranger, this ufurper, monfter,
Is by the oracle, the wife Tirefias,
Proclaim'd the murderer of thy royal Laius!
Jocafta, too, no longer now my fifter,
Is found complotter in the horrid deed.
Here I renounce all tie of blood and nature,
For thee, Oh, Thebes, dear Thebes, poor bleeding Thebes!
And there I wept; and then the rabble howl'd,
And roar'd, and with a thoufand antic mouths,
Gabbled revenge; revenge was all the cry.

   Pyr. This cannot fail; I fee you on the throne,
And OEdipus caft out.

   Cre. Then ftraight came on
Alcander, with a wide and bellowing crowd,
Whom he had wrought; I whifper'd him to join,
And head the forces while the heat was in them.
So, to the palace I return'd, to meet
The King, and greet him with another ftory.
But fee, he enters.

       Enter OEdipus *and* Jocafta, *attended.*

   OEdip. Said you that Phorbas is arriv'd, and yet
Intreats he may return, without being afk'd
Of ought concerning what we have difcover'd?

   Joc. He ftarted when I told him your intent;
Replying, what he knew of that affair

E 2

Would

Would give no fatisfaction to the King;
Then, falling on his knees, begg'd as for life,
To be difmifs'd from court: he trembled too,
As if convulfive death had feiz'd upon him,
And ftammer'd in his abrupt pray'r fo wildly,
That had he been, the murderer of Laius,
Guilt and diftraction could not have fhook him more.

   OEdip. By your defcription, fure as plagues and death
Lay wafte our Thebes, fome deed that fhuns the light
Begot thofe fears; if thou refpect'ft my peace,
Secure him, dear Jocafta; for my genius
Shrinks at his name.

   Joc. Rather let him go;
So my poor boding heart would have it be,
Without a reafon.

   OEdip. Hark, the Thebans come!
Therefore retire: and once more, if thou lov'ft me,
Let Phorbas be retain'd.

   Joc. You fhall, while I
Have life, be ftill obey'd:
In vain you footh me with your foft endearments,
And fet the faireft countenance to view;
Your gloomy eyes, my Lord, betray a deadnefs
And inward languifhing: that oracle
Eats like a fubtle worm its venom'd way,
Preys on your heart, and rots the noble core,
Howe'er the beauteous out-fide fhews fo lovely.

   OEdip. Oh, thou wilt kill me with thy love's excefs!
All, all is well; retire, the Thebans come.   *[Ex.* Joc.

   Ghoft. OEdipus!

   OEdip. Ha! again that ftream of woe!
Thrice have I heard, thrice fince the morning dawn'd
It hallow'd loud, as if my guardian fpirit
Call'd from fome vaulted manfion, OEdipus!
Or is it but the work of melancholy?
When the fun fets, fhadows, that fhew'd at noon
But fmall, appear moft long and terrible;
So when we think Fate hovers o'er our heads,
Our apprehenfions fhoot beyond all bounds,
Owls, ravens, crickets, feem the watch of death,
Nature's worft vermin fcare her god-like fons;
Echoes, the very leavings of a voice,

Grow

Grow babbling ghofts, and call us to our graves :
Each mole-hill thought fwells to a huge Olympus,
While we fantaftic dreamers heave and puff,
And fweat with an imagination's weight ;
As if, like Atlas, with thefe mortal fhoulders
We could fuftain the burden of the world.

                                [Creon *comes forward.*

  Cre. Oh, facred Sir, my royal Lord———
  OEdip. What now ?
Thou feem'ft affrighted at fome dreadful action,
Thy breath comes fhort, thy darted eyes are fix'd
On me for aid, as if thou wert purfu'd :
I fent thee to the Thebans : fpeak thy wonder ;
Fear not, this palace is a fanctuary,
The King himfelf's thy guard.
  Cre. For me, alas !
My life's not worth a thought, when weigh'd with yours !
But fly, my Lord : fly, as your life is facred.
Your fate is precious to your faithful Creon,
Who therefore, on his knees, thus proftrate, begs
You would remove from Thebes that vows your ruin.
When I but offer'd at your innocence,
They gather'd ftones, and menac'd me with death,
And drove me through the ftreets, with imprecations
Againft your facred perfon, and thofe traitors.
Which juftify'd your guilt : which curs'd Tirefias
Told, as from heav'n, was caufe of their deftruction.
  OEdip. Rife, worthy Creon, hafte and take our guard,
Rank them in equal part upon the fquare,
Then open every gate of this our palace,
And let the torrent in.   Hark, it comes.   [*Shout.*
I hear them roar : begone, and break down all
The dams that would oppofe their furious paffage.

                          [*Exit* Creon *with Guards.*

     Enter Adraftus, *his Sword drawn.*
  Adr. Your city
Is all in arms, all bent to your deftruction ;
I heard but now, where I was clofe confin'd,
A thund'ring fhout, which made my gaolers vanifh,
Cry, Fire the palace ; where's the cruel king ?
Yet, by th' infernal gods, thofe awful pow'rs,
That have accus'd you, which thefe ears have heard,

                                       And

And thefe eyes feen, I muft believe you guiltlefs;
For, fince I knew the royal OEdipus,
I have obferv'd in all his acts fuch truth
And god-like clearnefs; that to the laft gufh
Of blood and fpirits, I'll defend his life,
And here have fworn to perifh by his fide.

    OEdip. Be witnefs, gods, how near this touches me.

[*Embracing him.*

Oh, what, what recompence can glory make?

    Adr. Defend your innocence, fpeak like yourfelf,
And awe the rebels with your dauntlefs virtue.
But hark! the ftorm comes nearer.

    OEdip. Let it come.
The force of majefty is never known
But in a general wrack: then, then is feen
The difference 'twixt a threfhold and a throne,

  Enter Creon, Pyracmon, Alcander, Tirefias, Thebans.

    Alc. Where, where's this cruel king? Thebans, behold
There ftands your plague, the ruin, defolation
Of this unhappy——Speak; fhall I kill him?
Or fhall he be caft out to banifhment?

    All Theb. To banifhment, away with him.

    OEdip. Hence, you barbarians, to your flavifh diftance!
Fix to the earth your fordid looks; for he
Who ftirs, dares more than mad-men, fiends, or furies.
' Who dares to face me, by the gods, as well
' May brave the majefty of thundering Jove.'
Did I for this relieve you when befieg'd
By this fierce prince, when coop'd within your walls,
And to the very brink of Fate reduc'd?
When lean-jaw'd famine made more havock of you,
Than does the plague? But I rejoice I know you,
Know the bafe ftuff that temper'd your vile fouls:
The gods be prais'd, I needed not your empire,
Born to a greater, nobler, of my own;
Nor fhall the fcepter of the earth now win me
To rule fuch brutes, fo barbarous a people.

    Adr. Methinks, my Lord, I fee a fad repentance,
A general confternation fpread among them.

    OEdip. My reign is at an end; yet ere I finifh—
I'll do a juftice that becomes a monarch,

A mo-

A monarch, who, i'th' midst of swords and javelins
Dares act as on his throne encompast round
With nations for his guard.　Alcander, you
Are nobly born, therefore shall lose your head :

> [Seizes him.

Here, Hæmon, take him ; but for this, and this,
Let cords dispatch them.　Hence, away with them.

Tir. Oh, sacred Prince, pardon distracted Thebes,
Pardon her, if she acts by Heav'n's award ;
' If that th' infernal spirits have declar'd
' The depth of Fate, and if our oracles
' May speak, Oh, do not too severely deal,
' But let thy wretched Thebes at least complain :'
If thou art guilty, Heav'n will make it known :
If innocent, then let Tiresias die.

OEdip. I take thee at thy word ; run, haste, and save
I swear the prophet, or the King shall die.　[Alcander :
Be witness, all you Thebans, of my oath ;
And Phorbas be the umpire.

Tir. I submit.　　　　　　　　　[Trumpets sound.

OEdip. What mean those trumpets ?

> *Enter* Hæmon, *with* Alcander, &c.

Hæm. From your native country,
Great Sir, the fam'd Ægeon is arriv'd,
That renown'd favourite of the King your father :
He comes as an ambassador from Corinth,
And sues for audience.

OEdip. Haste, Hæmon, fly, and tell him that I burn
T' embrace him.

Hæm. The Queen, my Lord, at present holds him
In private conference ; but behold her here.

> *Enter* Jocasta, Eurydice, &c.

Joc. Hail, happy OEdipus, happiest of kings !
Henceforth be blest, blest as thou canst desire,
Sleep without fears the blackest nights away ;
Let furies haunt thy palace, thou shalt sleep
Secure, thy slumbers shall be soft and gentle
As infant dreams.

OEdip. What does the soul of all my joys intend ?
And whither would this rapture ?

Joc. Oh, I could rave,
Pull down those lying fanes, and burn that vault,
From whence resounded those false oracles,

> That

That robb'd my love of reft : if we muft pray,
Rear in the ftreets bright altars to the gods,
Let virgins heads adorn the facrifice ;
And not a grey-beard forging prieft come near,
To pry into the bowels of the victim,
And with his dotage mad the gaping world.
But fee, the oracle that I will truft,
True as the gods, and affable as men.

Enter Ægeon. Kneels.

OEdip. Oh, to my arms, welcome, my dear Ægeon ;
Ten thoufand welcomes, Oh, my fofter father,
Welcome as mercy to a man condemn'd !
Welcome to me,
As, to a finking mariner,
The lucky plank that bears him to the fhore !
But fpeak, Oh, tell me what fo mighty joy
Is this thou bring'ft, which fo tranfports Jocafta ?

Joc. Peace, peace, Ægeon, let Jocafta tell him !
Oh, that I could for ever charm, as now,
My deareft OEdipus ; thy royal father,
Polybus, king of Corinth, is no more.

OEdip. Ha ! can it be ? Ægeon, anfwer me.
And fpeak in fhort what my Jocafta's tranfport
May over-do.

Æge. Since in few words, my royal Lord, you afk
To know the truth ; king Polybus is death.

OEdip. Oh, all you powers, is't poffible ? What dead !
But that the tempeft of my joy may rife
By juft degrees, and hit at laft the ftars :
Say, how, how dy'd he ? Ha ! by fword, by fire,
Or water ? By affaffinates, or poifon ? Speak :
Or did he languifh under fome difeafe ?

Æge. Of no diftemper, of no blaft he dy'd,
But fell like autumn-fruit that mellow'd long :
Ev'n wonder'd at, becaufe he dropp'd no fooner.
Fate feem'd to wind him up for fourfcore years ;
Yet frefhly ran he on ten winters more ;
Till, like a clock worn out with eating time,
The wheels of weary life at laft ftood ftill.

' *OEdip.* Oh, let me prefs thee in my youthful arms,
' And fmother my old age in thy embraces.
' Yes, Thebans, yes, Jocafta, yes, Adraftus,

' Old

' Old Polybus, the king, my father's dead.
' Fires shall be kindled in the midst of Thebes;
' I' th' midst of tumult, wars, and pestilence,
' I will rejoice for Polybus's death.
' Know, be it known to the limits of the world;
' Yet farther, let it pass yon dazzling roof,
' The mansion of the gods, and strike them deaf
' With everlasting peals of thund'ring joy.
 ' *Tir.* Fate! Nature! Fortune! what is all this world?'
 OEdip. Now, dotard; now, thou blind old wizard
   prophet,
Where are your boding ghosts, your altars now;
Your birds of knowledge, that in dusky air,
Chatter futurity? and where are now
Your oracles, that call'd me parricide?
Is he not dead? deep laid in his monument?
And was not I in Thebes when Fate attack'd him?
Avaunt, begone, you visors of the gods!
Were I as other sons, now I should weep;
But, as I am, I've reason to rejoice;
And will, though his cold shade should rise and blast me,
Oh, for this death, let waters break their bounds,
Rocks, valleys, hills, with splitting Io's ring:
Io, Jocasta, Io Pæan sing.
 Tir. Who would not now conclude a happy end!
But all Fate's turns are swift and unexpected.
 Æge. Your royal mother, Merope, as if
She had no soul since you forsook the land,
Waves all the neighb'ring princes that adore her.
 OEdip. Waves all the princes! Poor heart! for what?
   Oh, speak.
 Æge. She, tho' in full-blown flow'r of glorious beauty,
Grows cold, ev'n in the summer of her age;
And, for your sake, has sworn to die unmarry'd.
 OEdip. How! for my sake, die, and not marry! Oh,
My fit returns.
 Æge. This diamond, with a thousand kisses bles'd,
With thousand sighs and wishes for your safety,
She charg'd me give you, with the general homage
Of our Corinthian lords.
 OEdip. There's magic in it, take it from my sight;
There's not a beam it darts, but carries hell,
Hot flashing lust, and necromantic incest:
        Take

Take it from thefe fick eyes, Oh, hide it frem me.
No, my Jocafta, though Thebes caft me out,
While Merope's alive, I'll ne'er return !
Oh, rather let me walk round the wide world
A beggar, than accept a diadem
On fuch abhorr'd conditions.

Joc. You make, my Lord, your own unhappinefs,
By thefe extravagant and needlefs fears.

OEdip. Needlefs ! Oh, all you gods ! By Heav'n I'd
Embrue my hands up to my very fhoulders   [rather
In the dear entrails of the beft of fathers,
Than offer at the execrable act
Of damn'd inceft : therefore no more of her.

Æge. And why, Oh, facred Sir, if fubjects may
Prefume to look into their monarch's breaft,
Why fhould the chafte and fpotlefs Merope
Infufe fuch thoughts as I muft blufh to name ?

OEdip. Becaufe the god of Delphos did forewarn me,
With thundering oracles.

Æge. May I entreat to know them ?

OEdip. Yes, my Ægeon ; but the fad remembrance
Quite blafts my foul : fee then the fwelling prieft !
Methinks I have his image now in view :
He mounts the Tripos in a minute's fpace,
His clouded head knocks at the temple-roof,
While from his mouth
Thefe difmal words are heard :
" Fly, wretch, whom Fate has doom'd thy father's blood
            to fpill,
And with prepoft'rous births thy mother's womb to fill."

Æge. Is this the caufe
Why you refufe the diadem of Corinth ?

OEdip. The caufe ? Why, is it not a monftrous one ?

Æge. Great Sir, you may return : and tho' you fhould
Enjoy the queen (which all the gods forbid)
The act would prove no inceft.

OEdip. How, Ægeon ?
Though I enjoy'd my mother, not inceftuous !
' Thou rav'ft, and fo do I ; and thefe all catch
' My madnefs ; look, they're dead with deep diftraction.'
Not inceft ! What, not inceft with my mother ?

Æge. My Lord, queen Merope is not your mother.
                                        OEdip.

OEdip. Ha ! did I hear thee right ? Not Merope
My mother !

Æge. Nor was Polybus your father.

OEdip. Then all my days and nights muſt now be ſpent
In curious ſearch to find out thoſe dark parents
Who gave me to the world ; ſpeak then, Ægeon,
By all the gods celeſtial and infernal,
By all the ties of nature, blood, and friendſhip,
Conceal not from this rack'd deſpairing king
A point or ſmalleſt grain of what thou know'ſt :
Speak then, Oh, anſwer to my doubts directly.
If royal Polybus was not my father,
Why was I call'd his ſon ?

Æge. He, from my arms,
Receiv'd you as the faireſt gift of nature.
Not but you were adorn'd with all the riches
That empire could beſtow in coſtly mantles
Upon its infant heir.

OEdip. But was I made the heir of Corinth's crown,
Becauſe Ægeon's hands preſented me ?

Æge. By my advice,
Being paſt all hope of children,
He took, embrac'd, and own'd you for his ſon.

OEdip. Perhaps I then am yours ; inſtruct me, Sir :
If it be ſo, I'll kneel and weep before you,
With all th' obedience of a penitent child,
Imploring pardon.
Kill me, if you pleaſe,
I will not writhe my body at the wound :
But ſink upon your feet with a laſt ſigh,
And aſk forgiveneſs with my dying hands.

Æge. Oh, riſe, and call not to this aged cheek
The little blood which ſhould keep warm my heart ;
You are not, mine, nor ought I to be bleſt
With ſuch a god-like offspring,   Sir, I found you
Upon the mount Cithæron.

OEdip. Oh, ſpeak, go on, the air grows ſenſible
Of the great things you utter, and is calm :
The hurry'd orbs, with ſtorms ſo rack'd of late,
Seem to ſtand ſtill, as if that Jove were talking.
Cithæron ! Speak, the valley of Cithæron !

Æge. Oft-times before I thither did reſort,

Charm'd

Charm'd with the converfation of a man
Who led a rural life, and had command
O'er all the fhepherds, who about thofe vales
Tended their numerous flocks : in this man's arms
I faw you fmiling at a fatal dagger,
Whofe point he often offer'd at your throat ;
But then you fmil'd, and then he drew it back,
Then lifted it again, you fmil'd again ;
'Till he at laft in fury threw it from him,
And cry'd aloud, The gods forbid thy death.
Then I ruſh'd in, and after fome difcourfe,
To me he did bequeath your innocent life ;
And I, the welcome care to Polybus.

   OEdip. To whom belongs the mafter of the fhepherds ?

   Æge. His name I knew not, or I have forgot :
That he was of the family of Laius,
I well remember.

   OEdip. And is your friend alive ? for if he be,
I'll buy his prefence, though it coft my crown.

   Æge. Your menial attendants beft can tell
Whether he lives, or not ; and who has now
His place.

   Joc. Winds, bear me to fome barren ifland,
Where print of human feet was never feen,
O'er-grown with weeds of fuch a monftrous height,
Their baleful tops are waſh'd wirh bellying clouds ;
Beneath whofe venomous ſhade I may have vent
For horrors that would blaft the barbarous world.

   OEdip. If there be any here that knows the perfon
Whom he defcrib'd, I charge him on his life
To fpeak ; concealment ſhall be fudden death :
But he who brings him forth, ſhall have reward
Beyond ambition's luft.

   Tir. His name is Phorbas ;
Jocafta knows him well ; but if I may
Advife, reft where you are, and feek no farther.

   OEdip. Then all goes well, fince Phorbas is fecur'd
By my Jocafta. Hafte, and bring him forth :
My love, my queen, give orders. Ha ! what mean
Thefe tears, and groans, and ftrugglings ? Speak, my fair,
Why are thy troubles ?

   Joc. Yours ; and yours are mine :

'Let

Let me conjure you take the prophet's counfel,
 And let this Phorbas go.
    OEdip. Not for the world.
By all the gods, I'll know my birth, though death
Attends the fearch : I have already paft
The middle of the ftream ; and to return
Seems greater labour, than to venture o'er.
Therefore produce him.
    Joc. Once more, by the gods,
I beg, my OEdipus, my lord, my life,
My love, my all, my only utmoft hope,
I beg you, banifh Phorbas : Oh, the gods,
I kneel, that you may grant this firft requeft.
Deny me all things elfe ; but for my fake,
And as you prize your own eternal quiet,
Never let Phorbas come into your prefence.
    OEdip. You muft be rais'd, and Phorbas fhall appear,
Though his dread eyes were bafilifks.   Guards, hafte,
Search the queen's lodgings : find, and force him hither.
                                        [*Excunt Guards.*

    Joc. Oh, OEdipus, yet fend,
And ftop their entrance, ere it be too late :
Unlefs you wifh to fee Jocafta rent
With furies, flain out-right with mere diftraction,
Keep from your eyes and mine the dreadful Phorbas.
Forbear this fearch, I'll think you more than mortal
Will you yet hear me ?
    OEdip. Tempefts will be heard,
And waves will dafh, though rocks their bafis keep.——
But fee, they enter.   If thou truly lov'ft me,
Either forbear this fubject, or retire.
              Enter Hæmon, *Guards, with* Phorbas.
    Joc. Prepare then, wretched prince, prepare to hear
A ftory, that fhall turn thee into ftone.
Could there be hewn a monftrous gap in nature,
A flaw made through the center, by fome god,
Through which the groans of ghofts may ftrike thy ears,
They will not wound thee as this ftory will.
Hark, hark ! a hollow voice calls out aloud,
Jocafta ! Yes, I'll to the royal bed,
Where firft the myfteries of our loves were acted,
And double-dye it with imperial crimfou ;
                        F   Tear

Tear off this curling hair,
Be gorg'd with fire, ftab every vital part,
And when at laft I'm flain, to crown the horror,
My poor tormented ghoft fhall cleave the ground,
To try if hell can yet more deeply wound.   [*Exit.*

OEdip. She's gone; and as fhe went, methought her
Grew larger, while a thoufand frantic fpirits   [eyes
Seething, like rifing bubbles, on the brim,
Peep'd from the watery brink, and glow'd upon me.
I'll feek no more; but hufh my genius up
That throws me on my fate.——Impoffible!
Oh, wretched man, whofe too too bufy thoughts
Ride fwifter than the galloping heav'ns round,
With an eternal hurry of the foul;
Nay, there's a time when ev'n the rolling year
Seems to ftand ftill, dead calms are in the ocean,
When not a breath difturbs the drowzy waves:
But man, the very monfter of the world,
Is ne'er at reft, the foul for ever wakes.
Come then, fince Deftiny thus drives us on,
Let's know the bottom.   Hæmon, you I fent:
Where is that Phorbas?

 Hæm. Here, my royal Lord.

 OEdip. Speak firft, Ægeon, fay, is this the man?

 Æge. My Lord, it is: though time has plough'd that
With many furrows fince I faw it firft;   [face
Yet I'm too well acquainted with the ground, quite to

 OEdip. Peace! ftand back a while.   [forget it.
Come hither, friend; I hear thy name is Phorbas.
Why doft thou turn thy face? I charge thee anfwer
To what I fhall enquire: wert thou not once
The fervant to king Laius here in Thebes?

 Phor. I was, great Sir, his true and faithful fervant,
Born and bred up in court, no foreign flave.

 OEdip. What office hadft thou? What was thy employment?

 Phor. He made me lord of all his rural pleafures;
For much he lov'd them: oft I entertain'd
With fporting fwains, o'er whom I had command.

 OEdip. Where was thy refidence? To what part o'th'
Didft thou moft frequently refort?   [country

 Phor. To mount Cithæron, and the pleafant vallies
Which all about lie fhadowing its large feet.

OEdip.

OEdip. Come forth, Ægeon. Ha! why ſtart'ſt thou,
     Phorbas?
'Forward, I ſay, and face to face confront him;
Look wiſtly on him, through him, if thou canſt,
And tell me on thy life, ſay, doſt thou know him?
Didſt thou e'er ſee him? e'er converſe with him
Near mount Cithæron?
    Phor. Who, my Lord, this man?
    OEdip. This man, this old, this venerable man:
Speak, didſt thou ever meet him there?
    Phor. Where, ſacred Sir?
    OEdip. Near mount Cithæron; anſwer to the purpoſe,
'Tis a king ſpeaks; and royal minutes are
Of much more worth than thouſand vulgar years:
Didſt thou e'er ſee this man near mount Cithæron?
    Phor. Moſt ſure, my Lord, I have ſeen lines like thoſe
His viſage bears; but know not where nor when.
    Æge. Is't poſſible you ſhould forget your ancient friend?
There are perhaps
Particulars, which may excite your dead remembrance.
Have you forgot I took an infant from you,
Doom'd to be murder'd in that gloomy vale?
The ſwadling-bands were purple, wrought with gold.
Have you forgot too how you wept, and begg'd
That I ſhould breed him up, and aſk no more?
    Phor. What e'er I begg'd, thou, like a dotard, ſpeak'ſt
More than is requiſite. And what of this?
Why is it mention'd now? And why, Oh, why
Doſt thou betray the ſecrets of thy friend?
    Æge. Be not too raſh. That infant grew at laſt
A king; and here the happy monarch ſtands.
    Phor. Ha! whither would'ſt thou? Oh, what haſt thou
     utter'd!
For what thou haſt ſaid, death ſtrike thee dumb for ever!
    OEdip. Forbear to curſe the innocent; and be
Accurſt thyſelf, thou ſhifting traitor, villain,
Damn'd hypocrite, equivocating ſlave.
    Phor. Oh, heav'ns! wherein, my Lord, have I offended?
    OEdip. Why ſpeak you not according to my charge?
Bring forth the rack: ſince mildneſs cannot win you,
Torments ſhall force.
    Phor. Hold, hold, Oh, dreadful Sir;
You will not rack an innocent old man.
        F 2   *OEdip.*

OEdip. Speak then.

Phor. Alas, what would you have me fay?

OEdip. Did this old man take from your arms an infant?

Phor. He did : and, Oh, I wifh to all the gods,
Phorbas had perifh'd in that very moment.

OEdip. Moment! Thou fhalt be hours, days, years, a
Here, bind his hands ; he dallies with my fury : [dying.
But I fhall find a way——

Phor. My Lord, I faid
I gave the infant to him.

OEdip. Was he thy own, or given thee by another?

Phor. He was not mine ; but given me by another.

OEdip. Whence? and from whom? What city? Of
      what houfe?

Phor. Oh, royal Sir, I bow me to the ground,
Would I could fink beneath it : by the gods,
I do conjure you to enquire no more.

OEdip. Furies and hell! Hæmon, bring forth the rack,
Fetch hither cords, and knives, and fulphurous flames :
He fhall be bound, and gafh'd, his fkin flead off,
And burnt alive.

Phor. Oh, fpare my age.

OEdip. Rife then, and fpeak.

Phor. Dread Sir, I will.

OEdip. Who gave that infant to thee?

Phor. One of king Laius' family.

OEdip. Oh, you immortal gods! But fay, who was't?
Which of the family of Laius gave it?
A fervant, or one of the royal-blood?

Phor. Oh, wretchd ftate! I die, unlefs I fpeak ;
And, if I fpeak, moft certain death attends me!

OEdip. Thou fhalt not die. Speak then, who was it?
While I have fenfe to underftand the horror ;   [Speak,
For I grow cold.

Phor. The queen Jocafta told me
It was her fon by Laius.

OEdip. Oh, you gods!—But did fhe give it thee?

Phor. My Lord, fhe did.

OEdip. Wherefore? For what?——Oh, break not
      yet my heart ;
Though my eyes burft, no matter. Wilt thou tell me,
Or, muft I afk for ever ; for what end,
Why gave fhe thee her child?

Phor. To murder it.   *OEdip.*

OEdip. Oh, more than favage! murder her own bo-
Without a caufe!   [wels!
    Phor. There was a dreadful one,
Which had foretold, that moft unhappy fon
Should kill his father, and enjoy his mother.
    OEdip. But one thing more.
Jocafta told me thou wert by the chariot
When the old king was flain. Speak, I conjure thee,
For I fhall never afk thee ought again,
What was the number of th' affaffinates?
    Phor. The dreadful deed was acted but by one;
And fure that one had much of your refemblance.
    OEdip. 'Tis well! I thank you, gods! 'tis wond'rous
Daggers, and poifons! Oh, there is no need   [well!
For my difpatch: and you, you mercilefs pow'rs,
Hoard up your thunder-ftones; keep, keep your bolts
For crimes of little note.   [*Falls.*
    Adr. Help, Hæmon, help, and bow him gently forward;
' Chafe, chafe his temples: how the mighty fpirits,
' Half-ftrangled with the damp his forrows rais'd,
' Struggle for vent! But fee, he breathes again,
' And vigorous nature breaks through oppofition.'
How fares my royal friend?
    OEdip. The worfe for you.
Oh, barbarous men, and, Oh, the hated light,
Why did you force me back to curfe the day;
To curfe my friends; to blaft with this dark breath
The yet untainted earth and circling air?
To raife new plagues, and call new vengeance down,
Why did you tempt the gods, and dare to touch me?
' Methinks there's not a hand that grafps this hell,
' But fhould run up like flax all blazing fire.'
Stand from this fpot, I wifh you as my friends,
And come not near me, left the gaping earth
Swallow you too——Lo, I am gone already.
        [*Draws, and claps his fword to his breaft, which*
            Adraftus ftrikes away with his foot.
    Adr. You fhall no more be trufted with your life:
Creon, Alcander, Hæmon, help to hold him.
    OEdip. Cruel Adraftus! Wilt thou, Hæmon, too?
Are thefe the obligations of my friends?
Oh, worfe than worft of my moft barbarous foes!
                    F 3.   Dear,

Dear, dear Adraftus, look with half an eye
On my unheard of woes, and judge thyfelf,
If it be fit that fuch a wretch fhould live !
Oh, by thefe melting eyes, unus'd to weep,
With all the low fubmiffions of a flave,
I do conjure thee give my horrors way;
'Talk not of life, for that will make fne rave:
As well thou may'ft advife a tortur'd wretch,
All mangled o'er from head to foot with wounds,
And his bones broke, to wait a better day.

Adr. My Lord, you afk-me things impoffible;
And I with juftice fhould be thought your foe,
To leave you in this tempeft of your foul.

Tir. Tho' banifh'd Thebes, in Corinth you may reign;
Th' infernal pow'rs themfelves exact no more:
Calm then your rage, and once more feek the gods.

OEdip. I'll have no more to do with gods, nor men !
' Hence, from my arms, avaunt. Enjoy thy mother !
' What, violate, with beftial appetite,
' The facred veils that wrapt thee yet unborn !
' This is not to be borne ! Hence: off, I fay;
' For they who let my vengeance, make themfelves
' Accomplices in my moft horrid guilt.
' *Adr.* Let it be fo: we'll fence Heav'n's fury from
' And fuffer all together: this, perhaps, [you,
' When ruin comes, may help to break your fall.'

OEdip. Oh, that, as oft I have at Athens feen
The ftage arife, and the big clouds defcend;
So now in very deed I might behold
The pond'rous earth, and all yon' marble roof
Meet, like the hand of Jove, and crufh mankind !
For all the elements, and all the pow'rs
Celeftial, nay, terreftrial, and infernal,
Confpire the rack of out-caft OEdipus.
Fall darknefs then, and everlafting night
Shadow the globe; may the fun never dawn,
The filver moon be blotted from her orb;
And for an univerfal rout of Nature
Through all the inmoft chambers of the fky,
May there not be a glimpfe, one ftarry fpark,
But gods meet gods, and juftle in the dark;

That

That jars may rife, and wrath divine be hurl'd,
Which may to atoms fhake the folid world.   [*Exeunt.*

END of the FOURTH ACT.

ACT V.

Enter Creon, Alcander *and* Pyracmon.

CREON.

THEBES is at length my own ; and all my wifhes,
    Which fure were great as royalty e'er form'd,
Fortune and my aufpicious ftars have crown'd.
O diadem, thou center of ambition,
Where all its different lines are reconcil'd,
As if thou wert the burning-glafs of glory !
    Pyr. Might I be counfellor, I would intreat you
To cool a little, Sir ;
Find out Eurydice ;
And with the refolution of a man
Mark'd out for greatnefs, give the fatal choice
Of death or marriage.
    Alc. Survey curs'd OEdipus,
As one who tho' unfortunate, belov'd,
Thought innocent, and therefore much lamented
By all the Thebans : you muft mark him dead :
Since nothing but his death, not banifhment,
Can give affurance to your doubtful reign.
    Cre. Well have you done, to fnatch me from the ftorm
Of racking tranfport, where the little ftreams
Of love, revenge, and all the under paffions,
As waters are by fucking whirlpools drawn,
Were quite devour'd in the vaft gulph of empire ;
Therefore, Pyracmon, as you boldly urg'd,
Eurydice fhall die, or be my bride.
Alcander, fummon to their mafter's aid,
My menial fervants, and all thofe whom change
Of ftate and hope of the new monarch's favour,
Can wifh to take our part. Away ! What now ?
                                    [*Exit* Alcander.
                                            Enter

Enter Hæmon.

When Hæmon weeps, ' without the help of ghosts,'
I may foretel there is a fatal cause.

   Hæm. Is't possible you should be ignorant
Of what has happen'd to the desperate king ?

  Cre. I know no more but that he was conducted
Into his closet, where I saw him fling
His trembling body on the royal bed.
All left him there, at his desire, alone :
But sure no ill, unless he dy'd with grief,
Could happen, for you bore his sword away.

  Hæm. I did ; and having lock'd the door, I stood ;
And through a chink I found, not only heard,
But saw him, when he thought no eye beheld him :
At first deep sighs heav'd from his woeful heart
Murmurs, and groans that shook the outward rooms.
And art thou still alive, O wretch ! he cry'd :
Then groan'd again, as if his sorrowful soul
Had crack'd the strings of life, and burst away.

  Cre. I weep to hear ; how then should I have griev'd,
Had I beheld this wond'rous heap of sorrow !
But to the fatal period.

  Hæm. Thrice he struck,
With all his force, his hollow groaning breast,
And thus, with out-cries, to himself complain'd.
But thou canst weep then, and thou think'st 'tis well.
These bubbles of the shallowest, emptiest sorrow,
Which children vent for toys, and women rain
For any trifle their fond hearts are set on ;
Yet these thou think'st are ample satisfaction
For bloodiest murder, and for burning lust :
No, Parricide ; if thou must weep, weep blood ;
Weep eyes instead of tears : O, by the gods,
'Tis greatly thought, he cry'd, and fits my woes.
Which said, he smil'd revengefully, and leapt
Upon the floor ; thence gazing at the skies,
' His eye-balls fiery red, and glowing vengeance ;
' Gods, I accuse you not, tho' I no more
' Will view your heav'n, till with more durable glasses,
' The mighty soul's immortal perspectives,
' I find your dazzling beings :' take, he cry'd,
Take, eyes, your last, your fatal farewel-view ;

Then

Then with a groan, that seem'd the call of death,
With horrid force lifting his impious hands,
He snatch'd, he tore, from forth their bloody orbs,
The balls of fight, and dash'd them on the ground.

Cre. A master-piece of horror; new and dreadful!

Hæm. I ran to succour him ; but, oh ! too late ;
For he had pluck'd the remnant strings away.
What then remains, but that I find Tiresias,
Who, with his wisdom, may allay those furies
That haunt his gloomy soul ?   [*Exit.*

Cre. Heav'n will reward
Thy care, most honest, faithful, foolish Hæmon !
But see, Alcander enters, well attended.

    Enter Alcander, *attended.*

I see thou hast been diligent.

Alc. Nothing these,
For number, to the crowds that soon will follow:
Be resolute,
And call your utmost fury to revenge.

Cre. Ha ! thou hast given
Th' alarm to cruelty ; and never may
These eyes be clos'd, till they behold Adrastus
Stretch'd at the feet of false Eurydice.
But see, they're here ? retire a while, and mark.

   Enter Adrastus *and* Eurydice *attended.*

Adr. Alas, Eurydice, what fond rash man,
What inconsiderate and ambitious fool,
That shall hereafter read the fate of OEdipus,
Will dare, with his frail hand, to grasp a scepter ?

Eur. 'Tis true, a crown seems dreadful, and I wish
That you and I, more lowly plac'd, might pass
Our softer hours in humble cells away :
Not but I love you to that infinite height,
I could (O wond'rous proof of fiercest love !)
Be greatly wretched in a court with you.

Adr. Take then this most lov'd innocence away :
Fly from tumultuous Thebes, from blood and murder ;
Fly from the author of all villanies,
Rapes, death and treason ; from that fury Creon.
Vouchsafe that I, o'er-joy'd, may bear you hence,
And at your feet present the crown of Argos.

   [Creon *and Attendants come up to him.*
          Cre.

Cre. I have o'er-heard thy black defign, Adraftus,
And therefore as a traitor to this ftate,
Death ought to be thy lot : let it fuffice
That Thebes furveys thee as a prince ; abufe not
Her proffer'd mercy, but retire betimes,
Left fhe repent, and haften on thy doom.

Adr. Think not, moft abject,
Moft abhorr'd of men,
Adraftus will vouchfafe to anfwer thee.
Thebans, to you I juftify my love :
I have addreft my prayer to this fair princefs ;
But, if I ever meant a violence,
Or thought to ravifh, as that traitor did,
What humbleft adorations could not win ;
Brand me, you gods, blot me with foul difhonour,
And let men curfe me by the name of Creon !

Eur. Hear me, O Thebans, if you dread the wrath
Of her whom fate ordain'd to be your queen,
Hear me, and dare not, as you prize your lives,
To take the part of that rebellious traitor.
By the decree of royal OEdipus,
By queen Jocafta's order, by what's more,
My own dear vows of everlafting love,
I here refign to prince Adraftus' arms
All that the world can make me miftrefs of.

Cre. O, perjur'd woman !
Draw all ! and when I give the word fall on.
Traitor, refign the princefs, or this moment
Expect, with all thofe moft unfortunate wretches,
Upon this fpot ftraight to be hewn in pieces.

Adr. No, villain, no ;
With twice thofe odds of men,
I doubt not in this caufe to vanquifh thee.
Captain, remember to your care I give
My love ; ten thoufand thoufand times more dear
Than life or liberty.

Cre. Fall on, Alcander.
Pyracmon, you and I muft wheel about
For nobler game, the princefs.

Adr. Ah, traitor, doft thou fhun me ?
Follow, follow,
My brave companions, fee the cowards fly.

[*Exeunt fighting :* Creon's *party beaten off by* Adraftus.

Enter

Enter OEdipus.

OEdip. O, 'tis too little this, thy loss of sight,
What has it done? I shall be gaz'd at now
The more; be pointed at, There goes the monster!
Nor have I hid my horrors from myself;
For tho' corporeal light be lost for ever,
The bright reflecting soul, through glaring opticks,
Presents in larger size her black ideas,
Doubling the bloody prospects of my crimes:
Holds Fancy down, and makes her act again,
With wife and mother. ' Tortures, hell and furies!
' Ha! now the baleful offspring's brought to light!
' In horrid form they rank themselves before me;
' What shall I call this medley of creation?
' Here's one, with all th' obedience of a son,
' Borrowing Jocasta's look, kneels at my feet,
' And calls me father; there a sturdy boy,
' Resembling Laius just as when I kill'd him,
' Bears up, and with his cold hand grasping mine,
' Cries out, how fares my brother OEdipus?
' What, sons and brothers! Sisters and daughters too!
' Fly all, begone, fly from my whirling brain;'
Hence, incest, murder; hence, you ghastly figures!
O gods! gods, answer; is there any means?
Let me go mad, or die.

Enter Jocasta.

Joc. Where, where is this most wretched of mankind,
This stately image of imperial sorrow,
' Whose story told, whose very name but mention'd,
' Would cool the rage of fevers, and unlock
' The hand of lust from the pale virgin's hair.
' And throw the ravisher before her feet?'
OEdip. By all my fears, I think Jocasta's voice!
Hence; fly; begone. ' O thou far worse than worst
' Of damning charmers! O abhor'd, loath'd creature!
' Fly, by the gods, or by the fiends, I charge thee,'
Far as the east, west, north, or south of Heav'n;
But think not thou shalt ever enter there:
The golden gates are barr'd with adamant,
'Gainst thee, and me; and the celestial guards,
Still as we rise, will dash our spirits down.

' *Joc.*

'*Joc.* O wretched pair ! O greatly wretched we !
'Two worlds of woe !
'*OEdip.* Art thou not gone then ? ha !
'How dar'ft thou ftand the fury of the gods ?
'Or com'ft thou in the grave to reap new pleafures ?
'*Joc.* Talk on; till thou mak'ft mad my rolling brain;
'Groan ftill more death; and may thofe difmal fources
'Still bubble on, and pour forth blood and tears.
'Methinks, at fuch a meeting, Heav'n ftands ftill;
'The fea nor ebbs nor flows: this mole-hill earth
'Is heav'd no more: the bufy emmets ceafe :
'Yet hear me on——
'*OEdip.* Speak then, and blaft my foul.
'*Joc.* O, my lov'd Lord, tho I refolve a ruin
'To match my crimes; by all my miferies,
''Tis horror, worfe than thoufand thoufand deaths,
'To fend me hence without a kind farewel.   [cafta.
'*OEdip.* Gods, how fhe fhakes me! Stay thee, O Jo-
'Speak fomething ere thou goeft for ever from me.
'*Joc.* 'Tis woman's weaknefs, that I fhould be pity'd;
'Pardon me then, O greateft, tho' moft wretched
'Of all thy kind: my foul is on the brink,
'And fees the boiling furnace juft beneath :
'Do not thou pufh me off, and I will go,
'With fuch a willingnefs, as if that Heav'n
'With all its glory glow'd for my reception.
'*OEdip.* O, in my heart, I feel the pangs of nature;
'It works with kindnefs o'er : give, give me way;
'I feel a melting here, a tendernefs,
'Too mighty for the anger of the gods !
'Direct me to thy knees : yet Oh forbear,
'Left the dead embers fhould revive.
'Stand off——and at juft diftance
'Let me groan my horrors—here
'On the earth, here blow my utmoft gale;
'Here fob my forrows, till I burft with fighing;
'Here gafp and languifh out my wounded foul '
     Joc. In fpight of all thofe crimes the cruel gods
Can charge me with, I know my innocence;
Know yours : 'tis fate alone that makes us wretched,
For you are ftill my hufband.
     OEdip. Swear I am,

And

And I'll believe thee; steal into thy arms,
Renew endearments, think them no pollutions,
But chaste as spirits' joys: gently I'll come,
Thus weeping blind, like dewy night, upon thee,
And fold thee softly in my arms to slumber.
   [*The ghost of* Laius *ascends by degrees, pointing at* Jocasta.
   Joc. Begone, my Lord! Alas, what are we doing?
Fly from my arms! Whirlwinds, seas, continents,
And worlds, divide us! Oh, thrice happy thou,
Who hast no use of eyes; for here's a sight
Would turn the melting face of Mercy's self
To a wild fury.
   OEdip. Ha! what seest thou there?
   Joc. The spirit of my husband! Oh, the gods!
How wan he looks!
   OEdip. Thou rav'st; thy husband's here.
   Joc. There, there he mounts
In circling fire among the blushing clouds!
And see, he waves Jocasta from the world!
   Ghost. Jocasta, OEdipus.   [*Vanish with thunder.*
   OEdip. What would'st thou have?
Thou know'st I cannot come to thee, detain'd
In darkness here, and kept from means of death.
I've heard a spirit's force is wonderful;
At whose approach, when starting from his dungeon,
The earth does shake, and the old ocean groans,
Rocks are remov'd, and tow'rs are thunder'd down:
And walls of brass, and gates of adamant
Are passable as air, and fleet like winds.
   Joc. Was that a raven's croak, or my son's voice?
No matter which; I'll to the grave and hide me:
Earth, open, or I'll tear thy bowels up.
Hark! he goes on, and blabs the deed of incest.
   OEdip. Strike then, imperial ghost; dash all at once
This house of clay into a thousand pieces;
That my poor ling'ring soul may take her flight
To your immortal dwellings.
   Joc. Haste thee then,
Or I shall be before thee: see; thou canst not see;
Then I will tell thee that my wings are on:
I'll mount, I'll fly, and with a port divine
Glide all along the gaudy milky soil,

G

To

To find my Laius out : afk every god
In his bright palace, if he knows my Laius,
My murder'd Laius !

OEdip. Ha ! how's this, Jocafta ?
Nay, if thy brain be fick, then thou art happy.

Joc. Ha ! will you not ? Shall I not find him out ?
Will you not fhew him ? Are my tears defpis'd ?
Why, then I'll thunder ; yes, I will be mad,
And fright you with my cries : yes, cruel gods,
Though vultures, eagles, dragons tear my heart,
I'll fnatch celeftial flames, fire all your dwellings,
Melt down your golden roofs, and make your doors
Of cryftal fly from off their diamond hinges ;
Drive you all out from your ambrofial hives,
To fwarm like bees about the field of heav'n :
This will I do, unlefs you fhew me Laius,
My dear, my murder'd Lord. Oh, Laïus ! Laius ! Laius !
                                      [Exit.

OEdip. Excellent grief ! why, this is as it fhould be !
No mourning can be fuitable to crimes
Like ours, but what death makes, or madnefs forms.
‘ I could have wifh'd, methought, for fight again,
‘ To mark the gallantry of her diftraction :
‘ Her blazing eyes darting the wand'ring ftars,
‘ T'have feen her mouth the heav'ns, and mate the gods.
‘ While with her thund'ring voice fhe menac'd high,
‘ And every accent twang'd with fmarting forrow ;’
But what's all this to thee ? Thou, coward, yet
Art living, canft not, wilt not find the road
To the great palace of magnificent death ;
Though thoufand ways lead to his thoufand doors,
Which day and night are ftill unbarr'd for all.
        [Clafhing of fwords : drums and trumpets without.
Hark ! 'tis the noife of clafhing fwords ! the found
Comes near : Oh, that a battle would come o'er me !
If I but grafp a fwoid, or wreft a dagger,
I'll make a ruin with the firft that falls.
        Enter Hæmon, *with Guards.*

Hæm. Seize him, and bear him to the weftern tow'r.
Pardon me, facred Sir ; I am inform'd
That Creon has defigns upon your life :
Forgive me then, if, to preferve you from him,
I order your confinement.   *OEdip.*

OEdip. Slaves unhand me.
I think thou haſt a ſword : 'twas the wrong ſide.
Yet, cruel Hæmon, think not I will live ;
He that could tear his eyes out, ſure can find
Some deſperate way to ſtifle this curs'd breath.
' Or if I ſtarve ! but that's a ling'ring fate ;
' Or if I leave my brains upon the wall !
' The airy ſoul can eaſily o'er-ſhoot
' Thoſe bounds with which thou ſtriv'ſt to pale her in :
' Yes, I will periſh in deſpight of thee ;
' And, by the rage that ſtirs me, if I meet thee
' In th' other world I'll curſe thee for this uſage.' [*Ex.*

Hæm. Tireſias, after him ; and with your counſel
Adviſe him humbly ; charm, if poſſible,
Theſe feuds within : while I without extinguiſh,
Or periſh in th' attempt, the furious Creon ;
That brand which ſets our city in a flame.

Tir. Heav'n proſper your intent, and give a period
To all our plagues : what old Tireſias can,
Shall ſtraight be done. Lead, Mantoe to the tow'r.
　　　　　　　　　　　　　　　[*Exeunt* Tir. *&* Man.

Hæm. Follow me all, and help to part this fray,
　　　　　　　　　　　　　　　[*Trumpets again.*
Or fall together in the bloody broil. 　　　[*Exeunt.*
Enter Creon *with* Eurydice, Pyracmon, *and his party,*
　　　　　giving ground to Adraſtus.

Cre. Hold, hold your arms, Adraſtus, prince of Argos,
Hear, and behold ; Eurydice is my priſoner.

Adr. What wouldſt thou, hell-hound ?

Cre. See this brandiſh'd dagger :
Forego th' advantage which thy arms have won,
Or, by the blood which trembles through the heart
Of her whom more than life I know thou lov'ſt,
I'll bury to the haft, in her fair breaſt,
This inſtrument of my revenge. 　　　　　　　[hand.

Adr. Stay thee, damn'd wretch : hold, ſtop thy bloody

Cre. Give order then, that on this inſtant, now,
This moment, all thy ſoldiers ſtraight diſband.

Adr. Away, my friends, ſince fate has ſo allotted ;
Begone, and leave me to the villain's mercy.

Eur. Ah, my Adraſtus ! call 'em, call 'em back !
Stand there ; come back, O, cruel, barbarous men !
　　　　　　　　G 2 　　　　　　　　　Could

Could you then leave your lord, your prince your king,
After fo bravely having fought his caufe,
To perifh by the hand of this bafe villain ?
Why rather rufh you not at once together
All to his ruin ? drag him through the ftreets,
Hang his contageous quarters on the gates ;
Nor let my death affright you.
    Cre. Die firft thyfelf then.
    Adr. O, I charge thee hold.
Hence from my prefence all : he's not my friend
That difobeys : fee, art thou now appeas'd ?
[Exeunt Attendants.

Or is there ought elfe yet remains to do,
That can atone thee ? flack thy thirft of blood
With mine : but fave, O fave that innocent wretch.
    Cre. Forego thy fword, and yield thyfelf my prifoner.
    Eur. Yet while there's any dawn of hope to fave
Thy precious life, my dear Adraftus,
Whate'er thou doft, deliver not thy fword ;
With that thou mayft get off, tho' odds oppofe thee :
For me, O fear not ; no, he dare not touch me ;
His horrid love will fpare me. Keep thy fword ;
Left I be ravifh'd after thou art flain.
    Adr. Inftruct me, gods, what fhall Adraftus do ?
    Cre. Do what thou wilt, when fhe is dead : my foldier
With numbers will o'er-pow'r thee. Is't thy wifh
Eurydice fhould fall before thee ?
    Adr. Traitor, no :
Better that thou, and I, and all mankind,
Should be no more.
    Cre. Then caft thy fword away,
And yield thee to my mercy, or I ftrike.
    Adr. Hold thy rais'd arm ; give me a moment's paufe.
My father, when he bleft me, gave me this ;
My fon, faid he, let this be thy laft refuge ;
If thou forego'ft it, mifery attends thee :
Yet love now charms it from me ; which in all
The hazards of my life I never loft.
'Tis thine, my faithful fword ; my only truft ;
Though my heart tells me, that the gift is fatal.
    Cre. Fatal ! yes, foolifh, love-fick prince, it fhall :
Thy arrogance, thy fcorn,
My wound's remembrance,

Turn

Turn, all at once, the fatal point upon thee.
Pyracmon, to the palace ; difpatch
The king : hang Hæmon up ; for he is loyal,
And will oppofe me.   Come, Sir, are you ready ?

Adr. Yes, villain, for whatever thou canft dare.

Eur. Hold, Creon ! or thro' me, thro' me you woun

Adr. Off, Madam, or we perifh both.   Behold,
I'm not unarm'd ; my poignard's in my hand :
Therefore, away——

Eur. I'll guard your life with mine.

Cre. Die both, then ; there is now no time for dallying.
                                        [*Kills* Eurydice.

Eur. Ah, Prince, farewel ! farewel, my dear Adraftus.
                                        [*Dies.*

Adr. Unheard-of monfter ! eldeft-born of hell !
Down to thy primitive flame.   [*Stabs* Creon.

Cre. Help, foldiers, help !
Revenge me !

Adr. More, yet more ; a thoufand wounds !
I'll ftab thee ftill, thus, to the gaping furies.
                    [Adraftus *falls, killed by the foldiers.*
Enter Hæmon, *Guards, with* Alcander *and* Pyracmon
            bound ; the affaffins are driven off.
Oh, Hæmon, I am flain ! nor need I name
Th' inhuman author of all villainies ;
There he lies, gafping.

Cre. If I muft plunge in flames,
Burn firft my arm ; bafe inftrument, unfit
To act the dictates of my daring mind.
Burn, burn for ever, Oh, weak fubftitute
Of that, the god, Ambition !   [*Dies.*

Adr. She's gone—Oh, deadly markfman ! in the heart !
Yet in the pangs of death fhe grafps my hand :
Her lips, too, tremble, as if fhe would fpeak
Her laft farewel.   Oh, Œdipus, thy fall
Is great ! and nobly now thou go'ft attended.
They talk of heroes, and celeftial beauties,
And wond'rous pleafures in the other world :
Let me but find her there ; I afk no more.   [*Dies.*
Enter a Captain to Hæmon, *with* Tirefias *and* Manto.

Cap. Oh, Sir, the queen, Jocafta, fwift and wild,
As a robb'd tygrefs bounding o'er the woods,

Has

Has acted murders that amaze mankind.
In twisted gold I saw her daughters hang
On the bed royal, and her little sons
Stabb'd through the breasts upon the bloody pillows.

Ham. Relentless Heav'ns! Is then the fate of Laius
Never to be aton'd. How sacred ought
Kings lives be held, when but the death of one
Demands an empire's blood for expiation!
But see, the furious, mad Jocasta's here.
SCENE *draws, and discovers* Jocasta *held by her women,*
· ' *and stabbed in many places of her bosom, her hair dishe-*
' *velled, her children slain upon the bed.'*
Was ever yet a sight of so much horror
And pity brought to view!

Joc. Ah, cruel women!
Will you not let me take my last farewel
Of those dear babes? Oh, let me run and seal
My melting soul upon their bubbling wounds!
I'll print upon their coral mouths such kisses,
As shall recall their wand'ring spirits home.
Let me go, let me go, or I will tear you piece-meal.
Help, Hæmon, help!
Help, OEdipus! help, gods! Jocasta dies!
Enter OEdipus *above.*

OEdip. I've found a window, and, I thank the gods,
'Tis quite unbarr'd. Sure, by the distant noise,
The height will fit my fatal purpose well.

Joc. What, hoa, my OEdipus! See where he stands!
His groping ghost is lodg'd upon a tow'r,
Nor can it find the road. Mount, mount, my soul!
I'll wrap thy shiv'ring spirit in lambent flames; and so we'll
But see, we're landed on the happy coast;   [fail.
And all the golden strands are cover'd o'er
With glorious gods, that come to try our cause.
Jove, Jove, whose majesty now sinks me down,
He who himself burns in unlawful fires,
Shall judge, and shall acquit us. Oh, 'tis done!
'Tis fix'd by fate upon record divine;
And OEdipus shall now be ever mine.   [*Dies.*

OEdip. Speak, Hæmon, what has Fate been doing
What dreadful deed has mad Jocasta done?   [there?
Ham.

Hæm. The Queen herself, and all your wretched off-
Are by her fury flain.   [fpring,
    OEdip. By all my woes,
She has out-done me in revenge and murder;
And I fhould envy her the fad applaufe:
But, Oh, my children! Oh, what have they done?
This was not like the mercy of the Heav'ns,
To fet her madnefs on fuch cruelty.
This ftirs me more than all my fufferings,
And with my laft breath I muft call you tyrants.
    Hæm. What mean you, Sir?
    OEdip. Jocafta, lo, I come!
Oh, Laius, Labdacus, and all you fpirits
Of the Cadmean race, prepare to meet me!
All weeping, rang'd along the gloomy fhore,
Extend your arms t'embrace me; for I come.
May all the gods, too, from their battlements,
Behold, and wonder at a mortal's daring:
And when I knock the goal of dreadful death,
Shout, and applaud me with a clap of thunder.
Once more, thus wing'd by horrid Fate, I come
Swift as a falling meteor; lo, I fly,
And thus go downwards, to the darker fky.
[*Thunder.   He flings himfelf from the window.   The The-*
    bans gather about his body.
    Hæm. Oh, prophet! OEdipus is now no more!
Oh, curs'd effect of the moft deep defpair!
    Tir. Ceafe your complaints, and bear his body hence;
The dreadful fight will daunt the drooping Thebans,
Whom Heav'n decrees to raife with peace and glory.
Yet, by thefe terrible examples warn'd,
The facred fury thus alarms the world.
Let none, tho' ne'er fo virtuous, great, and high,
Be judg'd entirely blefs'd before they die.
                              [*Exeunt.*

END of the FIFTH ACT.

EPI-

E P I L O G U E.

WHAT Sophocles could undertake alone,
    Our poets found a work for more than one;
And therefore two lay tugging at the piece,
With all their force, to draw the pond'rous mass from Greece.
A weight that bent ev'n Seneca's strong muse,
And which Corneille's shoulders did refuse.
So hard it is th' Athenian harp to string;
So much two consuls yield to one just king.
Terror and pity this whole poem sway;
The mightiest machines that can mount a play.
How heavy will those vulgar souls be found,
Whom two such engines cannot move from ground!
When Greece and Rome have smil'd upon this birth,
You can but damn for one poor spot of earth;
And when your children find your judgment such,
They'll scorn their sires, and wish themselves born Dutch:
Each haughty poet will infer with ease,
How much his wit must underwrite to please.
As some strange churl would brandishing advance
The monumental sword that conquer'd France;
So you, by judging this, your judgment teach,
Thus far you like, that is, thus far you reach.
Since, then, the vote of full two thousand years
Has crown'd this plot, and all the dead are theirs,
Think it a debt you pay, not alms you give,
And, in your own defence, let this play live.
Think them not vain, when Sophocles is shown;
To praise his worth, they humbly doubt their own.
Yet as weak states each other's pow'r assure,
Weak poets by conjunction are secure:
Their treat is what your palates relish most.
Charm, song, a shew, a murder, and a ghost!
We know not what you can desire or hope,
To please you more, but burning of a Pope.

Mr BRERETON in the Character of DON ALONZO.
Curse on her Charms! I'll stab her thro' them all.

BELL'S EDITION.

THE

REVENGE.

A TRAGEDY,

As written by E. YOUNG, L.L.D.

DISTINGUISHING ALSO THE

VARIATIONS OF THE THEATRE,

AS PERFORMED AT THE

Theatre-Royal in Drury-Lane.

Regulated from the Prompt-Book.

By PERMISSION of the MANAGERS.

By Mr. HOPKINS, Prompter.

Manet alta mente repoſtum.　　VIRG.

LONDON:

Printed for JOHN BELL, near *Exeter-Exchange*, in the *Strand*.

MDCCLXXVII.

PROLOGUE.

By a Friend.

OFT has the buskin'd muse, with action mean,
Debas'd the glory of the tragic scene:
While puny villains dress'd in purple pride,
With crimes obscene the heav'n-born rage bely'd.
To her belongs to mourn the hero's fate,
To trace the errors of the wise and great;
To mark th' excess of passions too refin'd,
And paint the tumults of a god-like mind;
Where mov'd with rage, exalted thoughts combine,
And darkest deeds with beauteous colours shine.
So lights and shades in a well-mingled draught,
By curious touch of artful pencils wrought,
With soft deceit amuse the doubtful eye,
Pleas'd with the conflict of the various die.
Thus through the following scenes with sweet surprize,
Virtue and guilt in dread confusion rise,
And love, and hate, at once, and grief and joy,
Pity and rage, their mingled force employ.
Here the soft virgin sees with secret shame
Her charms excell'd by friendship's purer flame,
Forc'd with reluctant virtue to approve
The gen'rous hero who rejects her love.
Behold him there with gloomy passions stain'd,
A wife suspected, and an injur'd friend;
Yet such the toil where innocence is caught,
That rash suspicion seems without a fault.
We dread awhile lest beauty should succeed,
And almost wish ev'n virtue's self may bleed.
Mark well the black revenge, the cruel guile,
The traitor-fiend trampling the lovely spoil
Of beauty, truth, and innocence opprest,
Then let the rage of furies fire your breast.
Yet may his mighty wrongs, his just disdain,
His bleeding country, his lov'd father slain,
His martial pride, your admiration raise,
And crown him with involuntary praise.

A 2

DRA.

DRAMATIS PERSONÆ.

MEN.

	Drury-Lane.	Covent-Garden.
Don *Alonzo,* the *Spanish* general,	Mr. Reddish.	Mr. Wroughton.
Don *Carlos,* his friend, ——	Mr. J. Aickin.	Mr. Lewis.
Don *Alvarez,* a courtier, —	Mr. Burton.	Mr. L'Eſtrange.
Don *Manuel,* attendant of Don *Carlos,* ——	Mr. Robſon.	Mr. Hurſt.
Zanga, a captive *Moor,* —	Mr. Holland.	Mr. Jackſon.

WOMEN.

Leonora, Alvarez's daughter, ——	Mrs. Baddeley.	Mrs. Jackſon.
Iſabella, the *Moor's* miſtreſs, ——	Mrs. Reddish.	Miſs Ambroſe.

SCENE, *SPAIN.*

THE

THE
REVENGE.

₄ *The lines marked with inverted commas, 'thus,' are omitted in the representation.*

ACT I.

SCENE, *Battlements, with a Sea Prospect.*

Enter Zanga.

WHETHER first nature, or long want of peace,
  Has wrought my mind to this, I cannot tell;
But horrors now are not displeasing to me: [*Thunder.*
I like this rocking of the battlements.
Rage on, ye winds, burst, clouds, and waters roar!
You bear a just resemblance of my fortune,
And suit the gloomy habit of my soul.
                Enter Isabella.
Who's there? My love!
  Isa. Why have you left my bed?
Your absence more affrights me than the storm.
  Zan. The dead alone in such a night can rest,
And I indulge my meditation here.
Woman, away. I choose to be alone.
  Isa. I know you do, and therefore will not leave you;
Excuse me, Zanga, therefore dare not leave you.
Is this a night for walks of contemplation?
Something unusual hangs upon your heart,
And I will know it, by our loves I will.
' To you I sacrific'd my virgin fame;'
Ask I too much to share in your distress.
  Zan. In tears? Thou fool! then hear me, and be
In hell's abyss, if ever it escape thee.   [plung'd
To strike thee with astonishment at once,

A 3

I hate

I hate Alonzo.   Firſt recover that,
And then thou ſhalt hear farther.
     Iſa. Hate Alonzo!
I own, I thought Alonzo moſt your friend,
And that he loſt the maſter in that name.
     Zan. Hear then. 'Tis twice three years' ſince that great
(Great let me call him, for he conquer'd me)   [man
Made me the captive of his arm in fight.
He ſlew my father, and threw chains o'er me,
While I with pious rage purſu'd revenge.
I then was young, he plac'd me near his perſon,
And thought me not diſhonour'd by his ſervice.
One day (may that returning day be night,
The ſtain, the curſe of each ſucceeding year!)
For ſomething, or for nothing, in his pride
He ſtruck me.   (While I tell it, do I live?)
He ſmote me on the cheek——I did not ſtab him,
For that were poor revenge——E'er ſince, his folly
Has ſtrove to bury it beneath a heap
Of kindneſſes, and thinks it is forgot.
Inſolent thought! and like a ſecond blow!
Affronts are innocent, where men are worthleſs ;
And ſuch alone can wiſely drop revenge.
     Iſa. But with more temper, Zanga, tell your ſtory :
To ſee your ſtrong emotions ſtartles me.
     Zan. Yes, woman, with the temper that befits it.
Has the dark adder venom? So have I
When trod upon.   Proud Spaniard, thou ſhalt feel me !
For from that day, that day of my diſhonour,
I from that day have curs'd the riſing ſun,
Which never fail'd to tell me of my ſhame.
I from that day have bleſt the coming night,
Which promis'd to conceal it ; but in vain ;
The blow return'd for ever in my dream.
Yet on I toil'd, and groan'd for an occaſion
Of ample vengeance ; none is yet arriv'd.
Howe'er at preſent I conceive warm hopes
Of what may wound him ſore, in his ambition,
Life of his life, and dearer than his ſoul.
By nightly march he purpos'd to ſurprize
The Mooriſh camp ; but I have taken care
They ſhall be ready to receive his favour.

                              Failing

Failing in this, a caft of utmoft moment
Would darken all the conquefts he has won,
  Ifa. Juft as I enter'd an exprefs arriv'd.
  Zan. To whom ?
  Ifa. His friend, Don Carlos.
  Zan. Be propitious,
Oh, Mahomet, on this important hour,
And give at length my famifh'd foul revenge ?
What is revenge, but courage to call in
Our honour's debts, ' and wifdom to convert
' Other's felf-love into our own protection ?'
But fee, the morning dawns ;
I'll feek Don Carlos, and enquire my fate.   [*Exeunt.*

SCENE, the Palace.

Enter Manuel and Don Carlos.

  Man. My Lord Don Carlos, what brings your exprefs ?
  Car. Alonzo's glory, and the Moors defeat.
The field is ftrew'd with twice ten thoufand flain,
Though he fufpects his meafures were betray'd.
He'll foon arrive. Oh, how I long to embrace
The firft of heroes, and the beft of friends !———
I lov'd fair Leonora long before
The chance of battle gave me to the Moors,
From whom fo late Alonzo fet me free ;
And while I groan'd in bondage, I deputed
This great Alonzo, whom her father honours,
To be my gentle advocate in love,
To ftir her heart, and fan its fires for me.
  Man. And what fuccefs ?
  Car. Alas, the cruel maid———
Indeed her father, ' who though high at court,
' And powerful with the king, has wealth at heart,
' To heal his devaftation from the Moors,'
Knowing I'm richly freighted from the eaft,
My fleet now failing in the fight of Spain,
(Heav'n guard it fafe through fuch a dreadful ftorm !)
Careffes me, and urges her to wed.
  Man. Her aged father, fee,
Leads her this way.
  Car. She looks like radiant truth,
Brought forward by the hand of hoary time———
You to the port with fpeed; 'tis poffible

Some

Some veffel is arriv'd.   Heav'n grant it bring
Tidings which Carlos may receive with joy !
        Enter Alvarez *and* Leonora.
    Alv. Don Carlos, I am labouring in your favour
With all a parent's foft authority,
And earneft counfel.
    Car. Angels fecond you !
For all my blifs or mifery hangs on it.
    Alv. Daughter, the happinefs of life depends
On our difcretion, and a prudent choice ;
Look into thofe they call unfortunate,
And clofer view'd, you'll find they are unwife :
Some flaw in their own conduct lies beneath,
' And 'tis the trick of fools to fave their credit,
' Which brought another language into ufe.'
Don Carlos is of ancient, noble blood,
And then his wealth might mend a prince's fortune.
For him the fun is labouring in the mines,
A faithful flave, and turning earth to gold.
His keels are freighted with that facred pow'r,
By which ev'n kings and emperors are made.
Sir, you have my good wifhes, and I hope   [*To* Car.
My daughter is not indifpos'd to hear you.   [*Ex.* Alv.
    Car. Oh, Leonora ! why art thou in tears ?
Becaufe I am lefs wretched than I was ?
Before you father gave me leave to woo you,
Hufh'd was your bofom, and your eye ferene.
' Will you for ever help me to new pains,
' And keep referves of torment in your hand,
' To let them loofe on ev'ry dawn of joy ?'
    Leon. Think you my father too indulgent to me,
That he claims no dominion o'er my tears ?
A daughter fure may be right dutiful,
Whofe tears alone are free from a reftraint.——
    ' *Car.* Ah, my torn heart !
    ' *Leon.* Regard not me, my Lord,
' I fhall obey my father.
    ' *Car.* Difobey him,
' Rather than come thus coldly, than come thus
' With abfent eyes and alienated mien,
' Suff'ring addrefs, the victim of my love.
' Oh, let me be undone the common way,

                                        ' And

‘ And have the common comfort to be pity'd,
‘ And not be ruin'd in the mask of blifs,
‘ And fo be envy'd, and be wretched too!
‘ Love calls for love.　Not all the pride of beauty,
‘ Thofe eyes that tell us what the fun is made of,
‘ Thofe lips, whofe touch is to be bought with life,
‘ Thofe hills of driven fnow, which feen are felt;
‘ All thefe poffefs'd, are nought, but as they are
‘ The proof, the fubftance of an inward paffion,
‘ And the rich plunder of a taken heart.
　　‘ *Leon.* Alas, my Lord, we are too delicate;
‘ And when we grafp the happinefs we wifh'd,
‘ We call on wit to argue it away:
‘ A plainer man would not feel half your pains:
‘ But fome have too much wifdom to be happy.'
　　Car. Had I known this before, it had been well:
I had not then folicited your father
To add to my diftrefs; as you behave,
Your father's kindnefs ftabs me to the heart.
Give me your hand——Nay, give it, Leonora:
‘ You give it not——nay, yet you give it not——
‘ I ravifh it.——'
　　Leon. I pray, my Lord, no more.
　　Car. ‘ Ah, why fo fad? You know each figh does fhake
‘ Sighs there, are tempefts here.——　　　　[me:
‘ I've heard, bad men would be unbleft in heav'n:
‘ What is my guilt, that makes me fo with you?'
Have I not languifh'd proftrate at thy feet?
Have I not liv'd whole days upon thy fight?
Have I not feen thee where thou haft not been?
And, mad with the idea, clafp'd the wind,
And doated upon nothing?
　　Leon. Court me not,
Good Carlos, by recounting of my faults,
And telling how ungrateful I have been.
Alas, my Lord, if talking would prevail,
I could fuggeft much better arguments
Than thofe regards you threw away on me;
Your valour, honour, wifdom, prais'd by all.
But bid phyficians talk our veins to temper,
And with an argument new-fet a pulfe;
Then think, my Lord, of reafoning into love.

Car.

Car. Muſt I deſpair then ? Do not ſhake me thus :
My tempeſt-beaten heart is cold to death.
Ah ! turn, and let me warm me in thy beauties.
Heav'ns ! what a proof I gave but two nights paſt
Of matchleſs love ! To fling me at thy feet,
I ſlighted friendſhip, and I flew from fame ;
Nor heard the ſummons of the next day's battle :
But darting headlong to thy arms, I left
The promis'd fight, I left Alonzo too
To ſtand the war, and quell a world alone.   [*Trumpets.*
   Leon. The victor comes. My Lord, I muſt withdraw.
   ' *Car.* And muſt you go ?
   ' *Leon.* Why ſhould you wiſh me ſtay ?
' Your friend's arrival will bring comfort to you,
' My preſence none ; it pains you and myſelf ;
' For both our ſakes permit me to withdraw.' [*Ex.* Leon.
   Car. Sure, there's no peril but in love.   ' Oh, how
' My foes would boaſt to ſee me look ſo pale !'
                    Enter Alonzo.
   Car. Alonzo !
   Alon. Carlos !——I am whole again ;
Claſp'd in thy arms, it makes my heart entire.
   Car. Whom dare I thus embrace ? The conqueror
Of Afric.
   Alon. Yes, much more Don Carlos' friend.
The conqueſt of the world would coſt me dear,
Should it beget one thought of diſtance in thee.
I riſe in virtues to come nearer thee.
I conquer with Don Carlos in my eye,
And thus I claim my victory's reward. [*Embracing him.*
   Car. A victory indeed ! your godlike arm
Has made one ſpot the grave of Africa,
Such numbers fell ! and the ſurvivors fled
As frighted paſſengers from off the ſtrand,
When the tempeſtuous ſea comes roaring on them.
   Alon. 'Twas Carlos conquer'd, 'twas his cruel chains
Inflam'd me to a rage unknown before,
And threw my former actions far behind.
   Car. I love fair Leonora.   How I love her !
Yet ſtill I find (I know not how it is)
Another heart, another ſoul for thee.
' Thy friendſhip warms, it raiſes, it tranſports
                                        ' Like

' Like mufic, pure the joy, without allay,
' Whofe very rapture is tranquility:
' But love, like wine, gives a tumultuous blifs,
' Heighten'd indeed beyond all mortal pleafures;
' But mingles pangs and madnefs in the bowl.'

      Enter Zanga.

 Zan. Manuel, my Lord, returning from the port,
On bufinefs both of moment and of hafte,
Humbly begs leave to fpeak in private with you.
 Car. In private!—Ha!—Alonzo, I'll return,
No bufinefs can detain me long from thee.   [*Ex.* Car.
 Zan. My Lord Alonzo, I obey'd your orders.
 Alon. Will the fair Leonora pafs this way?
 Zan. She will, my Lord, and foon.
 Alon. Come near me, Zanga;
For I dare open all my heart to thee.
Never was fuch a day of triumph known.
There's not a wounded captive in my train,
That flowly follow'd my proud chariot wheels,
With half a life, and beggary, and chains,
But is a god to me: I am moft wretched.
In his captivity, thou know'ft Don Carlos,
My friend, (and never was a friend more dear)
Deputed me his advocate in love,
To talk to Leonora's heart, and make
A tender party in her thoughts for him.
What did I do? I lov'd myfelf. Indeed,
One thing there is might leffen my offence,
(If fuch offence admits of being leffen'd)
I thought him dead; for (by what fate I know not)
His letters never reach'd me.
 Zan. Thanks to Zanga,
Who thence contriv'd that evil which has happen'd. [*Afide.*
 Alon. Yes, curs'd of heav'n! I lov'd myfelf, and now
In a late action, refcu'd from the Moors,
I have brought home my rival in my friend.
 Zan. We hear, my Lord, that in that action too,
Your interpofing arm preferv'd his life.
 Alon. It did—with more than the expence of mine;
For, Oh, this day is mention'd for their nuptials.
But fee, fhe comes—I'll take my leave, and die.
 Zan. Hadft thou a thoufand lives, thy death would
   pleafe me.   Un-

Unhappy fate ! My country overcome !
My fix years hope of vengeance quite expir'd !——
Would nature were——I will not fall alone :
But others' groans fhall tell the world my death.   [*Exit.*
                    Enter Leonora.
    Alon. When nature ends with anguifh like to this,
Sinners fhall take their laft leave of the fun,
And bid his light adieu.
    Leon. The mighty conqueror
Difmay'd ! I thought you gave the foe your forrows.
    Alon. Oh, cruel infult ! are thofe tears your fport,
Which nothing but a love for you could draw ?
Africk I quell'd, in hope by that to purchafe
Your leave to figh unfcorn'd ; but I complain not ;
'Twas but a world, and you are—Leonora.
    Leon. That paffion which you boaft of is your guilt,
A treafon to your friend.   You think mean of me,
To plead your crimes as motives of my love.
    Alon. You, Madam, ought to thank thofe crimes you
'Tis they permit you to be thus inhuman,   [blame ;
Without the cenfure both of earth and heav'n——
I fondly thought a laft look might be kind.
Farewel for ever.——This fevere behaviour,
Has, to my comfort, made it fweet to die.
    Leon. Farewel for ever !—Sweet to die !—Oh, heav'n !
                                                [*Afide.*

Alonzo, ftay, you muft not thus efcape me ;
But hear your guilt at large.
    Alon. Oh, Leonora !
What could I do ? In duty to my friend,
I faw you ; and to fee, is to admire.
For Carlos did I plead, and moft fincerely.
Witnefs the thoufand agonies it coft me.
You know I did.   I fought but your efteem ;
If that is guilt, an angel had been guilty.
' I often figh'd, nay, wept, but could not help it ;
' And fure it is no crime to be in pain.
' But grant my crime was great ; I'm greatly curs'd :
' What would you more ? Am I not moft undone ?
' This ufage is like ftamping on the murder'd,
' When life is fled ; moft barbarous and unjuft.'
    Leon. If from your guilt none fuffer'd but your felf,
It might be fo——Farewel.   [*Going.*
    2   *Alon.*

Alon. Who suffers with me?

Leon. Enjoy your ignorance, and let me go.

' *Alon.* Alas! what is there I can fear to know,

' Since I already know your hate? Your actions

' Have long since told me that.

' *Leon.* They flatter'd you.

' *Alon.* How, flatter'd me!

' *Leon.* Oh, search in fate no farther!

' I hate thee—Oh, Alonzo, how I hate thee!

' *Alon.* Indeed! and do you weep for hatred too?

' Oh, what a doubtful torment heaves my heart!

' I hope it most, and yet I dread it more.

' Should it be so; should her tears flow from thence,

' How would my soul blaze up in ecstasy!

' Ah, no! how sink into the depth of horrors!

' *Leon.* Why would you force my stay?'

Alon. What mean these tears?

Leon. I weep by chance; nor have my tears a meaning.
But, Oh, when first I saw Alonzo's tears,
I knew their meaning well!

    [Alon. *falls passionately on his knees, and takes her hand.*

Alon. Heavens! what is this? That excellence, for
Desire was planted in the heart of man;   [which
Virtue's supreme reward on this side heav'n;
The cordial of my soul—and this destroys me——
Indeed, I flatter'd me that thou didst hate.

Leon. Alonzo, pardon me the injury
Of loving you. I struggled with my passion,
And struggled long: let that be some excuse.

Alon. Unkind! you know I think your love a blessing
Beyond all human blessings; 'tis the price
Of sighs and groans, and a whole year of dying.
But, Oh, the curse of curses!——Oh, my friend!——

Leon. Alas!

Alon. What says my love? Speak, Leonora.

Leon. Was it for you, my Lord, to be so quick
In finding out objections to our love?
Think you so strong my love, or weak my virtue,
It was unsafe to leave that part to me?

Alon. Is not the day then fix'd for your espousals?

Leon. Indeed my father once had thought that way;
But marking how the marriage pain'd my heart,

Long he stood doubtful; but at last resolv'd,
Your counsel, which determines him in all,
Should finish the debate.

  Alon. Oh, agony!
Must I not only lose her, but be made
Myself the instrument? Not only die,
But plunge the dagger in my heart myself?
This is refining on calamity.

  Leon. What, do you tremble lest you should be mine?
For what else can you tremble? Not for that
My father places in your power to alter.

  Alon. What's in my pow'r? Oh, yes, to stab my friend!

  Leon. To stab your friend were barbarous indeed!
Spare him—and murder me. ' I own, Alonzo,
' You well may wonder at such words as these;
' I start at them myself; they fright my nature.
' Great is my fault; but blame not me alone:
' Give him a little blame who took such pains
' To make me guilty.

  ' *Alon.* Torment!   [*After a pause,* Leon. *speaks.*

  ' *Leon.* Oh, my shame!
' I sue, and sue in vain: it is most just,
' When women sue, they sue to be deny'd.
' You hate me, you despise me! you do well;
' For what I've done I hate and scorn myself.
' Oh, night, fall on me! I shall blush to death.'
  Alon. First perish all!

  ' *Leon.* Say, what have you resolv'd?
' My father comes; what answer will you give him?

  ' *Alon.* What answer! let me look upon that face,
' And read it there——Devote thee to another!
' Not to be borne! a second look undoes me.

    ' *Leon.* And why undo you? Is it then, my Lord,
' So terrible to yield to your own wishes,
' Because they happen to concur with mine?
' Cruel! to take such pains to win an heart,
' Which you was conscious you must break with parting.

    ' *Alon.* No, Leonora, I am thine for ever,
                              [*Runs and embraces her.*
In spite of Carlos—' Ha! who's that? My friend?
                        ' [*Starts wide from her.*

' Alas, I see him pale! I hear his groan!
                              ' He

' He foams, he tears his hair, he raves, he bleeds,
' (I know him by myfelf) he dies diftracted !
    ' *Leon.* How dreadful to be cut from what we love !
    ' *Alon.* Ah, fpeak no more !
    ' *Leon.* And ty'd to what we hate !
    ' *Alon.* Oh !
    ' *Leon.* Is it poffible ?
    ' *Alon.* Death !
    ' *Leon.* Can you ?
    ' *Alon.* Oh————
' Yes, take a limb ; but let my virtue 'fcape.
' Alas, my foul, this moment I die for thee !
                                    ' [*Breaks away.*

    ' *Leon.* And are you perjur'd then for virtue's fake ?
' How often have you fworn !—but go, for ever. [*Swoons.*
    ' *Alon.* Heart of my heart, and effence of my joy !
' Where art thou !—Oh, I'm thine, and thine for ever !
' The groans of friendfhip fhall be heard no more.
' For whatfoever crime I can commit,
' I've felt the pains already.'
    Leon. Hold, Alonzo,
And hear a maid whom doubly thou haft conquer'd.
I love thy virtue as I love thy perfon,
And I adore thee for the pains it gave me ;
But as I felt the pains, I'll reap the fruit ;
I'll fhine out in my turn, and fhew the world
Thy great example was not loft upon me.
' Be it enough that I have once been guilty ;
' In fight of fuch a pattern, to perfift,
' Ill fuits a perfon honour'd with your love.
' My other titles to that blifs are weak ;
' I muft deferve it by refufing it.
' Thus then I tear me from thy hopes for ever.
' Shall I contribute to Alonzo's crimes ?
' No, tho' the life-blood gufhes from my heart.
' You fhall not be afham'd of Leonora ;
' Or that late time may put our names together.'
Nay, never fhrink ; take back the bright example
You lately lent ; Oh, take it while you may,
While I can give it you, and be immortal !   [*Exit.*
    Alon. She's gone, and I fhall fee that face no more ;
But pine in abfence, and till death adore.
                    B 2   When

When with cold dew my fainting brow is hung,
And my eyes darken, from my fault'ring tongue
Her name will tremble with a feeble moan,
And love with fate divide my dying groan.   [*Exit.*

END of the FIRST ACT.

ACT II.

SCENE, *continues.*

Enter Manuel *and* Zanga.

ZANGA.

IF this be true, I cannot blame your pain
  For wretched Carlos; 'tis but humane in you,
But when arriv'd your difmal news ?
  Man. This hour.
  Zan. What, not a veffel fav'd ?
  Man. All, all the ftorm
Devour'd; and now o'er his late envy'd fortune
The dolphins bound, and wat'ry mountains roar,
Triumphant in his ruin.
  Zan. Is Alvarez
Determin'd to deny his daughter to him ?
That treafure was on fhore; muft that too join
The common wreck ?
  Man. Alvarez pleads, indeed,
That Leonora's heart is difinclin'd,
And pleads that only; fo it was this morning,
When he concurr'd: the tempeft broke the match;
And funk his favour, when it funk the gold.
The love of gold is double in his heart,
The vice of age, and of Alvarez too.
  Zan. How does Don Carlos bear it ?
  Man. Like a man
Whofe heart feels moft a human heart can feel,
And reafons beft a human heart can reafon.
  Zan. But is he then in abfolute defpair ?
  Man. Never to fee his Leonora more.
And, quite to quench all future hope, Alvarez
Urges Alonzo to efpoufe his daughter
This very day; for he has learnt their loves.

Zan.

Zan. Ha! was not that receiv'd with ecstasy
By Don Alonzo?
  Man. Yes, at first; but soon
A damp came o'er him, it would kill his friend.
  Zan. Not if his friend consented: and since now
He can't himself espouse her——
  Man. Yet, to ask it
Has something shocking to a generous mind;
At least, Alonzo's spirit startles at it.
Wide is the distance between our despair,
And giving up a mistress to another.
But I must leave you.   Carlos wants support
In his severe affliction.   [*Exit* Manuel.
  Zan. Ha, it dawns!——
It rises to me, like a new-found world
‘ To mariners long time distress'd at sea,
‘ Sore from a storm, and all their viands spent;’
Or like the sun just rising out of chaos,
Some dregs of ancient night not quite purg'd off.
But shall I finish it?——Hoa, Isabella!
                Enter Isabella.
I thought of dying; better things come forward;
Vengeance is still alive; from her dark covert,
With all her snakes erect upon her crest,
She stalks in view, and fires me with her charms.
When, Isabella, arriv'd Don Carlos here?
  Isab. Two nights ago.
  Zan. That was the very night
Before the battle——Memory, set down that;
It has the essence of the crocodile,
'Tho' yet but in the shell——I'll give it birth——
What time did he return?
  Isab. At midnight.
  Zan. So——
Say, did he see that night his Leonora?
  Isab. No, my good Lord.
  Zan. No matter——tell me, woman,
Is not Alonzo rather brave than cautious,
Honest than subtle, above fraud himself,
Slow, therefore to suspect it in another?
  Isab. You best can judge; but so the world thinks
      of him.
              B 3   *Zan.*

Zan. Why, that was well—go, fetch my tablets hither.
                                    [*Exit* Isab.
Two nights ago my father's sacred shade
Thrice stalk'd around my bed, and smil'd upon me;
He smil'd a joy then little understood——
It must be so—and if so, it is vengeance
Worth waking of the dead for.
Re-enter Isabella *with the tablets;* Zanga *writes, then reads*
                      as to himself.
Thus it stands——
The father's fix'd——Don Carlos cannot wed—
Alonzo may——but that will hurt his friend——
Nor can he ask his leave——or, if he did,
He might not gain it——It is hard to give
Our own consent to ills, tho' we must bear them.
Were it not then a master-piece, worth all
The wisdom I can boast, first to persuade
Alonzo to request it of his friend,
His friend to grant——then from that very grant,
The strongest proof of friendship man can give,
(And other motives) to work out a cause
Of jealousy, to rack Alonzo's peace?——
I have turn'd o'er the catalogue of human woes,
Which sting the heart of man, and find none equal.
It is the Hydra of calamities,
The seven-fold death; the jealous are the damn'd.
Oh, jealousy, each other passion's calm,
To thee, thou conflagration of the soul!
Thou king of torments, thou grand counterpoise
For all the transports beauty can inspire!
   Isab. Alonzo comes this way.
   Zan. Most opportunely.
Withdraw—' Ye subtle dæmons, which reside   [*Ex.* If.
' In courts, and do your work with bows and smiles,
' That little engin'ry, more mischievous,
' Than fleets and armies, and the cannon's murder,
' Teach me to look a lie; give me your maze
' Of gloomy thought and intricate design,
' To catch the man I hate, and then devour.'
                Enter Alonzo.
My Lord, I give you joy.
   Alon. Of what good Zanga?
   Zan. Is not the lovely Leonora yours?
                          Alon.

Alon. What will become of Carlos ?

Zan. He's your friend ;
And since he can't espouse the fair himself,
Will take some comfort from Alonzo's fortune.

Alon. Alas, thou little know'st the force of love !
Love reigns a sultan with unrivall'd sway ;
Puts all relations, friendship's self to death,
If once he's jealous of it. I love Carlos ;
Yet well I know what pangs I felt this morning
At his intended nuptials. For myself
I then felt pains which now for him I feel.

Zan. You will not wed her then ?

Alon. Not instantly.
Insult his broken heart the very moment !

Zan. I understand you : but you'll wed hereafter,
When your friend's gone, and his first pain assuag'd.

Alon. Am I to blame for that ?

Zan. My Lord, I love
Your very errors ; they are born from virtue.
Your friendship (and what nobler passion claims
The heart ?) does lead you blindfold to your ruin.
Consider, wherefore did Alvarez break
Don Carlos' match, and wherefore urge Alonzo's ?
'Twas the same cause, the love of wealth. To-morrow
May see Alonzo in Don Carlos' fortune ;
A higher bidder is a better friend,
And there are princes sigh for Leonora.
When your friend's gone you'll wed ; why, then the cause
Which gives you Leonora now will cease.
Carlos has lost her ; should you lose her too,
Why, then you heap new torments on your friend,
By that respect which labour'd to relieve him——
'Tis well he is disturb'd ; it makes him pause.. [*Aside.*

Alon. Think'st thou, my Zanga, should I ask Don Carlos,
His goodness would consent that I should wed her ?

Zan. I know it would.

Alon. But then the cruelty
To ask it, and for me to ask it of him !

Zan. Methinks, you are severe upon your friend,
Who was it gave him liberty and life ?

Alon. That is the very reason which forbids it.
Were I a stranger, I could freely speak :

In me it fo refembles a demand,
Exacting of a debt, it fhocks my nature.
	Zan. My Lord, you know the fad alternative.
Is Leonora worth one pang or not?
It hurts not me, my Lord, but as I love you:
Warmly as you I wifh Don Carlos well;
But I am likewife Don Alonzo's friend:
There all the difference lies between us two.
In me, my Lord, you hear another felf;
And give me leave to add, a better too,
Clear'd from thofe errors, which, tho' caus'd by virtue,
Are fuch as may hereafter give you pain——
Don Lopez of Caftile would not demur thus.
	Alon. Perifh the name! What, facrifice the fair
To age and uglinefs, becaufe fet in gold?
I'll to Don Carlos, if my heart will let me.
I have not feen him fince his fore affliction;
But fhunn'd it, as too terrible to bear.
How fhall I bear it now? I'm ftruck already.	[*Exit.*
	Zan. Half of my work is done. I muft fecure
Don Carlos, ere Alonzo fpeak with him.
		[*He gives a meffage to a fervant, then returns.*
Proud, hated Spain, oft drench'd in Moorifh blood!
Doft thou not feel a deadly foe within thee?
Shake not the tow'rs where-e'er I pafs along,
Confcious of ruin, and their great deftroyer?
Shake to the centre, if Alonzo's dear.
Look down, Oh, holy prophet! fee me torture
This Chriftian dog, this infidel, which dares
To fmite thy votaries, and fpurn thy law;
And yet hopes pleafure from two radiant eyes,
Which look as they were lighted up for thee!
Shall he enjoy thy Paradife below?
Blaft the bold thought, and curfe him with her charms!——
But fee, the melancholy lover comes.
		Enter Don Carlos.
	Car. Hope, thou haft told me lies from day to day,
For more than twenty years: vile promifer!
None here are happy, but the very fool,
Or very wife; and I wasn't fool enough
To fmile in vanities, and hug a fhadow;
Nor have I wifdom to elaborate

An artificial happiness from pains :
Ev'n joys are pains, becaufe they cannot laft.   [*Sighs.*
' Yet much is talk'd of blifs ; it is the art
' Of fuch as have the world in their poffeffion,
' To give it a good name, that fools may envy ;
' For envy to fmall minds is flattery.'
How many lift the head, look gay, and fmile
Againft their confciences ? And this we know,
Yet, knowing, difbelieve, and try again
What we have try'd, and ftruggle with conviction.
Each new experience gives the former credit ;
And reverend grey threefcore is but a voucher,
That thirty told us true.

   Zan. My noble Lord,
I mourn your fate : but are no hopes furviving ?
   Car. No hopes.   Alvarez has a heart of fteel.
'Tis fix'd, 'tis paft, 'tis abfolute defpair.
   Zan. You wanted not to have your heart made tender,
By your own pains to feel a friend's diftrefs.
   Car. I underftand you well.   Alonzo loves ;
I pity him.
   Zan. I dare be fworn you do.
Yet he has other thoughts.
   Car. What canft thou mean ?
   Zan. Indeed he has ; and fears to afk a favour
A ftranger from a ftranger might requeft ;
What cofts you nothing, yet is all to him ;
Nay, what indeed will to your glory add,
For nothing more than wifhing your friend well.
   Car. I pray be plain ; his happinefs is mine.
   Zan. He loves to death ; but fo reveres his friend,
He can't perfuade his heart to wed the maid
Without your leave, and that he fears to afk.
In perfect tendernefs I urg'd him to it.
Knowing the deadly ficknefs of his heart,
Your overflowing goodnefs to your friend,
Your wifdom, and defpair yourfelf to wed her,
I wrung a promife from him he would try :
And now I come, a mutual friend to both,
Without his privacy, to let you know it,
And to prepare you kindly to receive him.

                            Car.

Car. Ha! if he weds I am undone indeed;
Not Don Alvarez' felf can then relieve me.

Zan. Alas, my Lord, you know his heart is fteel.
'Tis fix'd, 'tis paft, 'tis abfolute defpair.

Car. Oh, cruel Heav'n! and is it not enough
That I muft never, never fee her more?
Say, is it not enough that I muft die;
But I muft be tormented in the grave?—
Afk my confent!—Muft I then give her to him?
Lead to his nuptial fheets the blufhing maid?
Oh!——Leonora! never, never, never!

Zan. A ftorm of plagues upon him! he refufes. [*Afide.*

Car. What, wed her?—and to-day?

Zan. To-day, or never.
To-morrow may fome wealthier lover bring,
And then Alonzo is thrown out like you:
Then whom fhall he condemn for his misfortune?
Carlos is an Alvarez to his love.

Car. Oh, torment! whither-fhall I turn?

Zan. To peace.

Car. Which is the way?

Zan. His happinefs is yours;
I dare not difbelieve you.

Car. Kill my friend!
Or worfe——Alas! and can there be a worfe?
A worfe there is; nor can my nature bear it.

Zan. You have convinc'd me 'tis a dreadful tafk.
I find Alonzo's quitting her this morning
For Carlos' fake, in tendernefs to you,
Betray'd me to believe it lefs fevere
Than I perceive it is.

Car. Thou doft upbraid me.

Zan. No, my good Lord; but fince you can't comply,
'Tis my misfortune that I mention'd it;
For had I not, Alonzo would indeed
Have dy'd, as now, but not by your decree.

Car. By my decree! Do I decree his death?
I do——Shall I then lead her to his arms?
Oh, which fide fhall I take? Be ftabb'd, or—ftab?
'Tis equal death! a choice of agonies!——
Ah, no! all other agonies are eafe
To one—Oh, Leonora!—never, never!

Go,

Go, Zanga, go, defer the dreadful trial,
Tho' but a day ; fomething, perchance, may happen
To foften all to friendfhip and to love.
Go, ftop my friend, let me not fee him now ;
But fave us from an interview of death.

Zan. My Lord, I'm bound in duty to obey you——
If I not bring him, may Alonzo profper.   [*Afide. Exit.*

Car. What is this world?—Thy fchool, Oh, Mifery !
Our only leffon is to learn to fuffer ;
And he who knows not that, was born for nothing.
' Tho' deep my pangs, and heavy at my heart,
' My comfort is, each moment takes away
' A grain, at leaft from the dead load that's on me,
' And gives a nearer profpect of the grave.'
But put it moft feverely——fhould I live——
Live long——Alas, there is no length in time !
Nor in thy time, Oh, man ! What's fourfcore years ?
Nay, what, indeed, the age of time itfelf,
Since cut from out eternity's wide round ?
' Away, then.   To a mind refolv'd and wife,
' There is an impotence in mifery,
' Which makes me fmile, when all its fhafts are in me.'
Yet Leonora——fhe can make time long,
Its nature alter, as fhe alter'd mine.
While in the luftre of her charms I lay,
Whole fummer funs roll'd unperceiv'd away ;
I years for days, and days for moments told,
And was furpris'd to hear that I grew old.
Now fate does rigidly its dues regain,
And every moment is an age of pain.
As he is going out, enter Zanga *and* Alonzo. Zanga
ftops Carlos.

Zan. Is this Don Carlos ? this the boafted friend ?
How can you turn your back upon his fadnefs ?
Look on him, and then leave him if you can.
' Whofe forrows thus deprefs him ? Not his own ;
' This moment he could wed without your leave.'
 Car. I cannot yield ; nor can I bear his griefs.
Alonzo !   [*Going to him, and taking his hand.*
 Alon. Oh, Carlos !
 Car. Pray, forbear.
 Alon. Art thou undone, and fhall Alonzo fmile ?
Alonzo,

Alonzo, who perhaps in some degree
Contributed to cause thy dreadful fate?
I was deputed guardian of thy love;
But, Oh, I lov'd myself! Pour down afflictions
On this devoted head; make me your mark;
And be the world by my example taught,
How sacred it should hold the name of friend.

    Car. You charge yourself unjustly; well I know
The only cause of my severe affliction.
Alvarez, curs'd Alvarez!—So much anguish
Felt for so small a failure, is one merit
Which faultless virtue wants. The crime was mine,
Who plac'd thee there, where only thou couldst fail;
Tho' well I knew that dreadful post of honour
I gave thee to maintain. Ah! who could bear
Those eyes unhurt? The wounds myself have felt,
(Which wounds alone should cause me to condemn thee)
They plead in thy excuse; for I too strove
To shun those fires, and found 'twas not in man.

    Alon. You cast in shades the failures of a friend,
And soften all; but think not you deceive me;
I know my guilt, and I implore your pardon,
As the sole glimpse I can obtain of peace.

    Car. Pardon for him, who but this morning threw
Fair Leonora from his heart, all bath'd
In ceaseless tears, and blushing for her love!
Who, like a rose-leaf wet with morning dew,
Would have stuck close, and clung for ever there!
But 'twas in thee, thro' fondness for thy friend,
To shut thy bosom against ecstacies;
For which, while this pulse beats, it beats to thee;)
While this blood flows, it flows for my Alonzo,
And every wish is levell'd at thy joy.   [to speak.

    Zan. [*To* Alon.] My Lord, my Lord, this is your time
    Alon. [*To* Zan.] Because he's kind? It therefore is the
‘ For 'tis his kindness which I fear to hurt.   [worst;
‘ Shall the same moment see him sink in woes, -
‘ And me providing for a flood of joys,
‘ Rich in the plunder of his happiness?
‘ No, I may die; but I can never speak.
    ‘ *Car.* Now, now it comes! they are concerting it?
‘ The first word strikes me dead—Oh, Leonora!
                                      ‘ And

' And shall another taste her fragrant breath?
' Who knows what after-time may bring to pass?
' Fathers may change and I may wed her still.   [*Aside.*
   ' *Alon.*' [*To* Zan.] Do I not see him quite possess'd
         with anguish,
' Which, like a dæmon, writhes him to and fro;'
And shall I pour in new?   No fond desire,
No love: one pang at parting, and farewel.
I have no other love but Carlos now.

   Car. Alas! my friend, why with such eager grasp
Dost press my hand, and weep upon my cheek?

   Alon. If after death, our forms (as some believe)
Shall be transparent, naked every thought,
And friends meet friends, and read each other's hearts,
Thou'lt know one day that thou wast held most dear.
Farewel.

   Car. Alonzo, stay—he cannot speak—   [*Holds him.*
Lest it should grieve me—Shall I be out-done?
And lose in glory, as I lose in love?   [*Aside.*
I take it much unkindly, my Alonzo,
You think so meanly of me, not to speak,
When well I know your heart is near to bursting.
Have you forgot how you have bound me to you?
Your smallest friendship's liberty and life.

   Alon. There, there it is, my friend, it cuts me there.
How dreadful is it to a generous mind
To ask, when sure he cannot be deny'd!

   Car. How greatly thought! In all he tow'rs above me.
                                         [*Aside.*
Then you confess you would ask something of me?

   Alon. No, on my soul.

   Zan. [*To* Alon.] Then lose her.

   Car. Glorious spirit!
Why, what a pang has he run through for this!
By Heav'n, I envy him his agonies.
' Why was not mine the most illustrious lot,
' Of starting at one action from below,
' And flaming up into consummate greatness?
' Ha! angels strengthen me!'—It shall be so——
' I can't want strength. Great actions, once conceiv'd,
' Strengthen like wine, and animate the soul,
' And call themselves to being. [*Aside.*]' My Alonzo!
Since thy great soul disdains to make request,

C

Receive

Receive with favour that I make to thee:
  Alon. What means my Carlos?
  Car. Pray obferve me well.
Fate and Alvarez tore her from my heart,
And plucking up my love, they had well nigh
Pluck'd up life too, for they were twin'd together.
Of that no more—What now does reafon bid?
I cannot wed—Farewel my happinefs!
But, O my foul, with care provide for hers!
In life, how weak, how helplefs is woman!
' Soon hurt; in happinefs itfelf unfafe,
' And often wounded while fhe plucks the rofe;
' So properly the object of affliction,
' That Heav'n is pleas'd to make diftrefs become her,
' And dreffes her moft amiably in tears.
Take then my heart in dowry with the fair,
Be thou her guardian, and thou muft be mine,
Shut out the thoufand preffing ills of life
With thy furrounding arms—Do this, and then
Set down the liberty and life thou gav'ft me,
As little things, as effays of thy goodnefs,
And rudiments of friendfhip fo divine.
  Alon. There is a grandeur in thy goodnefs to me,
Which with thy foes would render thee ador'd.
' But have a care, nor think I can be pleas'd
' With any thing that lays in pains for thee.
' Thou doft diffemble, and thy heart's in tears.
  '*Car.* My heart's in health, my fpirits dance their round,
' And at my eyes pleafure looks out in fmiles.
  ' *Alon.*' And can'ft thou, can'ft thou part with Leonora?
  Car. I do not part with her, I give her thee.
  Alon. O, Carlos!
  ' *Car.* Don't difturb me, I'm fincere,
' Nor is it more than fimple juftice in me.
' This morn didft thou refign her for my fake;
' I but perform a virtue learnt from thee;
' Difcharge a debt, and pay her to thy wifhes.
  '*Alon.* Ah, how?--But think not words were ever made
For fuch occafions. Silence, tears, embraces,
Are languid eloquence; I'll feek relief
In abfence from the pain of fo much goodnefs,
There thank the bleft above, thy fole fuperiors,
Adore, and raife my thoughts of them by thee.   [*Exit.*
                                            Zan.

Zan. Thus far fuccefs has crown'd my boldeft hope.
My next care is to haften thefe new nuptials,
And then my mafter-works begin to play.   [*Afide.*
Why this was greatly done, without one figh   [*To* Car.
To carry fuch a glory to its period.

Car. Too foon thou praifeft me. He's gone, and now
I muft unfluice my over-burthen'd heart,
And let it flow.   I would not grieve my friend
With tears ; nor interrupt my great defign ;
Great fure as ever human breaft durft think of.
But now my forrows, long with pain fuppreft,
   Burft their confinement with impetuous fway,
   O'er-fwell all bounds, and bear e'en life away.
So till the day was won, the Greek renown'd
With anguifh wore the arrow in his wound,
Then drew the fhaft from out his tortur'd fide,
Let gufh the torrent of his blood, and dy'd.   [*Exeunt.*

END of the SECOND ACT.

A C T   III.

Enter Zanga,

ZANGA.

O Joy, thou welcome ftranger ! twice three years
   I have not felt thy vital beam ; but now
It warms my veins, and plays around my heart :
A fiery inftinct lifts me from the ground,
And I could mount——the fpirits numberlefs
Of my dear countrymen, which yefterday
Left their poor bleeding bodies on the field,
Are all affembled here, and o'er-inform me.——
O, bridegroom ! great indeed thy prefent blifs ;
Yet ev'n by me unenvy'd ; for be fure
It is thy laft, thy laft fmile, that which now
Sits on thy cheek ; enjoy it while thou may'ft ;
Anguifh, and groans, and death befpeak to-morrow.
                    Enter Ifabella.
My Ifabella !
   Ifab. What commands my Moor ?
   Zan. My fair ally ! my lovely minifter !
'Twas well Alvarez, by my arts impell'd,

(To plunge Don Carlos in the laft defpair,
And fo prevent all future moleftation)·
Finifh'd the nuptials foon as he refolv'd them ;
This conduct ripen'd all for me, and ruin.
Scarce had the prieft the holy rite perform'd,
When I, by facred infpiration, forg'd
That letter, which I trufted to thy hand :
That letter, which in glowing terms conveys,
From happy Carlos to fair Leonora,
The moft profound acknowledgment of heart,
For wond'rous tranfports which he never knew.
This is a good fubfervient artifice,
To aid the nobler workings of my brain.

 Ifab I quickly dropt it in the bride's apartment,
As you commanded.

 Zan. With a lucky hand ;
For foon Alonzo found it ; I obferv'd him
From out my fecret ftand. He took it up;
But fcarce was it unfolded to his fight,
When he, as if an arrow pierc'd his eye,
Started, and trembling dropt it on the ground.
Pale and aghaft a while my victim ftood,
Difguis'd a figh or two, and puff'd them from him ;
Then rubb'd his brow, and took it up again.
At firft he look'd as if he meant to read it ;
But check'd by rifing fears, he crufh'd it thus,
And thruft it, like an adder, in his bofom.

 Ifab. But if he read it not, it cannot fting him,
At leaft not mortally.

 Zan. At firft I thought fo ;
But farther thought infoims me otherwife,
And turns this difappointment to account.
' He more fhall credit it, becaufe unfeen,·
' (It 'tis unfeen) as thou anon may'ft find.
 ' *Ifab.* That would indeed commend my Zanga's fkill.'

 Zan. This, Ifabella, is Don Carlos' picture ;
Take it, and fo difpofe of it, that found,
It may raife up a witnefs of her love ;
Under her pillow, in her cabinet,
Or elfwhere as fhall beft promote our end.

 Ifab. I'll weigh it as its confequence requires,
Then do my utmoft to deferve your fmile. [*Exit.*
                Zan.

Zan. Is that Alonzo proftrate on the ground ?——
Now he ftarts up like flame from fleeping embers,
And wild diftraction glares from either eye.
If thus a flight furmife can work his foul,
How will the fulnefs of the tempeft tear him ?

Enter Alonzo.

Alon. And yet it cannot be——I am deceiv'd——
I injure her : fhe wears the face of heav'n.

Zan. He doubts.   [*Afide.*

Alon. I dare not look on this again.
If the firft glance, which gave fufpicion only,
Had fuch effect, fo fmote my heart and brain,
The certainty would dafh me all in pieces.
It cannot——Ha ! it muft, it muft be true.   [*Starts.*

Zan. Hold there, and we fucceed. He has defcry'd me.
And (for he thinks I love him) will unfold,
His aching heart, and reft it on my counfel.
I'll feem to go, to make my ftay more fure.   [*Afide.*

Alon. Hold, Zanga, turn.

Zan. My Lord.

Alon. Shut clofe the doors,
That not a fpirit find an entrance here.

Zan. My Lord's obey'd.

Alon. I fee that thou art frighted.
If thou doft love me, I fhall fill thy heart
With fcorpions ftings,

Zan. If I do love, my Lord ?

Alon. Come near me, let me reft upon thy bofom ;
(What pillow like the bofom of a friend ?)
For I am fick at heart.

Zan. Speak, Sir, O fpeak,
And take me from the rack.

‘ *Alon.* And is there need
‘ Of words ? Behold a wonder ! See my tears !
‘ *Zan.* I feel 'em too. Heav'n grant my fenfes fail me !
‘ I rather would lofe them, than have this real.
‘ *Alon.* Go, take a round thro' all things in thy thought,
‘ And find that one ; for there is only one
‘ Which could extort my tears ; find that, and tell
‘ Thyfelf my mifery, and fpare me the pain.
‘ *Zan.* Sorrow can think but ill—I am bewilder'd ;
‘ I know not where I am.

C 3

‘ Alon.

' *Alon.* Think, think no more;
' It ne'er can enter in an honeſt heart.
' I'll tell thee then——I cannot——yet I do
' By wanting force to give it utterance.
    ' *Zan.* Speak, eaſe your heart ; its throbs will break
        your boſom.'
    Alon. I am moſt happy : mine is victory,
Mine the king's favour, mine the nation's ſhout,
And great men make their fortunes of my ſmiles.
O curſe of curſes ! in the lap of bleſſing
'To be moſt curſt !——My Leonora's falſe !
    Zan. Save me, my Lord !
    Alon. My Leonora's falſe !   [*Gives him the letter.*
    Zan. Then heav'n has loſt its image here on earth.
    [*While Zanga reads the letter, he trembles, and ſhews the*
        utmoſt concern.
    Alon. Good-natur'd man ! he makes my pains his own.
I durſt not read it ; but I read it now
In thy concern.
    Zan. Did you not read it then ?
    Alon. Mine eye juſt touch'd it, and could bear no more.
    Zan. Thus periſh all that gives Alonzo pain !
                                [*Tears the letter.*
    Alon. Why didſt thou tear it ?
    Zan. Think of it no more.
'Twas your miſtake, and groundleſs are your fears.
    Alon. And didſt thou tremble then for my miſtake ?
Or give the whole contents, or by the pangs
That feed upon my heart, thy life's in danger.
    Zan. Is this Alonzo's language to his Zanga ?
Draw forth your ſword, and find the ſecret here.
For whoſe ſake is it, think you, I conceal it ?
Wherefore this rage ? Becauſe I ſeek your peace ?
I have no intereſt in ſuppreſſing it,
But what good-natur'd tenderneſs for you
Obliges me to have.   Not mine the ' heart
' That will be rent in two.   Not mine the' fame
That will be damn'd, tho' all the world ſhould know it.
    Alon. Then my worſt fears are true, and life is paſt.
    Zan. What has the raſhneſs of my paſſion utter'd ?
I know not what ; but rage is our deſtruction,
And all its words are wind——Yet ſure, I think,
I nothing own'd——but grant I did confeſs,
        4   What

What is a letter? letters may be forg'd:
For heav'n's sweet fake, my Lord, lift up your heart.
Some foe to your repose——
   Alon. So, heav'n look on me,
As I can't find the man I have offended.   [shield :
   Zan. Indeed ! [*Aside.*]——Our innocence is not our
They take offence, who have not been offended;
They seek our ruin too, who speak us fair,
And death is often ambush'd in their smiles.
' We know not whom we have to fear.' 'Tis certain
A letter may be forg'd, and in a point
Of such a dreadful consequence as this,
One would rely on nought that might be false——
Think, have you any other cause to doubt her?
Away, you can find none. Resume your spirit;
All's well again.
   Alon. O that it were !
   Zan. It is ;
For who would credit that, which credited,
Makes hell superfluous by superior pains,
Without such proofs as cannot be withstood ;
Has she not ever been to virtue train'd ?
Is not her fame as spotless as the sun,
Her sex's envy, and the boast of Spain ?
   Alon. O, Zanga ! it is that confounds me most,
That full in opposition to appearance——
   Zan. No more, my Lord, for you condemn yourself.
What is absurdity, but to believe
Against appearance !——You can't yet, I find,
Subdue your passion to your better sense ;——
And, truth to tell, it does not much displease me.
'Tis fit our indiscretions should be check'd
With some degree of pain.
   Alon. What indiscretion ?
   Zan. Come, you must bear to hear your faults from me.
Had you not sent Don Carlos to the court
The night before the battle, that foul slave,
Who forg'd the senseless scroll which gives you pain,
Had wanted footing for his villainy.
   Alon. I sent him not.
   Zan. Not send him !—Ha !—That strikes me.
I thought he came on message to the king.

Is there another caufe could juftify
His fhunning danger, and the promis'd fight?
But I perhaps may think too rigidly;
So long an abfence, and impatient love————
  Alon. In my confufion that had quite efcap'd me.
By Heav'n, my wounded foul does bleed afrefh;
'Tis clear as day—for Carlos is fo brave,
He lives not but on fame, he hunts for danger,
And is enamour'd of the face of death.
How then could he decline the next day's battle,
But for the tranfports?——Oh, it muft be fo——
Inhuman! by the lofs of his own honour,
To buy the ruin of his friend!
  Zan. You wrong him;
He knew not of your love.
  Alon. Ha!————
  Zan. That ftings home.   [*Afide.*
  Alon. Indeed, he knew not of my treacherous love—
Proofs rife on proofs, and ftill the laft the ftrongeft.
' Th' eternal law of things declares it true,
' Which calls for judgment on diftinguifh'd guilt,
' And loves to make our crime our punifhment.'
Love is my torture, love was firft my crime;
For fhe was his, my friend's, and he (O horror!)
Confided all in me.   O, facred faith!
How dearly I abide thy violation!
  Zan. Were then their loves far gone?
  Alon. The father's will
There bore a total fway; and he, as foon
As news arriv'd that Carlos' fleet was feen
From off our coaft, fir'd with the love of gold,
Determin'd, that the very fun which faw
Carlos' return, fhould fee his daughter wed.
  Zan. Indeed, my Lord; then you muft pardon me,
If I prefume to mitigate the crime.
Confider, ftrong allurements foften guilt;
Long was his abfence, ardent was his love,
At midnight his return, the next day deftin'd
For his efpoufals—'twas a ftrong temptation.
  Alon. Temptation!
  Zan. 'Twas but gaining of one night.
  Alon. One night!

Zan.

Zan. That crime could ne'er return again.

Alon. Again! By heav'n, thou doſt inſult thy Lord.
Temptation! One night gain'd! O ſtings and death!
And am I then undone? Alas, my Zanga!
And doſt thou own it too? Deny it ſtill,
And reſcue me one moment from diſtraction.

Zan. My Lord, I hope the beſt.

Alon. Falſe, fooliſh hope,
' And inſolent to me!' Thou know'ſt it falſe ;
It is as glaring as the noon-tide ſun.
Devil !—This morning, after three years coldneſs,
To ruſh at once into a paſſion for me !
'Twas time to feign, 'twas time to get another,
When her firſt fool was ſated with her beauties.

Zan. What ſays my Lord? Did Leonora then
Never before diſcloſe her paſſion for you?

Alon. Never.

Zan. Throughout the whole three years ?

Alon. O never ! never !
Why, Zanga, ſhould'ſt thou ſtrive ! 'Tis all in vain :
Tho' thy ſoul labours, it can find no reed
For hope to catch at. Ah ! I'm plunging down
Ten thouſand thouſand fathoms in deſpair.

Zan. Hold, Sir, I'll break your fall—Wave ev'ry fear,
And be a man again—Had he enjoy'd her,
Be moſt aſſur'd, he had reſign'd her to you
With leſs reluctance.

Alon. Ha ! Reſign her to me !——
Reſign her !—Who reſign'd her ?—Double death !
How could I doubt ſo long ? ' My heart is broke.'
Firſt love her to diſtraction ! then reſign her !

Zan. But was it not with utmoſt agony ?

Alon. Grant that, he ſtill reſign'd her ; that's enough.
Would he pluck out his eye to give it me ?
'Tear out his heart ?——She was his heart no more——
Nor was it with reluctance he reſign'd her ;
By heav'n he aſk'd, he courted me to wed.
I thought it ſtrange ; 'tis now no longer ſo.

Zan. Was't his requeſt ? Are you right ſure of that ?
I fear the letter was not all a tale.

Alon. A tale ! There's proof equivalent to ſight.

Zan. I ſhould diſtruſt my ſight on this occaſion.

Alon.

Alon. And fo fhould I ; by heav'n, I think I fhould.
What ! Leonora, the divine, by whom
We guefs'd at angels ! Oh ! I'm all confufion.
   Zan. You now are too much ruffled to think clearly.
Since blifs and horror, life and death hang on it,
Go to your chamber, there maturely weigh
Each circumftance ; confider, above all,
That it is jealoufy's peculiar nature
To fwell fmall things to great ; nay, out of nought
To conjure much, and then to lofe its reafon
Amid the hideous phantoms it has form'd.
   Alon. Had I ten thoufand lives, I'd give them all
To be deceiv'd. ' I fear 'tis doomfday with me.'
And yet fhe feem'd fo pure, that I thought heav'n
Borrow'd her form for virtue's felf to wear,
To gain her lovers with the fons of men.
O, Leonora ! Leonora !   [*Exit.*
               Enter Ifabella.
   Zan. Thus far it works aufpicioufly.   My patient
Thrives underneath my hand in mifery.
He's gone to think ; that is, to be diftracted.
   Ifab. I overheard your conference, and faw you,
To my amazement, tear the letter.
   Zan. There,
There, Ifabella, I out-did myfelf.
For tearing it, I not fecure it only
In its firft force ; but fuperadd a new.
For who can now the character examine
To caufe a doubt, much lefs detect the fraud ?
And after tearing it, as loth to fhew
The foul contents, if I fhould fwear it now
A forgery, my Lord would difbelieve me,
Nay, more would difbelieve the more I fwore.
But is the picture happily difpos'd of ?
   Ifab. It is.
   Zan. That's well—Ah ! what is well ? O pang to think !
O dire neceffity ! is this my province ?
Whither, my foul ! ah ! whither art thou funk
' Beneath thy fphere ? Ere while, far, far above
' Such little arts, diffembling, falfhoods, frauds,
' The trafh of villainy itfelf, which falls
' To cowards and poor wretches wanting bread.'
                                                Does

Does this become a foldier ? This become
Whom armies follow'd, and a people lov'd ?
My martial glory withers at the thought.
But great my end ; and fince there are no other,
Thefe means are juft, they fhine with borrow'd light,
Illuftrious from the purpofe they purfue.
And greater fure my merit, who to gain
A point fublime, can fuch a tafk fuftain ;
To wade thro' ways obfcene, my honour bend,
And fhock my nature, to attain my end.
Late time fhall wonder ; that my joys will raife ;
For wonder is involuntary praife.   [*Exeunt.*

END of the THIRD ACT.

ACT IV.

Enter Alonzo *and* Zanga.

ALONZO.

OH, what a pain to think ? when every thought,
  Perplexing thought, in intricacies runs,
And Reafon knits th' inextricable toil,
In which herfelf is taken ! ' I am loft,
' Poor infect that I am, I am involv'd,
' And bury'd in the web myfelf have wrought !
' One argument is balanc'd by another,
' And reafon reafon meets in doubtful fight,
' And proofs are countermin'd by equal proofs.'
No more I'll bear this battle of the mind,
This inward anarchy ; but find my wife,
And to her trembling heart prefenting death,
Force all the fecret from her.
  Zan. O forbear !
You totter on the very brink of ruin.
  Alon. What doft thou mean ?
  Zan. That will difcover all,
And kill my hopes.   What can I think or do ?   [*Afide.*
  Alon. What doft thou murmur ?
  Zan. Force the fecret from her !
What's perjury to fuch a crime as this?

Will

Will she confess it then ? O groundless hope !
But rest assur'd, she'll make this accusation,
Or false or true, your ruin with the king ;
Such is her father's power.

   Alon. No more, I care not ;
Rather than groan beneath this load, I'll die.

   Zan. But for what better will you change this load ?
Grant you should know it, would not that be worse ?

   Alon. No, it would cure me of my mortal pangs :
By hatred and contempt I should despise her,
And all my love-bred agonies would vanish.

   Zan. Ah ! were I sure of that, my Lord——

   Alon. What then ?

   Zan. You should not hazard life to gain the secret.

   Alon. What dost thou mean ? Thou know'st I'm on the
I'll not be play'd with ; speak, if thou hast ought, [rack.
Or I this instant fly to Leonora.

   Zan. That is, to death. My Lord, I am not yet
Quite so far gone in guilt to suffer it,
Tho' gone too far, heav'n knows—'Tis I am guilty——
I have took pains, as you I know observ'd,
To hinder you from diving in the secret,
And turn'd aside your thoughts from the detection.

   Alon. Thou dost confound me.

   Zan. I confound myself,
And frankly own it, tho' to my shame I own it ;
Nought but your life in danger could have torn
The secret out, and made me own my crime.

   Alon. Speak quickly ; Zanga, speak.

   Zan. Not yet, dread Sir :
First I must be assur'd, that if you find
The fair one guilty, scorn, as you assur'd me,
Shall conquer love and rage, and heal your soul.

   Alon. Oh ! 'twill, by heav'n.

   Zan. Alas ! I fear it much,
And scarce can hope so far ; but I of this
Exact your solemn oath, that you'll abstain
From all self-violence, and save my Lord.

   Alon. I trebly swear.

   Zan. You'll bear it like a man ?

   Alon. A god.

   Zan. Such have you been to me, these tears confess it,
And

And pour'd forth miracles of kindnefs on me:
And what amends is now within my pow'r,
But to confefs, expofe myfelf to juftice,
And as a bleffing claim my punifhment?
Know then, Don Carlos————

Alon. Oh!

Zan. You cannot bear it.

Alon. Go on, I'll have it, though it blaft mankind;
I'll have it all, and inftantly. Go on.

Zan. Don Carlos did return at dead of night————

‘ *Enter* Leonora.

‘ *Leon.* My Lord Alonzo, you are abfent from us,
‘ And quite undo our joy.

‘ *Alon.* I'll come, my love:
‘ Be not our friends deferted by us both;
‘ I'll follow you this moment.

‘ *Leon.* My good Lord,
‘ I do obferve feverity of thought
‘ Upon your brow.   Aught hear you from the Moors?

‘ *Alon.* No, my delight.

‘ *Leon.* What then employ'd your mind?

‘ *Alon.* Thou love, and only thou; fo Heav'n befriend
‘ As other thought can find no entrance here.   [me,

‘ *Leon.* How good in you, my Lord, whom nations'
‘ Solicit, and a world in arms obeys,   [cares
‘ To drop one thought on me!

‘ [*He fhews the utmoft impatience.*

‘ *Alon.* Doft thou then prize it?

‘ *Leon.* Do you then afk it?

‘ *Alon.* Know then, to thy comfort,
‘ Thou haft me all, my throbbing heart is full
‘ With thee alone, I've thought of nothing elfe;
‘ Nor fhall, I from my foul believe, till death.
‘ My life, our friends expect thee.

‘ *Leon.* I obey.   [*Exit* Leon.

‘ *Alon.* Is that the face of curs'd hypocrify?
‘ If fhe is guilty, ftars are made of darknefs,
‘ And beauty fhall no more belong to heav'n————
‘ Don Carlos did return at dead of night——'
‘ Proceed, good Zanga, fo thy tale began.

‘ *Zan.* Don Carlos did return at dead of night;'
That night, by chance (ill chance for me) did I

D

Com-

Command the watch that guards the palace gate.
He told me he had letters for the king,
Difpatch'd from you.
 Alon. The villain ly'd !
 Zan. My Lord,
I pray forbear——Tranfported at his fight,
After fo long a bondage, and your friend,
(Who could fufpect him of an artifice ?)
No farther I enquir'd, but let him pafs,
Falfe to my truft, at leaft imprudent in it.
Our watch reliev'd, I went into the garden,
As is my cuftom, when the night's ferene,
And took a moon-light walk : when foon I heard
A ruftling in an arbour that was near me.
I faw two lovers in each other's arms,
Embracing and embrac'd.　Anon the man
Arofe, and falling back fome paces from her,
Gaz'd ardently awhile, then rufh'd at once,
And throwing all himfelf into her bofom,
There foftly ligh'd; "Oh, night of ecftafy !
When fhall we meet again ?" Don Carlos then
Led Leonora forth.
 Alon. Oh, Oh, my heart !　　　[*He finks into a chair.*
 Zan. Groan on, and with the found refrefh my foul !
'Tis through his heart, his knees fmite one another.
'Tis thro' his brain, his eye-balls roll in anguifh. [*Afide.*
My Lord, my Lord, why do you rack my foul ?
' Speak to me, let me know that you ftill live.
' Do not you know me, Sir ? Pray look upon me ;
' You think too deeply.　I'm your own Zanga,
' So lov'd, fo cherifh'd, and fo faithful to you ——
' Why ftart you in fuch fury ? Nay, my Lord,
' For heav'n's fake fheath your fword ! What can this
' Fool that I was to truft you with the fecret,　[mean ?
' And you unkind to break your word with me.
' Oh, paffion for a woman ! On the ground ?
' Where is your boafted courage ? Where your fcorn,
' And prudent rage, that was to cure your grief,
' And chafe your love-bred agonies away ?'
Rife, Sir, for honour's fake.　Why fhould the Moors,
Why fhould the vanquifh'd triumph ?
 Alon. ' Would to heav'n

           ' That

' That I were lower ftill !' Oh, fhe was all !—
My fame, my friendfhip, and my love of arms,
All ftoop to her, my blood was her poffeffion.
Deep in the fecret foldings of my heart
She liv'd with life, and far the dearer fhe.
But——' and' no more——' fet nature on a blaze,
' Give her a fit of jealoufy——away——'
To think on't is the torment of the damn'd,
And not to think on't is impoffible.
' How fair the cheek that firft alarm'd my foul !
' How bright the eye that fet it on a flame !
' How foft the breaft on which I laid my peace
' For years to flumber, unawak'd by care !
' How fierce the tranfport ! how fublime the blifs !]
' How deep, how black, the horror and defpair !'
    Zan, You faid you'd bear it like a man.
    Alon. I do.
Am I not almoft diftracted ?
    Zan. Pray be calm.
    Alon. As hurricanes : be thou affur'd of that.
    Zan. Is this the wife Alonzo ?
    Alon. Villain, no !
He dy'd in the arbour, he was murder'd there ;
' I am his dæmon though——My wife ! my wife !—
    Zan. Alas ! he weeps.
    Alon. Go, dig her grave.
    Zan. My lord !
    Alon. But that her blood's too hot, I would caroufe it
Around my bridal board.
    Zan. And I would pledge thee.   [*Afide*.
    Alon. But I may talk too faft. Pray let me think,
And reafon mildly.——Wedded and undone
Before one night defcends.——Oh, hafty evil !
What friend to comfort me in my extreme !
Where's Carlos ? Why is Carlos abfent from me ?
Does he know what has happen'd ?
    ' *Zan*. My good Lord !
    ' *Alon*. Oh, depth of horror ! He !——My bofom
    ' *Zan*. Alas, compofe yourfelf, my Lord.   [friend !
    ' *Alon*. To death !
'' Gaze on her with both eyes fo ardently !''
' Give them the vultures, tear him all in pieces !

' *Zan.* Moſt excellent !   [*Aſide.*
' *Alon.* Hark ! you can keep a ſecret.
' In yonder arbour bound with jaſmine——
' Who's that ? What villain's that ? Unhand her——
          Murder !——
' Tear them aſunder——Murder——How they grind
' My heart betwixt them !—— Oh, let go my heart !
' Yet let it go——" Embracing and embrac'd !"
' Oh, peſtilence !——Who let him in ? A traitor.
                         [*Goes to ſtab* Zanga, *he prevents him.*
' Alas ! my head turns round, and my limbs fail me.'
    Zan. My Lord !
    Alon. Oh, villain, villain, moſt accurſt !
If thou didſt know it, **why** didſt let me wed ?
    Zan. Hear me, my Lord, your anger will abate.
I knew it not, I ſaw them in the garden ;
But ſaw no more than you might well expect
To ſee in lovers deſtin'd for each other.
By heav'n I thought their meeting innocent.
Who could ſuſpect fair Leonora's virtue,
'Till after-proofs conſpir'd to blacken it ?
Sad proofs, which came too late, which broke not out,
(Eternal curſes on Alvarez' haſte !)
'Till holy rites had made the wanton yours ;
And then, I own, I labour'd to conceal it,
In duty and compaſſion to your peace.
    Alon. Live now, be damn'd hereafter ; for I want thee.
Oh, night of ecſtaſy !——Ha ! was't not ſo ?
" I will enjoy this murder"—Let me think——
The jaſmine bow'r—'tis ſecret and remote ;
Go wait me there, and take thy dagger with thee.
                                    [*Exit* Zanga.
How the ſweet ſound ſtill ſings within my ear !
" When ſhall we meet again ?"—To-night, in hell.
          As he is going, enter Leonora.
Ha ! I'm ſurpriz'd ! I ſtagger at her charms !
Oh, angel-devil !—Shall I ſtab her now ?
No, it ſhall be as I at firſt determin'd ?
To kill her now were half my vengeance loſt.
Then muſt I now diſſemble—if I can.
    Leon. My Lord, excuſe me ; ' ſee, a ſecond time'
I come in embaſſy from all your friends,
Whoſe joys are languid, uninſpir'd by you.
                                         Alon.

Alon. This moment, Leonora, I was coming
To thee, and all—but sure, or I mistake,
Or thou canst well inspire my friends with joy.

  ' *Leon.* Why sighs my Lord?
  ' *Alon.* I sigh'd not, Leonora.
  ' *Leon.* I thought you did; your sighs are mine, my
' And I shall feel them all.   [Lord,
  ' *Alon.* Dost flatter me?
  ' *Leon.* If my regards for you are flattery,
' Full far indeed I stretch'd the compliment
' In this day's solemn rite.
  ' *Alon.* What rite?
  ' *Leon.* You sport me.
  ' *Alon.* Indeed I do; my heart is full of mirth.
  ' *Leon.* And so is mine————I look on cheerfulness,
' As on the health of virtue.
  ' *Alon.* Virtue!————Damn————'
  Leon. What says my Lord?
  Alon. Thou art exceeding fair.
  Leon. Beauty alone is but of little worth;
But when the soul and body of a piece,
Both shine alike, then they obtain a price,
And are a fit reward for gallant actions,
Heav'n's pay on earth for such great souls as yours;
If fair and innocent, I am your due.
  Alon. Innocent!   [*Aside.*
  Leon. How! my Lord, I interrupt you.
  Alon. No, my best life, I must not part with thee,
This hand is mine. Oh, what a hand is here?
So soft, souls sink into it, and are lost!
  Leon. In tears, my Lord?
  Alon. What less can speak my joy?
' I gaze, and I forget my own existence;
' 'Tis all a vision, my head swims in heav'n.
' Wherefore! Oh, wherefore this expence of beauty?
' And wherefore? Oh!————'
Why, I could gaze upon thy looks for ever,
And drink in all my being from thine eyes;
And I could snatch a flaming thunderbolt,
And hurl destruction.————
  ' *Leon.* How, my Lord! what mean you?

D 3

Ac-

' Acquaint me with the fecret of your heart,
' Or caft me out for ever from your love.
  ' *Alon.* Art thou concern'd for me ?'
  Leon. My Lord, you fright me.
Is this the fondnefs of your nuptial hour ?
' I am ill-us'd, my Lord, I muft not bear it.'
Why, when I woo your hand, is it deny'd me ?
Your very eyes, why are they taught to fhun me ?
Nay, my good Lord, I have a title here,
[Taking his hand.

And I will have it. Am not I your wife ?
Have not I juft authority to know
That heart which I have purchas'd with my own ?
' Lay it before me then ; it is my due.
' Unkind Alonzo ! though I might demand it,
' Behold, I kneel ! See, Leonora kneels,
' And deigns to be a beggar for her own !'
Tell me the fecret, I conjure you tell me.
' The bride foregoes the homage of her day,
' Alvarez' daughter trembles in the duft.'
Speak then, I charge you fpeak, or I expire,
And load you with my death. My Lord—my Lord !
  Alon. Ha, ha, ha !
[He breaks from her, and fhe finks upon the floor.
  Leon. Are thefe the joys which fondly I conceiv'd ?
And is it thus a wedded life begins ?
What did I part with, when I gave my heart ?
I knew not that all happinefs went with it.
Why did I leave my tender father's wing,
And venture into love ? The maid that loves
Goes out to fea upon a fhatter'd plank,
And puts her truft in miracles for fafety.
Where fhall I figh ? Where pour out my complaints ?
He that fhould hear, fhould fuccour, fhould redrefs,
He is the fource of all.
  Alon. Go to thy chamber,
I foon will follow ; that which now difturbs thee
Shall be clear'd up, and thou fhalt not condemn me.
[Exit Leon.

Oh, how like innocence fhe looks ! What, ftab her,
And rufh into her blood ?————' I never can.
' In

' In her guilt shines, and nature holds my hand.'
How then ? Why thus——No more.; it is determin'd.
Enter Zanga.
Zan. I fear his heart has fail'd him.   She must die.
Can I not rouze the snake that's in his bosom,
To sting our human nature, and effect it ?   [*Aside.*
Alon. This vast and solid earth, that blazing sun,
Those skies through which it rolls, must all have end.
What then is man ? the smallest part of nothing.
Day buries day, month month, and year the year,
Our life is but a chain of many deaths ;
Can then death's self be fear'd ? our life much rather.
Life is the defart, life the folitude,
Death joins us to the great majority :
'Tis to be borne to Plato's, and to Cæfars ;
'Tis to be great for ever ;
'Tis pleasure, 'tis ambition then to die.
    Zan. I think, my Lord, you talk'd of death.
    Alon. I did.
    Zan. I give you joy, then Leonora's dead.
    Alon. No, Zanga, ' the greatest guilt is mine,
' Tis mine, who might have mark'd his midnight vifit,
' Who might have mark'd his tameness to refign her ;
' Who might have mark'd her fudden turn of love :.
' Thefe, and a thoufand tokens more ; and yet,
' (For which the faints abfolve my foul !) did wed.
    ' *Zan.* Where does this tend ?
    ' *Alon.*' To fhed a woman's blood
Would stain my fword, and make my wars inglorious ;
' But juft refentment to myfelf, bears in it
' A flamp of greatnefs above vulgar minds.'
He who, fuperior to the checks of nature,
Dares make his life the victim of his reafon,
Does in fome fort that reafon deify,
And take a flight at heav'n.
    Zan. Alas, my Lord,
'Tis not your reafon, but her beauty finds
Thofe arguments, and throws you on your fword.
You cannot clofe an eye that is fo bright,
You cannot strike a breaft that is fo foft,
That has ten thoufand ecflafies in ftore——
For Carlos ?——No, my Lord, I mean for you.

Alon.

Alon. Oh, through my heart and marrow! Pr'ythee
        spare me:
Nor more upbraid the weakneſs of thy lord.
I own, I try'd, I quarrell'd with my heart,
And puſh'd it on, and bid it give her death;
But, Oh, her eyes ſtruck firſt, and murder'd me.

Zan. I know not what to anſwer to my Lord.
Men are but men; we did not make ourſelves.
Farewel then, my beſt Lord, ſince you muſt die.
Oh, that I were to ſhare your monument,
And in eternal darkneſs cloſe theſe eyes
Againſt thoſe ſcenes which I am doom'd to ſuffer!

Alon. What doſt thou mean?

Zan. And is it then unknown?
Oh, grief of heart to think that you ſhould aſk it!
Sure you diſtruſt that ardent love I bear you,
Elſe could you doubt when you are laid in duſt——
But it will cut my poor heart through and through,
To ſee thoſe revel on your ſacred tomb,
Who brought you thither by their lawleſs loves.
For there they'll revel, and exult to find
Him ſleep ſo faſt, who elſe might marr their joys.

Alon. Diſtraction!—But Don Carlos well thou know'ſt
Is ſheath'd in ſteel, and bent on other thoughts.

Zan. I'll work him to the murder of his friend;
Yes, till the fever of his blood returns,
While her laſt kiſs ſtill glows upon his cheek.   [*Aſide.*
But when he finds Alonzo is no more,
How will he ruſh like lightning to her arms!
There ſigh, there languiſh, there pour out his ſoul;
But not in grief——ſad obſequies to thee!——
But thou wilt be at peace, nor ſee, nor hear
The burning kiſs, the ſigh of ecſtaſy,
' Their throbbing hearts that joſtle one another:'
Thank heav'n, theſe torments will be all my own.

Alon. I'll eaſe thee of that pain. Let Carlos die,
O'ertake him on the road, and ſee it done.
'Tis my command.   [*Gives his ſignet.*

Zan. I dare not diſobey.

Alon. My Zanga, now I have thy leave to die.

Zan. Ah, Sir! think, think again. Are all men buried
In Carlos' grave? You know not woman-kind.
When once the throbbing of the heart has broke
                                The

The modeſt zone, with which it firſt was ty'd,
Each man ſhe meets will be a Carlos to her.
   Alon. That thought has more of hell than had the
Another, and another, and another !   [former.
And each ſhall caſt a ſmile upon my tomb.
I am convinc'd ; I muſt not, will not die.
   Zan. You cannot die ; nor can you murder her.
What then remains ? In nature no third way,
But to forget, and ſo to love again.
   Alon. Oh !
   Zan. If you forgive, the world will call you good ;
If you forget, the world will call you wiſe ;
If you receive her to your grace again,
The world will call you, very, very kind.
   Alon. Zanga, I underſtand thee well.   She dies,
Though my arm trembles at the ſtroke, ſhe dies.
   Zan. That's truly great. What think you 'twas ſet up
The Greek and Roman name in ſuch a luſtre,
But doing right in ſtern deſpite to nature,
Shutting their ears to all her little cries,
When great, auguſt, and god-like juſtice call'd ?
At Aulis one pour'd out a daughter's life,
And gain'd more glory than by all his wars ;
Another ſlew his ſiſter in juſt rage ;
A third, the theme of all ſucceeding times,
Gave to the cruel ax a darling ſon.
Nay more, for juſtice ſome devote themſelves,
As he at Carthage, an immortal name !
Yet there is one ſtep left above them all,
Above their hiſtory, above their fable,
A wife, bride, miſtreſs unenjoy'd——do that,
And tread upon the Greek and Roman glory.
   Alon. 'Tis done !———Again new tranſports fire my,
I had forgot it, 'tis my bridal night.   [brain :
Friend, give me joy, we muſt be gay together ;
See that the feſtival be duly honour'd.
   And when with garlands the full bowl is crown'd,
   And muſic gives the elevating ſound,
   And golden carpets ſpread the ſacred floor,
   And a new day the blazing tapers pour,
   Thou, Zanga, thou my ſolemn friends invite,
   From the dark realms of everlaſting night,

Call

Call vengeance, call the furies, call defpair,
And death, our chief-invited gueft, be there;
He with pale hand fhall lead the bride, and fpread
Eternal curtains round our nuptial bed.   [*Exeunt.*

END of the FOURTH ACT.

A C T · V.

Enter Alonzo.

'OH, pitiful! Oh, terrible to fight!
' Poor mangled fhade! all cover'd o'er with wounds,
' And fo difguis'd with blood!—Who murder'd thee?
' Tell thy fad tale, and thou fhalt be reveng'd.
' Ha! Carlos?—Horror! Carlos?—Oh, away!
' Go to the grave, or let me fink to mine.
' I cannot bear the fight—What fight?—Where am I?
' There's nothing here—If this was fancy's work,
' She draws a picture ftrongly.————'
Enter Zanga.
' *Zan.* Ha!——You're pale.'
Alon. Is Carlos murder'd?
Zan. I obey'd your order.
Six ruffians overtook him on the road;
He fought as he was wont, and four he flew.
Then funk beneath an hundred wounds to death.
His laft breath bleft Alonzo, and defir'd
His bones might reft near yours.
Alon. Oh, Zanga! Zanga!
But I'll not think; for I muft act, and thinking
Would ruin me for action. ' Oh, the medley
' Of right and wrong! the chaos of my brain!
' He fhould, and fhould not die——You fhould obey,
' And not obey——It is a day of darknefs,
' Of contradictions, and of many deaths.'
Where's Leonora then? Quick, anfwer me:
I'm deep in horrors, I'll be deeper ftill.
I find thy artifice did take effect,
And fhe forgives my late deportment to her.
Zan. I told her, from your childhood you was wont

On

On any great furprize, but chiefly then
When caufe of forrow bore it company,
To have your paffion fhake the feat of reafon ;
A momentary ill, which foon blew o'er,
Then did I tell her of Don Carlos' death,
(Wifely fuppreffing by what means he fell)
And laid the blame on that.   At firft fhe doubted ;
But fuch the honeft artifice I us'd,
And fuch her ardent wifh it fhould be true,
That fhe, at length, was fully fatisfy'd.
  ' *Alon.* 'Twas well fhe was.   In our late interview
' My paffion fo far threw me from my guard
' (Methinks 'tis ftrange !) that confcious of her guilt,
' She faw not through its thin difguife my heart.
  ' *Zan.*' But what defign you, Sir, and how ?
  Alon. I'll tell thee.
Thus I've ordain'd it.   In the jafmine bow'r,
The place which fhe difhonour'd with her guilt,
There will I meet her ; the appointment's made ;
And calmly fpread (for I can do it now)
The blacknefs of her crime before her fight,
And then with all the cool folemnity
Of public juftice, give her to the grave.   [*Exit.*
  ' *Zan.* Why, get thee gone ! horror and night go with
' Sifters of Acheron, go hand in hand,   [thee !
' Go dance around the bow'r, and clofe them in ;
' And tell them that I fent you to falute them.
' Profane the ground, and for th' ambrofial rofe,
' And breath of jafmine, let hemlock blacken,
' And deadly nightfhade poifon all the air,
' For the fweet nightingale may ravens croak,
' Toads pant, and adders ruftle through the leaves ;
' May ferpents winding up the trees let fall
' Their hiffing necks upon them from above,
' And mingle kiffes—fuch as I fhould give them.' [*Exit.*

SCENE, the Bower.

Leonora fleeping. Enter Alonzo.
  Alon. Ye amaranths ! ye rofes, like the morn !
Sweet myrtles, and ye golden orange groves !
Why do you fmile ? Why do you look fo fair ?

Are

Are ye not blasted as I enter in ?
' Yes, see how every flow'r lets fall its head !
' How shudders every leaf without a wind !
' How every green is as the ivy pale !'
Did ever midnight ghosts assemble here ?
Have these sweet echoes ever learn'd to groan ?
Joy-giving, love-inspiring, holy bow'r !
Know, in thy fragrant bosom thou receiv'st
A——murderer ! Oh, I shall stain thy lilies,
And horror will usurp the seat of bliss.
' So Lucifer broke into Paradise,
' And soon damnation follow'd.' [*He advances.*] Ha ! she
          sleeps————
The day's uncommon heat has overcome her.
Then take, my longing eyes, your last full gaze.
Oh, what a sight is here ! how dreadful fair !
Who would not think that being innocent ?
Where shall I strike ? Who strikes her, strikes himself.
My own life-blood will issue at her wound.
' Oh, my distracted heart !—Oh, cruel heav'n !
' To give such charms as these, and then call man,
' Mere man, to be your executioner.
' Was it because it was too hard for you ?'
But see, she smiles ! I never shall smile more.
It strongly tempts me to a parting kiss,
                    [*Going, he starts back.*
Ha ! smile again. She dreams of him she loves.
Curse on her charms ! I'll stab her through them all.
                [*As he is going to strike she awakes.*
  Leon. My Lord, your stay was long, and yonder lull
Of falling waters tempted me to rest,
Dispirited with noon's excessive heat.
  Alon. Ye pow'rs ! with what an eye she mends the day !
While they were clos'd I should have giv'n the blow. [*Aside.*
' Oh, for a last embrace ! and then for justice :
' Thus heav'n and I shall both be satisfy'd.'
  Leon. What says my Lord ?
  Alon. Why this Alonzo says ;
If love were endless, men were gods : 'tis that
Does counterbalance travel, danger, pain——
'Tis heav'n's expedient to make mortals bear
The light, and cheat them of the peaceful grave.
  Leon. Alas, my Lord ! why talk you of the grave ?
                                        Your

Your friend is dead ; in friendfhip you fuftain
A mighty lofs ; repair it with my love.
   Alon. Thy love, thou piece of witchcraft ! I would fay,
Thou brighteft angel ! I could gaze for ever.
' Where hadft thou this, enchantrefs, tell me where,
' Which with a touch works miracles, boils up
' My blood to tumults, and turns round my brain ?
' Ev'n now thou fwim'ft before me.   I fhall lofe thee—
' No, I will make thee fure, and clafp thee all.
' Who turn'd this flender waift with fo much art,
' And fhut perfection in fo fmall a ring ?
' Who fpread that pure expanfe of white above,
' On which the dazzled fight can find no reft ;
' But, drunk with beauty, wanders up and down
' For ever, and for ever finds new charms ?'
But Oh, thofe eyes ! thofe murderers ! Oh, whence,
Whence didft thou fteal their burning orbs ? From heav'n?
Thou didft ; and 'tis religion to adore them.
   Leon. My beft Alonzo, moderate your thoughts.
Extremes ftill fright me, tho' of love itfelf.
   Alon. Extremes indeed ! it hurried me away ;
But I come home again—and now for juftice—
And now for death——It is impoffible——
' Sure fuch were made by Heav'n guiltlefs to fin,
' Or in their guilt to laugh at punifhment.'   [*Afide.*
I leave her to juft Heav'n. [*Drops the dagger, and goes off.*
   Leon. Ha, a dagger !
What doft thou fay, thou minifter of death ?
What dreadful tale doft tell me ?——Let me think——
            Enter Zanga.
   Zan. Death to my tow'ring hopes ! Oh, fall from high !
My clofe, long-labour'd fcheme at once is blafted.
That dagger, found, will caufe her to enquire ;
Enquiry will difcover all ; my hopes
Of vengeance perifh ; I myfelf am loft——
Curfe on the coward's heart ! wither his hand,
Which held the fteel in vain !—What can be done ?—
Where can I fix ?—That's fomething ftill—'twill breed
Fell rage and bitternefs betwixt their fouls,
Which may perchance grow up to greater evil :
If not, 'tis all I can ——It fhall be fo——   [*Afide.*
   Leon. Oh, Zanga, I am finking in my fears !
       E   Alonzo

Alonzo dropp'd this dagger as he left me,
And left me in a strange diforder too.
What can this mean ? Angels preferve his life !
   Zan. Yours, Madam, yours.
   Leon. What, Zanga, doft thou fay ?
   Zan. Carry your goodnefs, then, to fuch extremes,
So blinded to the faults of him you love,
That you perceive not he is jealous ?
   Leon. Heav'ns !
And yet a thoufand things recur that fwear it.
What villain could infpire him with that thought ?
It is not of the growth of his own nature.
   Zan. Some villain; who, hell knows; but he is jealous ;
And 'tis moft fit a heart fo pure as yours
Do itfelf juftice, and affert its honour,
And make him confcious of its ftab to virtue.
   Leon. Jealous ! it fickens at my heart.   Unkind,
Ungen'rous, groundlefs, weak, and infolent !
Why, wherefore, and what fhadow of occafion ?
‘ 'Tis fafcination, 'tis the wrath of Heav'n
‘ For the collected crimes of all his race.'
Oh, how the great man leffens to my thought !
How could fo mean a vice as jealoufy,
‘ Unnatural child of ignorance and guilt,
‘ Which tears and feeds upon its parent's heart,'
Live in a throng of fuch exalted virtues ?
I fcorn and hate, yet love him and adore.
I cannot will not, dare not think it true,
Till from himfelf I know it.   [*Exit.*
   Zan. This fucceeds
Juft to my wifh.   Now fhe, with violence,
Upbraids him ; he, well knowing fhe is guilty,
Rages no lefs : and if on either fide
The waves run high, there ftill lives hopes of ruin.
               Enter Alonzo.
My Lord———
   Alon. Oh, Zanga, hold thy peace ! I am no coward ;
But Heav'n itfelf did hold my hand ; I felt it,
By the well-being of my foul, I did.
I'll think of vengeance at another feafon.
   Zan. My Lord, her guilt——
   Alon. Perdition on thee, Moor,
For that one word ! Ah, do not roufe that thought !
                        I have

I have o'erwhelm'd it as much as poffible :
' Away, then, let us talk of other things.'
I tell thee, Moor, I love her to diftraction.
If 'tis my fhame, why, be it fo——I love her ;
' Nor can I help it; 'tis impos'd upon me
' By fome fuperior and refiftlefs pow'r.'
I could not hurt her to be lord of earth ;
It fhocks my nature like a ftroke from heav'n.
' Angels defend her, as if innocent.'
But fee, my Leonora comes—Begone.   [*Exit* Zanga.
                   Enter Leonora.
Oh, feen for ever, yet for ever new !
The conquer'd thou doft conquer o'er again,
Inflicting wound on wound.
     Leon. Alas, my Lord !
What need of this to me ?
     Alon. Ha ! doft thou weep ?
     Leon. Have I no caufe ?
     Alon. If love is thy concern,
Thou haft no caufe : none ever lov'd like me.
' But wherefore this ? Is it to break my heart,
' Which lofes fo much blood for every tear ?
     ' *Leon.* Is it fo tender ?
     ' *Alon.* Is it not ? Oh, Heav'n !
' Doubt of my love ! Why, I am nothing elfe ;
' It quite abforbs my every other paffion.'
Oh, that this one embrace would laft for ever !
     Leon. Could this man ever mean to wrong my virtue ?
Could this man e'er defign upon my life ?
Impoffible ! I throw away the thought.   [*Afide.*
Thefe tears declare how much I tafte the joy
Of being folded in your arms and heart ;
My univerfe does lie within that fpace.
This dagger bore falfe witnefs.
     Alon. Ha, my dagger !
It roufes horrid images. Away,
Away with it, and let us talk of love,
' Plunge ourfelves deep into the fweet illufion,
' And hide us there from ev'ry other thought.
     ' *Leon.* It touches you.
     ' *Alon.* Let's talk of love.'
     Leon. Of death !
                   E 2   *Alon.*

Alon. As thou lov'st happiness——
Leon. Of murder!
Alon. Rash,
Rash woman! yet forbear.
   ' *Leon.* Approve my wrongs!
   ' *Alon.* Then must I fly, for thy sake and my own.
   ' *Leon.* Nay, by my injuries, you first must hear me:
' Stab me, then think it much to hear my groan!
   ' *Alon.* Heav'n strike me deaf!'
   Leon. It well may sting you home.
   Alon. Alas, thou quite mistak'st my cause of pain!
Yet, yet dismiss me; I am all in flames.
   Leon. Who has most cause, you or myself? What act
Of my whole life encourag'd you to this?
Or of your own, what guilt has drawn it on you?
You find me kind, and think me kind to all;
The weak, ungenerous error of your sex.
What could inspire the thought? We oft'nest judge
From our own hearts; and is yours then so frail,
It prompts you to conceive thus ill of me?
He that can stoop to harbour such a thought,
Deserves to find it true.   [*Holding him.*
   Alon. ' Oh, sex, sex, sex!'   [*Turning on her.*
' The language of you all.'   Ill-fated woman!
Why hast thou forc'd me back into the gulf
Of agonies I had block'd up from thought?
' I know the cause; thou saw'st me impotent
' Ere while to hurt thee, therefore thou turn'st on me;
' But, by the pangs I suffer, to thy woe:'
For, since thou hast replung'd me in my torture,
I will be satisfy'd.
   Leon. Be satisfy'd!
   Alon. Yes, thy own mouth shall witness it against thee;
I will be satisfy'd.
   Leon. Of what?
   Alon. Of what!
How dar'st thou ask that question? Woman, woman,
Weak and assur'd at once! thus 'tis for ever.
Who told thee that thy virtue was suspected?
Who told thee I design'd upon thy life?
You found the dagger; but that could not speak:

Nor

Nor did I tell thee ; who did tell thee then ?
Guilt, confcious guilt !

Leon. This to my face ! Oh, Heav'n !

Alon. This to thy very foul.

Leon. Thou'rt not in earneft ?

Alon. Serious as death.

Leon. Then heav'n have mercy on thee.
Till now I ftruggled not to think it true ;
I fought conviction, and would not believe it.
And doft thou force me ? This fhall not be borne ;
Thou fhalt repent this infult.   [*Going.*

Alon. Madam, ftay.
Your paffion's wife ; 'tis a difguife for guilt :
' Tis my turn now to fix you here a while ;'
You and your thoufand arts fhall not efcape me.

Leon. Arts ?

Alon. Arts. Confefs ; for death is in my hand.

Leon. 'Tis in your words.

Alon. Confefs, confefs, confefs !
Nor tear my veins with paffion to compel thee.

Leon. I fcorn to anfwer thee, prefumptuous man !

Alon. Deny then, and incur a fouler fhame.
Where did I find this picture ?

Leon. Ha, Don Carlos !
By my beft hopes, more welcome than thy own.

Alon. I know it ; but is vice fo very rank,
That thou fhouldft dare to dafh it in my face ?
Nature is fick of thee, abandon'd woman !

Leon. Repent.

Alon. Is that for me ?

Leon. Faft, afk my pardon.

Alon. Aftonifhment !

Leon. Dar'ft thou perfift to think I am difhoneft ?

Alon. I know thee fo.

Leon. This blow, then, to thy heart——.
      [*She ftabs herfelf, he endeavours to prevent her.*

Alon. Hoa, Zanga ! Ifabella ! hoa ! fhe bleeds !
Defcend, ye bleffed angels, to affift her !

Leon. This is the only way I would wound thee,
Tho' moft unjuft. Now think me guilty ftill.

Enter Ifabella.

Alon. Bear her to inftant help.   The world to fave her.

Leon. Unhappy man ! well may'ft thou gaze and tremble :
But fix thy terror and amazement right ;
Not on my blood, but on thy own diftraction.
What haft thou done ? Whom cenfur'd ?—Leonora !
When thou hadft cenfur'd, thou wouldft fave her life :
Oh, inconfiftent ! Should I live in fhame,
Or ftoop to any other means but this
To affert my virtue ? No ; fhe who difputes
Admits it poffible fhe might be guilty.
While aught but truth could be my inducement to it,
While it might look like an excufe to thee,
I fcorn'd to vindicate my innocence :
But now, I let thy rafhnefs know, the wound
Which leaft I feel, is that my dagger made.
                                    [Ifabella *leads out* Leonora.

Alon. Ha ! was this woman guilty ?—And if not—
How my thought darkens that way ! Grant, kind Heav'n,
That fhe prove guilty ; or my being end.
Is that my hope, then ?—Sure the facred duft
Of her that bore me trembles in its urn.
Is it in man the fore diftrefs to bear,
When hope itfelf is blacken'd to defpair,
When all the blifs I pant for, is to gain
In hell, a refuge from feverer pain?   [*Exit.*

Enter Zanga.

Zan. How ftands the great account 'twixt me and ven-
Tho' much is paid, yet ftill it owes me much,   [geance ?
And I will not abate a fingle groan——
Ha ! that were well—but that were fatal too——
Why, be it fo——Revenge fo truly great,
Would come too cheap, if bought with lefs than life.
' Come, death, come, hell, then ; 'tis refolv'd, 'tis done.'

Enter Ifabella.

Ifab. Ah, Zanga, fee me tremble ! Has not yet
Thy cruel heart its fill ?—Poor Leonora——

Zan. Welters in blood, and gafps for her laft breath.
What then ? We all muft die.

Ifab. Alonzo raves,
And, in the tempeft of his grief, has thrice
Attempted on his life.   At length difarm'd.

                                                    He

He calls his friends that fave him his worft foes,
And importunes the fkies for fwift perdition.
Thus in his ftorm of forrow.   After paufe,
He ftarted up, and call'd aloud for Zanga,
For Zanga rav'd; and fee, he feeks you here,
To learn the truth which moft he dreads to know.

   Zan. Begone.   Now, now, my foul, confummate all.
[*Exit* Ifab.

Enter Alonzo.

   Alon. Oh, Zanga!
   Zan. Do not tremble fo; but fpeak.
   Alon. I dare not.   [*Falls on him.*
   Zan. You will drown me with your tears.
   Alon. Have I not caufe?
   Zan. As yet you have no caufe.
   Alon. Doft thou too rave?
   Zan. Your anguifh is to come:
You much have been abus'd.
   Alon. Abus'd! by whom?
   Zan. To know were little comfort.
   Alon. Oh, 'twere much!
   Zan. Indeed!
   Alon. By Heav'n! Oh, give him to my fury!
   Zan. Born for your ufe, I live but to oblige you.
Know, then, 'twas——I.
   Alon. Am I awake?
   Zan. For ever.
Thy wife is guiltlefs—that's one tranfport to me;
And I, I let thee know it—that's another.
I urg'd Don Carlos to refign his miftrefs,
I forg'd the letter, I difpos'd the picture;
I hated, I defpis'd, and I deftroy.
   Alon. Oh!   [*Swoons.*
   Zan. Why, this is well—why, this is blow for blow!
Where are you? Crown me, fhadow me with laurels,
Ye fpirits which delight in juft revenge!
Let Europe and her pallid fons go weep;
Let Afric and her hundred thrones rejoice:
Oh, my dear countrymen, look down, and fee
How I beftride your proftrate conqueror!
I tread on haughty Spain, and all her kings.
But this is mercy, this is my indulgence;
'Tis

Zan. This too is well.   The fix'd and noble mind
Turns all occurrence to its own advantage;
And I'll make vengeance of calamity.
Were I not thus reduc'd, thou wouldſt not know,
That, thus reduc'd, I dare defy thee ſtill.
Torture thou may'ſt, but thou ſhalt ne'er defpiſe me.
The blood will follow where the knife is driven,
The fleſh will quiver where the pincers tear,
And fighs and cries by nature grow on pain.
But theſe are foreign to the ſoul: not mine
The groans that iſſue, or the tears that fall;
They difobey me; on the rack I ſcorn thee,
As when my faulchion clove thy helm in battle.
   Alv. Peace, villain!
   Zan. While I live, old man, I'll ſpeak:
And well I know thou dar'ſt not kill me yet;
For that would rob thy blood-hounds of their prey.
   Alon. Who call'd Alonzo?
   Alv. No one call'd, my ſon.
   Alon. Again!——'Tis Carlos' voice, and I obey.
Oh, how I laugh at all that this can do!
                     [Shewing the dagger.
The wounds that pain'd, the wounds that murder'd me,
Were giv'n before; I am already dead;
This only marks my body for the grave.   *[Stabs himſelf.*
Afric, thou art reveng'd——Oh, Leonora!——   *[Dies.*
   Zan. Good ruffians, give me leave; my blood is yours,
The wheel's prepar'd, and you ſhall have it all.
Let me but look one moment on the dead,
And pay yourſelves with gazing on my pangs.
                 [He goes to Alonzo's *body.*
Is this Alonzo? Where's the haughty mien?
Is that the hand which ſmote me? Heav'ns, how pale!
And art thou dead? So is my enmity.
I war not with the duſt.   The great, the proud,
The conqueror of Afric was my foe.
A lion preys not upon carcafes.
This was thy only method to ſubdue me.
Terror and doubt fall on me: all thy good
Now blazes, all thy guilt is in the grave.
Never had man ſuch funeral applauſe:
If I lament thee, ſure thy worth was great.
                            'Oh,

Oh, Vengeance, I have follow'd thee too far,
And to receive me Hell blows all her fires.

                     [*He is borne off.*

  Alv. Dreadful effects of jealousy ! a rage
In which the wise with caution will engage ;
Reluctant long, and tardy to believe,
Where, sway'd by nature, we ourselves deceive,
Where our own folly joins the villain's art,
And each man finds a Zanga in his heart.

                     [*Exeunt.*

END of the FIFTH ACT.